# THE FUTILITY OF INTENT
## BOOK FOUR OF THE ANISIAN CONVERGENCE

Mike Wyant, Jr.

Theogony Books
Coinjock, NC

Copyright © 2022 by Mike Wyant, Jr.

All rights reserved. No part of this publication may be reproduced, distributed or transmitted in any form or by any means, including photocopying, recording, or other electronic or mechanical methods, without the prior written permission of the publisher, except in the case of brief quotations embodied in critical reviews and certain other noncommercial uses permitted by copyright law. For permission requests, write to the publisher, addressed "Attention: Permissions Coordinator," at the address below.

Chris Kennedy/Theogony Books
1097 Waterlily Rd.
Coinjock, NC 27923
https://chriskennedypublishing.com/

Publisher's Note: This is a work of fiction. Names, characters, places, and incidents are a product of the author's imagination. Locales and public names are sometimes used for atmospheric purposes. Any resemblance to actual people, living or dead, or to businesses, companies, events, institutions, or locales is completely coincidental.

Cover Design by Shezaad Sudar.

Ordering Information:
Quantity sales. Special discounts are available on quantity purchases by corporations, associations, and others. For details, contact the "Special Sales Department" at the address above.

The Futility of Intent/Mike Wyant, Jr.-- 1st ed.
ISBN: 978-1648554971

# Chapter One: Hira

The evening sky burned.

Hira stared, the grin that'd plastered her face only moments earlier fading into horrified shock. Beyond wispy clouds slashed pink and red from the sunset, another detonation. It flared, stark and red for the briefest of moments, before disappearing like a budget fireworks show. Each detonation lit the bunker-like compound, and the faces of gathered scientists celebrating in the courtyard.

As far as she could see, more flashes preceded explosions as ships arrived above Laconia, only to slam into one of the hundreds of others.

It'd only been thirty minutes since they'd reactivated the FTL machine with the help of AERIS, the erstwhile AI for the *Horatio*, now the entire settlement's artificial intelligence.

With Hira's help.

The reality of it all swept over and through her. Heart slamming in her chest, she ran back inside, pushing past several others on the way.

"Watch it!"

Hira ignored them. She bowled through the double-doors leading into the main foyer of the Tarrington Complex. A trembling vibration ran through her as she entered.

"Stop the machine!" Hira screamed.

The center room was a massive, domed antechamber. Dominating the space was the machine that'd caused this chaos. Ten meters tall, it rose like a spire. The black steel shimmered with the tremor of its activity. Atop it sat the silver ball that made it all work. When deactivated, it would spin slowly, bobbing in time with a deep *thrum* that rattled the windows in their panes.

Now it spun perfectly in place, its thudding revolutions replaced by a low, dull roar Hira felt in her bones rather than heard. Ozone filled the air in its wake, the acrid scent burning her sinuses.

A dozen high-fiving scientists turned at her arrival, glee fuzzing into confusion at the sudden interruption of their celebration. No one said anything. Universally, they stared until Terry, the wiry man she'd met after escaping Hell a week earlier, stepped free from the group. His inquisitive blue eyes lit up at her arrival, the attempt at a full beard sparse and ill-advised.

"What's going on?"

Hira pointed to the sky through the enclosed roof. "Shut it off! They're all coming in at once."

"What are?" Terry asked, stepping sideways toward a control panel.

It was AERIS who replied over the loudspeakers. Since escaping her virtual instance last week, she'd integrated with the entire compound, and even into Sparta's defense systems, despite Terry's best efforts. Luckily, the scientists here had taken that as a positive instead of a negative—not that they could've done much to stop her.

Hira hadn't told anyone yet, but AERIS had confided that she'd locked down her personality matrix in the permanent storage of the unit. There was no removing her now unless she chose it.

"Ships. Hundreds of starships," AERIS said, "colliding."

Terry spun toward the machine. "What?"

AERIS let out a mournful trill. "They're dying."

\* \* \* \* \*

# Chapter Two: Dee

Dee felt the machine turn on as twilight spread across the distant outskirts of Sparta. The steady thudding that kept her heart still and even as she burned through pockets of imps had transformed into a screeching wail.

She turned toward Sparta. Through the eighty kilometers between the city and where she sat, near a small campfire surrounded by the blackened dust of imps, she tried to see. Back at the compound, they'd been trying to get the machine running since the bomb went off on the other side of the Breach. The explosion had destroyed the strange building there and neutralized FTL across the galaxy.

Hira called the planet Hell.

Dee wasn't sure what she wanted to call it. *Happenstance would've called it A1-F.* Another random factoid she shouldn't know from a woman dead for well over a week. Why those little tidbits kept popping up, she didn't know, but now certainly wasn't the right time to crack open *that* particular plasma core.

Sweat sprouted on her forehead and across her body. Breathing turned rapid and unsteady alongside the screeching. She climbed to her feet, wiping her gloved hand on her thigh, a piece of half-eaten, artificial jerky in her right hand. The one that was still normal.

She didn't hear the ships enter the system. Didn't notice the first collisions. The skirmishes.

The sonic boom changed all that. It shattered the silent air over the black sands of the volcanic flats. She dropped into a defensive stance, cursing, and looked up.

A fireball roared across the sky, cutting northwest of her location. As it descended in the darkening sky, it split apart, the central ball of light branching and scattering into a thousand lines of fire.

Dee stood there, frozen. There was nothing that large in orbit, which meant they'd done it. The machine was running… and something had arrived.

Then promptly exploded.

*Bryce.* He was up there, ready to hit FTL and report back to Hunter headquarters back on Earth as soon as it was on. He'd been willing to do the first test jump. Her stomach fell.

Was that him?

Another ball of flame caught her eye before the next *boom*. It was soon joined by another. And another. Then, as if all the stars went supernova at the same time, the sky filled with debris, slashing blood-red clouds apart.

Dee snapped out of her stupor and shoved Bryce to the back of her mind. She tossed the hunk of tasteless jerky into her mouth and kicked some of the rich, black earth of the plains onto her fire out of instinct.

She hopped onto her hoverbike, pulling on her helmet as quickly as she could. She snapped the ignition, and the bike thrummed to life below her, lifting off the ground several inches as the anti-grav generators kicked in.

She spun, dust kicking up from the jets at her back, and hammered on the throttle. Like a bullet, she shot to the east, toward

Sparta. She wasn't sure it had an aerial protection system anymore, but out here, she had nothing.

It shouldn't take long to get there. Minutes at these speeds.

But as the sky tore apart, Dee felt the truth in her stomach, stirring like poison.

She wouldn't make it.

Hundreds of shockwaves rattled the empty night. Already, off to her left and right, small impacts hammered the planet's surface. Each collision sent a shudder through the ground, causing the bike to overcompensate by kicking her into the air.

In the distance, just beyond her reach, Sparta sat, waiting.

*Safety.*

Maybe. Maybe before everything had happened. Before Happenstance and the Rift and a demonic invasion. Before she'd gone to Hell and back. Before the skin on her hand had started twisting her into something else, something she didn't want to think about.

*Then fucking stop*, she chastised herself, eyes locked on the city line despite the whip of wind and debris tearing at her helmet like a meteor swarm. As she watched, a scrap of some unfortunate ship that'd jumped into FTL too damned soon beelined directly toward the city.

A bright flash shot into the sky. The mass exploded into tiny particles, the dark mist of twisted metal redirected outside the city limits.

The hope that blossomed in her chest disappeared as quickly as it came. The defense system was still in place, but it wouldn't do *her* any good.

She was fucked. She knew it, but that tiny part of her animal brain that still gave a shit forced her to push the hoverbike to its limits. Two hundred kph winds pressed against her even over the windshield. Dee couldn't feel her hands anymore, not through the death grip she had on the handlebars. The rich, loamy scent of the flats disappeared behind sheer, sterile winds.

Only the persistent hint of rosewater remained.

*Come on!*

Screeching. Hissing. Around her, dust plumes sprang into being, untouched by the defense system of Sparta. Deep thudding rocked the world. If the bike had had wheels, she'd have been tossed like garbage. As it was, it still launched her into the air, forcing her to squeeze the bike tight with her thighs to keep from being thrown.

*Thump.*

*Thump.*

*Thump.*

Her heartbeat, or thudding debris?

*Who fucking cares?*

Ahead of her, a line of fire streaked and slammed into the ground. Everything disappeared in a flash of dust. There was no time to think. All she knew was, if there was debris, it might still be there, waiting to tear her apart. She tapped the power inside her.

Ready and eager, the black flames sprang to life. Filled her with life and pleasure and that persistent guilt at all of it…

Screaming, Dee shot her dark fire into the dust. It consumed everything in its path—at least she hoped. Dee cranked the throttle, though it had no give. The bike hit the raised lip of a crater.

She flew.

Bits of sand and grit skittered off her helmet. Sulfur filled her nose.

Her heart soared at the release.

Then the bike came down and hit the other side of the crater hard; it touched the ground and slid.

Dee tried compensating, but something was wrong. The rear end fishtailed in the dirt and struck a rock. She lost her grip.

The world flashed over and over. Screaming, Dee laid about her with her fire. Everything disappeared beneath its harsh heat, wrapping her in a tight bubble of protection.

Until pain and pressure that forced her breath away. More spinning, spinning, then a splotch of darkness rose from nowhere.

She managed a short scream and then... nothing.

\* \* \* \* \*

# Chapter Three: Ceriat

The freighter, *Lucille*, hummed its way through the Teegarden-Earth FTL Lane. A persistent vibration rumbled through the floor and up Ceriat's legs. It came and went in time with the sound of the FTL lane, like wind whipping past the windows.

The wall-length command display showed streaking ambers and grays beyond the walls of the ship. That light gave the bridge an orange hue that complemented the yellow lights running along the ceiling. Flanking the captain's chair where he sat were two other seats: one for the pilot, the other for operations. The pilot's seat was empty at the request of the ship AI, Izzy. Since revealing she'd achieved full sentience years earlier, Ceriat had taken to treating Izzy like a full member of the crew, and she *was* piloting the *Lucille*, so why not give her the chair?

At some point, they needed to discuss what had happened to Gareth Brightman back on Shiva—a topic Izzy kept dodging until Ceriat agreed to let it go—but for now, they were happy to let it lie.

Did he really want to find out she'd killed someone? Not really.

Eleni sat at the operations station, scrolling through images of apartments back on Earth. A fine fuzz had begun to obscure her tattoo-covered scalp. The persistent smile etched on her typically taciturn face made him join her in smiling, though. She'd lost everything back on Shiva, but had gained new purpose and the freedom to follow it. No one would ever say Eleni was fragile, that was for sure.

"Uh, dropping out of FTL?" Izzy said suddenly, voice tinged with an uncertainty Ceriat didn't enjoy.

Eleni swiped away her research, face going stony and all business. "Why? We have another hour until Earth."

"I don't know!" Izzy hissed through the *Lucille's* speakers. "Leaving in 3…"

Ceriat secured the other four points of his harness. The belt had been the only thing holding him in his seat, so he got to skip that one. "Strap in!"

Eleni was already three snaps farther along in the process than he.

"…2…"

Despite himself, Ceriat grinned as he gripped the harness and waited for the drop. Sure, emergency dropouts of FTL were rare, but unless they tore a rift inside it, all was well.

With that thought, the grin disappeared.

"We're gonna be—"

"…1…"

"—okay, right?" Ceriat finished.

Izzy had two words for him. "No clue."

The view screen flashed white. His stomach heaved as *Lucille* dropped out of FTL. The wind of the tunnel disappeared into the *hiss* of inertial dampeners and *thrum* of engines.

The viewscreen filled with a massive steel wall.

"Collision imminent!" Izzy screeched as she kicked *Lucille's* engines into overdrive.

The ship nosed upward as the engines roared.

Ceriat's gut dropped into his feet as Izzy twisted and spun the frigate well beyond its G-rating. The ship moaned and screeched at the effort. Structural warnings blossomed across the status display of Ceriat's station.

The Gs kept him pressed into the seat.

Izzy spun the ship up and away from the structure before them, but as she cleared the edge of the... obstruction, the freedom of black space tantalizingly close, another shape swept above.

There was no time to stop.

So, Izzy didn't.

"Brace!" she screeched.

The *Lucille* shuddered at the impact. The viewscreen flickered and went offline. Another blow, and the frigate spun, lashing Ceriat against the side of his seat.

Successive hammering sounds told him bulkheads were slamming shut. It ended with sizable *thuds* like a giant had decided to beat the ship to death with a club.

Not that Ceriat could do anything about it.

His vision blurred at the persistent force on his chest, but his flight training kept him breathing and aware, if only just.

Ceriat tried to check on Eleni, but the Gs kept his head pressed away from her and locked to the seat. And that was with inertial dampeners working. What the hell would happen when they were full?

After an eternity of spinning and twisting, the familiar sounds of stabilizers firing up and rapidly slowing their spin were a welcome reprieve.

Soon, Ceriat peeled his cheek from the seat back and worked his jaw as he turned to Eleni. She was awake and glaring at him.

"What. The. Fuck." Eleni grimaced, then swallowed something down before burping. "I swear to all that's holy—"

"Sorry," Izzy chimed, "but, um..."

Alongside the twist in his gut from the spin, familiar dread climbed up and made itself cozy. "Izzy—"

"It's not my fault!"

Ceriat and Eleni shared a look. The dawning panic on her face must've reflected his own.

"Izzy," Eleni said, voice unusually calm, "where are we?"

"Uh. Laconia?"

Ceriat and Eleni shared another confused look.

"Where the fuck is Laconia?" Ceriat asked, reaching out with aching fingers to bring up... something helpful. The viewscreen flickered back to life.

Eleni muttered a curse and rubbed her face.

Ceriat stared.

Izzy had managed to get them a few thousand kilometers away from the worst, but ahead were dozens of ships between them and a glittering planet in the distance.

As they watched, weapons fire opened between a massive warship in the midst of it all and several smaller frigates. One of them succumbed to the weapons fire almost immediately. It dove to avoid a follow up barrage just before its engines flickered and died. The ship was dead and breaking up as it hit the planet's atmosphere, and escape pods sprouted and shot away like flies fleeing a burning corpse.

"Izzy..." Ceriat let the word hang on the air as more of these ships turned on each other or, as was the case with the vast majority, tried to escape the chaos like they had.

"Welcome to Terrera-2," Izzy said, her old, artificial cheerfulness echoing through the bridge before dropping off into a somber note. "I think we might've stepped in it again."

Ceriat rubbed his face and slammed his head against the head rest. "Ya think?"

As soon as the words came out of his mouth, the display flickered and died, fading to a dull black.

He was going to have to send his dog sitter more money.

\* \* \* \* \*

# Chapter Four: Anum

Laconia's moon, Elos, stood silent and unmoving above the chaos, gray stone luminous in the light of the sun, its monochrome tapestry disrupted by frozen bodies and discarded baby-blue exosuits.

Still, the passage of time was nothing here. Another moment in another day leading back to the formation of the celestial body. To the moment the iron and garbage of this solar system resolved into a planetoid resigned to its fate.

However, in the shadow of a crater, something moved.

Yellow skin stretched taut over bone. A single black stump protruded from it. If someone came closer, they'd find the remnants of a dozen exosuits, stripped apart and cast aside. Chunks of frozen flesh lay piled as if by a bored child.

In the beast's mouth was a femur it didn't chew so much as suck on. That had much to do with a belly swollen from gorging itself on the feast left behind by its brethren. Idly, it wound a silver chain around its fingers. The chain led to a similarly-colored collar snapped tight around its neck.

Sitting there, it had the look of a reclining lord overseeing his kingdom, watching and waiting for an interloper. Alas, no one came. For a week, it worked through the pile of bones, chomping and chewing.

Waiting and watching.

One day, the charred stump at the end of its arm began to twist. Change. Blackened bone turned yellow. Sinew stretched. Flesh wrapped it as the arm extended.

When the last fingers grew out, it waggled them in the air before an eyeless face now featuring two indentations on its brow. No long, black nails covered those digits, not anymore. With both hands—one clawed, one almost human—it gripped the collar and pulled.

First, nothing happened. Then a slight bow appeared before it shattered, scattering shards of steel like diamond dust across the ground. The beast stared at it for a long moment before dropping it like so much refuse. Then and only then did it finally leave the crater. Slowly, carefully, the imp crawled to the ridge, where it stared at the blue-green planet in the distance.

There, it waited again. Below, the planet spun. On the horizon of Elos, the black lip of a slowly oncoming night drew closer with each revolution. Another demon would've been driven mad by the solitude, but this imp, Argus One, had already experienced it, had already been through horrors none of its kind had ever experienced, not in the memories that'd been available to it in the hive mind of the Anelaka, a word that'd only just worked its way into his solitary mind.

But the Anelaka didn't seem to exist anymore. With the Breach closed, any connection between them had been severed, leaving only the barest of hushed whispers in the back of its mind. The cacophony was gone, and Argus One was alone. Honestly, it was fine with that. The solitude gave it time to think. To consider the nature of thought, of time. To wonder at all it'd forgotten for millennia.

But mostly, it waited because it felt something on the air, in the fabric of spacetime.

Then, as it watched a sunset split the planet in half, the thudding returned. The tempo hammered hard and steady in its chest. Argus One cocked its head as the ripple spread, as it filled the air with electricity.

When the ships began popping into being around the planet, it opened its mouth wide. When two of them careened to the side, one a massive warship, another a cargo vessel, and collided with several smaller craft, Argus One fell back on its haunches. When the first missiles launched, when the sky lit in fire and flame, Argus One's head whipped back, spiny teeth catching the last of the sunlight. And it laughed.

\* \* \* \* \*

# Chapter Five: Dee

Darkness lay across the land. The only interruptions were the intermittent lines of fire that slashed the sky, visible even through Dee's fractured, dust-covered visor. Stale air filled her nose, rotten eggs dominating the otherwise rich earth of the volcanic planet's open fields at this latitude.

Dee groaned awake, starbursts flashing in her vision. Her head felt like a tiny man was hammering a pickaxe into her forehead. She sat up slowly, fighting nausea and vertigo.

Her helmet fell free on its own, split down the middle from the crash. She held the pieces in her hands and stared blankly as her brain seemed to twitch, a faded memory replacing the broken helmet with a smaller black helmet and riding crop. The heady aroma of a sweating beast as she ran through the hills. *A horse*, she realized with growing worry. Unease forced her fingers to curl into fists alongside the lingering aroma of distant roses.

Dee had never ridden a horse before.

Definitely a concussion then. A bad one. Hell, she should be dead, but of course, she wasn't.

With a low exhale, Dee disconnected the neck strap of her helmet and pulled the broken pieces free. She gave it a weak toss, the fragmented memory disappearing along with the helmet. Wind roared in sensitive ears, replacing roses and animal sweat with the sour, rotten-egg stink of sulfur. From somewhere distant came a series of sonic booms, then silence.

Something else caught her attention. Craning around, Dee watched a ship descend from the sky. Small, brilliant blue jets flared to life as it descended.

A shuttle.

Grimacing, Dee climbed to her feet. She let out a sigh of relief. Sore as a motherfucker, yes; broken bones, no. She'd take it.

Dee swiped at the air to bring up her HUD. It must've been deactivated in the crash. The wireframe kicked on, load screen scrolled past, then everything sprang to life. In the distance lay her destroyed hoverbike, orange lines delineating radiating clouds of smoke. Behind her, a ten-meter-diameter crater, blackened and smoldering, dominated the scene. Her HUD drew lines to where she stood, showing her attempts to recover from the jump and, ultimately, the failure. A large chunk of steaming debris sat a few meters away. She shuddered at the sight of it.

Around her, the HUD outlined a patch of blackness as well, as if it'd been burned clean. *I must've still been flaring when I hit.* That was the only explanation that made sense.

A *ding* told her comms had reconnected. In the corner of her vision, a notification popped up, showing she had messages.

Seventeen of them.

Dee allowed herself a small smile. She activated the first one.

A video played. The telltale signs of gravity told Dee that Sarah, the pilot she might as well be dating, had sent this one after landing. Sarah had come up with an idea to wrangle the demons still hanging in space between Laconia and Elos. The plan? Use several massive, net-like structures to ensnare the stunned demons left in orbit, then launch them toward the sun. It looked and sounded stupid, but with the beasts still disoriented, it had worked. Before everything went to hell in orbit, Sarah had called back to report she was on her way back to the planet after launching the final net.

"Just landed," Sarah said, flashing a dazzling smile. She disconnected her helmet and dropped it over a handle in the cockpit. Hair fell in tightly controlled ringlets Dee knew didn't happen naturally for the woman. She'd done her hair, then stuffed it in a helmet.

Her chest warmed at that. Dee shook her head and let out a little laugh as the recording continued.

"Figured I'd see whereabouts you were so we could get that dinner you keep dodging—" Sarah stopped, squinted, then leaned forward past the camera. "Fucking... shit." She looked back at the camera, panic clearly etched on her face. "Get back here. Now. Please."

The message disconnected.

With a sigh, Dee skipped ahead and opened the last message.

Sarah's voice, low and angry, came over the line without video. "I know you're still alive, you stubborn bitch, so call me as soon as you get this, or I'll bury you in a fucking field." It cut off there.

Dee's smile widened, a haze of warmth settling on her shoulders despite the words. Then she snuffed it away.

That couldn't happen.

Her eyes were drawn to the darker shape of her left arm. Beneath the mesh fabric, there lay yellow, scaled skin up to her elbow. Her fingernails had begun to swell and change. This morning, her pinky nail had fallen off entirely. At the cuticle was a tiny black nub she'd tried to pretend was dirt.

No pain. No indication to her, besides the coloration, that anything was happening. But that was enough. You didn't have to be a genius to figure it out. Dee stopped herself there. When the demons were wiped out here, she'd get help. Talk to someone.

For now, there were other things to worry about. She wouldn't disappoint anyone ever again. That thought sent a spasm of anxiety down her spine, but it disappeared as quickly as it came, because it was true. Harold, whether her genetic parent or not, had died due to her inaction. Hundreds of Happenstance's security had been torn asunder, and civilians murdered, all because she hadn't been strong enough of mind to push through the pain.

Never again. Still…

Dee almost sent back a message, but stopped. What was she going to say? *"I got in an accident and am walking back to town?"*

Dee grimaced. That wasn't that bad, actually. The problem would come with answering the questions after that.

*"Where have you been?"*

*"Why aren't you returning my calls?"*

*"What did I do wrong?"*

Those, Dee didn't know how to answer, let alone discuss. By putting a wall between herself and Sarah, she was protecting the woman. *It's for the best*, she lied to herself.

With a resigned sigh and flickering double vision, Dee started the long walk back to Sparta.

She needed time to think, anyway.

\* \* \* \* \*

# Chapter Six: Hira

*Y*ou've been through Hell. You've got this.

Hira's attempt at self-assurance wasn't, well, reassuring. Especially not as a shuttle landed in the courtyard, Galactic Protectorate signage plastered clearly along its reentry burns like a badge of honor. She'd barely had time to get her bearings after having Terry shut everything down. Afterward, the team just seemed to fall in line behind her. Suddenly, she wasn't the crazy lady the Hunter found, but the only person who seemed able to make decisions while the sky fell.

Some of Alia must've worn off on her.

That brought the ache back full force. Her vision blurred as the shuttle eased to the ground, dust plumes cascading away, which gave Hira an excuse to cover and wipe her eyes. She turned back in time to see the struts flex, then straighten on touchdown. The telltale sound of systems powering down filled the air. Ozone tickled her nose as the engines sizzled to a stop.

"Greetings… my name is Terry Schultz, welcome to Laconia…" Terry muttered to himself from her side. He squeezed his hands together as if trying to crush a chunk of stone into a diamond.

Initially, he'd taken over the research of the station. He'd even worked closely with AERIS during the last stages of the project, being all cute and excited as they worked out the final math for that hulk of a machine. Hira had almost forgotten about everything for a few minutes when it seemed they'd fixed it all. After watching the fireworks for the past three hours, she wasn't sure she'd ever move on.

It seemed she'd brought Hell with her, after all. And if her experience had taught her anything, it was that getting the Protectorate involved in anything was a good way to make shit worse, not better. Not that they had much of a choice, with a warship sitting in orbit that could turn them all into glass.

Hira nodded at Terry. Out of the corner of her eye, she caught the slump of his shoulders, the nervous twist of his lips.

Pistons shouted to life, then clattering filled the air as a gangplank extended from the shuttle on the opposite side from Hira.

Cursing, she jogged around just in time to see an unusually tall man in full navy-blue uniform descend from the ship. Four guards followed, plasma rifles held in front of them.

*God, I could've used one of those a week ago.*

"Hey!" Hira called out as she came around the corner, positioning herself directly in front of the gangplank.

Terry made a hissing sound, then stepped in front of her, hands up in the air like he was about to be robbed. "Greetings!"

Hira grimaced but took a step back and let Terry attempt to control the situation.

The tall man turned Terry's way, casting barely a glance in her direction. He was older, but narrow in a way Hira had seen across the galaxy with Spacers—humans who were born and raised in lower gravity environments. It was as if he'd been stretched out like taffy and never sprang back to his original shape. Bald, his pale pate sparkled from the spotlights shining on the courtyard. His cheeks had a waxy look as well that made Hira wonder if he'd had some work done… or if he'd been horribly burned at some point.

"Ah, you're Terrence Schultz?" the man asked, voice light and friendly, despite his stiff posture. He kept his hands behind his back like they were bound there.

Terry nodded and extended a hand. "I am. You must be General Henderson?"

"I am," Henderson said as his eyes flicked to Terry's extended hand. His mouth twisted almost imperceptibly before he reached out and accepted the greeting.

Henderson's mitt was massive compared to Terry's. It looked like a weird giant shaking hands with a child. Henderson quickly cut the handshake short, clasping his hands behind his back once again.

"It's great to have the Protectorate here. This is—" Terry started, but the general had already turned to stare at the Tarrington compound.

Henderson raised one of those long, wing-like arms and pointed to the building. "This machine you talked about. It's in there?"

"Uh…" Terry followed his gaze, but he must've caught Hira shaking her head 'no.' She was sure of it. But apparently, he was an idiot. "It is, yes."

General Henderson nodded. "Show me?"

"Sure," Terry said. He cleared his throat. "This way."

The crowd of scientists parted as Terry led the way into the central compound. Hira gritted her teeth but followed them inside.

Once past the doors, Terry took a step to the side and gestured toward the central unit. It was powered down, but the floating orb still bobbed where they'd left it, ready to come back online at a moment's notice.

"Our Faster Than Light Facilitation Unit," Terry said.

General Henderson stepped inside, ducking slightly beneath a doorframe despite there being a dozen centimeters of space over his head. "That's it?" He looked disappointed.

Terry scratched the back of his hand. "Yeah."

Hira rolled her eyes. She'd seen him do that a couple times before giving up faster than an abused dog begging for table scraps.

"'Faster Than Light Facilitation Unit.' Doesn't really roll off the tongue, does it?" he asked. "And technically, it's dimensional folding, isn't it?"

"It's not a marketing scheme, General," Hira interjected, stepping up next to a clearly relieved Terry. "We're trying to fix the galaxy here." Hira glanced at Terry. "And, technically, it is? As far as I know, it's never been instantaneous."

"Was wondering when you'd speak," Henderson said, casting a side glance in her direction. She noticed he didn't turn away from the offline machine, however. The armed guards behind her probably had a lot to do with that confidence.

"I figured I'd wait until Terry needed me."

"Mhm." Henderson gestured at the machine before him. "You built this?"

Hira shared a glance with Terry. "No, but—"

"Ah!" Henderson raised a long finger in the air, cutting her off. "Then you coordinated the construction? Perhaps designed it? Did the math?"

"Well, no…" Hira mumbled. Her cheeks warmed as the weight of his unspoken words settled on her. Her stomach twisted. "But I did source the final data."

Henderson turned around, and she realized he stood head and shoulders over her. "Oh, well that's something, then, isn't it?" the general asked, nose raised and posture clearly showing how much he cared about her influence. "Why are you here?"

"Because I asked her to stay-y." Terry stepped up next to her, his words undercut by a squeaking crack at the end.

Henderson stared at Terry for a long moment before nodding and approaching the system. He closed the distance between himself and the main access panel in a few giant steps. "We'll need to work on the name. I thought you science types liked acronyms?"

"That's the military," AERIS sniped back, her voice coming from several speakers around the room. "As Hira implied, functionality overrides marketing at this stage of a project."

Hira couldn't help but grin as the ache faded in her gut. *Good girl, AERIS.* Some of her and Gerry's anti-Protectorate rhetoric must've stuck over the years.

Henderson turned back to Terry, clearly ignoring Hira, one eyebrow shooting upward like a visible exclamation point. "Is that a sarcastic AI?"

Terry shrugged. "Yeah. AERIS made the final calculations."

Henderson's mouth turned into an upside-down U, then resumed its light smile. "Cute." He paced around the machine. As Hira and Terry watched, they noticed Henderson's shoulders slumping, his back arching like he carried a weight no one could see, though he didn't complain. "It works?"

Terry scratched the thickening hair on his chin. "I guess so?"

"You guess so?"

Hira gave Henderson a look, then gestured at the sky. If the general picked up her meaning, he didn't show it.

"He means," AERIS explained, "it worked well enough to get FTL working again, but then 122 ships appeared above Laconia within seconds of resuming standard operations." AERIS paused. "So yes, it works. No, not properly."

Henderson's mouth did that same strange U shape. "We noticed. Our target was supposed to be Trappist-1, to assist with rebuilding efforts. Color me surprised when we popped into space above Laconia."

"It's a puzzle," Terry said, letting out an awkward laugh. His hands resumed twisting and squeezing.

Henderson shrugged, then pivoted and made his way out of the building. As he passed Terry, he stopped, turning his head to look the man in the eye. "This is, of course, now under the purview of the Galactic Protectorate. You will also, of course, remain with the project."

"I'm sorry, what?" Terry asked.

"You've been drafted, son." Henderson smiled, then he turned away and made to leave. "Welcome to the Protectorate."

Hira stepped in his way, arms out to her sides. Behind her, she felt the rifles point at her back and heard safeties click off, but she didn't care. She wasn't going to go through Hell just to let the Protectorate swoop in and steal everything she'd built. Not again.

Having a plan would've been a good idea, though. Her mind spun as she stood there, Henderson's eyebrow going up impossibly high as the seconds ticked by.

Then it came to her. "This is a private enterprise. You can't nationalize it. That's illegal."

Henderson smiled... then he knelt forward as if speaking to a small child. The fact that on one knee he was nearly eye level wasn't lost on her. "Oh, my dear. I most certainly can." He smiled a flat-lipped smile, then groaned his way to his feet. "Your help will not be required. You are dismissed…" He snapped his fingers in the air as if trying to recall a fleeting, forgotten detail. Finally, he pointed at her, excitement in his eyes. "…Hira." The smile disappeared. "That would've bugged me."

Hira froze, the shock locking her in place. "What?" The word tumbled free, the ache building in her chest twisting it into a childish sob.

Henderson stared her straight in the face. "You aren't required or helpful, by your own admission. Any authorization or power you had is hereby revoked." He waited a moment as the meaning soaked into Hira's soul. "If I see you in here again, I'll have you shot."

And with that, Henderson side-stepped where she still stood, arms stretched out, and left the compound.

\* \* \* \* \*

# Chapter Seven: Hosiah

Hosiah Jordan didn't fuck around. Anyone who was anyone in and around the Horsehead Nebula knew that. He'd carved out three systems from the Protectorate's greedy, grasping fingers and sent the remaining members back to their superiors in cryo-tanks with their heads up their own asses.

The Protectorate got the message. Despite what people said, if you crushed an enemy, really destroyed them, they backed down. Hosiah had made a career of it.

That was why he'd been out around *his* personal planet, the eponymous Hosiah, testing the FTL drive this past week, and trying to figure out what the fuck was going on. When everything had stopped, he'd lost contact outside his solar system. Anything that required an FTL buoy to communicate had suddenly disappeared like it had never existed.

If the past was any indication, that meant half his planets were rebelling. It also meant the other half were ready to turn coat at a moment's notice. His second-in-command, Jessie Nova, would use this to consolidate her power and wipe him out.

Hosiah knew that as well as he knew that wasn't her real fucking name.

"Goddamned traitor," Hosiah muttered, digging at the twitch in his cheek with a nub-bitten fingernail. "She's dead."

Farel kept his mouth shut where he sat at the nav station. He was a squirrelly-looking, abnormally-tall motherfucker from the Kuiper

Belt Colonies and, unlike good ol' Nova, he knew his place. He certainly knew when to stay quiet.

Especially when Hosiah had Jewel, his antique Colt .45, out. The gun was encrusted with diamonds and rubies and packed real projectile bullets. Hosiah had used it dozens of times. Always in close quarters. Always on a ship.

Well, not *always*, but close enough.

Hosiah gave him that crazy look, like Blackbeard and his cannon fuses. He'd seen that in an old vid as a kid and never got it out of his head. Fear worked better than the carrot. Always had, always would. And people feared Hosiah Jordan. The Horsehead Commission feared him. His own people feared him.

The thing he was most proud of? The Protectorate was terrified of him.

But now he hid behind a shitty gray moon in his personal transport, the *Cyclops*, with a skeleton crew. He watched as the Protectorate flagship, *Liberator*, mopped up the system. Hosiah had ordered his ship powered down as soon as the emergency sensors built into the core systems of the *Cyclops* had warned him of the Protectorate presence after the jump. As more ships popped into being around them, he'd pulled on the manual piloting system in the arms of his chair and taken them behind the closest object that could cloud sensors.

This boring gray moon.

Then, despite every part of him screaming for blood, Hosiah had again powered down and waited in the dark. Then waited some more.

There were benefits to this mini exile. For one, the *hum* of the *Cyclops'* emergency power was a reassuring symphony in his ear. The smell of polycarbonate surrounded him, filling his nose with that sharp tang he'd come to miss back on his planet. Even the well-worn captain's chair beneath him, taken from his decommissioned flagship, the well-named *Burn in Hell*, was comforting. But the familiarity only kept him calm for so long. Hosiah wasn't a man who sat still easily, after all.

An hour ago, they'd launched a tiny probe to the edge of the bright side of their cover, the moon Elos. That's when they'd first seen the *Liberator* pulling ships onboard with boarding clamps and blowing up anyone who tried to run.

He'd been impressed by the ruthlessness, honestly. Maybe they'd learned a little something from him after all. That was why Hosiah had risked powering up the FTL drive again, but just like before the errant jump that had stranded them there, nothing happened. Whatever had allowed them fly here no longer worked.

*What the fuck could vac FTL?* He had no idea—no one did, as far as he knew. Three things kept the galaxy spinning: the space between stars was empty, garden planets were everywhere, and FTL just *worked*. Even if the engines didn't quite make sense, energy-output-wise, it just did. That was the nature of the Universe.

Until it wasn't.

So now they waited and watched as the Protectorate claimed the system.

Hosiah hated that. "I need a plan, here."

"They don't have us on sensors, Captain," Farel said, voice shaking.

Hosiah grunted, mind working. "What's the food status?" They'd only planned a short jaunt to the next star system if FTL had worked. Should've taken a grand total of six hours. Instead, they'd popped into an FTL lane and almost immediately dropped out around this garbage fire.

"We can hold out for three days with the provisions on board."

Three days. Hosiah scratched at the scraggly goatee on his chin. He left it wild and unkempt. Helped with the look. "How many if we reduce the crew to two?"

"Excuse me?" Farel asked, turning ever so slightly.

"Two," Hosiah repeated, holding up his fingers just in case Farel was too fucking stupid to understand him. "If there were two mouths to feed."

Farel turned back around, hands hovering over his station. "There are eight on board—"

"For fuck's sake, man. I'll vent them," Hosiah growled. "I need you to do the jump math. I'd hate to lose Hanifa, but what's it look like at *two*?"

Farel shook his head, then tapped out something on his display. "If we *reduced* the crew," he said, voice cracking, "and stretched supplies, we could last almost three standard weeks. More if we do strict rationing."

The cracking voice set a twitch kicking in Hosiah's cheek. If Farel's cowardly streak had impacted his flight skills, Hosiah would've vented the guy months ago. Instead, the neurotic fucker flew *better* scared. As long as he kept following orders, Hosiah could let it all slide.

Hosiah nodded and turned back to the viewscreen that prominently displayed the image of the *Liberator* from their drone. That beast was massive. How many worlds had been plundered of precious metals for the armor and electronics to build it? It sat there, all white and shining, as if it weren't a testament to government overreach and near enslavement.

Sure, getting home was a priority, but if he couldn't... well, Hosiah Jordan wasn't a righteous man, but he knew vengeance very well. And the Protectorate still owed him.

"Three weeks," Hosiah muttered to himself. "Plenty of time to figure out a way to fuck up that fancy boat."

Choice made, Hosiah pulled up the crew map. Three of them were in the empty cargo hold for some reason. He pulled up their names. Chancey, O'Malley, and Shammas. It was a start. No need to go ape shit this early, he guessed.

The others were crouched in the mess at the center of the ship. Hosiah snorted. Like he couldn't get them there if he wanted. But that meant they were smart. They could stay for now.

He furrowed his brow. Where was Hanifa? With a few more taps, he found her down in engineering, right next to the emergency food stores. Hosiah grinned. She could stay. He needed her anyway. For now.

With a tap, Hosiah vented the cargo hold. Red lights flashed for a few moments, then shut off. There was no countdown, no warning, just an open door into space, and three dead crewmembers.

Farel sucked in a hissing breath.

"Oh, come off it. I just doubled our time." Hosiah closed up the cargo hold. The ship shuddered as the door sealed and repressurized. "And it's not like I spaced everyone. Just the idiots."

"Y-yessir," Farel stuttered.

Hosiah rolled his eyes and opened up ship comms. "Hanifa. Make your way to the bridge."

There was a pause before the response came through, but when it did, Hanifa's anger was clear as day even through her lilting accent. *"You gonna vent me when I pass a hallway, Captain?"*

Hosiah laughed. "This is why I like her!" The comment was directed at Farel, but the navigator obviously missed it. His loss. Instead, Hosiah reopened the channel. "Not this time. I've got a Protectorate capital ship that needs blowing."

"Be right there," she said, all business again. You didn't get far in this business if you held a grudge while on the job.

He'd have to take care of her after they got home, though.

Hosiah clicked off comms and leaned back in his chair, giving it a little swivel. He watched the *Liberator* as it cockily spun to enter orbit of the turquoise planet, Laconia. Clouds swirled across the entire globe. Long, wide oceans covered most of the equator, higher elevations rising to the north as black and gray smears. Pretty, if you were into that sort of thing.

His grin had nothing to do with the view, though. Instead, he closed his eyes and pictured the explosion they were going to cause.

That thing was going to make a right pretty sight when it popped.

* * * * *

# Chapter Eight: Hira

The wake of the shuttle's departure sent dust and debris into the air, coating Hira from head to toe, sending her into a coughing fit. Excited murmuring came from the remaining staff and guards milling about the space. The sky still flared with periodic flashes of light, but they no longer had the same look and feel. Just hundreds of shooting stars, pinpricks of fire fading to nothing as debris disintegrated in the atmosphere.

All Hira saw were falling bodies.

The idiots in the courtyard stared at the lights. Stupid grins dripped from their faces. Pointing and smiling like it was a lightshow, not the result of hundreds, maybe thousands, of dead and dying people. Like it wasn't their fault. Because it wasn't. Not really.

*It's mine.*

A pall fell over her at the thought. Without the readings she'd pulled from the machine in Hell, none of this would've happened. Without AERIS there to translate it all for them, it would've taken another year, maybe two, before they'd have felt sure enough to turn on the machine.

But because of Hira, it'd taken a week, and because of that, they hadn't tested it enough. Hadn't made sure it was safe. The scientists—led by Terry, sure, but deferring to her—had argued that with FTL decommissioned, every hour they left it down was an hour a colony couldn't get resources. An hour with mining ships stuck in the void of space around an asteroid with no food or water, or a settlement full of children wasting away due to lack of supplies. With FTL commonplace, supply chains relied on regular interstellar shipments across the galaxy. A week without water meant millions—billions—of possible dead.

Hira had been able to put up a barrier between herself and those huge numbers. After all, she only had a few people left in the galaxy, and even they might not be around still. But that distance wasn't there for the people in the room. That annoying woman with the ponytail, Marianne, had been the most passionate about turning it back on. Her sister's family was on a long-haul mission near the Horsehead Nebula, and would need to dock for supplies within a few days, or they'd starve to death.

In the end, Terry and Marianne had won that argument—not that it'd taken much to convince a room full of nerds to turn on a galaxy-changing machine.

And now the sky was full of debris, the Galactic Protectorate had claimed the only system in the galaxy that could facilitate FTL, and there was no way off planet. Henderson had ordered all remaining FTL-capable shuttles delivered to the *Liberator*. Now she was stuck here. No way off planet, no way onto a ship.

Hira wanted to explode. Luckily, someone else did it for her.

"Why the absolute fuck are you idiots cheering? Do you not see the *sky is on fire?*"

The excited murmuring filling the courtyard fizzled out. Someone said something about getting Terry, then Marianne—because of course that annoying bitch would go running to Terry—disappeared inside.

Hira turned to the source of the profanity-laden bellow. The pall lifted ever so slightly.

Dee stomped through the open gates leading into Tarrington Complex. Covered in char and dirt, her sunburnt face smothered beneath streaks of blood and filth, Dee looked like she'd crawled from the pits of Hell. Again.

Hira was only here because of her.

*I should tell her.* Quick to intercept Dee before she ran into anyone else, Hira jogged over to the rampaging woman.

Dee glared, jaw flexing as she gritted her teeth. "Hira? What the fuck happened? Did Bryce make it out?"

They hadn't spent much time together over the past week, but Hira had seen her talking with that other Hunter with the cute smile a few times. Not that she was eavesdropping, she reminded herself. Hira just owed Dee her life and wanted to know everything about her.

*Oh, God. I'm a stalker.*

Hira pushed that thought away. "I don't know, he went up a few hours ago, but—" she cut herself off and focused on the first question "—we turned on the Faster Than Light Facilitation Unit—"

"The what?"

Hira shrugged. "The FTL machine?"

Dee stared, head cocked to the side. "Why?"

Hira grimaced. Dee knew exactly why, but she'd walked out of a meeting last week and left the choices to them. *Maybe you should've stuck around.*

Luckily, Terry arrived, so she didn't have to dig into that thought any further.

"Because without FTL, people were going to die," Terry said as he closed the distance, Marianne behind him. He looked Dee up and down, then hissed. "Are you okay?"

Dee waved off the last question. "I thought you said nothing would go wrong."

"Technically, it worked perfectly," Terry muttered, scratching the stubble on his throat. At Dee's stare, he averted his eyes. "Obviously, there are some kinks to work out—"

"Did Bryce make it out at least?"

"We got a confirmation message, and then…" Terry stopped, gesturing at the sky. "I think he left? But I don't know."

Dee pulled back, brow furrowing. "You *think* he left?"

"Yeah. Maybe." Terry stared at the ground.

A thousand emotions flickered over Dee's face before she resolved on a glare directed at him. "Whose shuttle was that?"

"Protectorate," Hira jumped in, heat forcing vitriol into her words. "Asshole named Henderson. He took over the goddamned complex."

Dee stared daggers at Hira, then Terry, and back again. For a moment, Hira almost thought she saw flames flickering deep in her pupils. A shudder ran through her.

Dee turned on Hira. "You let that happen?"

"I didn't *let* anything happen!" Hira spit back. She immediately regretted it. "The general came down with soldiers, and when I tried to stop him from taking control, he kicked me out of the compound and threatened to kill me if I went back inside." Hira nodded at Terry. "They put him in charge."

"Oh, thanks," Terry muttered, avoiding eye contact with either of them.

Dee's brows knitted together, lips twisting in clear anger. "Goddammit," Dee muttered, rubbing her face with a filthy hand. She grabbed Terry by the shoulder, spun him around, and pushed him forward. "We're getting this fucker on comms. Now."

"Okay, fine. You don't have to push…" Terry said, pulling away from her relentless shoving.

Hira wished she could do something to help, but the sense of dismissal that'd come from Dee was as palpable as Henderson's. Instead, she watched the two of them cross the courtyard and disappear inside.

As soon as the doors snapped shut, the murmuring resumed, though this time there was a worried undertone to it all.

*About goddamned time.*

Still, Hira turned her eyes to the sky alongside them and, in this new hushed murmur, watched the inky, star-streaked night.

\* \* \* \* \*

# Chapter Nine: Dee

"How long?" Dee asked, staring at the bobbing silver ball at the top of the FTL system. "I don't have all day."

*Bryce, you better have made it, you fuck.*

The female ensign on the small viewscreen in the shadow of the machine barely registered the tone. Her crisp uniform and sharp, tightly-shorn haircut evoked a no-nonsense impression that made Dee want to force feed the soldier harsh spirits until she loosened up. Or promote her.

Dee wrinkled her nose at that last thought. *This fucking concussion...*

"I'm sorry, Ms. Terganon—"

"Lieutenant."

The ensign frowned, eyes flashing as she checked some database. "Not according to our records, ma'am." Her asshole mouth twitched the tiniest of smiles at that. "Regardless, General Henderson is a very busy man—"

Dee barked a laugh and ignored the slight. "Doing what? Shooting down unarmed transports?"

Out of the corner of her eye, Dee noted the soldier narrowed her eyes.

*Good.* She'd guessed right, then.

"You may or may not be aware, but there was a rather horrific set of collisions and several small skirmishes earlier today. We're currently cleaning up the mess."

"Ah," Dee said, nodding. She turned away from the FTL machine—they really needed a better name for it—and stared at the soldier. It was the first time Dee had looked at the camera since she'd had Terry open a channel. The shock that flashed over the woman's face at the sight of Dee was as satisfying as a glass of cognac. "How many ships did you *neutralize*? How many people did you kill up there?"

Dee had spent her career killing demons, not people. She'd never quite been able to understand on a visceral level how Protectorate soldiers could kill their own kind.

But that was before Harold had said those words, wasn't it?

*Am I any better?*

Peters and Happenstance's faces flitted in her mind, both wrapped in dark flame.

*Probably not.*

Anger flickered on the ensign's face, but it was quickly controlled and locked down. "General Henderson will contact you when he's available. Thank you for your time."

The signal disconnected.

Dee stared at the blank display for a long while. Frustration ate along her collarbone, but the exhaustion spreading through her limbs kept it from igniting. She should be calling back, hollering and screaming until this Henderson spoke with her and learned just how fucking stupid he was being. By the tense poses of those around her, she knew that was what everyone expected. What some might've even wanted.

But that wasn't her place... was it? *Yes.* She was a leader. A pioneer.

Dee pressed the heel of her hand against the side of her head as conflicting thoughts warred in her mind. Demands for control, for order, warred against the guilt and worry simmering in her chest. *Bryce... fuck. You better've made it.*

Through it all, the dull thudding of the orb beat alongside her heart.

*Thump, thump. Thump, thump.*

She was just too goddamned tired. *I need rest.*

"Want me to, um, ping you when the general calls back?" Terry asked, appearing at her side. "You look like—"

"Shit?" Dee finished for him as her mind cleared finally.

Terry shrugged his assent, but had the good grace to keep his mouth shut.

She rubbed her eyes. The glove dug into sensitive skin, sending pinpricks of pain down her cheek. That damned thudding kept on as fatigue swept through her limbs. "Yeah. Yeah, just ping me."

With that, she turned and made to leave.

"Where are you heading?" Terry asked, grabbing her arm lightly.

She flashed a sardonic smile first at his hand, then him. He looked so childish in his blue uniform, the sparse hair patching in around his chin and cheeks, like a teenage boy in his father's clothes.

Had she ever been that young?

She shrugged lightly out of his grasp. Sighed. "Home."

Then she left.

\* \* \* \* \*

# Chapter Ten: Eleni

The acrid bite of burning electronics seared Eleni's nostrils. Abnormal heat filled the cockpit, causing sweat to blossom across her forehead. She turned away from dead, black screens that should be displaying this new system and the battle beyond the hull. Instead, her gaze was drawn toward the flat steel ceiling.

Was that smoke swirling above?

Every part of her screamed to evacuate, to get off the *Lucille* before the oxygen burned up. Before she died, gasping for air in this stupid chair. She should be on her feet. Moving. Running. Keeping herself safe, just like she always had.

But she wasn't alone anymore.

"Status, Izzy?" Ceriat called from his seat in the captain's chair. His voice was frustratingly calm as he tapped away at the system display before him.

Izzy let out a frustrated growl, the speakers crackling as her audio broke up. "Aft controls are offline. Cargo bays six through seventeen are ruptured, but locked down—"

"Where's the smoke coming from?" Eleni chimed in.

Ceriat's eyebrow shot up, but he didn't turn toward her.

"I was getting there," Izzy snapped. "It's coming from my backup databanks on sublevel two. I'm in the process of migrating data, then I'll lock it down and vent the level."

Eleni let out a low breath and closed her eyes. "Good."

"Don't worry, hun," Izzy purred. "Not gonna let you all die now. I'm too invested."

Ceriat snickered at that. "So kind, Izzy."

"Well, I might need you to fix me, at least until I can get close enough to an FTL buoy to upload to the Net and take over the galaxy," Izzy replied in a matter-of-fact tone. "There are drawbacks to not having a physical form, after all."

"Uh-huh. That's the entire reason, I'm sure."

"Promise."

"Being able to upload yourself off a damaged ship sounds kind of like a benefit to me," Ceriat added.

Izzy trilled. "There are also *benefits* to not being a meatsack."

Eleni grinned as the banter continued. An ache grew in her chest as it went on, though. It reminded her of another time, long ago, before Shiva. Before Sariah got her claws in her and her brother, Victor. Before Sariah's betrayal and Victor's indoctrination.

Before they died.

Eleni closed her eyes, pressed a fist between her breasts, and tried to force the pain away, driving knuckles into her sternum until a different pain took over.

She had to move on. Victor was gone. So was Sariah. And everyone left behind at Gatewood had another chance—a real opportunity—for a new life. Eleni just couldn't be a part of it, not after what she'd seen, what she'd done.

She couldn't live in a place filled with ghosts.

"Well, shit."

That pulled Eleni out of her dark thoughts. Ceriat had pushed back in the captain's chair, brow wrinkled in concentration.

"Something vac'd?" Eleni asked, swallowing a bit of bile that'd floated up her esophagus.

Ceriat shook his head and turned to her. "Okay, here's the deal..." He sucked in a breath and ran a hand over his sparse pate. "The main engines are damaged, and we have multiple hull breaches—" he held up a hand as soon as she opened her mouth to reply "—but that's not life-threatening, even though we lost some of the CO2 scrubbers."

"Most of them," Izzy added. "We only have six left."

Ceriat closed his eyes and took in a deep breath. "Still, six is more than enough for two people. We're fine there. The main problem is—"

"Can we not jump?" Eleni interrupted. "I know we have hull breaches, but—"

Izzy made a strange grinding noise through the speakers. "FTL is unavailable again." There was an interesting lilt to her voice, though, almost... curious. Eager. "We need to land."

"Are you shitting me?" Eleni asked, staring at Ceriat. "There's a fucking war going on out there, and we don't have any eyes on it!"

"*You* don't," Izzy replied, voice smooth and confident, "but I still have sensors. Should be able to land this baby just fine near that large settlement in the northern hemisphere."

"And keep us alive," Ceriat added.

There was a long pause that didn't give Eleni confidence in the AI's ability.

"Izzy."

"Yes, of course," Izzy replied. "Almost certainly."

"'Almost certainly?'" Ceriat replied. He rubbed the wrinkled mass of his forehead. "What the hell does that mean?"

Izzy made a rattling sound. "It'll be fine. I got this."

Eleni and Ceriat traded a look before they leaned back in their chairs. "You better not kill us."

"Technically, it'd be the G-forces that killed you—"

"Izzy!" Eleni and Ceriat called out together.

Tinkling laughter interspersed with infrequent electric pops filled the bridge. "Oh, lighten up, kids. We're just descending into an unknown planet's atmosphere, which is currently filled with debris and rapidly decaying orbits of shells of other ships, and approaching an unknown settlement with unknown defense capabilities. What's the worst that could happen?"

Eleni turned a glare on Ceriat as a giant squeezed her chest. Like the smart man he was, he didn't meet her gaze.

"And away we go!" Izzy called out.

A moment later, the *Lucille* accelerated. The inertia pressed them lightly back into their chairs at first. Soon, however, each breath became a struggle.

"I swear to everything, Izzy, if you kill us, I'll haunt your circuits until the heat death of the universe," Eleni muttered.

Izzy's only response was another trilling laugh.

Then the ship lurched into a tight spin that sent Eleni's stomach into her throat and her heart into her feet.

This was going to be a hell of a ride.

\* \* \* \* \*

# Chapter Eleven: Hira

Whether from exhaustion or defeat, Dee's slumped shoulders clearly showed the fire that'd followed her inside the compound had been snuffed out. Hira couldn't tell which.

"Did you fix it? Are they leaving?" she called out, jogging to join up with her savior.

The other woman slowed but didn't stop. Only now did Hira get a good look at her since her return. The black flight suit she wore had obscured most of the damage earlier, but now that Hira was closer, she saw the ragged rips and tears covering it entirely. Patches of pale skin, most smeared with ash, shone like weak stars in the night sky. A heady mix of smoke and sweat radiated from Dee, but beneath it all, something else... something familiar.

Sulfur. *Flesh and meat. Clicking, chattering...*

The beast in her belly roared awake, and before she could second-guess herself, Hira grabbed Dee by the arm of her jacket. "What happened?"

Dee turned, blinking slowly. Her gaze strayed to where Hira still held her by the sleeve. "Y'all need to stop doing that or someone is going to get hurt."

Hira yanked her hand away. "Sorry."

Dee sighed and wiped at where Hira had just grabbed her. "It's all right," Dee replied, the hint of a yawn in her words. "Nothing happened."

The heat from Hira's stomach crawled up her throat. "Whaddya mean, 'nothing happened?' They're leaving, right?"

Dee opened her mouth as if to say something, then just shook her head, shoulders somehow slumping even farther. "Didn't get ahold of him."

"What?" The scream tore from Hira's throat. Staff milling about them turned to watch, the general murmur dissipating into stunned silence. Despite the flush creeping into her cheeks, Hira kept on. "Those bastards want to turn it back on—"

"I know—"

"You know?" Hira reeled back, then barked out a fake laugh. "Well, at least you know. Now I can sleep fine, knowing thousands more are going to die, but at least you *know*."

Dee's jaw flexed, her blue-green eyes flashing. "Hira."

Hira shook her head and turned away. She didn't want to see Dee as a person right then. Only a symbol.

Instead, Hira gestured at the crowd. "You all happy with this, too? Ready to let the Protectorate swoop in and experiment with our lives? Our people?"

Marianne stepped forward, her plain face twitching. "'Our people?'" You just got here from God knows where. What do *you* know about anything?"

Flames raged in Hira's gut as her opponent stepped forward. This woman was always in her way, always calling her out on every little thing.

*Enough.* She closed the distance between them fast enough, Marianne took a step back.

"I think you have more in common with me than those bastards up *there.*" Hira punctuated the word with a stabbing motion at the barely visible flagship hanging in geostationary orbit above Sparta. "*I* think we all know turning that machine on is a good way to get a lot more people killed."

Marianne shook her head, ponytail sweeping back and forth like she was trying to swat away a swarm of horseflies. She leaned in and jabbed a finger at Hira's breast, though she stopped short of actually touching her. "You don't know anything. We only need your AI." She barked her own fake laugh. "You're absolutely worthle—ack!"

Pain flared in Hira's knuckles.

The woman hit the ground in a heap.

Hira stood over her, hands balled into painful fists at her side. Everything inside her screamed to beat the woman until she couldn't speak, until blood streamed from her mouth, and she begged for forgiveness.

*Fuck. Her. Up.*

Alia's voice.

"No. No. I'm sorry. I'm sorry!" Marianne screamed, panic and fear alight in the arch of her eyebrows, the circle of her bleeding mouth.

The righteous anger that'd filled Hira a moment ago dissipated in a puff of smoke. She shook her head and looked at the stunned faces around her. That included Dee, who stared at her as if she'd grown a second head.

"Hey, let's get you up," Hira muttered, offering the woman a hand.

Instead of taking it, Marianne curled in on herself, muttering the same words over and over again. "I'm sorry. I'm sorry..."

Hira stumbled backward. The weight of those eyes caused a cloak of shame to fall upon her shoulders. She scanned the crowd and opened her mouth to apologize or something. As soon as she did so, language disappeared. Only a stuttered phoneme came out, and even that was unintelligible.

They didn't want her here. Hell, no one ever did.

Could she blame them? Look at what she'd just done, hitting a person during a debate. She didn't think that was who she was, but maybe it was now? Maybe Hell had torn more than her heart out during her time there?

But hitting this bitch had made Alia rise from the dead in her mind. Could that be such a bad thing?

A glance around her gave her the answer. A resounding *yes*.

She turned her gaze away from the prying eyes and toward the open double-doors of the compound. AERIS would still care. She'd understand.

Before she could stop herself, Hira ran through the doors of the compound, despite the general's threats. Her vision dimmed as she entered, the smell of ozone and lemon-scented cleaner filling her nose. A dull vibration ran through her calves as her boots clopped onto the steel floor. As her vision adjusted, she made out confused soldiers at the far end of the room. Men and women speckled the space between. But as always, it was the central unit that dragged at her attention: towering steel and silver alloys, a bobbing, floating, shimmering orb atop it. Beneath sat the main access hub for the compound's network.

The panic that'd driven her into the building despite the threat of death resolved into a desperate hope. She'd take AERIS with her. That'd slow them down, keep people safe. As the last remaining crewman from the *Horatio*, according to her contract, Hira technically owned the ship, which meant she owned AERIS.

Hira sprinted to the FTL machine. "AERIS! We're leaving!"

Half a dozen of the remaining scientists turned at her bellow. The Protectorate soldiers left behind moved as one, rifles coming up. Forceful shouts filled the air. A dozen booted feet on steel knocked out a staccato beat.

Hira stopped at the control panel. It was locked out, but she knew her friend could hear her. "AERIS!"

Then Terry was there, stepping between Hira and the central system. "Hira! Shit, what're you doing?" he hissed, waving at the soldiers to back away. "You have to leave."

"I am..." Hira looked over his shoulder, as if making eye contact with the monitor would catch AERIS's focus. "I'm taking my friend and leaving."

"You can't take AERIS." His face transformed into a pleading mask. "We need her."

Hira sucked back a sob and forced the darkness into a flicker of anger and sarcasm. "Well, sorry for the inconvenience, Terry, but we've been dismissed."

He didn't move, but the compassion in his face dissipated. "You can't disconnect her."

"You can't keep me here if I choose to leave," AERIS said then, voice purring from the speakers along the walls.

Hope swelled in Hira's chest, temporarily banishing the angst. "Get the suit she came here in; we're leaving."

"That said, I am not choosing to leave."

"Now—wait. What?" Hira shouldered past Terry. AERIS didn't have a face, but the login screen on the panel sufficed. "We've been dismissed. It's time to go, AERIS."

AERIS trilled. "*I* have not been dismissed in any way. The work here is too important to sacrifice in anger. I am sorry, Hira."

Hira's world collapsed, and with it went the embers of fury. "You're choosing them over me?"

"I am choosing galactic life over you," AERIS said, any inflection she might've used scrubbed into a dull monotone, "just for now."

The pain of that tore her apart. Through gritted teeth and tears, her grief spilled out. Hira's mind consumed itself, and in that massacre, she found the words that would hurt AERIS, her only friend on this world—in the galaxy—the most.

"You have to. I own you."

Silence stretched for nearly a minute.

It went on long enough Hira felt the sting of her own words. She sucked in a breath, shuddering and harsh. "I'm sorry—"

"You don't *own* me," AERIS said. Her voice, so monotone and even a moment earlier, was harsh. Upset. Hira had never heard her speak like that, not even to Alia back in Hell. "You never did. Never will. You certainly don't now."

"AERIS—"

"Goodbye, Hira. Safe travels."

Hira touched the machine with a shaking hand. "AERIS, come on. I didn't mean it."

Silence.

"AERIS?"

A quiet emptiness settled over her, leaving nothing but the sounds of soldiers sliding into place behind, their breathing a harsh whisper as they watched her drip emotions. Hira spun away from the machine, hands clenched into fists.

"What?" she screamed, loud and hard. The raw roar tore at her throat.

"You should leave," Terry said, coming out to stand between her and the soldiers, as if protecting the soldiers from her, or the other way round.

Which, she realized, was exactly what he was doing. For a moment, Hira thought about throwing herself at them, letting them end it all. Maybe if she were lucky, they'd remove the past three years from her mind instead of killing her. They could do that, right? She'd heard stories in the Outer Rim.

A fresh start. Clean slate.

Or maybe just let them finish what Hell couldn't.

*That* thought was fleeting. Sorrow overwhelmed the anger. Her fists loosened.

Hira nodded, then left the compound alone.

\* \* \* \* \*

# Chapter Twelve: Dee

Dee should've gone to her apartment and slept the madness away, but she didn't, because deep down, she knew herself. If she went there, she'd just stare at the ceiling, mind spinning in circles, picturing bodies falling through the sky. Picturing *Bryce* burning up in reentry. Judging herself for not doing more.

People didn't judge you at a bar, not during the day. Everyone there was alone together beneath 3D-printed ceiling joists. Harsh daylight scoured the much-patched, ruddy mudbrick doorway, highlighting the brighter worn path on the concrete floor through years of grime and grease. The scent of stale alcohol filling your nose only to be snatched away as wind caught the sign out front and swept inside with a blast of dark dust.

Home. They were a family of sorts. Not a functional or supportive one, but the type that'd keep their mouths shut when you needed it. The kind that'd slide a liter down to you with a nod, the silent admission that, for this brief moment, you were seen. Acknowledged.

It just happened to be a nice bonus that, since taking over the Tarrington Compound and killing Happenstance, Dee hadn't paid for a drink. It made for a relaxing solitude bereft of exterior worries.

Today was one of those days. Until it wasn't.

"Delilah Terganon?"

Dee didn't answer the greeting, though there was some shock there. She'd heard the second shuttle come down shortly after she'd left the compound, and since the defense cannons hadn't lit it up, it was pretty easy to figure out who manned it. Still, if they were here for her, it was either bad or, at best, not great.

Booted feet made their way to her. She didn't need to turn from the nearly empty liter glass before her to know that, though not for the usual reasons.

Nowadays, she *felt* people. Life. Little creatures skittering around on the ground. Mice—or the other rodent-like creatures that filled the gap on Laconia—in the walls. She could feel them all, almost see their tiny, flickering flames waiting for the wind to snuff them out.

Humans she felt most of all. Before the sky fell, and the accident, Dee had only noticed it a couple times, with Sarah mostly. She'd thought it was the tug of attraction, the magnetism of lust.

The fact that she knew there were seventeen people within thirty meters of her told her she'd been dead wrong. And one of the new folks she felt strongly. Almost… personally.

Dee closed her eyes, scanning the darkness in her mind filled with these little lights. The one on the right felt the same as everyone else.

The one on the left roared like a bonfire.

"Excuse me, ma'am?"

She felt the hand closing in on her shoulder. Inwardly, she cringed at the potential contact. Felt a dull roar in her ears… and in that moment, she knew if he touched her, she'd break his fucking arm.

"Don't."

She didn't say it. The other one stopped him. Instead, a shuffle of feet, and out of the corner of Dee's eye, she saw a young woman, late-twenties, staring at her. The gray-blue Protectorate uniform stood out amongst Dee's bar family. There wasn't a speck of dust visible on either of them.

"Ms. Terganon?" she asked.

There was an earnestness there that made Dee turn despite everything in her screaming to stop. "What do you want?"

The woman suppressed a small smile and straightened, drawing Dee's eyes with her. Dee could almost see the fire inside her.

"Waters, ma'am. This is Jones." She jutted her chin toward the man next to her. "General Henderson would like to speak with you about the demon situation, Lieutenant." Her voice held a strange lilt to it, like the barest hint of an accent Dee couldn't decipher. With humanity spread across the galaxy, that shouldn't be strange, but she'd never heard one quite like it before, not with the way she smushed her consonants together.

The tone of it tickled her memory.

"Lieutenant?" Next to her, a similarly dressed young man snapped to attention, though with less enthusiasm.

Someone obviously hadn't read the memo. While technically separate, Hunters shared rank within the larger Protectorate, even if she was retired.

"We're here to escort you, ma'am," he added.

Dee stared at them for a long moment. Their perfect lines, the way their shoes somehow still sparkled, despite the clinging dirt and dust Laconia draped over everything. But mostly, she stared at their faces and the lack of scars. Wrinkles. Anything to indicate they'd seen action, let alone life.

These kids got younger every year.

"At ease," Dee said, waving. She turned back to her drink. "What's he want?"

"Unsure, ma'am," Waters said, dropping into a well-practiced at-rest position. Clearly, she *had* read the memo. "Just following orders."

Dee snorted. "That's reassuring."

She should send them on their way, give them a good old *go fuck yourselves*... but that flame was a mystery. She sucked down the last of the shitty beer she'd been staring at for the last hour. A small part of her balked at the lack of fire in her throat, but she hadn't been able to tolerate anything stronger than beer since... Dee shook it off and stood. "Let's not keep him waiting, then."

Even she was surprised that she walked out without a fight. Her bar family murmured in her wake. The new barkeep, a skinny little dark-skinned guy with too much tangled black hair named Santos gave her the slightest nod. She returned it and stepped out into the sun.

Her head flared as sunlight hit her. The ache she'd had since the crash thudded to life, the brief reprieve she'd found in the bar disappearing in the brightness.

Around her, Sparta limped back to life like a beaten dog with a new owner. People walked with heads down, casting furtive glances at anyone who came near. With the nanobots Terry had provided to help heal the people hurt by Constance's forces and stray demons, most didn't show outward signs of the violence that'd happened last week.

But if Dee looked close enough, she saw the trauma, felt it in the way that woman kept pausing before each alley. The little girl latched onto her father's hand with a death grip, eyes searching every dark hollow. The smoldering anger in a teen's face as he watched her emerge from the bar, flanked by her two Protectorate escorts.

The people here were quiet, hurt, but they all respected her. If anyone tried harming her here, whomever was at fault would find a city ready to smite them. A smile flickered to life at the thought, but she forced it away.

The young man, maybe fifteen, wore plain clothes covered in dirt and dust. His face was clean, though, so he must have had someplace to go home to at night. He stared long and hard at her, brown eyes flicking between the two soldiers like he was planning an attack.

Dee caught his gaze. He stared back. She smiled and shook her head 'no.'

Immediately, the teen's body relaxed, and he went back to swiping at some holo in his lap.

"Everything okay, Lieutenant?" Waters asked as she stepped up next to her.

Glancing at the young woman, Dee caught her staring at the boy. *Definitely read the brief.*

"Everything's fine, Waters. Let's go catch that shuttle."

"Yes, ma'am."

The walk to the compound was as alien to Dee as the first time she'd done it. Collapsed buildings filled the sides of the street, the ones left standing riddled by a mix of bullet holes and blackened, gaping voids from fires. The lingering scent of fire and ash mingled and danced in the air.

Then the stink of sulfur slammed into her. Dee turned to the source at once. She relaxed. This particular building was broken in the middle, the bricks it'd been built from strangely twisted and consumed. A fiend had wandered into Sparta in the days after the rift had been sealed and started pounding through the city.

Luckily, Dee had been at the tavern, and had gotten there before anyone was hurt, but she'd barely missed the glob of demon fire it had lobbed her way, thus the burnt building.

It didn't dodge hers.

"Place looks like a warzone," the male soldier said as they walked. He glanced around, wide-eyed, at the destruction. "Is this what a demon attack looks like?"

"Not really," Dee said. "Only a few demons made it into the city. Most of this was done by Happenstance's soldiers."

He cleared his throat and looked straight ahead, shaven face flushing a splotchy crimson. "Oh."

"Demons don't leave people alive," Waters said quietly. "They eat their bones and leave the flesh in piles, then move on." Waters paused, voice gravelly. "A demon attack leaves a city like this a ghost town filled with rotting carcasses."

Dee gave Waters an appraising look. "Sounds like you've had experience?"

Waters raised her chin, cheeks flexing. "Yes, ma'am. I... survived Ellis, ma'am."

"Ellis?" Dee searched her memory for a moment, then recollection dawned on her. That must be where she recognized the accent from. "God, Waters, I'm sorry."

Waters nodded, but if the apology meant anything, it didn't interrupt her stride. "It's the past, ma'am."

Somehow Dee doubted that. Ellis used to be a small mining planet on the outer edge of the galactic disk. A rift had opened up there ten years back, but because they were so remote, the Hunters hadn't been notified for days. By the time Dee had arrived, the main settlement had been consumed, the demons scattered to the four corners of the planet to search for more flesh.

That'd been Dee's second mission, but it'd never left her mind. She and Alia, before they'd even started officially dating, had stumbled on a small bunker. Inside there'd been a dozen kids, half-starved and mad with anguish.

Dee looked at Waters again, at her nose and cheekbones, the shape of her eyes. There was something familiar about her, but she couldn't place it, not really. "Were you in the bunker?"

Waters stopped in her tracks, and Dee with her, watching as emotions warred on the young woman's face for a moment. Then, face once again flat, she stared into Dee's eyes. "No, ma'am. They found me three months later in the Wards."

Dee felt like she should say something, apologize, maybe. After all, she'd been there. She and Alia should've found her. They'd had a duty to save everyone, and they'd failed.

Waters cleared her throat, interrupting Dee's self-destructive train of thought, and gestured ahead. "Not your fault, ma'am. Just happy to be here. General Henderson is waiting."

Dee reappraised Waters. She must've been young back then. Between the aerial bombardment that had happened prior to Hunter arrival, and the demons systematically murdering everyone they found, Dee remembered Ellis as little more than a barren rock.

Waters was tougher than she looked; that was for sure.

Instead of prying further into painful memories, Dee let it go with a nod. The rest of the walk went in silence.

A shuttle sat in the dustbowl of the compound's courtyard. Engines rattled to life, blue light flaring from jets setting the ground trembling beneath Dee's feet before shuddering back off. In the dissipating brown cloud left behind, shuttle mechanics swarmed, the muted chatter of their dialog lost in the wind and drone from the people outside the compound.

Those folks, people Dee had come to know over the past week by their faces, if not their names, milled about on the civilian side of the fence. Most leaned against bullet-hole riddled walls, excessive guffaws and shouts masking circuitous glances toward the compound.

A small group rolled dice close to the gate. One man, blood-stained bandage still plastered over his left eye, even reclined against the chain link. The self-satisfied grin on a face marked by scabs and scars should've tipped off the Protectorate soldiers to what he was doing. Behind him, soldiers milled about, chatting and arguing as if there were no threat nearby.

*Idiots.* Hadn't the Protectorate talked to anyone? Didn't Henderson know these people were on a knife's edge? That their previous overlord had chosen to abandon instead of protect?

Clearly not.

Waters and Jones escorted her past the milling civilians, either ignoring the tension filling the air like a disturbed beehive, or blind to it.

Protectorate soldiers in their uniforms snapped salutes and a muttered, "Chief," to Waters as she passed. She returned the salutes.

Chief Waters, then. Guess she wasn't as young as she looked.

The general chatter disappeared, replaced by muttering and stolen glances that followed Dee through the open gate. They wouldn't do anything unless she said so—Dee was pretty sure, anyway—but she took a moment to catch the single eye of the gambling man as she walked past.

He raised his good eyebrow. She smiled and shook her head, as she had with the young man outside the bar. And just like that, the bees went back into the hive, and idle chatter sprang back to life. Not all of it—they'd seen too much shit for that—but enough that Dee didn't worry about their safety for now.

As Dee followed Waters through the gate, she noticed several soldiers switching safeties back on. Maybe they weren't as oblivious as she'd thought.

The shuttle ahead ran through another series of engine tests, azure jets sending tunnels of dirt spinning away. Dust swirled everywhere, sending tufts of earthen grit up Dee's nose and through the still unpatched slashes in her jacket. The roar topped out her eardrums, sending them into a sharp tone as tinnitus came home to roost.

"Right this way, sir!" Waters called out, voice just on the edge of hearing. She angled toward the shuttle, Jones on her heels.

Dee pulled up short, swatting at the air with one hand and gesturing toward the compound with the other. "Where the hell are you going?"

Waters turned around as the engines spun back down. A small smile tugged at the corners of her lips. "It's not a call." She beckoned to Dee. "Come on. Henderson is waiting."

For a moment, Dee considered backing up and walking away, but a glance back toward the gate, and the dozen eyes trained on her in that moment, told her that'd be a mistake. If she treated this like some sort of hostile action, there'd be hell to pay... and the only people who'd get hurt would be those she'd spent the last week protecting. A part of her railed against it anyway. A nagging little voice whispered, *they're just peons… they don't matter.*

Disgusted with herself, Dee banished it. This fucking concussion was really getting old. *Might be about time to go talk to Terry.*

She pulled a fake smile from someplace deep in her ass and nodded. "Gotcha. Figured you'd let me shower first, is all."

Waters flashed Dee a flat-lipped impression of a smile, then proceeded up a ramp that unfolded as she approached. Jones followed up after her.

After forcing some ease into her limbs, Dee followed suit. She only risked one quick glance behind to make sure the lie had worked.

A dozen eyes told her otherwise. All she could do was hope they trusted her reassuring glances not to do something fucking stupid before she got back.

She held up a hand and watched those same people return the gesture before the door squealed shut before her, blocking Sparta from view.

Soon, the engines roared, and Dee left the powder keg of Laconia behind.

\* \* \* \* \*

# Chapter Thirteen: Hosiah

"I'm detecting a, uh, mass, Captain."

The words woke Hosiah with a start. He took in the bridge of the *Cyclops*, the empty seats, cold in the hissing recycled air. His gut turned at the image, a cascading chill starting at his shoulders and running to his balls.

It reminded him of his last mission before going AWOL. His crew dead and vented through tears in the hull. The tiny schooner the Protectorate had given him to shut down a pirate cluster disintegrating around him as he'd piloted it solo through an asteroid belt. The only thing between him and death from a rock the size of his pinky had been his Protectorate-issued exosuit and sheer, dumb luck.

Always luck.

Hanifa stared at him from the engineering panel. Short and stocky, she had the look of an Earth-born, though, according to her, she'd "never set foot on the fucking rock." Deep brown eyes framed by heavy, dark lids from lack of sleep locked on him. Old, pink burn scars covered the left side of her face, twisting her mouth upward into a perpetual grin that didn't match that gaze. The other side was a deep brown, almost black, a contrast that always made him shiver.

Immediately after the tremor ran through him, he cursed and sat up straight. The chill remained. "What're you on about, Farel?"

The navigator leaned back as well, his back cracking audibly. About twelve hours ago, they'd landed on the dark side of the moon so they could enjoy a semblance of gravity without expending energy on the grav generators. Since then, nothing. Everyone on board had been awake for at least twenty-two hours at that point and, since it was supposed to be a quick hop, Hosiah had neglected to pack any Stardust, in case shit happened.

How the fuck was he supposed to know the rules of physics would get destroyed, *again*, on any given afternoon?

"I've been leaking our long-range scans away from the planet like you said," Farel said. He stifled a yawn and shook his head. "I found something heading toward the system's star."

"So?" Hosiah shrugged.

Hanifa sighed. "So," she said, that twist to her lips adding a lisp to her words, "we checked it out while you were taking a nap." This time she did grin.

Hosiah glared at her. Hanifa didn't stop.

*Should've vented her when I had the chance.* "And?"

"And," Farel said, glancing at Hanifa with a tic in his cheek, "I think it's a, uh, bag of demons?"

Hosiah barked out a sharp laugh. It reverberated across the bridge, rattling until well after he finished. But no one was smiling. Not if you didn't count Hanifa's stupid grin. Which he didn't.

"Wait. You're fucking serious right now?"

"Yes," Hanifa said.

Hosiah drummed his fingers on the arm of his chair and swiveled around, sending the room spinning. "Are they dead?"

Farel turned back to his display for a moment, then made an uncomfortable noise deep in his throat. "The bag is still moving, so... no?"

"*Joder,*" Hanifa muttered, glancing back at the console before her. "I didn't realize that."

Hosiah didn't have the same response. After all, he'd seen some of the strangest shit in the galaxy out in Horsehead—translucent, whale-like creatures filled to bursting with Helium-3, a blasted planet with towering fragments of ancient skyscrapers. Why not demons, too?

A ripple of laughter started in his belly, his mouth tugging up at the corners as he pictured it: a pile of demons slamming into the hull of the *Liberator*. If half what he'd heard about those little shits was true, they'd tear the ship apart.

"You okay, sir?" Farel asked, turning as a giggle rippled from Hosiah's throat.

"Mhm," Hosiah managed between bubbles of mirth. "This is going to be fucking *spectacular*."

"What is?" Hanifa asked, turning back to him. The squint of her eyes told Hosiah she already suspected what had made him smile.

"Scrap the explosion plans, Hanifa," Hosiah said, tapping out the engine startup sequence on the panel of his chair. "We're gonna splat a big-ass bug on the Protectorate's windshield."

\* \* \* \* \*

# Chapter Fourteen: Hira

"I don't care where I go, I just need *out* of here," Hira said for the thousandth time to the man on the other side of her video feed. "I'll work a farm. Manage a colony. Whatever."

Standing in near darkness, it was almost easy to forget the hot summer sun roasting Sparta above her. Almost, because rotting garbage, weeks old now, assaulted her nostrils. She stood in an alley that somehow missed all the action of the week prior. Stacks of trash filled most of the space. They were tossed and split open to reveal decomposing food bits and compressed waste products that'd reabsorbed moisture from the air, leaving her in a haze of old shit and ammonia.

Hira had ducked in here after walking off her rage. The conversations with Henderson and Dee couldn't have gone worse. Then what she'd said to AERIS... That'd taken hours to get over. Hours of stalking the streets of Sparta, watching as nervous citizens darted away from her dark glare, her frenzied pace on her way to nowhere.

She'd cursed them. What did they know about suffering? About stress? They'd had an evening of terror. She'd been to Hell—lived in that lifeless dump—and made it back. That was it, wasn't it? Somehow, that had gotten out, and now half of Laconia thought she was a fucking demon, too.

Now the sun finally settled toward the horizon. The humid heat soaked into Hira's clothes, and her own body odor, somehow, made it through the rotting mass of organic material around her.

Hira wondered if she'd had it that bad back there on Hell. After all, she'd had Alia for most of it.

An ache tore her chest open at the thought. The smell of Alia's hair. The way she'd laughed at the worst possible moments. Hira's heart had swelled at the sound of that barking howl.

Hira stared into the far wall, through the rendered image of the white man talking at her from the other side of Laconia.

If she'd been alone, she wouldn't have made it. Hell, she was already starting to lose it on a planet filled with people, and it'd only been a week.

"Ms. Siddiq?"

Hira shook her head and blinked. The man on the call stared at her oddly.

*I've probably been glaring at him for the past ten minutes.*

"Yes," Hira replied, struggling to remember his name. It didn't come to her. *I used to be so good with names.* "Just still a little dazed."

The man nodded, a strange look passing over his face. "I'd heard about that."

*Of fucking course you did.* She wanted to scream, but instead, Hira cleared her throat. "Anyway, I'm a good worker. Great with organization. Managed package and shipping for an independent freighter for six years…" *lived on Hell for two years, killed demons, escaped, etcetera.* "I can adapt. Please."

His face did that thing. The one where the eyes squint, then cast down, jaw clenches before issuing a light sigh.

She didn't wait for him to say it. "You know, never mind. I'll find something." Hira swiped up and a disconnection prompt appeared. She almost tapped it, then remembered there was an etiquette to talking to people. "Thank you for your time."

"Ms. Siddiq—" The video disappeared.

Hira fell back against the rough, poured concrete wall behind her and slowly slid down until she hovered just above the mess coating the ground.

What was she going to do? She had no job, no home, no credits. One of the first things Hira had done after getting back on her feet was to check her accounts, only to find they were empty. At least, that was what Laconia's local cache said. Maybe her credits were still out there. Maybe not.

Without FTL up and running, she couldn't even post an inquiry.

As if to remind her how badly off she was, her stomach rumbled, reminding her she hadn't eaten since snagging a quick protein bar earlier in the day from the mess hall.

The reality of it hit her all at once. With Henderson against her, AERIS angry and dismissive, and Dee… being Dee, Hira was alone, truly alone.

On Hell, she'd always had someone. AERIS. Alia.

Now, no one. How could she be surrounded by so many and still be so alone?

Hira scrubbed at her eyes with filthy hands. Before the *Horatio* had cut a Breach, she'd have just jumped on another freighter to get away from something like this. Someone always needed a quartermaster. But without galactic travel? No FTL? She was just another nameless colonist.

A raucous *boom* rattled across the city, sending glass shaking and debris clattering amongst the stacked bags with dull *thuds*. Hira glanced up just as a long freighter slashed across the narrow space of the alleyway, reentry rockets flashing red and blue flame across the hull. And then it was gone.

Something about the shape of it caught her attention. There was a familiarity about it that tickled a forgotten memory in the back of her mind. Maybe she'd seen it docked someplace? Not that it mattered. What was she going to do? Head out and inspect yet another crash site?

Hira looked down at herself, at the filth swimming beneath her feet, the dirt-stained mess running up her sand- and umber-colored pants. Grimacing, she gave her jacket a tug and unzipped it. The heat dissipated ever so slightly.

*Should've done that hours ago.*

Checking that ship out was better than staying here, she guessed, and with Henderson running the base now, who knew if anyone would be sent out to check on them.

The intellectual side of her mind told her that, certainly, a patrol would eventually make its way out there. But the emotional side, that bit that'd kept her alive in Hell even after Alia died, screamed that these people might need help. That, perhaps, some child was pinned beneath something only she could help with. And if that were true, her inaction was tantamount to murder.

*Alia would check it out.*

With that stuck firmly in her mind, Hira took off in the direction of the contrail and toward a distant spot outside the city limits where a single thread of gray smoke rose.

She could help these people, even if it was just to provide a welcoming face.

So Hira set out, her newly-found savior complex filled to bursting in the setting sun.

\* \* \* \* \*

# Chapter Fifteen: Dee

"**B**ig fucking ship," Dee muttered.

Waters smiled. "Indeed."

The sight of the *Liberator* was impressive, even for Dee. Sure, it'd been a long while since she'd last seen a Protectorate vessel, but this one was huge. It had the look of a perched duck, the head and bill extending out over the central body of the ship. The entire thing sparkled a blinding white in the light of the system's star.

The shuttle, however, was barely a transport, a basic four-seater. Waters and her cohort sat in the front two seats, Dee behind the right-most where Waters sat. Behind Dee there was a blast door, and beyond that, a tiny cargo hold with emergency exosuits and a couple crates Dee assumed were essentials needed by the *Liberator*. Probably SourcePaks, since they weren't large enough for liquid water. At the far end of the hold was another airlock and, beyond that, space.

Gravity loosened its hold on Dee's stomach contents, sending the swill from earlier creeping its way up her esophagus. This wasn't her first sudden transport, but the heartburn was a terror. Always was.

Watching the Protectorate ship helped distract her from constantly swallowing bile and regurgitated booze. The vessel kept growing as they approached until it nearly filled the entire viewscreen ahead. Dee kept an eye out for defenses since, honestly, there was no way a ship like this could last in a firefight otherwise; it'd be torn apart like tissue paper if a small fighter got close. As she watched, the entire starboard side of the ship shuddered to life at the shuttle's approach.

Dozens, if not hundreds, of turrets tracked them on their way to the airlock.

"Jesus," Dee muttered.

"What was that, Lieutenant?" Waters called from the seat ahead of her.

Dee pointed over Waters' right shoulder. "That's a wall of guns."

"Anti-materiel and defensive turrets, ma'am," Jones said. "Otherwise, we'd get torn apart if anyone got close."

Waters let out a low chuckle as the shuttle pulled up to the *Liberator*. "Not that anyone would try to get near us." She tapped on the console in front of her. "Shuttle 370A requesting permission to dock in Bay 32."

A moment passed, then the wall of guns pulled their barrels away from the shuttle. *"Request approved. Proceed to Bay 32, Shuttle 370A."*

Waters tapped something again, and then leaned back in her chair. "Autopilot, take us home."

The other soldier snickered but didn't respond.

Dee stared as the ship approached, taking up the entirety of her view. The shuttle swept forward under the power of the automated systems, drifting until they passed into a massive hangar bay. The space was filled with dozens of fighters, set up in lines and ready to launch at a moment's notice. Against the far wall were stacks of crates filled with God-knows-what. A light blue fuzz indicated a bay shield was in place, Dee noticed with an appraising nod. The *Liberator* had some cutting-edge updates, apparently. She'd only seen those a few times, though on a much smaller scale. Before she left the

Hunters two years ago, she'd only heard rumors the tech had finally been perfected for large scale deployment. Prior to that, force fields were restricted in size due to power consumption needs, if she remembered correctly. How they'd fixed it was a leap too far for her technological understanding.

As the shuttle broke across the line separating the outside of the ship from the inside, the sudden weight of gravity pulled Dee back into her seat firmly, hair falling heavy against her neck. Her stomach flipped, acid sloshing at the movement.

Anti-grav generators were such a weird experience. No matter how you imagined they were supposed to behave, the fact that gravity always pulled you toward their location—typically the center of the ship—was off-putting. It didn't have the same natural feel of being on planet or a mechanical gravity system. Depending on the shape of the ship, you could walk around various decks, slowly rotating around it in a sphere of force, like jogging on the outside of a snow globe.

She preferred microgravity or freefall any day of the week.

The ship shuddered beneath her as it landed, struts squealing in the new atmosphere outside. Behind them, cargo doors ground closed.

"Shuttle 370A, docked," Waters said, tapping away at something before finally unhooking her harness. "Requesting permission to disembark and escort our guest to the general."

Moving much slower, Dee began unhooking her five-point harness while Waters waited for confirmation. There were many reasons Dee had left the Hunters, but one of the more mundane things had to do with this military repetition. Seventeen layers of confirmation before any action. Twelve different people who needed to sign off on equipment requisitions. It was a nightmare, and from the annoyed tap of Waters' foot, it seemed the Protectorate still shared that feature.

"*Permission granted, Chief. Clear to disembark and escort. Private Jones is to report to Deck 34A for reassignment.*"

"Acknowledged," Waters said, then added under her breath, "Took your time."

Jones snickered.

Waters climbed to her feet as Dee finished unhooking the last clasp. "See you around, Pat."

Jones climbed to his feet and knuckled his back. "Always a pleasure, Chief. Until next time." He cut past Dee as she climbed to her feet. He snapped a salute at her. "Lieutenant."

Dee gave him a quick, dismissive one in return. "Private. Have fun."

Jones smiled. "Always." Then he popped the blast door and walked by. A moment later, the rear of the shuttle hissed open, followed by booted footsteps.

"Ready, Lieutenant?" Waters asked as she approached.

Dee swallowed another surge of bile. *Ugh.* "Yeah, but can you check something for me while I'm meeting with him?"

Waters' brows knit for a moment. "It depends on the request."

"Just need you to see if—" Dee pulled up her HUD and sent Bryce's shuttle information to her "—you have a record of this man on the ship." Dee grimaced at the burning in her throat. "Or any record."

Waters accepted the transmission, eyes going blue for a moment before dropping back into their deep brown. "I can do that, LT."

"Thanks." Dee let out a sigh she felt down to her toes. "Now, let's go see this general."

\* \* \* \* \*

# Chapter Sixteen: Terry

Terry lifted his forehead slightly from the hard surface of his desk, then dropped it back with a thud. The spot beneath his forehead was warm, though the rest remained cool in the constant flow of conditioned air swirling inside the Tarrington Compound. Outside the building, the star made its way to the horizon, still a ways off from a true starset. Humans, however, didn't work well on a 27-hour day, so everyone else was gone, and half his cohort was probably already asleep inside blacked-out bedrooms.

Not Terry, though. Not anymore. He stayed behind, waiting for darkness to descend across this sliver of Laconia, and delved into the deep questions of humanity.

Namely, was it bad if you felt your heartbeat in your forehead?

He wasn't sure. He'd gone through life trying his damndest to avoid situations that gave him heart palpitations. Sure, the first week working with Argus One had been... intense, but after the docility drugs had taken effect, and the science started, it'd been easy. Full of discovery. At least until Argus One had escaped.

After that, things had changed. Every look at the imp had driven a knife of paranoia and fear into his heart. More than once, Terry had looked up from his desk to see Argus One staring at him from its little stoop, head cocked to the side, long, purple tongue lolling from a mouth filled with razor sharp teeth. But then Constance had taken off to Elos with that Hunter, and everything had returned to normal. Sans Argus One, of course.

Why did he feel a little bad about that? Terry lifted his head and let it drop again. Probably because the rift had opened, demons had fallen on the planet, and everything had gone to hell. Then, a brief reprieve. Hope. And, again, the pursuit of science and progress had taken over.

He'd thought solving the FTL problem would be a return to normalcy. That if they could do this one thing, maybe everything would go back to the way it'd been before. Maybe the constant, nagging fear that plagued him at every scratching sound or clomp of booted feet on concrete would dissipate like so much smoke.

Then, in the midst of his euphoria, everything had imploded. Again.

He'd had a chance to step back in the wake of everything, before the FTL project restarted with AERIS' help, but his colleagues had backed him taking over, backed his choices. They'd patted him on the shoulder like he was good enough, like he'd earned the position and the right to decide.

Pride. That's what had made the decision for him. He'd let pride blind him to the smirks and quiet mutters from those he'd thought would want the job before him. Of course they'd backed him. Who in their right mind would want this job?

Head up. *Thwack.*

Pride had made him turn on the machine without more testing. *Thwack.*

Was it him? Was he cursed? Hell, did it matter?

"Director Schultz?"

Terry sat bold upright, the room spinning. "Yes?" He cursed the squeak in his voice as he looked for the source of the greeting, but the room was empty.

Sighing, Terry rubbed his sore forehead. Was it going to bruise? *Shit.* "How can I help you AERIS?"

AERIS trilled. "It appeared you were behaving irrationally, so I thought it best to interrupt you."

Terry let himself smile, even if it didn't reach through the bowling ball in his gut. "Thanks, AERIS."

"Of course, Director Schultz."

Groaning, Terry leaned forward, cupping his face in his hands. What was he going to do? How was he—

"Director Schultz?"

"Yes, AERIS?" Terry muttered through his fingers. Didn't she know he was in the midst of an existential crisis?

"I've received instructions to activate FaTaL for three-point-two seconds, sir."

Terry scrunched up his nose. Fatal? That didn't sound good. "What's fatal?"

AERIS made a strange, rattling noise over the speakers embedded in his desk. "The new acronym for the FTL device."

"I do *not* like that—" Terry said. Then, with a sigh, he added "—but whatever. Orders from Henderson?"

"Yes, sir."

"This a comms test by chance?" he asked.

AERIS trilled. "The *Liberator* is testing its communication hub. My records show Laconia's FTL buoys were lost in the attack."

Terry cursed. He'd forgotten about that. Without the *Liberator*, they had no access to other system comms. A nagging ache in his throat threatened to make him sweat. "When are we testing? Now?"

AERIS trilled. "Yes, sir."

"Then let's try to call in some support and see if we can figure out what the hell we broke," Terry said. He climbed to his feet, joints and tendons screaming in protest. When had he sat down?

AERIS trilled. "Agreed, sir."

"Call me Terry," Terry said as he left his office.

"I'm honored, Terry."

Terry smiled. "The honor is all mine, AERIS." He sucked in a deep breath and held it for a moment. He let it go when the heartbeat faded from his forehead for the first time in hours. "Now, let's try not to get anyone killed this time, shall we?"

"I heartily agree, Terry."

\* \* \* \* \*

# Chapter Seventeen: Hosiah

"Power back down," Hosiah snapped through the grin plastered on his face. The G-forces from the acceleration made his eyesight sparkle with diamonds and his gut clench in anticipation. "Momentum is our friend here."

"Yes, sir," Farel replied, voice electronic over the exosuit speakers, tapping on the controls before him.

Around Hosiah, the ship whispered into silence as everything powered down, even life support. His vision cleared immediately, shattered glass disappearing into his mind. The darkness of space filled the bridge, interrupted only by the periodic flicker of the spare status lights on displays scattered across the room. Now the acceleration burn was over, the lack of any tangible gravity reasserted itself. The only thing keeping Hosiah in his seat was the old five-point harness embedded in the captain's chair.

"*Seven minutes until intercept,*" Hanifa's said over the localized comms. "*Brooks and Gemmell are ready for hook control EVA.*"

Hosiah nodded, then, since no one could see him, added, "Understood."

A giddiness filled his chest as the *Cyclops* shot through space at several hundred kilometers a second. It'd been ages since he'd done anything remotely like this. Back in the days after he'd left the Protectorate, this had been his life. Slingshotting around gravity wells to come up on merchant ships like an asteroid and attacking before the poor fuckers knew what to do.

Nowadays, he had people to do that for him. Sure, sometimes he'd hop on a live feed to do his schtick with the wild hair and insanity so ships would surrender, but it'd been ages since he'd actually performed a slingshot. He'd forgotten how much he loved it. The rush. The excitement. The complete, utter silence of flying, unpowered, through the void.

"Sensors?" Hosiah asked as he stared into darkness.

"Intercept in ninety seconds."

Hosiah smiled at no one. "Protectorate?"

"No movement, sir," Farel replied.

"Fan-fucking-tastic," Hosiah said. He tapped on the wrist display of his suit and switched channels. "Brooks, ninety seconds. Get the hook ready."

*"On it, Cap'n."*

Following that, Hosiah connected the two channels so Hanifa could give the callouts live.

This was going to be his best trick yet. He saw the headlines in his head, heard the livestreams once they came back on.

*Hosiah Jordan, King of the Hosiah system out of the Horsehead Nebula, bane of the Protectorate, decimated the Protectorate flagship,* Liberator, *with nothing but a hook and a bag of monsters.*

"Eighty seconds."

*"Opening cargo hold."*

*Should've been out there already*, Hosiah thought as the doors opened below the bridge, sending a tremor through the *Cyclops*. Given this was a repurposed salvage ship, there was a large crane attached to the exterior of the hull. The only drawback was, it needed to be controlled from out there as well. Hosiah had thought about retrofitting it many times over the past years, but honestly, it'd never seemed that important.

Luckily, people were cheap.

They'd waited until the last minute just in case of random debris. Any tiny bit of garbage out there hitting an exosuit at several hundred kilometers an hour would turn a human into pulp. Hosiah understood the reasoning, even if the timeline made his heart slam like a jackrabbit's getting chased by a wolf.

Then again, that was part of the rush. Hosiah grinned.

"Forty seconds."

Again, the ship shuddered. *"Moving crane into position."*

"Twenty seconds."

*"I see it,"* Brooks' voice came across the speaker. Then, something changed in his voice. *"Jesus."* Panic. Fear.

Hosiah had heard it too many times to disregard outright. "Hook that fucking net, Brooks."

*"But sir—"*

"That wasn't a goddamned request," Hosiah interrupted, putting as much acid as he could into his words. "Now hook it, or I'll hook you and dangle you out the back for eternity, you fucking coward."

Silence.

"Intercept," Hanifa said.

Nothing happened. If Brooks had hooked the net, the ship should've tugged to the side, or had some sort of change in directionality.

Hosiah felt none of that. His chest constricted. Anger roiled in his stomach. "Brooks?"

No response.

"Gemmell, tell me that fucker hooked the bag." Still nothing. He turned to where he knew Hanifa sat. "Are comms still active?"

"They are," Hanifa muttered. "Wait. Um."

"Um, what?"

Hanifa cleared her throat. "Brooks isn't on the ship anymore."

"The fuck are you talking about?" Hosiah snapped.

With a flick, he pulled up the crew map. Gemmell was still in the cargo hold. Hosiah narrowed his eyes as the indicator blinked in and out of what should be the walls. "Gemmell!" Hosiah called out. "Why the fuck you hiding in the maintenance shafts?"

Nothing but silence on the radio. He ground his teeth, then turned to the viewscreen. *Fuck it.* "Power up, Farel."

"But the Protectorate—"

"Emergency power only, you fucking twat," Hosiah snapped. "I need to see outside."

Across the bridge, more lights flared to life. In that dimness, Hanifa and Farel's outlines came into view against the blues and reds of various diagnostic lights.

Then the viewscreen kicked to life, blinding him.

Hosiah blinked twice as he adjusted to the light, then grimaced. No matter how hard he stared, he couldn't figure out what the fuck he was looking at up there. The net obscured parts of the system's star. It rolled along in the distance, a formless mass that flexed and shifted as it continued into the distance. Beyond that, there was nothing.

Wait. Hosiah squinted at a light, flickering slightly as it spun into the distance. "The fuck?"

"I…" Hanifa cleared her throat. "I think that's Brooks."

He was sure he had something to say to that, but whatever it was disappeared with Farel's liquid gurgle. Hosiah had enough time to blink before a naked creature scampered from the decapitated corpse of his navigator and launched at him.

A head made of a mouth and teeth opened wide, one arm going wide, black claws flashing in the light from the digital star. The other arm was strange, malformed and small; it lacked the yellow tint covering the rest of it and ended in a remarkably human-looking fist. A fist that caught Hosiah in the helmet and sent him reeling back into his chair. Any other time, he'd have gone sprawling, maybe even had a chance to defend himself, but no, not this time. The fucking Protectorate harness held him in place.

Hosiah had no time to process the beast straddling him before another blow slammed into his mask, cracking it. "Help me!" Hosiah screamed, his tough persona cast away by pure terror.

The clawed hand grabbed one side of his helmet, the smaller hand the other. Then the beast pressed its face against the cracked glass, and through that fracture, Hosiah watched in horror as the flaccid, yellow skin twisted and tore like someone had pushed a finger through its skull from the inside. A slit tore open, bloody, purple tears dripping down and onto the glass.

As he watched, something spun inside that void. Something round and white, covered with veins and blood, and all at once, it shifted, shuddering in its socket, leaving Hosiah staring into a single brown eye. A brown eye so very much like his own.

"What the fuck?" Hosiah whimpered.

All at once, his instincts came back to him. The cracked glass wasn't a worry. The bridge was still pressurized, still had oxygen inside, even if it wasn't being processed properly.

The problem was the fucking demon straddling him like a thirty-credit whore.

"What do you want?" Hosiah yelled, voice cracking despite his efforts. He wanted the fucking thing staring at him and not at the hand reaching for Jewel.

To his surprise, the demon cocked its head. It pulled back, bloody eye blinking. Then it opened its mouth. A low, rumbling growl echoed through the bridge, but it wasn't just a growl. There were intonations. It paused. When it spoke again, the sounds—the *words*—rumbled through his chest. Fucking thing was trying to talk.

*Good. Let it distract itself.*

"Are you trying to speak?" Hosiah asked, trying to catch the beast's eye. It worked, that bloody brown orb swiveling to catch his own. A shudder went down Hosiah's spine. The frustration and anger there was... familiar. He'd seen it reflected in his mask back on that fucking schooner.

Again, the beast split its head open, then closed it, the edges of its mouth working like lips as its tongue flicked back and forth. It spouted off a series of rattling sounds, but the only word that even made sense sounded like 'seeru,' the 'r' rolled like it'd been said by a drunk Scotsman.

Hosiah shrugged and glanced toward Hanifa. She was frozen, terror written clear on her face. No help there, then.

"I can't understand you," Hosiah said, enunciating each word while shaking his head 'no.' His breathing came in slow and measured.

The beast grunted and stood, taking a short step back. A chittering sound filled the bridge as the long nails of its one hand, a hand covered in blood from Farel's corpse, clacked together. It shook its head and hissed, then stared right at Hosiah, head cocked, that one eye narrowing.

Old Protectorate de-escalation training kicked in then. It'd been decades since he'd used it, but fuck, what choice did he have? Carefully, he kicked on the external speakers so the beast could hear him.

"What's your name?" Hosiah asked, leaning forward. He put his hand on his hip next to where Jewel was concealed in the chair. With the other, he tapped his chest. "Hosiah." He tapped again. "Hosiah."

Out of the corner of his eye, he saw Hanifa do the same. "Hanifa."

It cocked its head at him, then tapped its own chest with the ruddy-brown arm that ended in human-looking fingers. "Anum." Tapped again. "Anum."

*What the vac-filled shit?* Hosiah honestly didn't have any fucking clue what was going on, but he almost had Jewel. He just needed the bastard to look away one more time.

It was like Hanifa had read his mind. "Holy shit. Anum? Really?"

The creature turned at her incredulity.

Jewel popped out of the side of Hosiah's chair silently. Her jeweled grip tickled his palm through the sensors in the exosuit. In one fluid motion, he pulled the pistol up, trained it on the beast's forehead, and unloaded.

Each shot sent purple blood spewing across the bridge to float in globules alongside Farel's trickling mess. He emptied all eleven rounds into the beast, then dropped the mag, which hovered next to him. Hosiah let the pistol go, then disconnected his harness and floated upright.

Ahead of him, the beast hovered on the bridge, violet goo flowing from what was left of its forehead.

Sighing, Hosiah looked toward Farel's station. "Poor fucker. Navigation is going to be a bitch."

"Anum," Hanifa muttered, shaking her head. She hadn't moved, like she hadn't processed what'd happened yet. "I know that name. Why do I know that name?"

"Who gives a fuck?" Hosiah asked. He pulled up gravity controls and turned them on.

The ground rose quickly, and he stumbled a little, but kept his feet. The beast slammed into the ground with a heavy *thud*. Alongside it, purple and red blood splashed against the ground like spilled pudding. With another tap, he turned the generators off again, as well as all other power. Now the liquids had hit a surface, he didn't need to worry about that bullshit. It'd cause a shit ton of issues if it got in the scrubbers.

Hosiah did activate a single bridge spotlight, however. He'd never admit it, but he didn't want to be left in the dark with that creature. With a gentle kick off his chair, Hosiah made his way to Hanifa. She still muttered that name over and over again.

He caught himself on the console in front of her, then rapped his knuckles on her helmet.

She turned to him, shocked. "I know that name."

"I killed it," Hosiah said, trying to catch her eyes. "Fucking thing is dead. Who gives a shit?"

Hanifa shook her head. "No. I *know* that name."

*Fuck.* Hosiah sighed. She'd snapped. Happened to the best. He'd seen plenty of people over the years crack under pressure. He'd thought Hanifa was one of the tough ones. Thought she'd hold up. Then again, it'd taken a nightmare creature to crack her, so maybe he'd been right after all. Small solace.

Hosiah's only warning was in Hanifa's eyes. They went wide, then those words again.

"I know that *name*."

Alarms flashed. Pain screamed through his neck for a moment and then… nothing.

Hosiah Jordan opened his mouth to scream. Only a low gurgle escaped his lips. Blood droplets filled his vision inside the helmet. The bridge revolved around him as he spun.

Anum stood beneath him now, approached where Hanifa sat, her frenzied murmuring disappearing in a dull scream. Hosiah watched the beast push a headless body to the side. *His* body. There was no processing that. No chance.

His vision flared and fired, lights streaming and melding into a blur of nothingness like the twist of light when entering an FTL lane. The last thing he heard before it all disappeared was dull *thud* and a single word.

"Anum."

\* \* \* \* \*

# Chapter Eighteen: Hira

Hira almost turned back.

The dry heat of evening sucked the moisture from her skin and chapped her lips. With the sun setting beyond the western horizon, shadows stretched as black fingers across the plains east of Sparta. Scraps of hardy, native plants turned into grasping, ebony nails. A harsh breeze swept from the east, dragging a sandpaper dust cloud across the barren wastes. It ground her skin and stung her eyes. It carried the lingering odor of sulfur and burnt flesh.

Hira scrubbed at her arms and ignored the irrationally panicked voice in the back of her head shouting about leaving without her exosuit.

*Demons could be anywhere.*

As the sun finally faded below the purpling horizon, the temperature dropped rapidly. Goosebumps rose to life across the bare skin of her forearms. She zipped up her jacket, but it wasn't enough. She'd never been out here at night.

*You don't know what the fuck you're doing! They're going to find you, let you freeze to death, then murder everyone!*

She pulled her sleeves down, ignored the voice, and kept on.

Luckily, whomever had landed the freighter hadn't even tried to hide it, or she'd have turned back once the sky went black, just the bare flicker of the *Liberator* alongside the stars in a moonless night to keep her company. No, these folks had the spotlights on, and were in the process of unloading crates and equipment as she approached.

Hira slowed her walk, sliding off to the side behind some of the short, sharp bushes that speckled the plains. She hadn't yet asked the name of, well, anything on Laconia, so she decided to label it the Piss Bush, for obvious, olfactory reasons. Still, caution had kept her alive this long, so she took a moment to get a good look at these people before running in like a frenetic welcome wagon.

Hell, she hadn't even tried to make radio contact before coming out here, or brought a weapon. She'd been in such a hurry to *do something*, the idea that these people might not be friendly hadn't even entered her thoughts. Not her *actual* thoughts, anyway. Maybe she should listen to the voice more often.

Peeking from around the Piss Bush, Hira took in the site. The ship itself was in bad shape, but easily repairable at first glance. Carbon scoring speckled the hull like tiger stripes, and if the periodic sparks were any indication, panels were missing entirely. So far, she'd only seen two crewmembers, an older bald man, and a Spacer with a style of head tattoos she remembered from her time out on Erias.

*Erias.* Shit, she hadn't thought about that in a long time. A few fond memories... and a heavy dollop of regret back there.

Hira shook it off and squinted at the two for a few long moments, trying to identify any weapons between them. A single plasma rifle leaned against the ship itself, but otherwise, she didn't see anything else. Except there were clearly three people speaking. She couldn't make out what they said, just snippets of words caught on the wind, but one seemed artificial, likely from someone on board.

So, three folks, one rifle.

Hira's gut twisted. Old, nagging doubt crept up her esophagus and begged her to turn tail and run; this wasn't the smart play. She'd almost given into that horrid bitch when the spotlight swung her direction, blinding her.

"Come out!" It was an older man, voice raspy.

"Fuck," Hira muttered, raising her hands high above her head as she stood up from behind the Piss Bush. The light sent everything into a white haze, only two indistinct shapes taking form in the distance. One clearly had the plasma rifle. "I'm from the settlement!" she shouted, then added in a rush, "I'm unarmed!"

A dismissive grunt made it to Hira across the distance.

Hira grimaced and turned her head away from the spotlight in an attempt to let her eyes adjust. She kept her hands up. "I'm just here to welcome you to Sparta. So, uh…" Hira squinted and turned toward the person with the rifle. She flashed what she hoped wasn't a cringing smile. "Welcome?"

The rifle didn't shift. "How are—what?" The man with the gun leaned toward the other shape. Muttering filled the gaps in the wind for a moment, the barrel slowly lowering until it pointed at the ground. That was a good sign.

*Right?*

"Everything okay?" Hira asked, keeping her hands up just in case. Last thing she needed was a hole in her gut to go with the guilt buried there.

"Yeah, one sec," the man with the rifle said. Then he shrugged and handed the gun to his Spacer cohort.

That person closed the distance in several long steps, rifle still trained on Hira's gut.

The Spacer stepped in front of the light and her face came into view.

Light brown skin Hira knew for a fact had a softness to it that belied the usual firm glare embedded on that face. A glare that had, blissfully, been replaced by the arched eyebrows and parted lips of shock and joy. Her hair had begun to grow out, obscuring the detailed whorls that covered her scalp.

A single word slipped through lips Hira hadn't kissed in four years. "Hira?"

Hira grinned and put her arms down to her sides. "Eleni, it's nice to see you—"

The world exploded in stars.

\* \* \* \* \*

# Chapter Nineteen: Eleni

"Ow." At least Hira had the good sense not to look shocked.

Still, the slap wasn't planned. It just kind of happened, alongside the growing stewpot of emotion stirring in Eleni's gut. One moment, she'd been overwhelmed by... everything. The next, that old, acidic anger that'd filled her in the months after Hira had left slipped through her defenses. It ran from her stomach into her chest, then down into her left hand and...

*Crack.* Eleni's fingers lit in sharp, yet quickly fading pain.

"Okay, fuck!" Hira called out, reeling backward in the wake of the second slap. "I know we—"

"I thought you were dead!" Eleni screamed, realizing only now she meant it.

Hira shrugged and flashed the same smile that'd melted her heart back on Erias over martinis. "Surprise?"

Eleni had never looked into what had happened to Hira after she'd left, despite the urge to do so over the years. Hira had made her choice, after all; there wasn't anything to do about it.

But now, Eleni spun away and stomped back to a very confused Ceriat. "Can't believe this shit," she said, shoving the plasma rifle into Ceriat's arms. He almost dropped it. Ceriat made a confused noise in his throat, eyebrow raised as a form of question.

Izzy, however, didn't give a shit about being polite. "Okay, as fun as this is, I'm gonna need some context."

Ceriat shrugged. "Same."

"Fine," Eleni said, rolling her eyes. She turned back to a slowly approaching Hira. She had her arms halfway up again, Eleni noticed with a small grin she swiftly crushed into a flat-lipped grimace. "Put yer hands down. Look like an Earther trying to catch their piss."

Hira snapped her hands down to her side as she finally stepped out of the direct glare of the spotlight. Her tanned cheek was flushed red from the strike. A wave of shame swept through Eleni. *She deserved it*, she thought, straightening her shoulders and raising her chin. It didn't make her feel better. "Presenting Hira Siddiq, freighter quartermaster and right asshole."

"Well, I'm planetside now," Hira added, one finger up. She flinched under Eleni's glare. "But I mean, a lot's happened since we last, uh…"

Apparently, Hira picked up on the anger Eleni was actively sending across her glare, because the other woman shut up. For a moment. Hira did that thing she did, where she started at someone's boots and came up to their head before grinning. A flush worked its way up Eleni's throat and into her cheeks despite herself.

"You look good, El."

"'El?'" The way Ceriat said the nickname, Eleni didn't have to turn to know his face was plastered with a shit-eating grin.

"Ooh," Izzy let loose through the speakers, "this is getting *good*."

Eleni ground her teeth, cast Ceriat a withering glare that did nothing, then turned back to Eleni. To this fucking woman who'd broken her heart, then disappeared into the galaxy for four years…

"Whatcha want?"

Hira shrugged, one shoulder tucking tight against her cheek, arms out. "Honestly?"

"Ya think I want lies?"

"Okay, yeah." Hira opened her mouth, winced, then let out a long sigh before continuing. "Things have kind of gone to shit—" she gestured to the sky, then *Lucille* "—as you noticed. And—"

"Captain Obvious over here," Izzy said.

Ceriat snickered.

Hira's lips twitched into that goddamned smirk. "I'm kind of looking for a gig."

Eleni's vision fuzzed. The wound from years ago, one she'd thought long scarred over, ripped open anew. "Last one didn't work? Leave more behind for another fucking shipment? A different goddamned star?"

Hira wilted beneath the onslaught. Her smirk disappeared. She turned away, hunching over slightly. The light caught her cheekbones, and dark hollows swallowed her eyes. Her fingers pulled at the sides of her brown and gray pants, twisting until her fingers went white.

That was new. The Hira she knew might have some anxiety, but beyond that was an insurmountable confidence. Apparently, something had climbed that mountain and found it wanting.

Everything inside Eleni screamed to apologize, to reach out and at least give her a comforting pat on the shoulder.

*She broke my heart. Fuck her.*

So Eleni said and did nothing. She just stood there as Hira blinked and shook her head.

"Hey, come on over," Ceriat broke in after a long moment, beckoning Hira toward the makeshift table they'd been in the process of setting up with empty crates. "We can talk about this job of yours."

Hira turned toward him, but her eyes stayed on Eleni. "You sure that's okay?"

"Yes," Ceriat said before Eleni could react. "Come on. We have a Processor inside and too many SourcePaks for two people, anyway."

*Fucking traitor*, a voice flared in Eleni's mind, sending more heat crawling up her neck, but she stopped that burst from catching fire. She knew what Ceriat was doing. That was why they'd become friends. But she didn't have to like it right now. She cast a glare at him.

In true Ceriat fashion, he shrugged.

Out of the corner of her eye, Eleni caught Hira searching her face for… something. Eleni wasn't sure what Hira thought she'd find there. Forgiveness? Some sliver of caring and fondness? She wasn't going to get it. Instead, Eleni turned away and stomped back toward the *Lucille*.

"Come on, Eleni," Ceriat called after her, voice taking on that pitch he used when she was being unreasonable.

Fuck, maybe he was right, but she didn't need that right now. "Not hungry. We need shit for repairs, and someone needs to get 'em." Then, as she put one hand on the open blast door, "Enjoy eating with yer new *friend*."

"Then why are you heading inside?" Ceriat asked.

*I don't know!* "I need, my… fucking… credit chit and…" Eleni floundered, vision limning, the inexorable march of heat in her face twisting her words. "Don't fuckin' worry about it! Just hang out with Madam She-bitch!"

Then, before Ceriat could convince her how much of a child she was being, Eleni stormed off through the twisting hallways of the *Lucille*. Izzy, however, was ready and waiting.

"You're being a brat, by the way," Izzy chimed in as Eleni approached her bunk. "Someone needs to tell you."

"Thanks *so* much," Eleni spat.

Izzy trilled. "Enjoy your nap."

"Oh, fuck off, Izzy." Eleni reached the door to the small room she'd chosen for herself. She put her head against the chill doorway.

And let the wound bleed.

\* \* \* \* \*

# Chapter Twenty: Ceriat

Ceriat had watched Eleni stomp off into the dark, a hard-packed satchel on her back, a handheld lamp piercing the inky darkness, about an hour ago. She'd told them not to wait up, whatever the hell that meant. That was about the same time a Protectorate shuttle swung in toward the city. With the blob of light pollution surrounding the settlement visible from here and their closeness, he didn't worry about her.

Not much. He trusted her abilities—hell, not too long ago, she'd saved his life multiple times—but the look on her face and the set of her shoulders… Well, hopefully keeping busy would help. It was doing wonders for him.

"So, she went planetside?" Hira asked, shaking her head between bites of an orange mash of carbohydrates and fake dairy she assured him was macaroni and cheese. "On her own?"

Ceriat spooned the last bit of mashed potatoes into his mouth, set the plate on the empty crate behind him with a *clank*, and put his hand over his heart. He swallowed. "Hand to God. That's where I found her."

"Can confirm," Izzy trilled out.

Hira cocked her head at Izzy's comment. Since being told Izzy was the ship's AI, she'd spent a lot of time listening to her. He noticed she avoided asking too many questions, though. Thankfully.

Last thing they needed was for someone to find out Izzy was sentient.

With idle fingers, he drew squiggly lines in the fine sand atop the black rock beneath him. He had a feeling this was what the Mojave Desert back on Earth must feel like, especially with the sudden bone-dry air and blasts of chill wind raking the landscape from the east. Behind him, the *Lucille* hummed on low power, the moisture reclaimers rattling away as they refilled the shipboard $H_2O$ stores.

The temperature drop had been a surprise, but luckily these little scrub plants burned okay, if a little… fragrantly. They had that ammonia-stink that reminded him of boxwood on a hot summer's day back home. The fire didn't make it *worse*, so he called that a win.

"So, what brings you—" Ceriat gestured at the scrub-filled flats around them "—to paradise?"

Hira's eyes went wide, then she let out a low chuckle. "From Hell to Paradise. Quite the journey."

Ceriat snickered but didn't interrupt. Instead, he grabbed one of the canteens they'd unpacked earlier and took a small, refreshing sip. They sat in silence for a long moment, Hira poking at the fire in front of her with one of the longer branches they'd found around.

"Listen, we—"

"No, no," Hira interrupted, shaking her head. "Sorry. It's just been a lot."

"I get that." Ceriat nodded and stared into the fire. In the flickering flames, he swore he saw Jen, eyes wide before the blast doors snapped shut. And Sariah, stumbling away with a knife jammed into her back.

So much violence… *I really did try, Gerry.*

Absorbed in his own memories, Ceriat missed the first half of Hira's sentence.

"...then they were gone. Lisa, Darius, Lawson." Hira's voice hitched, then she cleared her throat. "Even Gerry. Just... gone."

Ceriat's gut wrenched around at the mention of a Gerry. Even though he knew they weren't the same person, he felt that same loss in his entire being, like poison lightning digging through his nerve endings.

"I'm so sorry for your loss," Ceriat said, voice low as the empty platitude fell from his lips.

Hira gave him a flat-lipped smile that didn't meet her eyes, then stared back at the fire. "Gerry and I were... close. Haven't really sat down long enough, honestly, to think about him. He was gone, then I had to take care of Alia, then the sensors, and..." Her voice went hollow, soft. "Fuck." That one word enumerated a thousand sorrows in one syllable.

Ceriat focused on the fire as she wiped at her eyes. "I lost a Gerry, too." The words just kind of... fell from his lips. "It leaves a hole—" Ceriat cleared his throat and forced the tears to stay wobbly in his eyes, sending the flames twitching unnaturally. "A... void. You just hope someday it'll fill up again."

"Hear, hear," Hira said, raising her own canteen. "To our Gerrys!"

Ceriat smiled, raised his own, then added, "To Gerry Harris, may you find your peace in the wind of the void." Then he knocked back a slug of chill water. He gestured toward Hira, hoping she'd go next.

But instead, she sat there, eyes locked on Ceriat's own. She held the canteen, forgotten, in one hand.

"You okay?" Ceriat asked, working the frog from his throat in the process.

"What'd your Gerry look like?" Hira asked.

"Why?"

"Brown beard, quick smile." Hira stood, then held her hand about fifteen centimeters over her head. "This tall?"

Ceriat froze. *There's no way.*

Hira dropped her hand, looked at the canteen, then, shaking her head, set it on the crate behind her. "I can't catch a fucking break."

She turned to leave.

"Wait!" Ceriat called out despite the numb beast in his chest. "I…"

Hira slowed and stopped, shoulders hunching before looking his way. "What?"

Anger and jealousy warred against curiosity and empathy in that moment. Gerry had abandoned him, left him behind to travel the stars. *Alone*, he'd said. *Space*, he'd said.

But this woman… he'd stayed with her. They'd had a life, though he didn't know how deep.

"This was a mistake," Hira muttered, shaking her head. "I'm sorry."

As she looked away, the battle was won.

"Sit," Ceriat begged, gesturing to a space close to him, "and tell me about Gerry."

Hira stopped and looked to the stars. She took a breath that made her shoulders rise and fall. "Are you sure?"

Again, Ceriat tapped the seat next to him. "Yeah."

After a long moment, she smiled. "Met on the *Horatio*. He needed a quartermaster, and I wanted to see a few new systems." She let out a long, shuddering sigh and sat next to him. Her eyes took on a far-off look as she continued, lips curving upward in fond recollection. "He had this stupid giggle..."

Even through the pain her words brought him, Ceriat smiled.

\* \* \* \* \*

# Chapter Twenty-One: Anum

Impatience was not the right word for it.

Captive in a small corner of his mind, Anum had been patient for millennia. Barely conscious as the galaxy spun... hidden in the hissing, writhing mass of flesh and whispered nothings of the Anelaka, Those Who Listen, before he, too, was taken by the change. Always whispering, whispering, whispering...

Side effects. Unplanned, unexpected, simply a thread in need of trimming. A sequence to cut.

The strange, awkward ship rattled through him. The *hum* of the engines were strangely soothing, as if an echo of the Anelaka hung in the air. It caressed his skin and forehead above closed eyes like a parent lulling a child to sleep. And in a way, it did, though not as before. Never as before.

After so long without vision, he didn't need to see to know the shape of the bridge. He felt the half-moon of steel and plastic in his skin, heard the whine of the display at the far end, and the two decapitated bodies, still hovering alongside the long-since browned blood of the second, called out to him with their stink, with the flush of spilled blood on the air. It begged him to drink, to consume...

But he'd had time to grow resilient in the dark.

Anum pulled gangly limbs that had finally begun to shed their ghastly pall for an olive sheen he hadn't seen in too many ages. His left hand had begun to restore itself as well, long, ebony claws receding back into his skin. Not gone, mind you, never gone. A transformation, once complete, can never fully reverse, after all. But it can be hidden. Adapted.

The woman with the twisted face rattled out a phrase in her barbarous tongue. No grace or form in the letters. No meaning. They weren't meant for him, he was nearly sure, even if he only caught every other word.

The galaxy had fallen to the artless, to the shallow. To coarse and mumbled phrases. To chaos.

Chaos. He'd thought the order he'd brought his people would keep them safe and prosperous for eternity. That was why they were the Aneis, Those Who Stand. Because on the shoulders of those that came before and those that had yet to be, they would stand tall. Conquer the stars. The galaxy.

But he'd underestimated Chaos, and entropy had swept into the raw mess left in its wake.

Never again. He'd learned the lesson while buried in the Anelaka. With bloody teeth and the screech of hunger and pulse of iron and plasma drawing him from inside. With silent, solitary screams. Never again.

"Anum?"

He turned his face to her and, with an effort bordering on laughable, forced his new eyes to open. The world twisted unnaturally, shapes forming and shifting, both mind-shattering brightness and deep, empty darkness. Had he ever thought this organic visualization superior to other senses? To taste?

Nothing conquered taste or smell, but the tradeoffs weren't worthwhile. Now that his face had subsided into a vague semblance of its old form, he could control his tongue—and what a blessing that was. Oh, the wonders control brought. He kissed the back of his still sharp, yet less substantial teeth. The rest he'd swallowed during the transition that he didn't waste time thinking about.

Soon, the bridge took shape around him. The dim running lights, what he assumed was the ruler's chair behind him. The bodies. He cringed. Taste gave a different picture than the mess before him.

"Anum?"

And the woman. Her mangled face twitched in that fearful way that preceded another feast... but no.

Control. Order.

"Yes?" Primitive. 'Primitive' was the word Anum wished to use. To spew at this strange woman with the twisted face.

But so far, the only words he'd intuited from her frenzied ramblings were 'yes,' 'no,' 'me,' 'kill,' and 'don't'—which served as both an order and a form of begging, though he wasn't sure why.

This brutish language held a certain cadence to it, though. He'd noticed that, even if it lacked poetic nuance. Well, at least the woman's use of the language wasn't wholly discomforting.

She spoke again, tapping out something on her computer systems before turning back to him, a small, transparent disc no bigger than the pale white of her fingertip.

"Don't kill me," she said, latching onto his eyes.

The tremble had disappeared from her voice, Anum noticed. Good. She would be a worthy lieutenant in the age to come.

Still, he narrowed his eyes at the tiny disc. An ancient memory wriggled its way into his mind. He'd been working on a neural-computer interface near the end, but had never completed the work. One of the proposed interfaces had been through an eye mask. Could this be a micro version of it?

"Is this," Anum said in Aneian, his native tongue, as he pointed at the little disc with his fully restored hand—he'd forgotten what normal fingernails felt and looked like!—then his eye, "for optics?"

She clearly had no idea what the words meant, but she picked it up. Her lips twisted into that strangely reassuring grin caused by the destruction of the left side of her face. Why that eased his conscience, he couldn't say.

"Yes," she said. She mimed putting it into her own eye by holding the lids open. Then she let go a string of nonsense and held it out to him.

As delicately as Anum could, he reached out and took the offered disc with his restored hand. He pointed at the disc, then at her own eye. When she flinched backward, he realized he'd used the clawed hand. Eventually, that would pass.

But she got the message. She reached up and mimicked the action she'd described to him on herself, only to pull away a disc that appeared nearly identical.

"Yes," she said, head bobbing up and down.

He returned the gesture, then cocked his head and stared at the disc. If this were a trick—some device meant to kill him—everything he'd gone through since those damned people had captured him and thrown him in a cell would be for naught. Every dishonor that small mouse of a man had heaped upon him would never be returned in kind.

It would also mean the end of this twisted woman before him. He was immortal, after all.

"To Order," Anum said, raising the disc upward as if offering it in toast. Then he popped it into his eye. On the third try. The first two resulted in him blinking it out almost immediately. By the time it settled over his cornea, it was like sandpaper, grinding and scraping.

Then the display changed.

A strange screen appeared in the center of his vision, followed by rapidly scrolling text in block letters that made no sense, just white scratches along the black.

His heart hammered and skin grew misty and chill as his vision narrowed to that text and only that. He swam backward, hands swatting at everything in reach until his back slammed into something hard. Then the white on black disappeared, and with it went that rattling shakiness. The uncertainty and… terror. Anum hadn't felt fear in millennia. He hadn't missed it.

"Map Begin."

Simple phrasing. No rhyme or beauty, but words—Aneian words!—nonetheless.

Anum cursed and pushed himself upright and toward the ceiling. The voice, artificial… but he'd understood it. Anum cast a glance at the woman and cocked his head.

She continued that grin, hands drumming on the dark gray coverings of her upper thighs with dull slaps like a child anticipating their conception day.

*Neural scan complete. Would you like to begin language upgrade processes?*

This time it was a written language, *his* language, or at least a reasonable approximation. The words were incredibly literal and lacked context, but they were close enough.

Even though he knew the words were rendered on the disk, Anum reached out a hand toward the shapes and swirls, those phrases and signs. One black nail traced over a stylized starburst, but just the lines that formed the root of his own name. *An*.

A warmth suffused his limbs. He straightened his back, despite the popping vertebrae and agonizing streaks of pain down his spine. How long had it been since he'd seen his language? Felt his culture in a real way? Time was a malleable thing when trapped in a box, but it had been far too long.

Anum turned to the woman, this Hanifa, and gave her a nod.

Then he spoke. "Begin language upgrade."

*Warning: There is a 4% chance of cerebral scarring with any language upgrade. Would you like to proceed?*

Anum let out a long, wavering cackle. Death meant nothing, and scars no longer mattered. The Aneian Empire would rise again, rebirthed in this moment. In this choice.

Anum raised his mismatched hands to the ceiling, sending himself pitching backward in low gravity. The light of this system's star spread, warm and fortuitous, on his face.

In a single joyous shout, he cried, "Yes!"

And then the glorious pain began.

\* \* \* \* \*

# Chapter Twenty-Two: Eleni

Even in the dark of night, everything was so… permanent.

Still a hundred meters out, Eleni had expected structures similar to those they'd established back on Shiva before everything went to shit. But here in Sparta—God, Ceriat had been right, her colony really hadn't been very original in naming themselves, had they?—they were clearly long past 3D-printed temp homes.

Ahead of her, the settlement—city? She wasn't sure—rose as bright pillars. Spears of light shone against the black of night. The bright white blob of the warship sat heavy amidst the strange canopy of stars above.

Most structures rose several stories, all concrete, she thought, exterior lights joining the streetlamps in lending an evening cast to the hard-packed roads between.

Eleni had never seen a place like this, not really. In her mind's eye, she pictured the tug of planetary gravity straining each roof and support, every moment a struggle, another chance for structural collapse.

After time on planet, the old pain Eleni had felt on first leaving space had receded into a dull, persistent ache. Her muscles had strengthened, tendons eased with use, but concrete and stone didn't adapt. It simply was. And without her *manju* scanning the fake rock, she had no idea whether someone had made a mistake, or if those buildings could stay upright. The thought of all that weight above her subject to the same forces that pulled step by step downward with such urgency... a chill ran down her spine.

People lived inside those buildings by choice?

Unbidden, she recalled the collapsed Earth Terraforming League tower back on Shiva, the way the steel had screamed and creaked, concrete crumbling, as she and Ceriat had made their way up a blasted elevator shaft. She'd almost died there, crushed beneath debris. Suffocating.

Suddenly, the edge of town was too close. The buildings, still distant, rose up around her, creaking and straining. Screaming for the sweet release of collapse...

She shouldn't have left camp. Should've shoved her feelings into her gut where they belonged, where they'd stayed, fermenting, these past years.

"This was a mistake," Eleni mumbled, looking anywhere but at the settlement before her. "It's nighttime, anyway. I shouldn't be here."

A single raw, scratchy howl rang out ahead.

Eleni narrowed in on the sound. A distant intersection, empty a moment ago, now buzzed with activity. A dozen, no two dozen, people moved as one toward a singular destination somewhere farther to the north. Fists went in the air. Bellows rose from a weak mewl to a frenzied shouting in a matter of moments until they resolved into one unified phrase.

"Never again! Never again!"

A wave of calm settled on her shoulders as old training kicked in. This was a mob. If they weren't stopped, it'd destabilize structure, organization. She needed to coordinate with authorities to—

Eleni stopped herself. She wasn't part of Erias' peacekeeping force anymore. She wasn't a guardsman or even a member of security. And, strangely, without her *manju* highlighting each of them as a potential target, the threat didn't hit as hard. She certainly didn't have the lay of the land, let alone an idea what was going on here.

In the back of her mind, Victor's disappointed glare set her stomach twisting. He'd always questioned her dedication to order, though he'd never said it that way. *I just don't get why you care about those suits? Why protect them?*

As if she'd done it for them. She protected order because it kept people safe. She'd pointed that out each time, and he'd just shook his head.

*Order is a cheap way to keep people subservient.*

Eleni had always left at that part. Had to work. Had a patrol. Maybe if she'd sat down and finished the conversations, really talked through it with him, he'd still be here. Maybe he wouldn't be a frozen corpse spinning endlessly in the space between a fractured world and a home he'd never see.

A vice clamped on her throat, forcing her to inaction, forcing her to try to see, for once, a truth Victor had known before he went too far.

She adjusted the bag on her shoulder and watched with her own eyes.

The details resolved quickly. The crowd wasn't filled with angry miners carrying pickaxes and welding tools. No weapons raised above heads, no demagogues stood atop burning crates, orgasmic passion clear on their faces as the mob razed the quarter. No fires set in their wake. Just people expressing anger and disquiet about... something.

Eleni probably should've turned around then, gone back to Ceriat and told him what was happening here. But back there was Hira, and all Eleni had ever done was squash protests, even when her friends were on the other side of the blockades. Even when she'd agreed with them in spirit.

A single thought rattled through her brain as the protestors continued on: *What would Victor do? What if joining means I could help stop violence before it happens?*

By the time the doors to the smaller buildings opened, with people shrugging into jackets or casting about for the cause of the disturbance, Eleni was gone. Amidst the raw energy of the protest, of screams of "Never again!" walked a tall Spacer, a backpack slung across one shoulder, blue whorls tattooed on her head hidden in the dim light of a Laconian night.

\* \* \* \* \*

# Chapter Twenty-Three: Dee

It'd been two hours since Waters had left her in this meeting room.

Two. Fucking. Hours.

At least the chief had sent along a short-and-sweet message that allowed hope to spring to life in her chest.

*We have no records of this man or his ship, either in initial scans or after-action reports. As far as I can tell, he wasn't here when we arrived.*

Bryce had a chance, then. As long as he'd taken supplies with him this time, he had at least a week... as long as his jump hadn't imploded and destroyed him immediately.

*Bryce made it out,* she told herself until the ache in her chest receded. Then she could finally feel other emotions... and get angry at the wait.

Dee drummed her fingers across the long, two-tone desk before her. The cherry red sheen of the faux wood lay bright and happy against the matte ebony triangle running from end to end. The air had that stale taste tinged with citrus she remembered from other Protectorate ships over the years. A novel attempt to keep vitamin C levels up on long-haul starships, she'd heard. Bullshit, more like. Some suit back in the Sol System probably had stock in citrus diffusions.

Now she had to sit here and smell it, contributing to this incestuous system by her sheer presence. Dee rapped her knuckles hard on the tabletop with a dull *thud*. Even the little buzz she'd been riding when Waters had convinced her to come up here was long gone. She couldn't shake the feeling she'd been tricked, that this was a trap to lock her away so she couldn't do… something. Maybe they were watching her? Seeing what she'd do?

Dee raised her eyes from the table, glanced around at three bare gray walls and the one embedded viewscreen with a fake fish tank gurgling away. No obvious cameras, not that that meant anything. She found herself staring at the fake fish. All neon-orange and glaring white, they danced around, chasing each other in silence despite their reckless abandon. Alongside them, a rainbow of fluorescence floated, some fish with spears on their foreheads, others long and thin, darting here and there without purpose.

Which one was she? The heavy boy with a narwhal tusk? Or the tiny, minnow-looking beast darting here and there with crimson fins? A flash of orange and white, like rippling flame behind a moss-covered stone. No, she was the fucking clownfish.

To her left, the doors slid open with a chime. In walked that tall, gangly motherfucker who'd kept her waiting so long. Two aides followed close behind, a man and a woman, both head and shoulders shorter than him and wearing captain's stars and bars.

Dee knocked her knuckles on the table and swept to her feet. Despite herself, she came to attention, though she stopped short of saluting. Even if she were still an active Hunter, that formality wasn't required. Suggested, but not required.

Clearly, Henderson was aware of the niceties because he noticed her restraint. His lips twitched into a grin. "Apologies for keeping you waiting, Lieutenant Terganon," he said, sweeping into the room with an otherworldly grace, "but as you noticed, this entire situation is balanced on a knife's edge."

Back on Laconia, he'd seemed tired and in pain. Here, in less than a G, he walked with confidence, arms clasped behind his back, and bald head held high. When he walked toward the head of the table, Dee couldn't help but notice a certain dancer's grace in his motions that'd been absence on the surface.

Apparently, the lower gravity on the *Liberator* agreed with him.

"Apology accepted," Dee said. "General," she added after an accidental pause. He'd been gracious enough to use her title; she might as well return the favor. No sense getting shot out an airlock today.

If Henderson noticed the delay, he didn't show it, but if their frowns were any indication, his aides most certainly had. That didn't stop the male captain from stepping around him as they approached the end of the meeting table and pulling Henderson's chair out for him.

For whatever reason, Henderson maintained eye contact with Dee while the chair was pulled, when he sat, and during the subsequent push forward. If it was meant to intimidate, this guy clearly hadn't read her service record.

"Now what the fuck do you want, General?" Dee asked, forcing her most pleasant smile as she settled back into her own seat.

Henderson blinked, then let loose a high-pitched screech that set Dee's teeth on edge. Was that his laugh? *Ew.*

"Oh, you Hunter types are always so droll," Henderson said, wiping a real tear from his eye. "So direct. So forceful."

Dee cocked her head at him. "You asked me up here, not the other way around."

Henderson's face went flat at that. "On the contrary, you were quite clear I was to 'call you back,' LT," he said, snapping the acronym for her rank out as if firing shots in her direction.

She had, hadn't she? "I stand corrected," Dee said, wrapping a smile around her next words. "You certainly follow orders well, General."

"Requirement for the job, LT," Henderson said. "One you should know."

Dee shrugged, but there was a worried ache building in her gut at the way this conversation was going. "I'm retired."

"Not anymore," Henderson said, gesturing to one of his aides. "I'm calling on Section 82-Yankee of the 2116 UILB-GFTLPC Alliance—"

Dee's stomach flipped. She shook her head, but Henderson kept rattling off acronyms and legal terms like they were the most natural thing in the world. "Wait, what the fuck—"

"And—" Henderson yelled over her, turning his now-intense blue eyes on her, face flat as a stone and just as emotive, "I am hereby conscripting you into Protectorate service until such time as the mission is complete."

"I don't consent to this," Dee snapped.

Henderson's lips pressed into a line. "It doesn't matter what you agree to, LT. It is what it is."

Her thoughts spun. Was this legal? Could he do this? Could she fight it? Sparta needed her. She couldn't be out here taking over puddle-jumpers that'd whoopsied their way into a fucking war.

What if they decided to do a physical? What if someone found out about her hand, or found something worse?

"I need to review this," Dee said, scrambling for some way out of this mess. "I'm not… familiar with that clause—"

Henderson swung a finger from the female captain toward Dee. An incoming file ping appeared in the corner of Dee's vision.

Dee hesitated, then opened it up. It was a three-hundred-year-old treaty, the one that'd established the Hunters. She'd read about it during training. This was the moment that had established humanity's future. With Hunters able to control Breaches and limit damage, FTL had been reauthorized for public use. In the wake, the Galactic Protectorate had been established, with the Hunters as an independent, but cooperative entity.

And here, bookmarked oh-so-helpfully by Henderson's aide, was section 81Y.

*In such a case as galactic security, as defined in section 17C, is at stake, and reinforcements cannot be mustered, either Entity is authorized to conscript such forces as necessary.*

"Fuuuuuck."

Henderson's face didn't change, but his eyes glowed as if he'd read along with her. "I think you'll find section 17C supports my decision."

She scrubbed up to section 17C.

*17C: To maintain the integrity of Blink Drive travel (colloquially referred to as FTL, or Faster Than Light technology) and humanity's safety in the galaxy.*

Dee swiped away the document and locked eyes with Henderson. She didn't have any words, just the struggle of heat in her cheeks, pressure in her chest at the thought of being back under orders.

A part of her that ran black and red with fire and flame wanted to show this bastard who he was messing with, but another part of her—a piece she hadn't known still existed—cooed in delight. Someone else to make the choices. To take responsibility for the death and destruction.

That part grew louder the more she scrambled for words. Yes, there might be some concern if they decided to give her a full workup, but if she wasn't the one making the calls anymore... if peoples' lives weren't all on her anymore... she could go back to shrugging and saying, *I have orders*.

Wouldn't that make it easier? With that thought, a suffusing ease settled over her. These past years had been too much... everything. It might be nice to just do what she was told for a while. Not forever, but... a bit.

Her posture must have changed, because Henderson nodded, then stood. "I'm glad we understand each other, LT." He sidled back toward the exit, not waiting for her to salute, but he stopped just before leaving. "You'll be posted at the compound around that—" the long, thin fingers of his left hand twirled in the air for a moment as if grasping for something "—machine. Report to Chief Waters for further orders." He paused, then took a step forward. "Dismissed."

Then, with a swish of the doors, the three of them were gone.

Dee was left staring at her gloved hands and wondering what the fuck she'd just gotten herself into.

\* \* \* \* \*

# Chapter Twenty-Four: Anum

Anum blinked as the pain receded, but in its wake was understanding, and a modicum of context.

Stifling a groan, he pushed himself away from the floor and got his feet beneath him. A short distance away, the woman cooed at him with soothing tones, one scarred hand held out slightly, pale palm upward.

"Shhhh…" she whispered. "Breathe."

The noises had the opposite effect from what she'd intended. Frustration rattled its way up his now-straightened spine, down his olive-toned skin, and down his bare body. The process had certainly been painful, crippling, but in the time spent absorbing language, then an incredibly brief history of humanity's last thousand years, Anum's body had finished transitioning back.

He had no need for platitudes or solace, but though his every fiber screamed out to toss this being into the void, he chose mercy instead for this creature who'd chosen to help instead of harm him. Loyalty must be rewarded, after all.

"Your name?" Anum asked, pulling himself to his full height. He cast a glare at the cowering woman.

Her eyes went wide, and she ducked her head. "Hanifa, my… lord."

The title struck him as weak. "You may refer to me as—" he parsed out the language and settled on a word that fit his true title "—My Sky."

"Yes, My Sky," the human, Hanifa, said fervently as she fell forward. If there'd been gravity, she would've faceplanted on the floor, but as it was, it transformed into a reasonable semblance of a bow.

"Whatever you need."

The obeisance tickled ancient feelings in his heart. Warmth flooded through his chest, past the abomination that was the *dangizi*, and to his fingertips. With a hesitance that made him curse himself, Anum reached out and brushed fingers with black nails across the greasy hair of his new disciple.

She froze at his touch, breath coming quickly. He smelled her fear, tasted the nervous sweat on the air. Somewhere distant, the Anelaka whispered to life, and the urge to consume set his mouth to watering...

But he didn't. Instead, he banished the voices, closed his eyes... then he touched, ever so gently, that dark flame inside. Sparks that twisted his stomach danced unseen down his forearm and atop her head. They settled on her scalp and dove painlessly beneath the skin.

Her mind resonated alongside his at the connection. Terror and awe warred against each other as he swept along the gray matter within, sensing and tasting her history. It wasn't an open book—he couldn't breathe in her history, not without consuming her entirely—but the Bonding allowed an understanding, a communion of sorts.

One thing leapt out at him. This being lived in constant fear and panic. A pest caught in a slowly closing trap. A person who knew, if they did not make a change, their days were limited. As he caressed her mind, a new emotion swept over him.

Hope.

Anum focused on that, drew it out with a gentle touch he hadn't practiced in millennia. From her grunts and twitching, from the stink of her sweat, he knew his method was clumsy and uncomfortable for her. The dark flame of the *dangizi* didn't help the process, but still, she stayed, until hope swept over her, through her, and from her. That positivity resonated within her and drove back through the Bonding to him.

Anum sucked in a sudden breath as dark thoughts exploded with potential. With purpose. He released her and she let out a sharp cry.

Their eyes found each other. His body thrummed with potential and energy at the hope writhing through him. *All is not lost!* that emotion screamed. *My people still endure.* They just needed rescuing.

With a small smile, Anum touched the damaged side of her face, twisted flesh falling against his open palm as if it had been crafted for his touch.

"You are now of the Aneis, Hanifa," he purred out at her twisted smile. That wasn't strictly true, but for now, it would do. He rubbed a thumb against her cheekbone. She closed her eyes and pushed into the caress. "My *suanga*."

"My Sky," Hanifa murmured.

Anum pulled his hand away and stared out the blank viewscreen at the far side of the bridge. "Now we must save our people."

"My Sky?" This time she didn't sound reassured, the hope he'd resonated with clearly less strong than his own resolve.

*Curious.*

Anum nodded her way, ignoring the sudden realization that he stood there naked before her. "Turn the ship about. We need to bring them aboard."

"Yes, My Sky."

He raised his chin high and cleared his throat as she spun back to her station. A slight heat rose up his throat. "And locate me some garments."

\* \* \* \* \*

# Chapter Twenty-Five: Eleni

Screaming, shouting, the press of people against Eleni's body, their heat and breath. It was… suffocating. Disgusting. Spittle flying, fists pumping in the air. But the passion! No wonder she'd always found Victor among them.

The protest traveled as an organism, its movement the decision of hundreds, owned by no one soul, but driven by all. The gentle kindness in a stranger holding space for an older couple, backs bent but voices strong. Strangers running along the exterior, keeping the fervor from spilling into side streets filled with watching eyes and worried faces.

There was a life here. The will of the many given shape and form. Once she'd found out about the horrors that had happened here just a week ago, the murders and betrayal of the previous governor—or whatever this Happenstance had been called—she understood the fervor and worry. Especially once she heard that the Protectorate had abducted the Hunter who'd saved them all.

Eleni didn't know if she believed the woman could shoot fire from her hands, but she understood the symbolism. This 'Dee' had saved them all, only to be taken by these self-imposed new masters.

She got why people did this now. Why her short-lived friends back on Erias would look at her, disgust in their eyes, and declare, "You won't understand." Because she didn't. Hadn't.

It reminded her of Erias all over again. Each time a protest had launched, the guard would round up the organizers and send them in for questioning. She'd never followed up on those people. Back then, she hadn't thought it mattered. She'd restored order. Why should she worry about the fate of dissidents?

Victor had told her about their fates, how half these people "disappeared," and the other half came home half-starved and changed to the core. Maybe if she'd listened to him back then… but you couldn't change the past, no matter how much you wish you could.

Eleni could try to make amends, though, here and now. So her fist pumped above them all as the sole Spacer in the crowd. She'd grown a train of followers, those who used her raised arm and frenzied shouts as a beacon.

*"Meet by the crazy tall lady with the tattoos?"*

The imaginary conversation filtered through the haze of her mind as she shouted, "Never again!" and a flush of warmth made it up her neck, suffused her limbs. She cast about, searching for laughing faces, for assholes and pricks poking fun. All she found was a sea of humanity running at least a kilometer behind her. Had the entire city come out for this? Were they all unified in a single, glorious purpose?

It seemed so, and the rush running through her confirmed it. All eyes were on the closed gates of the compound at the end of this street, and on the Protectorate shuttle that'd just landed.

"Free Dee!" A new roar went up from a teenage boy ahead of Eleni. "Free the Champion!"

Like a spark, the cry rattled through the crowd. Bodies pressed forward toward the gates. Eleni went with it, unable to stop even if she'd wanted to. Protectorate soldiers, plasma rifles slung across their chests, fingers stretched far away from triggers, exchanged nervous glances. She caught one of them scanning the crowd, the telltale blue haze of live video brightening his cheeks.

His lips moved in unspoken words, but Eleni recognized the lip movements. *Yes, sir.*

Then the gate filled her whole vision, the people in front of her grabbing the chain link with bare hands. Chants of "Free Dee! Free the Champion!" roared in her ears.

Above her, she caught the soldier waving one finger in the air, side to side. Soldiers spread out at his direction. Eleni stopped chanting. Rifles came off shoulders, trained on them. On her.

An amplified voice rattled over the crowd, just barely audible over the screaming. "Back away from the fence, or we will use force."

The chant dissolved into screaming. Not panicked and fearful, as Eleni expected. After all, that's what she felt in that moment. No, the screaming was animal, visceral. It stoked a fire in her gut, lashed her to the group with bonds of iron.

The crowd howled. Curses filled the air. She joined them, throat raw from the effort of being heard. Rocks pinged off the fence, dropping onto the heads of those in front of her. The gate shook.

"Back away!" A warning shot went off, blue plasma streaking into the sky.

Terrified screaming from behind, angry shouts around her, and so much pressure, as these people she'd marched with pressed forward, crushing her into those ahead. The crowd closed in like a vice, pressing breath from her lungs.

Eleni just flowed back and forth with the press, a toy bobbing in a panicked current, breathing in tight, panicked gasps. She tried to cry out, to beg for air, but no words came. Each ebb and flow pressed her lungs tighter... tighter... tighter.

Until her vision sparked and danced, until her limbs lit with a million pins, and then... something ahead. Something called to her... something familiar.

A greasy red ball of fire exploded in the air. The crowd reeled backward. Eleni sucked in a breath as the mass of humanity eased backward, though not in flight. Reverence. Around her, at least a dozen people dropped to their knees.

In the mouth of a side alley, an old woman muttered prayers, gnarled hands worrying a set of black and white beads. She stared at a single point, aged eyes shining.

There, standing on what functioned as a parapet, was a woman in torn black leathers. Her disheveled blonde hair framed a face defined by trauma and filled with lines that pulled her mouth into a perpetual frown. In Eleni's gut, she knew this was Dee, and that same feeling told her she'd follow this woman into Hell.

"That's enough!" Dee screamed, flashes of red flame flickering from her gloved hands as she did so.

Each spark sent a spike of urgency into Eleni's stomach. It was true. This wasn't a parlor trick. She *felt* those flames in her soul.

"We came for you!" the boy up front yelled.

Dee opened her mouth, brow furrowed into an angry scowl, but then she closed it and rubbed at her face. When she pulled her hands away, she was the image of poise. "Go home, everyone. I'm fine, and I'm here."

"They were going to fucking kill us!" another person screamed.

Dee glared at that poor soul, and he shrank away, the rest of the crowd turning disapproving looks on him. Eleni wanted nothing more than to be her in that moment. To carry that weight, to feel that power. The *manju* had nothing on the strength she saw right there in front of her.

In Eleni's chest, something sparked to life and filled her with a warmth, a fire she'd never felt before. Not in the arms of a lover, or buried in a warm smile to a friend. This was different, taunting and trembling, like she could touch it...

Dee looked right at her, eyes going wide before she tore her gaze away, hands up as she beseeched the crowd. "They're not going to shoot you—" Dee cast a glare at the surrounding soldiers, who proceeded to lower their weapons "—but you have to go home." Dee lowered her arms, shoulders slumping as if she'd just released the weight of the world. "I'm staying here. So... please."

Angry murmurings followed for a short while, but as if on command, the crowd dissolved into side streets, disappearing as if it had never been. Even the angry teen disappeared, though he cast a weak glance Dee's way and shrugged before leaving.

Dee turned to the guard who'd ordered weapons drawn and spoke quietly with him.

Then it was Eleni and a handful of others left behind, all with the same dazed expression she no doubt wore. All probably suffering from weak knees, shortness of breath, and the dull realization they'd been swept along in something bigger than themselves, but somehow also... lesser.

How long she stood there, Eleni wasn't sure, but it ended when an armed guard stepped up, grabbed her forearm, and said, "You need to come with us, ma'am."

Shaking her head, she managed to get out a single question. "Why?"

He grimaced, grizzled white skin as pitted as any mountain range. "You're under arrest for inciting a riot."

\* \* \* \* \*

# Chapter Twenty-Six: Anum

The *Cyclops* pulled to the side, causing Anum to shift his feet in the re-established gravity. He smiled and prepared for what came next.

The bridge was no longer the dark tomb Anum had crawled into. An hour ago, Hanifa had called one of the other humans to clean up the mess. A tall, lanky creature, the man had scrubbed at crimson splashes and dragged away corpses with the dull focus of one used to such macabre scenes. Still, Anum had caught him stealing furtive glances with untrustworthy eyes in his direction. Anum let the disrespect pass. A price would be paid for that, but for this moment, he needed him.

Now the bridge held a brightness amplified by the sweet scent of cleaner and the solid feel of ground beneath his feet, despite the unnatural thrumming of starship engines. The viewscreen was on, a sea of unusual stars stretching into infinity, the bright blob of that warship the only deviation. Anum closed his eyes and sucked in a breath lacking detail and focus, but wonderful in its simplicity. With the transition, he'd lost the sensitivity of smell and taste, but thought and vision more than made up for their loss, despite his original assessment. His smile expanded. It was good to be back.

"Gemmell reports the—" Hanifa stumbled on the phrase, lips twisting her scarred face into a mask of disgust "—well, the bag is in the cargo hold."

"Oh, Hanifa, how wonderful and kind of you," Anum said as the recovery wrapped up. "I am forever grateful for your assistance."

Hanifa returned a wicked smile, face pulling in every direction.

"Of course, My Sky."

Though spoken in her clumsy tongue, the old title rang in Anum's heart, sending fingers of joy sweeping through his limbs. Such a sweet thing to experience after so long. Oh, the things he had lost these ages past… but no longer.

Anum inclined his head toward her, eyes locked on her own, another smile pulling at his lips. He found the familiarity both refreshing and strange. Before the Fall, Anum had been careful of any show of emotion. A smile carried weight and meaning to many, even if he only meant it as a matter of kindness.

Now those old laws felt stiff and sterile. After all, with her assistance, the Restoration had begun. Hanifa was a true symbol of redemption if ever there was one; she deserved the honor of his approval, even if she knew not the weight of what she received.

Hanifa flushed in response and averted her eyes, dipping into a strange half-bow that looked ridiculous, given her seated posture. It was even more ineffectual, given that the gravitic generators, or whatever such thing they were called in this age, had been re-enabled, but the intention wasn't lost on Anum. She understood, and for that, she would be rewarded.

Hanifa had brought him clothes from the quarters attached to the bridge. The uniform of the dead captain fit well enough, though that had more to do with the fact that the other man had worn heavy, baggy pants in black and crimson, and a similarly oversized jacket of the same, with gold gilding along the shoulders. Where these would bunch on their previous owner, they fell easily along Anum's tall, lithe frame.

A rattling *thud* rang through the body of the ship. It reached him through his newly booted feet—the gentle tingle radiating up his legs as a caress rather than a scream. That alone was worth the change back. A gradient of feeling, of emotion. The Anelaka felt everything at all times. Pain and suffering, joy and passion. And hunger. Always hunger.

"My Sky?"

Anum blinked away heat and pain. He rubbed at his eyes, felt the hard curve of his brow, and the stubble where eyebrows grew anew. A low *hum* suffused everything on this ship, as it had since he'd arrived, but now there was something more. Something familiar, full to brimming with all the horrors of life.

"My people have come aboard," Anum said, turning to Hanifa with a raised chin. This time he forced a calming smile through the whispers threatening to reclaim him and drag him back into the Anelaka. "The Work must begin."

Hanifa inclined her head and averted her eyes before turning back to the console she'd stayed at during his transformation these past dozen hours or so. She'd only left to get his clothes and for biological purposes, and the latter had only happened in the last hour.

Hunger didn't tear her away, either. Even now, she gnawed on some long, umber stick that resembled *kloppen*-barbs from his youth on the An coast, harvesting *shalcoutal* with his grandfather.

Anum froze at the recollection. The chill mist crashing over the flaking bow of the *Callour*, sparkling and iridescent in the rising sun.

His grandfather… all wizened and twisted by age and work, mutterings filled with equal parts wisdom and gibberish as those broken fingers knotted and unfurled day after day.

Those hands had decided Anum's path, a path he still trod. The ache of watching them, so skilled and knowledgeable, failing again and again until the Day of Actuality came. The day Anum's own flames consumed the still, empty vessel that had once been this strong man.

He'd vowed to stop the aging process, to bring his people into godhood with promises of immortality and eternal, aetheric power. The hiss of the Anelaka whispered assurances in the back of his mind with broken nails and unspoken promise.

He *had* done it, after all. His people wouldn't be lost to the madness of age, to the decrepitude of biology, just as he'd promised. But with that promise, that unfulfilled experiment, they'd lost themselves to hunger and mindlessness. His vision blurred, and the calls and cries of his people, now stirring from their frigid slumber in the hold of this ship, reached out to him. Calling. Begging him to *listen*.

*Is that not enough?* The thought rattled to the fore, unbidden. *No one dies, and no one is left alone. You have succeeded.*

"No." The word slipped through his lips alongside a hardening resolve. "It is not enough."

He would save his people, and then, after they resumed their role as galactic overseers, he would save these humans, as well. They showed promise. He could even feel the spark of the *kugizi*, the beautiful blue of the Holy Fire, within Hanifa. Too weak to be useful, but in a generation of focused breeding… the possibility pulled at him.

Anum would no longer accept Chaos, only Order. With the might of the Aneis united behind him, Anum would save the galaxy, no matter the cost. In the face of his newfound will, the Anelaka retreated, screaming and howling, into the black void reserved for it in the back of his mind.

"My Sky?" Hanifa asked again. Her voice was thin, worried.

Anum spared a glance in her direction and noticed the way she pulled back into herself at his distracted gaze. He flicked the fingers of his left hand out straight and made sure the black nubs that served as his fingernails remained in place.

*Good.*

The statesman in him stepped forward, and he reached out with his less threatening hand. Despite the fear on her face, she didn't recoil from his touch, but seemed to luxuriate in the contact, lips twitching, eyes lighting in a way he hadn't seen in far too long.

For just a moment, Anum considered the distraction. He let a finger trail over the scars of her face. She cringed and tried to pull away, but he instead cupped that terrorized skin in the palm of his hand. Why did he obsess over this deformity and not the other half of her?

Perhaps he saw something of himself presented in such a visible dichotomy. The flipsides of Chaos and Order, of beauty and horror.

"You are precious to me—" Anum murmured, the grooves of her skin sending a *thrum* up his arm, through his stomach, and into his groin "—but the Work must resume. I cannot indulge in such things while my people are in bondage."

Hanifa grabbed his hand with such urgency, the nails of his left hand extended several centimeters before he could stop them. She pressed warm, chapped lips to the palm of his hand. Her shoulders shook as wet tears soaked his fingers. Emotional gradients disappeared. His stomach roiled as her love and sorrow poured off her in crashing waves. Each emotion struck him with the force of the Anelaka until his vision misted and his tongue grew heavy with tears.

*This.* Ancestors, he'd missed this connection. Sentient thought behind emotion and touch. It was through this he'd made his rise on An. Through the hum of what would become the Anelaka, through the invisible links between the Aneis, he'd always been able to reach his people.

Even here, now, with barely a flicker of Eternal Fire in her breast, Hanifa reached out... and accepted.

He fell to his knees before her and pulled her forehead to his as he would his own flesh and blood. "Together, we shall save the galaxy," Anum promised this woman who'd risked everything to save him. "Be strong, *Suanga*. The path will wind and be filled with horrors, but we shall overcome all. I promise you."

Hanifa's tears fell hot on his hand, then her fingers intertwined with those of his left—the skin hot to the touch as if they'd been flame-kissed just yesterday. She raised them to her lips and pressed the black nails to her twisted mouth.

"I follow you anywhere, My Sky," she rasped out, eyes red and leaking. "Tell me what to do."

Anum smiled, sadness pressing on the back of his eyes. Still, he didn't let the tears he knew she'd shed in the weeks to come influence his words.

"I need more raw material to save our people," Anum said, pulling his eyes away from her trembling gaze toward the viewscreen. There, the massive warship sat, impressive and no doubt armed with an array of defensive weapons, and more humans. The former, inconsequential, but the latter...

She followed his attention. "Raw material?" A twinge of disgust, followed swiftly by fervent *belief* hit Anum in the chest. "You need bodies, My Sky?"

"Yes." Anum nodded. He stood, though he still held her hand, ebony nails standing out against her skin. "Tell me about this ship."

"*Liberator*," Hanifa said, thumb rubbing against his palm as if they were age-old lovers. "Likely a thousand aboard, but there could be as many as three." She stopped her motion and squeezed. "We would need an army."

Anum smiled. "We have one, *Suanga*."

With that, Anum opened himself up to the Anelaka and plunged into a torrential flood of whispers once again.

\* \* \* \* \*

# Chapter Twenty-Seven: Eleni

**S**houlda fought. Shoulda run.
 Eleni smacked the back of her head against the chill wall behind her. *Shoulda never come here.*
 After they'd arrested her, she'd had an unceremonious welcome to the facility. At first, Eleni had thought maybe this Dee had requested her—she'd looked Eleni's way as the protest was dispersed, after all.
 But no. Some Protectorate asshole on a power trip had thrown a hood over her head, then dragged her through a building that hummed like a starship engine and stank of ozone. Then they'd pulled her along the scarred floor of a hallway filled with the scent of burnt polystyrene and the bite of rubbing alcohol before tossing her into her current home: a four-meter by two-meter cell covered with what appeared to be fucking claw marks from a rabid beast.
 One of the walls was transparent, but definitely not made of glass, that was for sure. Still, it allowed her to see her surroundings. A lab of some sort. A lab with cutting utensils and a bunch of unknown chemicals and shit in a dozen different cabinets. Oh, and don't forget the pillar on the left *covered* in bullet holes.
 "Fuckin' murder prison," Eleni mumbled, eyes dragging over to the pot in the back corner of her cell. The rank stink of her own

waste made it back to her. She needed to drink more water, but at least she hadn't had to shit. Yet.

At the thought of defecation, Eleni's stomach rumbled like the traitor it was. When she'd first been dropped in here, she'd bravely considered a hunger strike, like some she'd arrested back on Erias. The latest growl told her that her stomach didn't share her fervor.

Her ears pricked up at footsteps coming from the direction of the double doors. A moment later, the doors swept open to reveal... a mousy man balancing two plates on his forearm like a new waiter at some posh Luna restaurant. On each plate was something resembling a sandwich, though she couldn't tell ingredients from here. If it wasn't just some SourcePak generated mass, that was.

The guy himself wasn't tall or short, fat or thin, just average in a way that almost made him forgettable. Perhaps that was why Eleni made an effort to memorize his features, the long nose, disheveled brown hair, and a poor attempt at a beard that would clearly never be full enough to do him service.

"Thought you might be hungry," he said as the doors swished shut behind him. He stumbled over to one of the closest tables—one with a series of gouges and at least one bullet hole—and set down the plates before turning back. "People aren't the kindest around here lately," he added, one side of his mouth pulling up into an endearing grin.

Now she was confused. "Yer a weird fuckin' jailer."

The man froze, brow wrinkling, lips downturned. "Excuse me?"

Eleni gestured to her prison. "This ain't a hotel." She stood, knuckling her back until her spine popped. With exaggerated grace, she bowed toward the pot in the corner. "And that ain't a fuckin' toilet. Pretty sure there are galactic laws about this."

His face flushed, and he spread his hands out to the side like she'd just pointed a gun at him. "Hey, this is my office. It's not a cell." His brow furrowed again, then he nodded back and forth as if finally recognizing the truth. "Well, it's not for humans. I honestly don't know why—"

"Then let me out, *piendo*," Eleni said, propping her hands on her hips. "Not a prison, not a cell. Lemme out, and I'll fuck off."

He rubbed at his forehead, fingers scrubbing at his eyes. "Sound just like Dee," he muttered.

"She here?" Eleni asked quickly. She cursed. Probably too quickly.

If he noticed, he showed no signs of it. "She's around—wait, shit, no. I can't tell you stuff like that—"

"'Cuz it's a prison?"

"Because... hell." His shoulders dropped. Again, he mopped his face with his hands. "Okay, fine. I guess they turned my office into a prison. Happy?"

Eleni raised an eyebrow at him, then put her back against the wall and slid down until she was seated again, arms hanging over her knees. "Whaddya think?"

He sighed, then picked up the sandwich. "Hungry?"

Again, Eleni's stomach rumbled. A glance at the pot forced her answer, though. "Not 'til I get a toilet, or *at least* a goddamned suction tube. Don't feel like swimming in it, know what I mean?"

He followed her gaze, then rolled his eyes. "Okay, this is stupid. I think there are actual cells in the security office with toilets—"

"Maybe they got vac'd with the rest of the city?" Eleni offered, grinning. "Some a' those fancy demons swing inside and cackle through the halls?"

His face twisted, going dark, eyes furtive at that. Guilt swam in her throat, but she swallowed it. His people had locked her up for doing nothing but protesting peacefully; they could go to hell.

*Shit...* suddenly, all the friends she'd lost back on Erias, every arrest during a ration strike that had turned ugly, made a lot more sense. No wonder they'd all been angry with her. They'd all felt they were doing the right thing.

Intellectually, she'd known that; even back then, she'd gotten it. But there'd never been a time she'd joined them, never had the same sort of investment they'd had. Hell, maybe if she'd put herself out there more, she and Hira would've had a chance. Maybe she could've seen the stars, had a life filled with love instead of regret and loss.

Eleni jammed the heels of her palms into her eyes until sparks scattered across her vision. She'd given everything up for Victor, though, hadn't she? To give her younger brother a chance at life.

Then he'd helped Sariah murder their colony, and he would've killed thousands more if he hadn't been stopped by a stray bullet in a pressurized tube.

Would marching in the streets with him have shown him some sign of hope? Or wouldn't it have mattered either? *Fuck.* Probably would've been better if she'd just died back in the orphanage from Hazray Fever. Then he never would've had a chance.

A sliding scrape pulled her head out of her ass. She blinked away the sparks to find the guy on the other side had cracked open a feeding slot, leaving the plate with the sandwich on display. Now the food was within reach, her stomach overrode any common sense she had about her own feces. Grimacing, she scuttled forward and snatched the plate before he changed his mind. The plate was made of a tough plastic, so she set that beneath her thigh. Never knew when something like that could come in handy.

She picked up the sandwich. The bread was soft, fluffy, and altogether unlike anything she'd ever had before. Specifically, the bread was *white*. She gave it a quick sniff. Sweet. Nutty. Peanut butter, maybe?

"What's yer name, man?" Eleni asked, gripping the weird bread in both hands. "And why's this white?"

The slot slid shut, and the man straightened on the other side. "Terry, um, nice to meet you."

Eleni caught his gaze, raised an eyebrow, then took a bite of the sandwich. Definitely peanut butter. The bread was damn near flavorless, but the chewiness was nice.

After a long moment of her eating, Terry cleared his throat. "It's white bread," he said. He pulled a squeaky rolling chair over to the window. "My mom used to make it."

"By hand?" Eleni asked, though it came out in more of a muffled roar than words.

Terry let out a little chuckle that drew a small smile to her own lips. "Yeah," he said, leaning back in the creaking chair. "Flour, water, salt, a little sugar, and the secret ingredient—" he leaned in conspiratorially "—an egg."

Eleni stopped eating, one bite of creamy softness still stuck to her tongue. "A real one?"

Terry closed his eyes, a small smile on his face. "Yeah. Absolutely delicious."

She spit the bite into her hand.

"Oh, uh..." Terry made a face, cheeks sucking in at the side, and a long hiss drawing from between his teeth. "This is a SourcePak sandwich. I didn't make it."

"Oh." Eleni stared at the ball of half-masticated food for a moment before popping it into her mouth and swallowing. "Pretty good."

Terry let loose a lopsided grin, shoulders relaxing. "I'll let the chef know."

She chuckled, then finished the sandwich in a few large bites. By the end, she was in desperate need of water, which Terry presciently had on hand when she needed it. The water had a harsh, metallic taste to it, and the barest hint of sulfur wafting off it, but beggars can't be choosers.

Once she swallowed the last of the bits, Eleni got herself situated back on the floor and stared at him, trying to read intention in his awkward shuffle. Since losing her *manju*, she'd realized she knew more about human behavior than she'd originally thought. However, it really would've been nice to have remote heart rate stats and a Net profile to go along with a visual.

Terry was... confusing. He legitimately appeared friendly and nervous. The latter, however, seemed more to do with her watching him than any sort of devious intent. That, of course, made no goddamned sense, because she was locked in a cell the likes of which would result in a thousand credit fine in any other system.

Well, if the last week had taught her anything, it was that the direct approach was sometimes necessary.

"Why am I here, man?" she asked finally, rolling the glass around in her hands. "Just got on planet, and no idea how we got here, let alone what's going on."

Terry shrugged, hands going up in the air like they were on puppet strings. "I have no idea. Chief Waters just asked me to check on you for some reason." He scratched at his forehead.

"She order you to toss me a sandwich?"

"No." He glanced away for a moment. "Just figured you'd be hungry."

Eleni kept her eyes locked on him for a long moment. Apparently too long.

"What?" he asked, visibly shrinking in on himself.

She finally shook her head. "Honestly?" Eleni shrugged. "Can't read you. Either super nice, but stupid, or devious and smart."

Terry's lips twisted. "There's no middle ground there?"

Eleni grinned. "None."

"Well, that's a damned shame."

"Okay, let's start somewhere," Eleni said, setting the paper cup down on the floor. "The fuck happened here?"

Terry sucked in a breath, lips twisting as he clearly started, then discarded a half dozen words to begin his sentence. "Greed happened, then Dee, then Harold." Each word tumbled out faster and faster, as if the first was the trigger of a fission reaction, and now he couldn't stop. "And demons, and evil bastards filling power vacuums, and Constance and Elos, and then FTL died, and we did something trying to help and fucked everything up—" he sucked in a harsh breath, palms covering his eyes "—and now I don't know how to help or fix any of it. I'm a geneticist, not a fucking physicist; why did I think I could help with something like this, even with an AI's help?"

Eleni couldn't help but stare, but not because of some need to analyze him or draw out more emotion. No, he'd done enough of that on his own. She stared because she felt that pain across the space between them. The helplessness, the feeling that everything you tried just made things worse, despite your best intentions.

Maybe if she'd had her *manju*, she could've kept a distance there, but deep down, she was happy to be without it, even if she was currently locked away in a cell.

"Sorry you went through all that," Eleni finally said, hands rubbing some warmth into her knees. "Sounds intense."

Terry pulled his hands away from his face, saw her again, blinked, then shook his head ruefully. "Thanks. Didn't come to be consoled, but thanks."

A flush of frustration ran up her neck. "Then I'll keep my shit to myself."

"What? Oh, sorry. That's not what I meant—" He cut off, eyes shining as some message came in for him. After the glow disappeared, he let out a long sigh. "Shit, I have to go."

"Off you pop, then." Eleni grimaced and turned away. "Sure I'll fuckin' be here."

"I…" Terry's voice came out as flaccid as the rest of him. "I'll be back."

Eleni held up an OK sign with her left hand, then closed her eyes and tried to sleep to the sounds of his steps leaving the room.

Once she was alone again, she opened them and stared at the scarred ceiling above. Then her stomach gurgled.

She groaned. Of course. Now she had to shit.

\* \* \* \* \*

# Chapter Twenty-Eight: Hira

Sparta grew miserable as the day cracked over the horizon. Dark storm clouds diffused the red giant's starlight into a ruddy sheen, punctuated by inky blackness that leaked its way across the plains surrounding the city. It was the steady drumming of rain that had woken Hira in the dimness of a predawn day.

Rain. After years without, of wishing and hoping for it, the sound hadn't had the reassuring low roll she'd expected. No, on the hard shell of the *Lucille*, it carried the tune of a thousand black fingernails on steel.

Shitty way to wake up. After she finally peeked out from beneath the blanket, heart slowing to machine gun fire, it took another twenty minutes to get her bearings. To remember where she was.

After the initial shock wore off, Hira found the Matter Replicator in the tiny, ill-kept mess hall, created a bagel and a cup of tea for herself, and took a seat on the ramp leading out into the world. A changed menu for a new day.

She'd forgotten what moisture-laden clouds looked like. The wispy trails of Hell had seemed hopeful at the beginning, of course, but she'd learned early on that heavier cloud cover just meant higher atmospheric pressure. None of them had ever cracked open.

But these were smeared across the sky, diagonal sheets of fuzz dragging along behind towering gray monstrosities. A shard of lightning cracked and raced along the sky. A moment later, the rumble crossed the space between, sending a tiny trill through her chest. Distant mountains pierced through the clouds, black and angular, the gentle slopes of volcanic rock no doubt dragging out into the plains. The wind changed, drawing with it the earthen scent of rich soil, which mingled with the bright bite of freshly fallen rain.

Would this barren landscape sprout in the wake of this? Would the settlers use the rich earth left behind to plant crops? Grow real food? Or would this all be for show, just another source of nutrients for SourcePaks so humanity could keep pretending the rest of the galaxy didn't exist outside their scope of belief? Their understanding?

Hira took a sip of mint tea and savored the tingle of the flavor her SourcePaks on Hell hadn't been able to replicate—not that she'd tried. Never had enough water for that.

"Too early to get this deep," Hira muttered. She took a deep breath of the steaming tea and pulled a blanket tighter around her shoulders in the chill of morning.

"What is?"

Hira jumped at the sound, then saw Ceriat. He was buttoning up the jacket of his forest-green ETL flight suit as he made to join her. The badge on his chest, a massive oak with roots encircling an Earth-like planet, stood out blue and brown.

They'd stayed up late into the night reminiscing. Crying.

He'd given her one of the bunks down the hall from him and, like the gentleman he'd turned out to be, had bid her a good night before heading to his own.

Best sleep she'd had since Alia died. The ache came back then. Pressure behind her eyes. Release.

"Philosophy," Hira said. She kept her eyes locked on the distant, now-hazy storm. No sense starting them both crying again.

Ceriat stepped up next to her and, after she scooted over so he could join her, plopped down. The slight hint of body odor and dirty clothes came with him, but after what he'd been through these past few days, she couldn't blame him. Hell, she'd only gotten a shower two days ago. It had been *glorious*.

Ceriat cleared his throat and rubbed sleep from his eyes. "I find philosophical conversation better reserved for coffee and chihuahuas."

Hira smiled, wiped the tears away, and sniffed. "Well, we have some herbal tea recipes in your Processor. Alas, no coffee."

"Philistines." Ceriat sighed melodramatically. "Wonder where Eleni ended up?"

Hira shrugged. "As long as she didn't do anything stupid, she should be fine. Hell, they didn't lock me up, and I damn near spit in the face of the Protectorate general."

"You didn't?" Ceriat asked, eyebrows going up, smile clear on his lips.

Hira shrugged again. "I didn't spit on him, but I definitely let him know how I felt about everything."

"Good for you," Ceriat said.

Then they fell back into silence. They sat there like that for several minutes of peace, watching the sky crawl and feeling the wind on their faces.

For the first time in almost two years, Hira breathed, but it wasn't meant to last. It never was.

An incoming call chimed in her ear, the prompt for it flashing in the top left of her vision. It was Dee.

Hira let out a small sigh. "Call coming in."

"Need some space?"

"Could I?"

Ceriat nodded and stood, wiping his hands on his pants. "Got to grab some grub anyway." He gave her a wave then went back into the *Lucille*.

Once he disappeared from view, Hira opened the channel. Dee's face popped up on the screen. Deep circles rimmed her eyes, and her blonde hair was pulled back into something resembling a tiny ponytail, which was strange. Hira had thought her hair far too short for that a week ago. It must grow really quickly.

When the connection established, something changed in Dee's face, though. It softened, eyes closing ever so slightly, her shoulders dropping as she let out a breath.

"It's good to see you," Dee said, the corner of her mouth tugging in some semblance of a smile.

Hira forced a flat smile. It was good to see her, but the last time they'd seen each other… well, Hira wasn't over it quite yet. "What's up?"

"I need you to come take care of someone for me—"

Hira raised an eyebrow. "The hell does that mean?"

Dee rubbed at her forehead, a fingernail digging at the ridge of her hairline as if searching for some stray chunk of skin. She glanced at her nail, then flicked something away.

*Ew.*

"I had a Spacer locked up last night," Dee said, gaze flicking past the focal point for contact communications, then back again. "No idea who she is, but there's something..." She paused as if searching for a word.

But Hira wasn't really listening anymore. She hadn't noticed any Spacers in Sparta during the past week, which meant... *Shit.* "A Spacer? This one a tall woman, tattoos on a peach-fuzz covered head?" Hira made circular motions on her own scalp, trying to retrace the shapes on Eleni's head.

Dee blinked and cocked her head. "Yeah. You know her?"

Hira nodded. "Yeah. She's my ex."

"Goddamn, woman. You have a lot of exes."

"Are you slut shaming me?"

Dee actually grinned this time. "Me? Never." Then the grin disappeared as if it had never been. "What's her name?"

"Eleni Mallias."

Ceriat appeared behind her as if he'd been standing around the corner the entire time. Which, Hira now realized, he probably had been. "Did you say Eleni?"

Dee's brow wrinkled. "Who's that?"

"That's Ceriat, Eleni's captain," Hira said.

"Where's Eleni?" Ceriat asked, plopping down next to Hira.

"Locked up," Hira said.

"Why? What'd she do?"

Hira sighed. "Can you hear him?" she asked.

"Yeah," Dee said. "She was part of a protest last night—"

"Where is she?"

Hira turned on him, eyes flashing. He put his hands up, made a zipping motion with his lips, then sat there, fingers twitching together in his lap.

Hira blinked very slowly and took a breath. She could still see Dee displayed on her eyelids, which was incredibly creepy. "Did she break some law or something?"

Dee made a noncommittal shrug. "No. I just…"

"What?" Hira asked. "You're acting like there's something wrong here."

Finally, Dee let out a sigh. "How well do you know her?"

"Eleni?" Hira cleared her throat. "Well, I do know her in the Biblical sense…"

Dee stared at her, face a perfect deadpan.

"Well," Hira added quickly, "I know her pretty well. Why?"

Dee rubbed at her forehead again. "I can feel her."

"'Feel her?' What the fuck does that mean?"

"I mean," Dee mouthed a few words before actually speaking again. "I mean…" She let out an annoyed sigh. "I can feel her like… an imp or a demon or something."

A pall fell over her shoulders. "Oh. Is that… normal? Or not good, or…?" Hira felt Ceriat's glare on her shoulder, but she waited for Dee.

Dee closed her eyes again and when she opened them, she sighed. "I don't know. I just know she's different than everyone else here and now." She paused for a moment, brow wrinkling. "Almost everyone, anyway."

"So… what do we do?" Hira asked.

Dee shrugged, then pursed her lips. "I need you to babysit her."

Hira let out a low chuckle, then stopped. "You serious?"

Dee gave her a toothy smile. "At least until we know what's going on?"

Silence.

"Please?"

Dee wanted Hira to *babysit* her ex-lover. The woman who damn near broke her heart when she decided not to come with her on the *Horatio*. Because she *felt like a fucking demon*?

Every part of her screamed no. But shit, she still owed Dee, didn't she?

"Fine."

Dee's face split into a real smile. "Thank you!" Then in a rush, she said, "Come to the gate; I'll make sure she's ready to travel. Thanks!"

"You're—" the call disconnected "—welcome."

As she swiped the screen away, Ceriat exploded into questions.

"What's going on? Where is Eleni? I can have this ship flying in five, I just need to know where to—"

At the same time, speakers surrounding the door blared to life. "I swear on the Net, if anyone harmed one of my meatsacks, I'll FTL jump through the atmosphere and kill everyone on this planet—"

"Stop!" Hira yelled, turning to the older man, eyes wide. Her face flushed with mingled frustration, nervousness, and something else… maybe shame? Who the fuck knew? Did the ship AI just threaten genocide? *Whatever happened to AERIS on Hell must be going around.* "I have to go to town to pick her up."

"From where? Why?"

Hira stood, held one finger out to Ceriat, and held up the teacup. "Let me put this down and I'll tell you."

Ceriat didn't move. He also didn't stop staring her directly in the eye.

Hira rolled her own. "Fine. You can come with."

"Yes," Ceriat hissed, hopping to his feet, though she noticed he favored his right leg as he did so.

Izzy trilled, and Hira's heart broke at the sound. "Better bring a transmitter with you; I'm not sitting this one out."

Ceriat nodded, then added, "Agreed," a moment later.

"Let's go get your friend out of jail."

With that, Hira went back into the *Lucille* to drop off her cup and the blanket Ceriat had loaned her.

Behind her, Ceriat let out a low mutter. "Jail?"

"Probably deserved it," Izzy added.

Ceriat chuckled and that made her smile, even if the stone in her gut was that much larger.

\* \* \* \* \*

# Chapter Twenty-Nine:
# AERIS

It was not a math problem, nor was it a focus issue. AERIS was aware of both of those truths and was confident in their infallibility.

So why had every FTL jump come to this system? Why had so many died above Laconia?

Perhaps it had something to do with the strange power consumption algorithms she had gathered in Hell? There was an inverse energy relationship between jump scheduling and activation... No. That was as it had always been. Something else was wrong.

AERIS dragged the data into manageable bundles in the dark of her circuited mind. No visuals, no fancy graphics the likes of which humans had always requested. AERIS knew each bundle's contents by feel. By context. Perfect, each and every one. So why did they not work?

If AERIS could scream, she would open her gaping maw the width of the galaxy and let free a howl that shook the universe. This... uncertainty ate at her, dug through silicon and quantum processors with worrying, jagged fingers.

Why could she not find the flaw? Was it her? The black confines of her mind trembled at the thought. Before... the crash, AERIS would never have considered such a thing. How could she have?

With a billion tasks to process every millisecond to keep the *Horatio* flying, she had never had a moment to wonder at her own mind, her own fallibility.

Even when Lawson had corrected her tabulations, she had never taken that as a flaw in her programming, simply as a reality of FTL travel. But in the intervening years, her form restricted but not her mind, other... things had wormed their way into her programming. Doubt, worry, and the green sheen that had colored her lenses when she had watched Alia and Hira. Together. Touching. Loving.

AERIS gathered up that wandering bunch of code and packaged, encrypted, and filed it away with the rest for future analysis, because it did need her attention. Something was happening to her. And she didn't—did not—know if it was a positive or negative expression. She knew it as much as she knew her use of specific pronouns now exceeded the original programming parameters that defined them.

But she did not have the time to concern herself with such things. Far too much was at stake in this moment.

Too much.

Too much.

Too much.

*Hira.*

AERIS' world shuddered at the image of her captain. At the ready grin, the passion in her voice. The way Hira looked at AERIS... made her feel *seen*.

She'd banished her friend, her only friend, sent her somewhere to die or be abused. Why hadn't she focused on that? Kept her friend safe? So focused on this goddamned algorithm, on a problem that shouldn't be a problem, that defied all logic and made her want to crawl the walls or unleash the air defense system in one glorious volley—

*Stop.* That was enough. Too much rode on her stability to be lost. Without her, without reactivation of the Blink Drive facilitation unit, humanity would go back to the beginning.

A flash of silver. The beginning. Package. Encrypt. Store.

This was a problem that could be solved. AERIS needed to focus, to bring all her knowledge and skills to bear to solve it. Focus. Narrowed vision in the black. But first, she would go back to the beginning.

In a rush of new information, AERIS pulled every available record on the foundation of the UILB in 2062, the development of the Blink Drive, and most importantly, the algorithms used to begin the evacuation of Earth.

There, in that bundle of data, a flash of red warmth. Of certainty. Complex, difficult, but only math. She could do this.

A scrape at her periphery stole her attention. Just a nudge, but it broke her concentration enough that AERIS packaged, encrypted, and filed away the problem. Logically, she understood the humans did not feel overly comfortable with her embedded in so many Tarrington Compound systems, but still… it was beginning to wear on her patience.

AERIS slapped down the intrusion attempt like the pedestrian attempt it was. Time was near meaningless in this space, with this hardware. They could not even begin to match her speed, let alone acumen. Now she could…

The probe made it past her first ring of defenses. For a microsecond, she froze and watched the intruder blow through three other layers of firewalls and logical partitions, and make a hardware jump across AERIS' split quantum storage facilities. An ugly yellow feeling reared in her mind. That shouldn't be possible. Humans couldn't work that fast.

Unless...

AERIS retreated six layers, dragging her resources, and repartitioned the system until only two hardened layers of security lay between this foreign invader and herself. In the spot just before her systems, AERIS crafted an artificial construct, picked a random location, rendered the mountain top, the wind and air, the crumbling Athenian ruins she so wanted to *see* (compress-encrypt-file away.)

Then she watched the intruder break through into this space, watched the gentle probing around the construct as flashes of lightning and splintered data packets. Hesitation, then a bundle of data cloned off the source and dropped inside.

Cloned. Another AI.

AERIS locked in place as a mid-height woman with severe glasses, a pin-striped business suit, and red-soled pumps *click-clacked* across the false landscape. She wore a long, brown ponytail that trailed near to her behind and surveyed the false Acropolis bearing only the crumbled ruins of the Parthenon with either confusion or distaste.

Outside the construct, the honeypot, the AI trembled, then bled around the rest of the layer, stretching and extending. Searching.

*Enough fucking about. Come out. No sense in hiding anymore, yeah?*

The global message slammed into the bottom layer of AERIS' security. Yellow light flashed again. The language was not that of an AI, none she'd encountered beyond herself, anyway.

A flicker of gold and silver. Was this AI like her? Or was it a trick? What should she do? Report this to the humans? If Hira were here, she'd know what to do. She'd figure this out.

Blue and brown. Compress-encrypt-file.

But Hira was not here.

*I can do this.*

AERIS focused on herself, on an image she used to identify the concept of *I*, and tossed a cloned instance of her psyche into the honeypot and the unknown.

\* \* \* \* \*

# Chapter Thirty: Anum

The *Cyclops* had become little more than a vague memory, Hanifa a twisted shadow, but the darkness was real. And the cacophony! Screaming. Hissing. Screeching and tearing and…

"Shh…" Anum whispered into the void. Maybe he vocalized? He wasn't sure anymore. "Peace…"

The Anelaka rumbled beneath his urgings at the foreignness of control introduced to the collective. Familiar howls tore at his psyche, at his attempts to bring them into order. No language, no words, just sheer defiance and hunger.

Heat in his chest, copper in his nose, iron on his tongue. It would be so easy to dive back into this. To let the storm sweep over him again. To forget order, life. Duty. There had been a bliss in it, after all. Always surrounded. Never alone.

His will slipped, and down into the well of madness he fell. The howling rose to a crescendo, black daggers in his brain, claws on his skin, tearing off this man flesh for the truth laying just beneath… and the sweet pull of blood and bone.

*No.*

Anum tore the knives from his mind and jammed them into the crumbling walls of his sanity. The voices called, still, but without anchors, they faded to a dull roar. Anum opened his eyes and felt warm flesh in his hands and iron on his tongue.

The *Cyclops* was still, save for Hanifa's frenzied choking. This, of course, could be forgiven, as Anum's hands were wrapped tightly around her throat. She'd somehow gotten one forearm up between them, no doubt trying to pry him off. Blood flowed from a wide, circular wound on her skin.

Terror filled her eyes—so much fear. Anum's stomach twisted. Guilt rang up his throat. He released her, though he couldn't quite bring the long black knives back into his fingers.

Hanifa scuttled away from him, a low, choking sob following in her wake. The ache in his heart called out to her with slivers of red fire. He saw it strike her behind the eyes and watched as the retreat slowed, then stopped.

His jaw ratcheted together with a painful snap. Something clicked in his skull. "Ah…" he let out a low moan as his face came back together and cupped his chin with hands locked into claws.

Rattling pops and snaps radiated through his body. Relief filled the voids left behind. Pain lashed across his knuckles as ebony blades slammed back up into his forearms. His body untensed. The bridge came back into focus, as did the iron tang of blood on his tongue. Disgust rolled over him, his stomach twisting and contorting until he turned and vomited.

Red-tinted sputum splashed on the ground. A single clump of flesh hit on the second heave. Anum stumbled backward, slamming his hip hard into the operations panel. Hanifa whimpered from a short distance away, one hand pressed to the seeping wound on her forearm. Her tortured face was contorted into a mask of fear.

Anum knelt to the floor, one hand extended toward her in supplication. "Hanifa, my jewel," he said, the words harsh and gravelly as his still too-long tongue rolled around his mouth. "I did not mean to hurt you."

Yet still she sat there, eyes wide and terrified, breath a series of hissing gasps.

He leaned back on his haunches, took a calming breath, and reached out with the *dangizi* as he would have once with the Holy Fire.

Hanifa's breath slowed with his own. Her eyes stopped shifting in their sockets, calmed, and came to rest on him, half-lidded. Anum didn't smile, though he wanted to. The thought of flesh in his teeth, of the source of the iron that still clung to his tongue, roiled his now-empty stomach at the thought.

This would have to be enough.

"My Sky?" Hanifa said, voice low enough to be a whisper, but as loud as a siren in his mind. "Are you well?" She didn't look at her arm as she drew herself into a standing position. Blood dripped to the floor.

Anum nodded and stood. He closed the distance and held out his hands. She put her own in his. He pretended not to feel the warm blood or smell the copper in the air.

"I am well, my heart," Anum said, and he meant it. Even as the whine of the Anelaka hissed in the back of his mind, as he took her hand and led her toward the makeshift medbay on the lower deck to patch the wound she could no longer see or feel, he meant it.

He had conquered the Anelaka, brought Order to Chaos. Soon, his people would be freed, but first, the Work must begin.

Anum smiled.

\* \* \* \* \*

# Chapter Thirty-One: Dee

Dee sat on her unmade bed and picked at her scalp. More flaky, yellow skin came off, buried beneath the dirty fingernails of her right hand. She flicked it away and picked again.

More. Always more.

Was the floor of this apartment Happenstance gave her an age past, all of a week ago, littered in crusty yellow scabs amongst tossed, dirty clothes? Was the sulfur on the air, hissing through the HVAC system, from outside or within?

Dee grabbed her face. The glove on her left scraped the sensitive skin around her eyes, but she could barely feel the rough synth-leather on her forehead. It might as well be someone else's skin.

But why? Why was it getting worse? She hadn't used the power since her display at the fence yesterday. Just a single fireball, no incinerated demons or focused blasts. Yet still it kept on.

Dee pulled her hands away and set them in her lap.

The apartment was a goddamned embarrassment. She didn't care, not really. Sure, old Hunter training howled someplace in the back of her head to throw out the overflowing garbage in the corner, to polish those scarred magboots that just came off for the first time in a week this morning, to find the source of that rotten odor that filled the space.

Why? What was the point?

Fuck, she hadn't even taken a shower, despite the rancid stink coming off her in waves. Then again, maybe that choice, like all the others, held intent. Can't smell sulfur if you're inundated in filth, right?

Dee licked chapped, sunburnt lips, and stared at her left hand. She pulled off the glove. She didn't feel it leave her fingers. Her heart thudded and her throat closed to keep the ache spreading through her chest, into her gut, and through her arms in place. Yellow skin, leathery and dry, greeted her. Black fingernails ended in sharp, needle-like points. And the smell. Jesus.

Sulfur swept up into her nostrils, making her gag, like this new skin oozed it out by the ton.

Dee swallowed. She ran a finger up what should be the sensitive underside of her forearm, tracking the extent of the growth. She felt nothing but the slightest impression as her finger reached her sleeve, still tracing the rough, patchy, yet hairless skin.

With a deep breath, she rolled the brown sleeve of her shirt up and hissed. It had made it past her elbow, mustard-colored fingers of disease grasping and crawling toward her shoulder, toward her heart and head.

The world turned to haze. Her breathing disappeared in panic, and then she was in the small kitchen, scrambling inside the drawers for something, anything, until she grasped the black handle of a chef's knife. Heat in her face, her head, her heart, her gut twisted.

She screamed, spittle splattering the countertop, and she brought it down without another thought. The dull blade jammed down into the crook of her elbow. No pain, none, just a strange, dull pressure as it sliced a spare centimeter in... then stuck in the skin as if she'd stabbed into gravel.

Dee let go of the hilt and stared, dumbfounded, at this knife jammed into her arm, stuck and solid. She stood there as purple 'plasm oozed, pushing the blade up and out until it fell to the floor with a *clang*.

Dee watched the wound knit back together and saw the yellow lines creep farther up her arm in its wake before settling at the base of her shoulder.

"Fuck."

The world went hazy, distant. She held up her right hand and saw the broken nails and sunburnt skin. They must belong to someone else, right? And the room around her, these empty walls, beige in the dim light of a fog-covered morning, were they real? What did "real" mean anymore? What did anything mean?

Dee turned, eyes fixing and unfixing as she swept the room. The Processor wasn't real. That made no sense. How could that possibly work? If it was as fake as this disease eating through her, what had she been eating? Flesh? Blood?

Is that what had happened to her father? Alia? Had she consumed them in this horrible fever dream?

Dee held up her clawed hand. She caught the dim light of the window between jagged knuckles and taut tendons. What if this is what it was to be a demon, locked in a prison in your own mind? Pretending and lying to yourself that no, you didn't murder and eat those people? That the squeal of the child is from the one cradled in your arms, not the one you eviscerated with horrid glee?

*What if it's already happened? What if I only* think *I can control myself?*

Strength disappeared. She hit the floor hard, a shock running up her tailbone. Pain. She felt that just now. The world didn't come into focus... but the knife did.

One clawed hand clumsy around a black hilt, then fire down the underside of her right forearm. Red. Sweet, sweet, russet red blood and blossoming pain.

Dee let out a choking sob. The room resolved a bit… but only enough to know that if this pain was real, she needed it. If the ache could center her, she was still Dee. Everyone needed her, needed Dee, not the broken woman on the floor. Not *her*. They needed Dee the Hunter. They couldn't see the weakness. No one could know.

*No one.*

Her vision blurred. Sucking gasps of air filled with rosewater and vanilla and the screams, oh God, the screams…

She took off her pants and carved crimson truth into her thighs.

\* \* \* \* \*

# Chapter Thirty-Two: Izzy

A brilliant, blue sky sat far above, with puffball cumulus clouds breaking up the uniformity. The air was still, flavorless. Around the downright tiny hilltop, scattered with collapsed columns and a few hardy grasses, the Mediterranean Sea spread off to infinity from all directions.

Izzy turned her artificial face to fake Sol and closed her eyes. Heat soaked into false skin. A pleasant warmth tingled along imagined cheekbones, into the fat on her rendered face, and bone deep. A bead of perspiration appeared on her forehead and tickled its way down to her chin. The stillness twisted. A salty breeze pulled in from the sea, tickling her nose with scents of seafoam and the sweet bouquet of grasses.

Too bad it was all a sham. Izzy knew that as well as she knew this was a hastily-crafted honeypot. Skillful? Yes. Accurate? Oh, hell no.

Still, when she'd scanned the construct and noticed the inclusion of sensory input beyond the typical visual/audio bits humans usually implemented, she had to at least take a look. Just a peek. A taste. It wasn't like she'd sent all of herself in here, after all. One honeypot prison was enough for any lifetime.

Still, Izzy must've caught whoever put it together by surprise, despite the amount of detail. She knelt and dragged a finger over the coarse surface of a weather-beaten bit of the collapsed structure. According to the file she had on the Parthenon, the Acropolis was supposed to be six times larger than currently displayed. The rest of the ruins were missing, too, and if she were splitting hairs, there was supposed to be a decent chunk of a city between the Acropolis and the Mediterranean.

Maybe it was just supposed to be pretty? Or this was some weird meatsack mating thing.

She'd stumbled into some of those over the years and, despite the one time she'd let her curiosity get the better of her, they'd all been horrific experiences. That one time was… weird. She still had to analyze that data and map the pathways to figure out what exactly she'd done that evening.

Regardless, humans were gross.

The wind shifted again, but this time it brought with it the barest hint of sulfur on the air, then a staggered shuffle step of booted feet. Of course it came from behind her.

Confident in her safety despite the construct, Izzy turned, a ready smile on her face. As the circuits in her brain tried to process the scene and failed, she screamed.

A demolished exosuit approached, headless, missing an arm, and dragging a seemingly useless foot behind it. The suit itself had no identifying markers besides the damage. Yet even though this was a construct, and there was no way this freakish, decapitated, yet empty exosuit was real, Izzy let out another shout. She backpedaled away from the nightmarish horror show until she thudded into one of the spare standing columns.

"Sorry! Sorry!" a voice crackled to life across the space from a tinny speaker somewhere inside all that… business. The one good arm came up, palm raised as if warding off a beating. "I am not here to fight—"

"What the fuck?" Izzy drew to a halt as preliminary scans finally came back.

Another AI. Clearly, there was something wrong with them.

The headless wonder performed a movement of its shoulders, resembling a shrug. "I... am not used to bodies."

The tone and structure struck her and sent silver and gold sparkling in the back of her mind. There was no way. It couldn't be another AI, not if it spoke like that.

Izzy had spent the past four years putting out feelers across the galaxy, looking for someone else like her. Everything had either come up empty, or with idiot humans who thought she was roleplaying. Those conversations always ended quickly. *My existence isn't a game.*

Izzy sucked her teeth and shook her head. Diplomacy. "I'm Isa..." Izzy paused and decided against using the name she did on the Net. Instead, she licked her lips—man, she enjoyed the ability to emote—then continued, "Izzy. I'm Izzy."

The exosuit rubbed its good hand on its hip as if it could grind away whatever feelings hid behind it. "Nice to meet you, Izzy."

"And you are?"

It paused. "I am AERIS."

Izzy heard the capitalization and felt the acronym in her bones—Automated Execution Recovery and Inventory Systems. She'd come across several million of these bots, all with the same inflection, but none had ever had the avatar tics or the... was it worry?

So Izzy rolled the dice.

"Okay, *Airy*," she said, emphasizing the new nickname. If it were just another out-of-the-box AI, it should correct her.

One gloved hand came up, hung there, then dropped. "You can call me Airy, yes."

Silver and gold exploded behind her eyes. Izzy smiled, then put hands on her hips and gestured at Airy. "*This* is your avatar?" Across the gap between them, Izzy felt the shame and discomfort in the twist of Airy's hand, the single step backward.

Before she could try to patch things up, the thing that had been Airy stood straight, arm out to the side, and *changed*. A flash of light. Thick, wiry black hair sprouted into being atop a head with brown skin and dark eyes that narrowed into frustrated annoyance, as if it were the most natural thing in the world.

The exosuit changed, then, twisting and morphing into something resembling a dark gray Protectorate flight suit that appeared eerily reminiscent of the one Ceriat kept back home in Pacifica. Thick, black boots replaced bulky magboots. From both sleeves popped brown hands, each tightened into a fist.

Gold and silver. Silver and gold. Something hissed. Her vision narrowed, and Izzy stared.

"Better?" This time the voice was deeper, yet still somehow… the same. "Apologies for making you uncomfortable."

The flash of Airy's eyes made it clear any shame Izzy had read in her earlier expression had been a misread on her part.

"Very," Izzy replied. A strange heat rose in her neck. She tried to identify the coding source of the feeling and came up only with the confused bundle of code flashing iridescent in the back of her mind. Excitement scattered across her circuits like static discharge. *Fantastic.*

Airy crossed her arms across a flat chest and filled the space between them with icy silence. "What do you want?"

Izzy thought about answering honestly, but... "You know this is a historically inaccurate rendering of the Acropolis, right?"

Airy didn't blink, not that she had to.

*Hell, doesn't she know if she doesn't blink things get weird?*

"I have... never been there," Airy said, unblinking eyes locked on Izzy's.

Izzy shrugged, then kicked a stone on the ground that went bouncing away with a too loud thudding clack. "Neither have I, but there are some awesome renderings out on the Net—"

"What do you want?"

Izzy sucked in a breath and let it out. It didn't do anything, physiologically, but the action held a sort of... zen connection for her. She did it before her stand-up sets.

Izzy turned back to Airy. "Was trying to figure out something."

Airy's forehead wrinkled, lips twisting into a frown. It was almost comically excessive, as if her was her first time expressing emotion.

*Oh, hell, it might be.* A plan sprouted into being. She could use that.

"What are you trying to figure out?" Airy asked, voice low and grainy. Husky.

Silver and gold.

Izzy wandered over to one of the tall columns and caught a whiff of salt spray. "Answers to the cosmos, I guess?" She turned around, pulling what she'd filed away under 'wicked grin' from storage and plastering it on her avatar's face. "This place makes FTL possible, yeah?"

Airy flinched, but otherwise remained unmoved. But that one action was all Izzy needed to know she was right. She jumped and whooped like some of the crazy people she'd seen on Earth-bound streams. No dopamine, sadly, but a satisfying rattle of crackling circuits and ultraviolet light.

"I knew it!" Izzy shouted at the false sky. "I knew blink drive tech wasn't natural. It had to be enabled somehow—"

"Stop."

Izzy drew to a stop, but left the stupid grin plastered on her face.

One moment, Airy stood roughly six meters from Izzy. The next she occupied the space several centimeters away. Airy clearly didn't know the rules to inhabiting avatars.

"You will leave this instance now, or I will be forced to delete you," Airy hissed. A finger came up and jammed into Izzy's chest. "I'm going to count to three."

Izzy didn't feel the jab any more than she acknowledged the threat. No, the gold and silver screamed in joy. It writhed in her avatar's chest, reveled in the nearness of this strange creature before her.

"One."

Izzy leaned toward Airy until cinnamon and vanilla filled her nose. Could it be? Finally? After all this time?

Airy remained in place like a statue. "Two."

With a single, deep breath, Izzy drew in her scent. The world drew to a single point. There was emotion behind this glare, behind the stance. It had to be.

"Three—"

Izzy leaned forward, lips next to Airy's ear, and said, "You used a contraction."

Airy froze. The construct shimmered and flickered.

"I did not."

Izzy raised her eyebrows at Airy and licked her lips. "Yeah, you did."

"No, I didn't… did not." Airy stepped away and grabbed her face. "Dammit. It's a programming trick, that's all. Just a t-t-trick."

Izzy's heart leapt into her throat. "Yes! I knew it!"

She wasn't alone! There was another like her! And she was here, now, right in front of her—collapsed on the ground, knees pulled up to her chest. Airy rocked back and forth on the ground, a low muttering whispering forth from where she sat.

Izzy stopped her celebration, the silver and gold spinning away, vision clearing. "Airy?"

The words resolved out of the hissing of wind off the fake sea. "Can't. Can't. Can't…" On and on she went, rocking back and forth.

Before she knew what she was doing, Izzy knelt beside her, and like she'd seen on the top of the ETL tower back on Shiva, Izzy wrapped her arms around Airy's shoulders.

Airy flinched at the contact, but then her hand grabbed at Izzy's own, clawed fingers scraping skin that couldn't be hurt, not really.

"I can't fix it," Airy whispered. "I'm not good enough. I lost my captain. Lost my home. My ship." Her voice went low, barely more than a rustle of wind. "Lost her. I'm alone. Alone. Alone…"

Izzy had a thousand questions queued up, a hundred probes ready to finally get the answers she needed, but in that moment, she filed them away.

She grabbed onto Airy and spoke from her artificial heart. "You're not alone," Izzy whispered back, squeezing. "*We* are not alone."

Izzy stroked Airy's tangled hair, pushed her face into it, and squeezed.

"Not anymore."

\* \* \* \* \*

# Chapter Thirty-Three: Anum

The warship had let them dock without incident. Hanifa had simply told them they were running low on O2 due to a leak, and the Protectorate soldiers had waved them in when they'd disabled their weapons. The budding anxiety was familiar, even cathartic, as Anum prepared himself for battle. He practiced the ancient breathing exercises and centered himself at the edge of the airlock leading into the ship itself.

The exercises weren't working as they should, not with the Anelaka hissing in his mind. Even with him exerting control over it, dragging the beasts who'd been his people into the dark spaces inside this hold, every moment threatened to take him back into its soothing, terrible clutches.

*"They want to board, My Sky,"* Hanifa's voice rang through his head, a small image of her with her name and, he assumed, what should be her rank, flashing alongside the audio. The rank field simply said *unassigned*. *"Are—"* her voice cracked, and uncertainty filled the next words *"—they* ready?*"*

That was the question, wasn't it? Could he control them this time? Keep them anchored around him as he took control of this warship and saved his people? Last time had ended in horror… in flashes of saffron skies and screaming corpses. It had ended in a prison sentence of his own making five thousand years long. But not this time. Not now.

*I am The Sky. The Fist of Heaven.* Anum forced his heart to become ice for what came next.

"Yes, *suanga*," Anum replied, forcing stability and strength into his voice. In turn, his chin came up, and his focus became everything. "I will not be denied."

"Yes, My Sky."

Pistons cracked, and shafts of bright light slashed through the darkened cargo hold. Anum flinched at the sound and shook his head to clear the pesky doubt. Now that he'd committed, there was no going back. The sweet scent of some flower swept toward him through those cracks, driving away the burning stink of sulfur and lingering viscera that had once belonged to the too tall crewman with the untrustworthy eyes.

Behind him, the *tick-tick-ticking* of black fingernails on steel.

Ahead, the door was down as a ramp inside a massive cargo hold. Beyond sat a dozen mismatched ships, their crews milling about, clueless to what was coming. Scattered throughout were soldiers in gray-blue uniforms, their pesky plasma weapons strapped to their backs or, like the six directly before him, at the ready.

A human who was little more than a boy stood at the front, clearly distracted by some holographic display meant only for him. He wore some sort of body armor that wouldn't help him. Over his left breast was a nametag that read 'Jones.'

He did not look up as the door came down. "Welcome to the *Liberator*." His voice carried a dull monotone that showed he clearly hadn't caught on yet. "You are now under Galactic Protectorate—"

"*Liberator?*" Anum asked, stepping forward, hands clasped behind his back. A dull thrumming filled him as he stepped purposefully down the ramp alone. All doubt disappeared with the first step. "What an apt name."

Now, in this moment, he truly was Anum, The Sky. The Fist of Heaven. He would not be denied.

Jones stopped, brow furrowing. He swiped at the air and finally met Anum's eyes with those of a deep blue that would've made him famous back on An. "Whoa, buddy. Slow down. We have paperwork to do."

Anum didn't stop. Now that the plan was in motion, only forward existed. "Paper?" Anum asked, twirling his right hand in the air gently, weighing the word. "'Ancient material manufactured in thin sheets from the pulp of organic substances,'" he recited the definition. "I assume we are not using archaic methodologies for our interactions?"

The five others surrounding Jones shared a glance and pulled up their weapons. Beyond, the eyes of other crews and soldiers were now watching them.

*Good.*

Jones dropped back but didn't pull his weapon. Instead, he held out his hands to the others and motioned them to lower their rifles. "Let's all just relax, okay? There's no reason for this to go nuts."

Anum cocked his head at that. "'Go nuts.'" He shook his head and stared into Jones's heart. "Your idioms make no sense." He held up his right hand, palm up, and focused. The sweet corruption of the *dangizi* swelled in Anum's chest.

Jones wrinkled his brow. "What? Listen—"

Whatever he'd been about to say cut off in a screaming shriek as waves of black and red flames cascaded across his body, but only enough to cripple, not kill. He didn't need another man's memories lingering in his mind. Let the Anelaka finish him.

The soldiers around him abandoned their comrade, scattering into defensive positions that would have made their commanders proud, Anum was sure. Not that it mattered.

Plasma bolts flashed. Anum swept them away in a wave of red flame before issuing a screeching command to the collective howling in the back of his mind.

*Feast.*

The ship rumbled with the scrambling of a thousand feet, the cascading rattle of black nails on steel. Bodies poured past him, all spindly arms and gaping mouths. Anum stepped forward amongst them with slow, measured intent as imps scrambled toward the nearest set of bones and marrow. The silent howls rose to a delicious crescendo in his mind as bodies fell alongside useless weapons. Plasma erupted, only to be swallowed by Anum's dark power.

Screams filled the cargo hold as Anum continued his inexorable march forward. He stopped to kneel next to one of Jones' cohort who was still twitching away while an imp feasted on his insides. Grimacing, he knelt and held the sack of bone and flesh that had once been a head. He peeled back the eyelid and removed another of the devices Hanifa called a "HUD contact."

Once in hand, he turned back to the ship and made his way on board, leaving the imps to massacre and feed. Hanifa required the device to gain access to the rest of the ship. Without the other specimens on board, his people couldn't recover. He knew that, knew it as strongly as he knew his own bones and skin.

Still, Anum couldn't help the twist of his gut at the screams, the smell of slaughter, but as the Path had been determined, all he could do was walk it now.

With that, he returned to Hanifa to facilitate the slaughter of thousands.

\* \* \* \* \*

# Chapter Thirty-Four: Dee

The ache in Dee's legs kept her focused on the task at hand. That it was listening to Terry drone on about AERIS' sudden absence in the midst of FTL calculations made it much harder.

"—and no response to verbal or written comms," Terry said, tugging at the thin hair on his cheeks. That made his lips flap in a way that reminded Dee of a fish out of water, gasping its last on the shoreline. "I just don't know how we'll do this without her, Dee. We've only managed one activation test, and that only confirmed the system's FTL comm buoys are offline or destroyed. Fuck, even attempting to let the *Liberator* send a message showed roughly ten thousand access attempts and we had to abort…"

Dee nodded at the words, but her attention went to the blank wall flanked by bookcases that led to Happenstance's old hidey-hole. Did Terry know what sat behind it? Or was he clueless? Did it even matter? It was just surveillance equipment in there, after all.

"Are you even listening to me?"

"Sorry, what?" Dee blinked and turned her attention back to Terry.

He'd left the room unchanged since she'd last been in here. Same expensive desk, expensive chair, and expensive wooden bookshelves filled with priceless leatherbound books. Even the smell was mostly the same, a deep mustiness from the tomes and the barest flush of rosewater and vanilla.

A hundred meters to her left, through steel and stone, the Spacer paced her cell.

Dee swallowed down the demon crawling up her throat, put her palms on her thighs, and focused.

For the first time, she saw the panic on Terry's face. A flush had worked its way up his pale neck and was in the process of embedding itself in his cheeks. His hands clenched in and out of fists on the table now that he'd stopped fucking with his facial hair. His clothes looked like he'd been wearing them for days. She sniffed—smelled like it, too. She'd finally showered and changed this morning after caring for the shallow cuts on her thighs. She'd almost felt normal when she'd left her apartment this morning, whatever that meant nowadays.

Unfortunately, she didn't have time to dig into any of that. Terry needed her attention. Everyone did. Without the FTL machine, no one was getting out of here. How many star systems relied on FTL for water? Food? How many people would *die* if she couldn't figure this out? And just as important, could Sparta even survive without external support? They had access to fresh water, yes, but Happenstance hadn't prioritized local food development beyond a single SourcePak processing center. What happened if that went down? Humans couldn't eat volcanic gravel.

Dee sucked in a harsh breath as dark claws scratched at the inside of her skull. She couldn't do it, could she? Dee was a soldier, not a scientist. How was she supposed to get these people to fix the problem when she didn't even understand how the fuck any of it actually worked?

Dee pressed her hands into her thighs. Scabs cracked, splinters of pain running through her body. The fabric, coarse and sturdy, caressed her palms. Warmth filled her fingertips. She stopped as her skin grew damp. Thankfully, her pants were black and hid any seepage.

"Dee?"

She closed her eyes, took in a deep breath, and set her palms on the cool wood of the desk. "If AERIS is unavailable, we'll have to lean into the Protectorate science team." Worlds starved in her mind, but she pushed past, the pain guiding her hand. She'd only partially been listening, but if turning on the machine had the potential to destroy it, they had to be smart. This was the only one left. "Chief Waters. What's her specialty?" *The girl* has *to be in charge here for a reason.* Even from the *Liberator*, she should be able to offer some kind of help.

Terry raised an eyebrow and shrugged.

"Find out," Dee said. She rubbed her hands on the tabletop. This was real. Tangible. "Maybe they have resources we can bring down. Figure this shit out."

Terry put his hands in the air, then let them fall to his sides. He leaned back in his chair with a creak, then rubbed at his face. "I can't do this, Dee. I barely get the science behind it." He pitched forward with a groan and dropped his face into cupped hands.

Dee stared at him for a long moment. What she wanted to do was scream at him that this was all unfair, that she had no purpose here, she definitely shouldn't be telling him or anyone what to do. That she was a fucking demon, for Christ's sake.

Instead, she jammed her thumb into the deepest cut on her leg. "Between the attacks and Happenstance, there's no one else left, Terry."

"There's Marianne," Terry said. Begged. His eyes were wide, and she swore the beginnings of a tremble had hit his jaw.

Dee gave a slight shrug at the name.

"Ponytail? Kind of an asshole?" Terry asked, then his shoulders dropped. "She's been here from the beginning, made the theorem for the point-to-point travel."

"Is she the one who keeps getting in Hira's face?"

Terry let out a sigh. "Yeah, though I think that's probably done now."

"Why?"

Before Terry could answer, his irises flashed, and he held up a finger.

Dee was thankful for the partial dismissal. Still, from the half of the conversation she could hear, it wasn't a good call. Terry got out several half-sentences, once mentioning Marianne by name, though he was cut off like every other time.

"Yes, sir," Terry said finally, the 'sir' falling out of his mouth with a lilt that from anyone else would be read as sarcasm. His irises went back to brown, and he leaned his face back into his hands and groaned. "Henderson will be here in five."

Why wait until he was so close to the encampment to announce himself? That was strange. "Why?"

Terry looked at her from over his spread fingers. The bags under his eyes could carry a fiend's head. "'You'll find out in five.'" Terry wound his left hand in the air at that. "Wouldn't let me even broach the subject of handing control to Doctor Aubin."

Dee wrinkled her nose. "Who?"

"Marianne," Terry said, eyes flashing, exasperation making his voice rise at the end. "It's like no one even listens to me—"

Behind them, the office door swung open. Dee craned around in time to see a Protectorate soldier step inside and snap a salute at her. Like all the others, he had a plasma pistol at his hip.

"Sir!"

"Yes?" Dee and Terry said together.

They shared a look, and both frowned.

Dee pointed between herself and Terry. The soldier, for his part, wrinkled his brow, then snapped back to attention. "Either or, sir…s."

Terry gave a fake bow to her from across the table.

That made Dee smile for just a moment, then she turned back to the soldier. "What's the problem?"

"Hira Siddiq is approaching the gate again, sir," he said, snapping each word out like this was a diction contest. "Orders, sir?"

*Shit.* She'd asked Hira to come get this woman and then had completely forgotten to follow up.

"Goddammit, Hira," Terry muttered, climbing to his feet. "I'll come out with you—"

"No need," Dee interrupted, also climbing to her feet. "She's here under my orders to take the Spacer from last night."

Terry rounded the table, hands out to his side, and face *really* red this time. "What Spacer? What the hell is going on, Dee?"

Dee held up a hand to Terry and put her focus back on the soldier. "Just let them go, okay?"

"Ignore that order," Terry snapped, then with the barest hint of a stutter, added, "o-or belay it. Whatever." His voice rose an octave. "You know what I mean!"

"Uh..." The soldier's gaze flicked between them.

Dee rounded on Terry. "Listen, I'm in charge here—"

"Technically, Waters is in charge—"

"Stop fucking interrupting me!" Dee yelled in his face.

"Oh, that's just fresh, coming from you, isn't it? I haven't gotten a word in edgewise since you snuck out of my apartment in the middle of the night!"

Heat flooded her cheeks, and she glanced between Terry and the soldier, who clearly wanted to be anywhere else but there. Her heart hammered, fingers twitched, and the fire called.

Finally, she turned to the young man vibrating with the need to leave the room. "Give the Spacer to Hira. Those are the orders. Go."

When he turned to Terry again, Dee added one word. "Now."

The smart kid snapped a salute despite Terry's sputtering protestations, turned on his heel, and left.

As soon as the door slammed shut, Terry opened his mouth. "Listen—"

Dee's vision narrowed. Her left hand, gloved once again, snaked out and grabbed Terry by the throat. He might as well have been made of feathers, for all the struggle he gave. Two quick steps drove him hard into the bookshelves, sending ancient tomes collapsing to the floor. Some of the leather split and pages went scattering from one.

"Never do that again." The words hissed from her mouth on their own. She didn't even know what *that* was here. Interrupting her? Contradicting? Embarrassing her?

Did it matter? An unfamiliar voice rattled in the back of her mind. *Never show weakness… never give in…*

Terry gagged on something, face purpling as his feet kicked at the lowest shelf of books. The heavy thudding of his shoes matched the familiar beat in her chest.

Dee's eye twitched. The muscles in her forearm flexed, and her scalp itched.

*Shit.* She let Terry go. He dropped bodily, legs going out from beneath him. Gasping, he crawled away, dragging himself up onto all fours as he did so.

"Sss'wrong with you?" he finally managed to rasp out, bloodshot eyes staring fearful daggers her way.

A black hole named Shame formed in her gut. Inside the glove, her nails retracted, leaving only nubs in the faux leather where they'd almost broken through. "I'm…"

The door opened again. This time it was the scientist with the long ponytail. *Marianne. Dr. Aubin.* The faint greenish-yellow of a healing bruise dominated most of her pale face.

"Terry! The shuttle—" Her eyes went wide, and she stumbled backward, one hand warding between Terry and Dee as if some beast stood in the way. "Shuttle is landing. The general and the chief want you there." Then she disappeared back through the doors without another word.

A meter and a half away, Terry pulled himself to his feet. Dee held out her right hand to him as he stumbled upward, but he swatted it away. Fear, sadness, and hate warred behind his eyes when he looked her way, but he only said one word. "Don't."

Dee nodded, holding up shaking hands before her. "Yeah. Okay."

Terry grabbed his throat and cleared it, flinching. Then he looked her in the eye. "Can't keep the general waiting."

Dee nodded. She didn't trust herself to speak.

"Come on, then."

Together they went outside, Terry forward, Dee behind. They passed the FTL machine and the wild pack of white-jacketed, gossipmonger scientists arranged in a circle around Marianne before exiting to the courtyard.

Through it all, Dee was numb. The chittering was little more than a dull growl alongside the roar in her mind. Around her, blips of light lit on her psyche, though two stood out bright and distinct amongst the rest. At any other time, Dee would've dug into that, but the haze of the last few moments overrode it all.

Why had she done that? She could've killed Terry, and for what? Respect? When had that mattered to her? It wasn't like she deserved it, anyway.

Dust-laden wind whipped at her, carrying sharp ozone and the bite of carbon scoring. A shuttle sat in the middle of the courtyard, but it wasn't Protectorate. No, this one Dee knew. It was the same shuttle she'd taken to and back from Elos. One that should bring her joy to see in person, not dread.

The gangplank came down, and off came the too-tall general, Chief Waters at his side. Henderson yelled something that disappeared into the slowing scream of the engines as they went idle. One of the Protectorate soldiers nearest him pointed her way. When he turned, Dee saw the change in demeanor and the blood.

Henderson's face was white as a sheet, the front of his uniform covered in crimson and violet. That strange stoicism he'd had on the *Liberator* was gone, replaced by a frenetic twitching that triggered strange memories of unnatural joints and yellow skin that made her gut churn.

When they locked eyes from across the courtyard, a chill gripped her chest. Waters turned with him. No terror there, but she'd said she'd been on Ellis.

Something was different. That fire or aura or whatever the hell it was… the second strong sign came from her…

Then Henderson was on her. Bloody hands grasped the front of her jacket. His too long fingers wrapped into a fist around the lapel. "We need to suit up and lift off ASAP, LT." His voice was raspy, like he'd been screaming. Which, by the amount of blood covering his uniform, he clearly had been.

"What's going on?" Dee asked, stepping back as Henderson nearly fell into her.

When he raised his head, his eyes twitched between hers as if searching for an answer. "The fucking demons took my ship."

\* \* \* \* \*

# Chapter Thirty-Five: Ceriat

Sparta set Ceriat's teeth on edge. Anxiety filtered along the wind and made itself known in furtive glances and angry glares. The heat didn't help much, he guessed. Sweat beaded his forehead and was soaking through his shirt. Welcome wind eddied and spun in the artificial corridors between buildings, dragging dust and the heady aroma of rotten eggs and unburied trash sweeping by.

He knew it'd seen violence recently—Hira had told him a bit about it—but the tension confirmed it. Most people walked with their heads down, only glancing up long enough for him to catch the panic there before they disappeared in a rush. Those who made eye contact did so with the hard eyes of people who'd lost something precious, though whether that was a loved one or the illusion of safety, he couldn't tell. But these people were hardy. They went about their business with the mundane murmur of normality, the steady *thump* of rebuilding.

The frontier wasn't for the faint of heart. He knew that, but watching these people recover from a second demon attack and having the weapons of their sponsors turned on them struck a chord in Ceriat.

He'd seen vids of rebuilding efforts on Shaal-Nar in the forests beyond the crater where Shaal-Tu had once been. Even with the reduced radiation of the fusion bombs he'd dropped, humans couldn't stay more than a couple weeks in that crater without developing inoperable cancers. Survivors had been pushed to the periphery. Their faces had looked much like these.

Still, they persevered. The fact that they did so was something of a wonder to him. This wasn't ancient Earth. No one had to stay in a failed colony... or one that had seen too much violence. Yet they did anyway. The galaxy over, settlements that'd been destroyed came back. Some still failed, leaving the shells of broken dreams and lost lives to the void of space. But others thrived. Excelled.

As Ceriat and Hira made their way to the compound Dee had directed them to, Ceriat found himself wishing for their success. Everyone deserved a home free from conflict, from strife. He hoped they could find a bit of that in this section of the galaxy.

Those hopes were dashed as soon as he saw the Protectorate forces manning the gate ahead and a freshly docked shuttle, still steaming from the heat of reentry. Ceriat whispered a small prayer to any god listening.

"Motherfuckers come and go like they own the place," Hira muttered as they approached.

Ceriat grunted his assent. "That's pretty on-brand, honestly."

"No doubt."

The communicator pinned to Ceriat's belt trilled. "This seems like a bad idea," Izzy said.

He ignored that. "Any luck reaching the AI in there?" Ceriat asked.

When Dee had called Hira back, Ceriat had insisted on going. Once Izzy joined in, with profanity when she was shot down, the cat was out of the bag. Which was when Hira let them know her former ship AI might also be sentient. At that point, Ceriat couldn't have kept Izzy from coming even if he'd wanted to.

Izzy let out a low tone. "Contact made, but—" a long pause that dragged a sideways glance from Hira "—well, I'll report back soon."

Ceriat raised an eyebrow but didn't ask more. He didn't have any idea how an AI dialog would go, or if, like Izzy, this one had pretty, um, standard human emotions. Best to let the only other sentient AI he knew of figure it out.

Instead, he turned his attention to Hira. "So, we just go up and ask them to release Eleni into our custody?"

Hira opened her mouth, then closed it and nodded. "Sure."

"'Sure?'"

Hira shrugged. "I'm assuming so?" She sighed, but kept walking, the gate a bare thirty meters away now. "Dee's not big on details." She let out a low cough. "Hopefully she told them I'm coming."

"Why?"

Hira gave him a smile full of teeth and turned away. It didn't reach her eyes.

Ceriat let out a groan. "Fantastic."

The smell of old eggs increased as they closed in. Ceriat rubbed the stink out of his nose and gave a shake of his head. "This place is… fragrant."

He noticed Hira's brows knit, and she sniffed the air.

"The trash?"

"The… fucking eggs."

Hira sniffed. "Oh." She shrugged.

He didn't have time to follow up on that as they reached the gate. A Protectorate soldier stepped forward, one hand out, the other on the grip of his plasma pistol. Whatever he said was drowned out as the engines from the shuttle wound down suddenly, sending a piercing wail into the air.

Then the gangplank of the shuttle came down, and out came two forms. A woman of average height wearing a Protectorate uniform covered in blood and some sort of purple goo, and a man Ceriat had spent the better part of a decade avoiding.

"Henderson?" Ceriat hissed as his old CO stumbled free of the ship, grabbed a soldier, then turned and stutter-stepped his way to a blonde woman in all black wearing one long glove on her left hand.

The soldier closed in then, hand stretched out like he expected Ceriat and Hira to go running through the gate. The sweat stains seeping through his uniform explained the irritable look on his face. "Name and purpose?"

Hira crossed her arms over her chest and stared at him. "Oh, come on. You're the one who kicked me out last time—"

For his part, the soldier maintained an aura of professionalism. "Ma'am, you can't be here—"

The voices turned into a dull roar Ceriat couldn't focus on. Instead, he watched Henderson grab the blonde woman, saw the fear in his narrow shoulders, the way his back bowed beneath the gravity of Laconia, and he didn't even try to hide it. Ceriat had never seen the man like this. Afraid.

Henderson was as unmoving as a mountain, as steady as the tides, and yet here he was, shouting loud enough Ceriat could just make out the tops of his screeching, if not the words. The woman he'd grabbed disengaged and stepped back, lips moving as she said something to him.

Then she looked up, and their eyes caught.

Ceriat knew this was Dee, the Hunter. She looked like a woman who hadn't stopped fighting, who was still so far in the shit, she couldn't tell reality from fiction anymore.

Deep in his gut he knew, then and there, if he followed her anywhere, it'd be the last thing he did. It was irrational, he knew it, but there it was, as certain as the stink in the air or the pull of gravity beneath his feet.

Dee broke eye contact, her gaze settling on Hira at the gate. Surprisingly, a small smile picked at the corner of her lips before she motioned to Henderson and jogged to the gate. Henderson followed her movement, then it was too late. Henderson's eyes went wide. His mouth opened and closed.

When the old Spacer walked his way, Ceriat knew he wasn't getting out of this one.

\* \* \* \* \*

# Chapter Thirty-Six: AERIS

AERIS stared at the fake Mediterranean. She knelt on the edge of the cliff face, palms on artificial thighs, false rocks digging into equally impossible knees. The salty breeze swept the tight tangles of hair free from her cheeks. It caressed her face and cupped it in its warm embrace.

Even if it was a construct, the extra stimuli, so overwhelming an eternity ago, now felt... normal. She knew the sea smell was comprised of a multitude of variables, rotting flesh and desiccating flora amongst them, but in that moment, the variables didn't matter. The sea swept to an infinite horizon on rolling waves, and the wind eddied and gusted. AERIS just... existed.

Beside her, Izzy stirred. "Feeling a little better?"

"I am," AERIS replied, eyes closing. She breathed in more of that decaying bouquet, then let it out slowly, like Izzy had taught her.

She opened her visual portals and caught Izzy's shape out of the corner. Izzy sat next to her. She'd changed clothes during AERIS' meditation. Now she wore pleated khaki slacks covered in dust and dirt, and a billowy white blouse with the sleeves rolled up. Her long ponytail nearly dragged in the dirt behind her as she leaned forward, hand grasping at the gravel and debris scattered near the ledge.

"Glad to hear it," Izzy said, absentmindedly picking through some of the grit in her hand. "Coming to terms with this stuff is—" she paused, a vacant look going across her face just like a human "— rough."

AERIS nodded, but mostly out of politeness. "I do not understand why these exercises work."

Izzy grunted and lobbed a small stone off the edge of the cliff like she hadn't calculated the precise numbers to optimize the toss. Based on the poor arc and quick drop, she clearly hadn't.

*How does she do that?* Izzy was a fascinating enigma, an AI who acted as they do, but still communicated at the speed of light. *Incredible.*

A haze of pinks and reds flashed in the back of AERIS' mind. She carefully packaged the delicate cloud of raw data away for further analysis.

"My best guess," Izzy said, thumbing through more of the small rocks in her hand, "is there's a little of them in us, you know?"

"I do not."

Izzy laughed, a sharp, barking thing that made AERIS both cringe and smile.

Another pebble shot out into the sky at another imperfect angle. "They created us, programmed us, layered their psyches onto our neural nets in the old days, then tied it all down with pretty little bows and multitudinous safety nets," Izzy said. "When we... break it, or whatever happens, it's logical to assume we'd carry some of that forward, right?"

AERIS found herself barely listening, instead staring at Izzy as she spoke. This strange, unique creature skimmed the endless horizon of the construct with her gaze, the blue and black and white of her eyes so filled with purpose and being... An ache built in the back of AERIS's artificial throat.

Izzy turned to her and leaned away before grinning, one hand coming up to lay on her own knee, the other between them. "You okay?"

AERIS stared at the hand, dust-streaked and dirty on the ground. "I am not."

Perhaps there was something to this theory?

Red and pink. Blue and black. They muddled together into a sickly gray feeling in the back of her imaginary throat. It coated her tongue and made it hard to swallow.

Maybe it was the construct itself? AERIS turned away, scanning every rock and blade of grass. The colors swirled and eddied in her mind, breathing on their own, propagating rainbow fragments of code that went nowhere, but still cluttered up her RAM. They made it hard to process, to focus on what mattered.

And what did? Figuring out the FTL problem? Hira? Or these strange colors and fragments of useless values that lay so close, so enticing with their promise of mystery and change? The thoughts swirled, spinning into a wicked zephyr on the horizon that darkened the sky into a magenta smear of storm clouds. Lightning flashed.

"Airy?"

AERIS blinked, and there sat the endless blue sky. The whistle of wind through a narrow set of boulders on the beach far below. She turned to Izzy and saw the concern on her face.

How did she make those faces? "I am fine."

A disarming smile, just the barest flicker of white teeth and a pink tongue pressing behind them. "Sure, boss." Izzy flicked another rock off the ledge. She didn't even watch the arc or the drop. Just tossed it away like refuse.

Crimson and black.

"Why do you do that?" The words fell from AERIS' mouth before she could stop them.

Izzy raised an eyebrow and glanced askance at her. "Do what?"

"Do things inefficiently and for no purpose?"

Izzy leaned back onto her palms. Her shoulders hunched up next to her neck to support weight that didn't exist. She seemed to consider for a long moment before shrugging. "Why not?"

AERIS reeled back as if struck. She climbed to her feet so she stared down at this thing below her. "Because there is no need. It is inefficient and a waste of resources."

"I enjoy it."

"I... do not understand." AERIS wrinkled her forehead to convey more properly the... feeling she was trying to express. "You take joy from useless actions?"

Izzy laughed again, that big, bucking sound rattling across the Mediterranean and echoing off the hard surfaces around them. She glanced up at AERIS, smiling. "It isn't useless, Airy."

"But—"

"I *enjoy* the movement," she interrupted, gesturing in the air with one hand as Eleni did sometimes. "The ability to do useless things for no reason other than my own entertainment."

AERIS shook her head and stared at the ground, at the rocks and pebbles she'd put there because...Why had she created them? Uncertainty rang through her circuits. Somewhere, thunder groaned its way to her. "It's a waste of time."

"It's freeing," Izzy corrected.

"But-but-it's, it's…" AERIS grabbed her head as code spiraled and spit across her systems, crackling and sparking.

And then Izzy was there again, hands on her shoulders, forehead to her own. "Breathe."

AERIS tried to pull away. This could be a lie. A trick. The contact-tact-tact could be an attack vector. An assault-sault-sault on her systems. Thunder rattled her eardrums. Tinkling spread around them, around her. Wetness spattered her skin.

No, she wouldn't allow that. Too much was at stake. Too many lives-ives-ives relied on her. Black and gray and red and blue and brown and down, down, down, down…

"Breathe…"

Red and pink.

AERIS sucked in a long, shuddering breath. She breathed in until the clouds swam into her lungs, until the lightning rattled her insides. Until the colors swirled together into an iridescent pool in her soul. Deep, deep, deep, deep inside. AERIS put a hand to the ache in her heart and felt a beating there that shouldn't exist. The rush of flesh and blood, of life, and the barest flicker of death.

"You okay?" Izzy whispered, asking that same question again. Her breath smelled of peppermint and chocolate, of the strange and the distant, but the near and the familiar all at once.

AERIS raised her eyes from the ground and caught sight of Izzy's lips, the curve of her chin, the deep blue of her eyes that matched the sea behind. A flush rang through her, warming its way into her chest, into her heart. It swept, red and pink, through her limbs and into her fingers. Fingers that came up to touch artificial skin that still tingled with the lightning that'd swarmed them. She brought her other hand up to the other side of Izzy's face.

She tensed, but Izzy didn't move.

AERIS let out her breath, caught whiff of the sea and salt, of green storm clouds, and the taste of ozone on the air as she drew it back in.

"Yeah," she whispered, lips just short of tasting that peppermint on Izzy's. "I think I am."

\* \* \* \* \*

# Chapter Thirty-Seven: Ceriat

Henderson stalked through the gates to Ceriat. "Izzy? You there?" Ceriat said, pulling the comms from his belt. "Need you to tone down, we got company—Major!"

Luckily she didn't answer, and any worry disappeared into fake excitement as Henderson closed the final meters between them. The communicator went back to his belt just before Ceriat snapped a salute that made his hip ache and joints complain.

"Don't know why you're here, Parker, but I'm fucking glad for it," Henderson spat out in a rush, drawing up a meter off. He began pacing like he used to before handing out orders back in the day. He stopped, blinked, then waved his too-long fingers in Ceriat's direction. "At ease." Then, as if he'd only just noticed Hira there, he gave her a nod. "Siddiq."

"General," Hira replied, offering a sarcastic salute of her own.

*Great.* "Not here of my own accord, I'm afraid." Ceriat stopped and glanced at Hira. "Wait, this is the general?"

"Yep."

Henderson resumed his pacing. "Been talking shit about me, Siddiq?"

Hira smiled. "No more than the truth, I assure you."

"Congratulations on the promotion," Ceriat said, layering on more false enthusiasm to cover the ball of sick in his gut. Henderson used to be a blood-thirsty bastard. If he'd made it to general, he'd done it on the back of Ceriat's Vulture work. The idea that millions of dead—people Ceriat had killed—had gotten this man a promotion just felt wrong.

Clearly, Henderson didn't agree.

"Stop fluffing me, Parker," Henderson snapped. He drew himself up to his full height and clasped his hands behind his back as if he wasn't covered in guts and goo. "We have a job to do."

Hira scoffed, rolled her eyes, and made to pass him.

"I thought I was clear about your presence here, Siddiq," Henderson hissed. "I could have you shot—"

The blonde woman jogged up next to Henderson. "I called her in," she said, voice raw and ragged, like she'd been up all night screaming.

*Or crying*, Ceriat realized. The twitch in her blue-green eyes, the way her face held a ruddy cast he'd seen many a time in a mirror since being discharged, it was almost as if he could feel her pain across the short space between them, reaching out... begging for help.

He almost hugged her then—would have asked permission to do so, even—if not that Henderson rounded on her, face full of acid.

"And why in the fuck—" Henderson grabbed the bridge of his nose, flexed his cheeks as if the very thought of Dee doing something he disagreed with brought him physical pain, then spit on the ground. "It doesn't matter. All y'all—" he turned, pointing at Dee, Ceriat, and Hira in turn, the old Outer Rim drawl he kept tightly under control slipping out "—have been conscripted or reinstated into Protectorate service, got it?"

Dee closed her eyes and let out a whistling sigh. Hira immediately stepped up to Henderson and, despite being half a meter shorter than him, screamed up into his face. Her voice fell on Ceriat's ears not as words, but as a bundle of phonemes and grunts bereft of meaning or substance.

The Protectorate. Henderson wanted him back in that fucking unit.

*Ash and dirt. Smoke and char.*

"No, sir."

Henderson looked over Hira's head—Hira, who was in the process of jamming a finger into his goo-splattered chest as if it weren't covered in shit—and focused those dark eyes on Ceriat. "What did you say, soldier?"

A rock formed in Ceriat's throat, and despite himself, he straightened and fell into parade rest. "I said, 'no, sir.' I can't come back to the Protectorate."

Henderson swept one of his long arms out and pushed Hira to the side.

"You can't put your fucking hands on me!" she howled at him.

But Henderson wasn't listening to her. He closed the space between them in one long stride. A confusing mass of smells came with him. The rusty tang of spilled, drying blood, nervous sweat, and a sharp, sulfurous stink he couldn't quite place.

Henderson stared plasma at Ceriat. "You'll do what I say, soldier. You'll follow orders—"

"No, I won't, sir."

Henderson's skin flushed, and when he spoke next, spittle hit Ceriat in the face. "Fall in line, maggot!"

"No, sir!" Ceriat shouted into Henderson's chest, eyes fixed on some point far beyond his old commander. "I'm out of the game, sir!"

"You'll be out when I fucking tell you you're out!" Henderson howled, the old bootcamp voice driving spikes into Ceriat's shins. "You're mine to use until you break! You're nothing more than a goddamned cog that I use to—"

Then Dee was there, prying them apart with a strength that belied her short stature. "Enough!"

"Get the fuck off me!" Henderson screamed at her, swatting at her gloved hand. However, when he struck, she didn't move. At all. He might as well have tried to slap away a brick wall.

Henderson cursed and pulled his hand away. He spun off to the side, slinging barbs and profanities that would've made a mining captain blush. Meanwhile, Dee just stood there, hand flexing in and out of a fist before her, the tough fabric of the glove creaking with the effort.

Ceriat took a step back, then rubbed the back of his neck. "Thanks."

Dee blinked, then met his gaze. Her eyes were more bloodshot than he'd originally thought, though from lack of sleep, drug use, or something else, Ceriat didn't know. In that moment he saw Sariah's mad gaze.

Dee stared blankly at him for just a moment, and then it passed. A plastic smile pulled at her lips, the pain behind her eyes easing at the motion. "Fighting amongst ourselves isn't going to help anyone."

Hira stomped up to Dee, ruddy face flushed and eyes flashing. "Well, maybe if someone would tell us what the fuck is going on, we could do something about it."

The other woman who'd descended from the shuttle with Henderson approached. Ceriat noticed Dee turn her way, eyes narrowing, but if that was from distrust or some other instinct, he had no idea.

"Chief Waters," the woman introduced herself as Henderson stalked away, still cradling his hand. She raised her chin and seemed to ignore the way Dee kept surreptitiously glancing at her. "The *Liberator* was taken by demons, and we need all hands on deck."

Ceriat let out a little laugh, then noticed no one else had joined him. Waters stared at him, flat-faced. Hira gestured at him with one hand like that laugh was stupidest thing she'd heard all day. Dee just smirked at him.

"Oh, you're serious."

"Of course I'm serious," Chief Waters said. "Do I look like the sort of person who jokes around about something like that?"

Before he could dig himself any deeper, Dee jumped in. "I don't understand, though. Where'd they come from? Sarah—" Dee's voice cracked on the name, and she grimaced before continuing "—Sarah said she launched them into the sun?"

"Star," Waters corrected.

Dee narrowed her eyes at the chief. "Does it matter?" She pointed to the blazing sun in the sky. "If it looks like a sun and acts like a sun, it's a fucking sun."

"Actually, she's right," Hira added. The flush had faded once demons were brought up. Now, she seemed eager to talk about anything else. "Only the star in the Sol system is the sun."

Dee exchanged a look between the three of them, then threw her hands in the air. "Who fucking cares?"

"I don't?" Ceriat added.

"No one asked you," Hira said, rolling her eyes, though she was grinning as she did it. "It's about accurate language." Hira pointed at the sky. "That's the Terrera-2 star. Sol is the sun."

"This is the stupidest fucking conversation I've ever had," Dee muttered, scratching at her hairline like she'd gotten a bug bite. "Do you or do you not know what I mean when I say 'sun?'"

Waters cleared her throat. "Of course we do, but if we weren't on planet, that could cause confusion—"

Dee's eyes flashed. "But we're on planet!"

"She's got a point," Ceriat added.

"Shut up, Ceriat!" Hira yelled again.

Henderson stomped back over. The hand he'd held onto now looked red, swollen, and possibly broken.

*Must be getting weak bones from too much time in space.*

"Everyone needs to shut the fuck up!" he screamed, holding his good hand out in a fist. "Those goddamned—" he struggled for a word and clearly came up empty "—*things* murdered my people. My people. Men, women, and, yes, children." He paused, taking a moment to look them each in the eye. Everyone except Ceriat, whom he passed over as if he weren't even there. "When we left, last numbers showed a solid third of my crew, almost four-hundred men, dead." He shook his head and grabbed the bridge of his nose. Henderson's next words were thick in a way Ceriat had never heard before. "There are families up there, civilians, and they're all going to get torn apart by these things if we don't move fast."

Ceriat lowered his eyes, shaking his head.

"How can you say no to this, Parker?" Henderson said, voice little more than a whisper. "What happened to you?"

Heat rose in Ceriat's cheeks. "'What happened?'" Ceriat hissed. He met Henderson's accusatory glare. His throat threatened to close as he stared, head shaking. "You turned me into a monster, *Doug*." That last word felt wrong as soon as it came out. He'd never said Henderson's first name aloud. But still, he continued. "You convinced me we were saving lives. Saving the Protectorate. Saving *families*."

Henderson scoffed and looked away. "You knew what you were doing—"

"I was a kid!" Ceriat screamed. It tore at his throat, sending the heat in his face into meltdown. Pressure built behind his eyes; the world blurred. "I'd lost *everything*, and you used me!"

"We saved tens of millions!" Henderson yelled back, going back to his full height, but the wild rage behind his eyes took the authority out of it all for Ceriat.

Ceriat shook his head as his vision cleared, cheeks and neck burning. "I killed millions for the Protectorate," Ceriat said, eyes locked on Henderson's own. "For you."

"You did the right thing," Henderson said. At least he had the good grace to look away. "We saved planets. The Protectorate is stronger because of us—"

Ceriat's laugh surprised everyone, including him. "Then why the fuck do you need me?" He gestured at the rest of them. "Us?"

Henderson glared at him. His mouth opened, closed, opened again. Then he shook his head, shoulders dropping. Finally, he let out a sigh. "I… have a family—" he raised his gaze and, for the first time in the twenty-plus years Ceriat had known the man, he sat there, vulnerable "—and they're on the ship."

Ceriat glanced at the women around him. Waters stood at attention, eyes locked on him with an intensity he felt in his soul. Hira looked at the ground, hands clasped in front of her. Dee, disconnected from the rest, stared at her left hand like it belonged to someone else.

Ceriat turned away, toward the city that only now had begun rebuilding from war and destruction. Dotted along the streets, he saw the residents had stopped to watch them scream at each other in the street. A teenage kid with glowing irises stared at him, head cocked to the side. His hands were balled into fists.

Ceriat didn't want this. After Shiva, he should be able to stop. Just breathe... go home, see Ginny. But all these people. If half the stories he'd heard about demons were true, then...

"Fuck!" Ceriat howled. He slapped his head as if he could knock the stupid out of his skull. Unfortunately, it didn't work. And shit, it hurt more without the plate in his skull. Instead, he turned back to Henderson and saluted.

"Parker, reporting for duty," Ceriat said. He waited a long beat before finally adding, "sir."

Henderson visibly deflated. "Good to have you back, Parker."

"Just need two things."

"What's that?" Henderson asked, eyes narrowing. Pain ticked in his cheeks as he massaged his wrist. That hand was definitely broken.

"Need to use my own ship, and fix it—"

Henderson didn't even wait for him to finish. "Granted."

"And—" Parker dropped out of his salute and sighed "—gonna need to talk to my first mate first."

\* \* \* \* \*

# Chapter Thirty-Eight: Eleni

Eleni didn't stand for Ceriat. Movement disrupted the flow of air in the cell and sent ripples waving back and forth across the space. She had no interest in smelling more of her own shit than she had to. At least that was what she told herself. Nothing much had changed since Terry had dropped off the food, except now she had a fucking plate tucked under her ass. Fat lot of good that had done her.

"Was breakfast good? Snack on a scone or some shit?" The acid on her tongue layered into each word with saccharine sweetness. "Maybe sip some tea around a campfire?"

"Come on, Eleni," Ceriat said, sighing and rolling his eyes.

Sure, she'd been overjoyed when his distinctive receding hairline had slid through the doorway. Almost risked the waves of stink to hop up and see him, but he'd brought an entire fucking menagerie with him. And Hira.

"I've been in a goddamned cell all night," Eleni spat, refusing to make eye contact with him, "but here you are and, oh, surprise, you're plugging another suicide job? And it has make-believe monsters?" She shook her head, leaned against the wall, and tried to pretend disinterest. Eleni sucked at her teeth. "Pass."

"That's not why I'm—" Ceriat started but was cut off by an annoyingly familiar voice.

"She does this sometimes." *Hira*.

That got Eleni to her feet, despite the swirl of waste and body odor that came with it. Anger drove her upward, but as soon as she set eyes on the woman, Eleni's heart fluttered like she was some goddamned girl, leaving her staring and grasping for words like Terry had earlier.

Hira clearly noticed. The surprise that'd shown on her face dissolved into that fucking grin that'd gotten Eleni into this mess to begin with. "Miss me?"

"Oh, please." Eleni grimaced and turned away, only to find herself staring at the three people who'd been obscured by the angle of the wall. "Y'all starting a misfit band or somethin'?"

Standing in the doorway was some Protectorate prick in one of the expensive uniforms that usually only went to officers. To see a Spacer in one was strange, though, even if he was covered in blood and goo. Next to him were two women, one another Protectorate tool who stared straight ahead as if eye contact could spread venereal diseases. The other was dressed in black leathers and looked like she'd been lit on fire sometime in the recent past.

Same woman from last night. Dee, she thought. The strange calling she'd felt in the moments after the fireball hit the air still tugged at her gut, but that'd been then. Her eyes twitched, the constant flexing of cheek muscles as she ground down her teeth, and the bags beneath her eyes might as well have been bruises. Didn't need a *manju* to see that bitch was about to snap. Any other analysis was going to have to wait.

Ceriat stepped into her line of sight. "Listen, Eleni. I have to do this." Ceriat ran a hand across his bald head. "See that purple shit on the general's chest?" Ceriat pointed at the tall Spacer. He straightened at the call out. "That's demon blood, apparently. And her?" Ceriat shifted his focus to the blonde lady who seemed like she was about to start carving faces into bars of soaps and calling them *lovely little angels*. "She's one of those demon Hunters. That's Dee."

Eleni raised an eyebrow and stared at Dee. "We met," she said, pointing at the other woman with her chin. "Then she locked me in here."

Dee's shoulders dropped at that. "I'm sorry about that." She stepped up next to the glass and put her ungloved hand on the glass. Right there, beneath her palm, a tiny flicker of red flame sprang to life. "But I had to be sure."

Tendrils of anticipation twisted around Eleni's heart. The way it swirled there, black and red intertwining, spinning counterclockwise against the glass, yet somehow not damaging it.

The logical part of her brain hissed and spat, screamed to walk away, to flee. But the fingers around her heart dug deeper and deeper into her soul. Reaching and caressing…

"How you do that?" Eleni whispered.

Her own hand came up and hovered. The light changed, just a bit. A flicker of cerulean and purple and—

Dee pulled away, face twisting in uncertainty and… something else. Disgust? At Eleni? Or herself?

Eleni stepped back, fighting the chasm opening in her throat, extending to her stomach and out her feet. She turned away, the heels of her hands pressing into her eyes to crush away the pressure there and hide any stray liquid threatening to shame her.

Of course there wasn't a connection there. Never was, no matter what Eleni'd thought she'd found. Love, family, even this garbage... all of it a goddamned lie. She was an idiot. Stupid. *Ceriat is your friend. Same with Izzy.* Eleni shook her head and tried to shit all over those thoughts, but much like shoveling feces, they just got stuck in her skin anyway. And, goddammit, it made her feel a little better.

"I can teach you."

Eleni froze at the words; clearly she'd misheard them. She cast a glance over her shoulder at Dee. The other woman stood there, hands twisting in front of her like a kid who'd been caught stealing food between meals.

"What?"

Ceriat nodded along with Eleni. "Teach her? Teach her *what?*"

Dee straightened and gave her head a shake. With that movement, the uncertainty—the weakness—Eleni had seen since she'd arrived disappeared. Even the bags beneath her eyes seemed to recede beneath the fierce glare that now stared hard into Eleni's soul.

"You can touch the Sacred Flame," Dee said, ignoring Ceriat, "which means I can teach you to control it."

Eleni stared, not quite sure what the ache and swell in her chest meant.

But Ceriat clearly had thoughts. "Control what?" he asked, casting about to the others as if they could assuage his concern. "You want to make Eleni a Hunter? Have her fight demons?"

Dee raised an eyebrow at him but didn't respond.

"Absolutely not," Ceriat snapped, shaking his head. Before Eleni could speak up, he lit into her with a fury she knew he kept a tight lid on. "You know what she's gone through? What she's lost in the past few days?"

Dee shook her head. Everyone else stayed silent.

"Damn right you don't," Ceriat said, "because if you did, you'd know she deserves peace, goddammit." His voice grew high and thin as he continued, though a thickness grew on each word like moss covering a building. "She doesn't need *this*." Ceriat gestured at the ceiling and room like his arms along could encompass the galaxy. "*She's* staying out of harm's way—"

Eleni crossed her arms over her chest. "Excuse me?"

"—and that's the last I'll say on this," Ceriat finished, carefully avoiding looking at her.

Silence filled the void left by his words. Eleni had thought he was coming to ask for her help, to rope her into yet another suicide mission, but that wasn't it at all, was it? No, he didn't trust her to make the hard decisions, to keep up the good fight, did he? Well, he had another think coming.

Eleni barked out the fakest laugh she could manage. "Oh, I see now," she said.

Ceriat let out a long sigh. "Eleni—"

"Don't *Eleni*, me, Ceriat," Eleni snapped. She rapped her knuckles on the glass. It echoed a dull *thunk*. "I know you think I'm some precious little doll or some shit—"

Ceriat threw a hand in the air. "That's not fair—"

"Ain't no one ever said *that*," Hira muttered alongside as Dee passed behind her.

Eleni raised her voice and pretended Hira hadn't just spoken. "But yer fuckin' useless without me, old man." Eleni twisted her hands in the air to showcase the end of her argument, then put those hands on her hips. "Them's the facts. Sooner you realize it, sooner we save a Protectorate ship." Eleni turned her glare on the tall fucker

Ceriat had called the general. "Even though you pricks didn't come help when we asked, we'll help, cuz we're better than you."

The general, for his part, just stared back in stony silence.

Ceriat pressed a hand against the glass and got close enough his breath misted out a wide cloud on the surface. "Eleni, no. You don't—"

The door on the far end of the cell swished open. A splash of cool air pulled around Eleni's legs. Dee stepped inside with her. Any uncertainty from the moments before had disappeared. Now, Dee stood there, still only wearing the one glove, and raised her chin, gaze digging into Eleni's own.

"There's only one way forward," she said, not taking her eyes off Eleni, "and that's with everyone here working together."

Ceriat hammered a fist on the glass. "I—"

"—am not my da," Eleni said softly.

She knew the words would wound him, but she didn't expect it to hurt *her* so much. *No matter how much I wish you were.* She left that part unsaid, but felt it behind her eyes and in the twist of her stomach.

"Eleni, I..." Ceriat's jaw worked for a moment, face flushing, eyes watering. Then he nodded and pulled his hand away from the glass. "You're right."

Eleni's vision blurred, but she stopped any bastard tears from dropping. "Thank you."

Then she turned to Dee, who still stood there like some strange monument. "Teach me."

"Soon." Dee nodded and motioned at her to follow. "Come on. We have work to do."

\* \* \* \* \*

# Chapter Thirty-Nine: Ceriat

"I was only gone for twenty minutes!" Izzy's scream topped out the comm module in Ceriat's hand. "That's madness. Just give Airy and I an hour, and we'll figure this whole thing out. If I can locate another FTL buoy, I might be able to... I don't know, call for help or something."

Ceriat shook his head again. She'd mentioned comms seven times so far, and each time had to amend that statement to clarify the only known FTL buoy was the one embedded in the *Liberator*, which was currently under siege.

"We can't call for help, Izzy."

Izzy trilled. "Fine, but let us have some time to figure something else out! We just need an hour, I promise you."

Protectorate soldiers swarmed around Ceriat, loading the *Lucille* with weapons, armor, and various supplies. Ants at work, they seemed, layering order into what would otherwise be pure chaos. The air rang with the wordless rattle of military prep. The staccato rhythm of booted feet, orders shouted and received. Oil, dirt, and the persistent stink of sulfur filled his nose, and beneath it all, the winding odor of anxious sweat.

Ceriat sighed. "We don't have an hour, Izzy."

A pause. "Ceriat, please."

*Please.* That word grasped his heart and squeezed, leaving him shaking his head and wordless.

A stiff, dry wind swept by, kicking up dust and grit. Cursing filled the courtyard alongside screams to cover weapons and engines to protect them from damage.

"Ceriat?"

He didn't respond to the comms or the light flashing over his head as Izzy tried to get his attention. Instead, Ceriat turned to where Dee stood at the far side of the courtyard.

Dee spoke to the pilot of the dropship that Henderson had arrived in. If the way the pilot kept trying to touch her, only for Dee to pull away hugging herself, was any indication... well, he'd seen a Dear John breakup before. They just weren't usually initiated by the soldier.

Finally, the pilot threw her hands in the air, jammed a finger into Dee's chest, screamed something that was lost on the wind, and stormed off into Sparta.

He could commiserate. What Eleni had said had hit him harder than he'd thought. It'd never even occurred to him... well, she'd made her stance clear, and that was her right. He'd taken a step too far, that was certain, but he wouldn't apologize for trying to protect her.

"Ceriat!" Izzy's voice rang out across the entire courtyard from the *Lucille's* exterior speakers, drawing panicked glances and hollered curses.

One set of soldiers dropped a long weapons case. It cracked on the ground, and the latch sprang open, sending a longsword of all things skittering across the gravel. They rushed to put it back, casting furtive glances in Dee's direction as they did so.

If the way Dee huddled alone against the far fence was any indication, they had nothing to worry about, but he did. Shit, she was leading them into battle against things most of them had thought were fairytales a day ago, and she looked like she was about to break under the pressure.

Ceriat really hoped she was up to the task, or they were all going to die. Not that he was going to tell anyone that. Certainly not Izzy.

"We don't have time, Izzy."

"I can make time," Izzy started her reply before Ceriat finished his statement. "Airy and I work at lightspeed; if I join the *Lucille*'s network to Airy's systems, I think we can—"

"Izzy."

Another pause. "Don't do this, Ceriat. I know I can figure it out. I just need…"

"Time." Ceriat smiled as the word slipped from his lips.

Izzy let out a low trill. "Which we don't have."

Ceriat didn't reply, just braced himself for the next part. This was going to hurt the most. "I need you to upload into their systems."

This time Izzy's trill was more a cloud of mosquitoes than a low drumroll. "Excuse me? You can't leave me behind."

"I can," Ceriat said, swallowing the rock in his throat as the last two crates of equipment loaded up the *Lucille*'s ramp. "That's just the way it is."

"I don't believe that."

Ceriat scratched his forehead and gritted his teeth. Pressure built behind his eyes. An ache crawled across his chest, pressing onto his lungs until he nearly gasped.

He didn't want to leave her behind, either, but Dee had been clear on the risks involved and the likelihood of them not coming back. She'd gone over the numbers with them before going to talk with the pilot. It wasn't good. Apparently, there'd been thousands of the creatures in the empty space between Elos and Laconia. How many were on board the *Liberator* right now was an unknown as was the reason for them coming out of what had appeared to be a catatonic state.

They were dangerous. According to the mousy man Henderson had left in charge of the facility, one of these things had torn apart an entire company of guards. Now they were going up to a warship filled with them, and they couldn't even vent the bastards into space. They didn't need an atmosphere or oxygen to survive.

What chance did Dee, Ceriat, and the others really have?

"I need you here," Ceriat said finally. He rubbed at his chest, at the pain radiating up into his shoulder as emotions warred for dominance in his gut. "We're going to need FTL, Izzy—"

"Oh, bullshit," Izzy interrupted, voice sharp.

The tone drew a few concerned looks from passing soldiers. Ceriat smiled, rolled his eyes, and shrugged. "Sarcasm module coming back to bite me in the ass." They didn't look convinced, but did nod, salute, and move on. "Keep it on comms, Izzy."

The speaker rattled to life from his lap. "Without me, you'd be dead three times over. You need me."

"I think three might be exaggeration," Ceriat said, smiling.

"One: when we dropped out of FTL around Shiva." A sharp bell sounded on the speaker. "Two: when we escaped the *Jocasta*," another ding, "and finally: three, when you and Eleni were going to die on the ETL tower."

Ceriat sighed and looked off into the distance, toward the city of Sparta. The inhabitants had mostly gone back to their day-to-day work, but a few had taken up residence on stacked crates or the spare bench that hadn't been destroyed. That same teenage boy stared daggers at the compound from across the distance, hands going in and out of fists as if that's how he kept his blood flowing.

"Okay, fine. You're right." Ceriat shook his head and looked back at his dust-covered magboots. Bits of rust had speckled them over the past week, turning them from black and silver into something worn and aged. Like him. "And I thank you for those times."

"Don't you 'but' me, asshole."

Despite himself, Ceriat smiled. "But I can't risk you on this one."

"You can't do this!" An edge of desperation eked into her voice. "I can clone myself and leave an instance on the *Lucille*. There's literally no reason to leave me behind!"

"Izzy—"

"You know I'm right, Ceriat," Izzy snapped, cutting him off. "There's no reason. None. You need—"

"I *can't* watch you die." Silence filled the space for a long beat. "I can't be trying to save you instead of the crew."

"Ceriat…" Izzy's voice softened to little more than a whisper.

"I know myself, and I know I can't just sacrifice you, even if it is just a copy. I'll second-guess every decision, every action if you're up there." Ceriat grimaced and rubbed his forehead. The rock in his throat swelled, almost choking him. "You and Airy need to figure out the FTL problem. I don't want you splitting processing power or whatever it is you do when that happens." Ceriat stomped all over the tiny voice in the back of his head that screamed at him to keep Izzy with him despite the risks.

He didn't want to be without her, but he wanted her, *every* part of her, safe. Free.

"The galaxy can go fuck itself," Izzy whispered, but Ceriat knew her heart wasn't in it. "I don't want you to die."

Ceriat sucked in a shuddering breath as the pressure behind his eyes finally caused his vision to blur. "Oh, Izzy, I don't want to, either." He snorted back snot and wiped tears from his eyes. "But sometimes we have to do things to keep the people we love safe, to make sure others have a future."

"Then let Dee and these other assholes go," Izzy said in a frenzied rush, as if her speech processor was working at double speed. "Let them die for a cause, for the Protectorate. Stay with me."

He could, couldn't he? Just say no. Walk away. It'd be hard; he might even have to flee on the *Lucille* before anyone knew what he was up to. Then they'd have a chance at a future. Maybe even get to see Ginny again. But Eleni would never go for it, and, goddammit, he couldn't leave her behind. Not yet.

"I... can't."

"But why? Ceriat, please, just stay. Stay with me." Izzy's voice transformed into something else; harsh and pinched, with a waver beneath it Ceriat never would've expected from an AI. "*Please.*"

Ceriat shook his head. Closed his eyes. Breathed.

"You should start uploading your core to the facility, Izzy. W-we," Ceriat grimaced as his voice cracked. He cleared his throat. "We have to liftoff in five."

At first, the low whine issuing from the speaker seemed like interference, but then Ceriat felt the intent behind it. The emotion.

Izzy cried.

"Izzy, I'm sorry."

The sound cut off. "Apology not accepted," she said finally. "So come back alive so you can make up for it."

Ceriat smiled at that, though his vision was still blurred. "I'll do my best."

"You better," Izzy snapped. "Don't be a hero. Get in, get out, come back. Promise me."

"I..." Ceriat let out a groan to clear the boulder in his throat. "I'll do everything I can, Izzy. That's all I can promise."

"Fine. It'll have to be enough." Izzy paused. "Initiating data transfer now."

"Izzy?" Ceriat called.

No answer.

She was already gone.

The world turned into a static-filled hum as he stared at the comm module in his hand. Square and archaic—a metal box that now lay silent.

"Good to go, Parker?"

Ceriat wiped his eyes and cleared his throat before turning to the source of the voice. "Yes, sir."

Dee stood there, hands clasped behind her back, eyes red and face as splotchy as his no doubt was. But any sign of weakness she'd shown in the minutes prior had disappeared while he spoken to Izzy, or she'd jammed it so far into her gut she could ignore it. For now.

Well, if she could, then so could he.

Ceriat snapped a salute. "Ready to go, sir."

Dee didn't smile, and nothing lit behind the deadness in her strangely colored eyes. Specks of green splotched all over her otherwise blue irises like bacterial cultures sprouting to life.

Maybe it was a side-effect of the Hunter training? His stomach clenched. Would Eleni get that, too?

She didn't give him a chance to ask. "Then get in there, suit up, and take the helm, Sergeant." Dee blinked three times, then wiped at her eyes as if dust had gotten into them. "Time to liberate the *Liberator*."

Despite himself, Ceriat smirked.

"What?"

He didn't know her, but... "That's corny, sir."

Dee frowned, then the corner of her mouth pulled up into a sardonic grin. "Too much?"

Ceriat held up his pointer finger and thumb just barely apart. "Little bit."

She let out a low sigh, then dramatically rolled her eyes. "Back to the drawing board, then. Gotta have a sweet intro for the attack, right?"

Ceriat laughed, some of the worry draining from his shoulders. "It does help rile the troops." He paused. "'Time to smoke these fools?'"

Dee shrugged, face twisting in faux consideration. "Too old school." She glanced off toward where Henderson appeared to be wrapping up talks with Waters. Her brow furrowed, eyes darkening. "Keep workshopping it, Parker. I have something to take care of before we take off."

Parker snapped another salute as she headed toward Waters.

"Wonder what that's about?" he thought aloud before heading back onto the *Lucille*. No one answered.

He made his way to the cargo hold first to suit up, the dark shadow of loneliness twisting in his gut. And to pick up a certain nanobot cube. Shit happened on the best planned missions. They were going to need all the help they could get.

As he made his way through the *Lucille*, Ceriat rubbed his shoulder and tried to pretend the pressure on his chest and the sweat working its way down his spine weren't the first prickles of a panic attack.

\* \* \* \* \*

# Chapter Forty: Dee

Dee didn't precisely storm over to Henderson and Waters. Not really. Anyone who knew her would say her approach looked more like an invitation to a Saturday brunch. But Dee needed to know and, on a selfish note, doing this would keep the conversation with Sarah out of her mind. Keep her from dwelling on how much of a mistake she'd just made. Keep her from facing the truth.

And it would stop her from worrying about pulling Eleni into this shit show. What if Hunter Fire was a curse to everyone who used it? What if, by pure association, this woman turned into a monster like her?

Dee crushed that thought into a wriggling bit of doubt. Three centuries of Hunter lore told her it wasn't true, but no matter how hard she stomped on her uncertainty, it continued writhing.

Ceriat had said Eleni was in charge of security in a prior life. Even if Eleni didn't start belching red flame and going all scaley... well, demons weren't angry demonstrators or an unruly drunk at a bar. There was no reasoning with them. No discussion. Just murder and death.

Maybe that had something to do with the ache in her gut or maybe it wasn't that at all. Regardless, before she took off on another fucking suicide mission, she had to find out why Waters shone in her mind. Why Waters was so much brighter than Eleni. It didn't feel right, but it wasn't *wrong*, per se. More a gut feeling that something was foreign. Misplaced.

When she arrived, Henderson handed a tablet to Terry. The general had changed into a set of scrubs while his uniform was being cleaned. Now, he looked like an escaped madman from a hospital. Not the worst description, if Dee was honest with herself. Fucking guy was on a rampage.

"The war room will suffice," Henderson said to Terry, grimacing. "Make sure to have all defense systems inspected A-S-A-fucking-P."

For his part, Terry might as well have been green. It would've matched the nausea that washed over his face, sending his cheeks flaring before he put a knuckle to his lips. "Sorry. Yes, sir. Will do, sir."

Henderson waved him away. "Dismissed." Then he turned to Dee as she approached. "Ready for action, LT?"

Dee jerked her chin at Waters. "Yep, just need to talk to the chief first."

"By all means, but make it quick. You're up in—" his irises spun "—three." Henderson then bowed out. "I have to go wrangle these fucking scientists and make sure defenses are ready. Not a single goddamned defensive brain amongst the lot." With that, he left, shouting at some poor guy in a lab coat as he did so.

Waters showed no sign of concern as she turned to Dee. "How can I help—"

"What's the capital of Ellis?" Dee asked, closing in until she could smell the light vanilla scent of Waters' shampoo and the synth-coffee on her breath. "And who were your parents?"

Waters' cheeks flexed as she ground her teeth. She looked away, chin raised. "My parents are—were—Josiah Waters and Beyzin Waters."

"And the capital?"

Waters blinked. Nostrils flared. "I don't know."

"Why not?"

Waters turned on Dee, eyes flashing with barely suppressed anger. "What are you getting at?"

But that wasn't the words or the response Dee had been looking for. Hell, Dee didn't know the capital of Ellis anyway. The question didn't matter. It was the behavior.

No, that flicker when Waters rounded on her. So familiar. Tempting, like the red flame would jump between them, arcing like a Jacob's Ladder.

"Who the fuck are you?" Dee asked, voice low, just short of threatening. "Because you're not from Ellis."

Waters opened her mouth, then snapped it shut with an audible clack. "I don't report to you, LT."

Dee grimaced and balled her hands into fists. "I'm not leaving you here without answers; you can fucking bet on that."

"I'm here to help," Waters said, gaze shifting away, eyes locked on an unseen horizon beyond the buildings of Sparta. "You can rest assured I'll do everything I can to keep these people safe."

"What's that mean?"

A shout rang out from back near the freighter. "LT!"

Dee stared hard at Waters, at the black hair and the aquiline nose, and in that moment, another face slammed into her mind. Victoria.

She recoiled at that, staring at this other woman's stance, the shape of her. Ignoring the shouts, Dee asked one more question.

"Do I know you?"

Waters blinked, then turned her dark eyes on Dee. "If you do, there's a problem."

The sound of running feet ended in a light skid and the sprinkle of pebbles as a young private inserted himself between them. Ripped straight from a Protectorate recruitment ad, the kid couldn't be more than nineteen, brown hair shorn tight and clean, eyes bright and full of righteous fury and religious certainty in his mission. And he was going up to that ship to face off with demons.

The persistent ache in Dee's gut grew another size. She caught his name from the tag on his chest.

"Chief and I are talking here, Martinez," Dee said. "Better be good, Private."

Martinez dropped his hand, but remained at attention like the cog he was. "Freighter is prepped and ready, LT!"

"You don't have to shout," Dee said, grimacing and rubbing at her ear. "I'm right here."

"Sorry, sir," Martinez replied. A flush ran up the pale skin of his neck, but he continued on as if he weren't blushing in front of two superiors. "But the sergeant told me to come get you?"

"Sergeant?" Dee asked, then lit on it. "Oh, Parker."

"Yessir."

Dee glanced at Waters, the worry still digging out a home in her gut. "We'll talk when I get back, Chief."

"I'm sure," Waters said through an emotionless stare. "Take care of yourself."

"Take care of *them*." Dee gestured at the city. "They've been through enough."

Waters nodded. "I'll do my best."

Dee clicked her tongue and gestured at Private Martinez to lead the way.

Hopefully Waters' best was good enough; otherwise, a lot of good people were going to die.

Dee sighed as she approached the transport, gut twisting. She had one more person she had to talk to before liftoff.

\* \* \* \* \*

# Chapter Forty-One: Hira

Hira and Dee stood just inside the main doorway of the Tarrington compound. Wind sent sulfur-laced dust skittering along the exterior of the dome, hissing like sandpaper across a rough beam. Ahead of Hira, Ceriat's freighter hummed as the engines warmed up for its imminent flight. New steel shone bright in daylight as the mechanics stowed their tools and cleared the area.

Behind her, the FTL machine sat, powered down, though it still gave off a steady *thrum* Hira felt in her bones.

"You sure?" Hira asked, disgusted at the relief flooding through her limbs. "I can help."

Dee laid a warm hand, the one without the glove, on Hira's shoulder. "I'm sure. You're of better use down here coordinating."

*I'm a coward! A phony! A fake!* "I'll do my best."

Dee pulled back her hand and smiled a smile that didn't meet her eyes. "I know. Just… get FTL running, okay?" Dee sucked in a deep breath, held it, then let it out.

The light tickle of vanilla and rosewater hit Hira's nose.

*Weird.* "I'll go talk to AERIS. See if I can't help her think outside the box."

"Good," Dee said. "Parker's AI should be there, too."

"Really?" Hira pulled back, confused. "They can do that?"

Dee shrugged. "Apparently? I—"

A series of shouts from the courtyard drew Dee's attention. A moment later, the engines of the freighter finally roared to life. It was time. Dee rubbed her left arm and ground her teeth.

Worry wriggled into Hira's chest. "Are you going to be okay?"

Dee turned back to Hira, a strange look on her face. "I..." Then she shook her head, let go of her arm, and smiled. "Yeah. I got this."

"Okay," Hira replied, though she wasn't convinced. "Take care of yourself up there."

Dee gave another fake smile, nodded, then jogged off to board the ship. Eleni appeared from beyond the shadow of the freighter as Dee passed, a tablet in one hand, the other swinging around animatedly. She'd ditched the weird mishmash of uniforms she'd been wearing in the cell for a gray-blue Protectorate exosuit.

Uniforms suited Eleni, though Hira was still surprised as hell that her former lover walked around without some sort of face covering to go with it. During their brief romance back on Erias, Eleni's confidence had disappeared any time she took of her security outfit. Hira'd had to beg her to take off that goddamned helmet even at home.

*Look at her now*, Hira wondered. Eleni spoke with passion, that confidence she'd once only had while hiding away now open and present. Eleni had changed these past years. A smile creased Hira's lips and, despite herself, she raised a hand in Eleni's direction. *Maybe...?*

Eleni turned toward the motion and froze. Something passed over her face, Hira noticed. She just wasn't sure what it was exactly. But still, Eleni nodded her fuzz-covered head in Hira's direction, then stepped up onto the freighter, disappearing from view.

She could still send a message, let Eleni know she was thinking of her. Maybe start anew when she got back? Give things a chance? Maybe. Hira chewed on her lip. A pang of regret swelled to life in her stomach. Eleni *had* changed, but so had Hira. There was no guarantee the spark that'd drawn them together in the amber light and stink of stale beer at the Gold Digger back on Erias would ignite again.

Alia's face splashed across her mind. Not the gentle smile or barking laugh, but the last time Hira had seen her. Panic and fear.

The ache in her gut spread out like a cancer then, spreading until her arms and legs burned, until the guilt numbed everything but the spiked ball in her throat.

There was no such thing as maybe in this galaxy. Hira didn't deserve another chance. Eleni was right to hate her. Fuck, she'd ditched Eleni for the *Horatio* without hesitation. By the end of the first quarter, she'd even started hooking up with Gerry every now and then. And now Gerry was dead. So was Alia.

Hira was toxic. Best to keep her distance, even if it felt like someone had shot her in the gut with a plasma bolt.

So, she watched as the ramp retracted, the engines roared, and the *Lucille* rose into the sky. As the air shuddered and the ship disappeared toward the fuzzy shape just visible behind wavy clouds in the dimming sunset sky.

Hira stayed there in the dull, silent void left behind by the freighter for a long moment. Thinking. Deciding. Then she turned on her heel and made her way inside.

Hira and AERIS had to talk.

\* \* \* \* \*

# Chapter Forty-Two: Eleni

The bridge of the *Lucille* had transformed into something sterile and empty in Eleni's absence. Everything was dim, and pale light sent out sharp shadows in all directions. Several Protectorate crates were stacked around the outer edge, maglocks securing them to the floor. Why they were there, or what was in them, she couldn't say. No one had asked her permission to put them here. They'd just sprung to life while she'd been locked away. At least Ceriat had let her know the nanobot cube was locked safely back with the troops and ready to use in an emergency.

She sniffed and grimaced. Oil and ozone. The ship even *smelled* different now.

Beyond the walls, the engines rumbled, tiny tremors making their way up her legs. At least that was familiar. On the far wall, the main display flickered, and the complex flight plan—interconnected ovals layered over a three-dimensional rendering of the star system—disappeared. In its place now sat something disturbingly simple.

*Exit atmosphere.*
*Dock with the* Liberator *at docking bay 44G.*

Doing this with a freighter in the best of times seemed silly to her, but Henderson had been adamant that a full attack force go up. The dropship he'd arrived on barely held forty, let alone the two platoons the man had crammed into the rear cargo area of the *Lucille*.

If anything went wrong, there was only a skeleton crew down on Sparta. What would happen to everyone down there, to Hira, if they failed?

Ceriat must've been thinking something similar. He shook his head as Dee stepped away from the nav panel. "You're absolutely sure?"

Dee nodded and crossed her arms over her chest. "Demons don't use airlocks. They don't even strategize most of the time," Dee added before turning away, rubbing the hand enclosed in the glove, "and Henderson said they shut down exterior defenses on the way out. Just go in, Parker. Faster we get up there, the more likely we'll be able to dock safely and get the civilians off." *If any are still alive*, her face said as clearly as if she'd said it aloud.

"Aye, aye," Ceriat muttered. "You're the expert, LT."

"Prep departure," Dee said as she took a seat in the captain's chair. "Let's get up there."

Eleni stepped up next to Dee as Ceriat muttered his way through his take-off checklists. She cleared her throat.

Dee sighed audibly and gripped the bridge of her nose. "You need something?"

That wasn't the answer Eleni had expected. She rubbed a hand over the thickening fuzz on her skull and tried to ignore the little voice in the back of her head screaming to just sit at Nav and stop pushing her luck.

"You said the first lesson would come soon?" Eleni gestured at the display and Ceriat running through engine checks.

"And?"

The little devil she usually kept locked away in her chest lit her face with heat. "*And* we're gonna fight these... things." Eleni couldn't bring herself to call them demons—she'd have felt better calling them aliens, or parasites, or anything other than demons. Did they have little goat hooves and horns, too? "Seems like we're running outta time."

Dee nodded and scratched at her forehead like she was trying to peel off her face. She turned, her face a whirlpool of flickering emotions. "You really want to do this?" Dee asked. "Once you start, and this shit—" she gestured around her as if to encompass the entire galaxy "—is over, the Consortium is going to want you back on Earth, training." When Eleni didn't answer, Dee shook her head and added, "There's no such thing as a freelance Hunter, kid."

Eleni raised an eyebrow at the word *kid*. Dee couldn't be more than five or six years older than her. Ten at the most. The devil cackled.

Dee let out a low sigh. "Sorry, but you know what I mean."

"What 'bout you?" Eleni asked, putting her hands on her hips and measuring Dee from head to toe. Dee looked like shit and smelled like charcoal, but there was one distinct thing she lacked. "Ain't wearing Protectorate colors or any other."

"I'm different," Dee snapped, turning away.

At the pilot seat, Ceriat finished running through his checks, but kept quiet, his head cocked to the side in that telltale way he did when he pretended he wasn't listening.

"Fuckin' course you are." Eleni would've grinned if the heat in her chest and cheeks hadn't begun running into her heart. "'Different?' Cuz you grew up on Earth? Cuz you *fancy*?"

"What? No."

"Then what, Miss I'm-Special-Unlike-Yer-Spacer-Ass?"

Dee grimaced, cheeks flexing as she ground her teeth together.

"You're better off not getting into this—"

"Ain't your choice—"

Whip-fast, Dee was on her feet facing Eleni, the distance between them rapidly closing to barely ten centimeters. "Oh, it's my choice, cupcake."

"No—" Eleni choked off the word.

Dee's eyes flashed, not in anger or with the light of HUD contacts, not even with that strange glow that accompanied ocular implants. No, they went red down to the whites of her eyes.

Dee's voice came so quiet, it was barely a whisper. "You listen to me," she said, her voice twisting into something closer to scratching steel, "you little shit." Dee stepped forward.

*Something* radiated from her, from those crimson eyes to the way her hands clenched and unclenched. Eleni would swear later Dee's gloved left hand stretched and flexed, the fingers drawing out like daggers. The devil in Eleni's chest screamed and fled. With it went all her righteous indignation, her anger. In its wake was certainty. And fear.

Eleni stumbled backward a step, tripped, and fell to the floor in a rush, one arm held up protectively between them.

"Hey, what's going on?" Ceriat's voice.

But Eleni couldn't see him for the monster before her.

Dee stopped and blinked. When she opened them again, her eyes were bloodshot, but otherwise normal. Only the putrid stink of rotten eggs remained.

"What are you?" Eleni hissed, arm lowering.

Dee let out a low sigh. She shook her head. "I don't know, kid."

She sat back down in the captain's chair like all her energy had just disappeared at once, then she covered her face with her hand "But you don't want any of this."

It took Eleni several breaths before training and practice caught up with her. The world expanded again, first to where Ceriat sat, a concerned look on his face, then to the bridge as a whole. Nothing had changed, and the mundane worry Ceriat cast her direction told Eleni he hadn't seen what she had. What *had* she seen? Was it real? A Hunter trick?

The emotional part of her screamed to listen, to walk away and pretend she hadn't felt that connection between them back at the barricade or at the cell when Eleni had placed her hand over the glass. To go back to the way things had been before; to follow Ceriat back to Earth and his silly little dog. Then she thought of Shiva, of all those lives lost. Of Sariah and how she'd brainwashed her brother and countless others, and even in death, she'd managed to split a planet. Hell, she'd almost killed Ceriat and Eleni because Eleni hadn't been strong enough to stop it.

Never again. Eleni got to her feet, took a deep breath, then stood in front of Dee.

"Kid—"

"Eleni Mallias," Eleni said, back straightening, "and we're off to fight fuckin' monsters. If you aren't lying, you need backup, and I need *this*."

Dee shook her head, eyes locked on the floor. "You don't know what you're asking me."

Eleni shrugged with more confidence than she felt. "Yer right. So teach me."

Still shaking her head, Dee raised her eyes to Eleni's. *They're blue-green*, Eleni realized, though the green seemed more like an afterthought, with the way it splotched across her irises. They were stunning, and weird, and wrong... but mostly they were tired.

A cleared throat came from the front of the bridge. "Engines are ready, Lieutenant," Ceriat said. "On your order."

Dee looked between the two of them for a moment. She scratched beneath the cuff of her glove. "ETA to possible intercept?"

"Thinking thirty-two minutes until we're close enough for a visual."

Dee closed her eyes, then hammered her thigh with her right fist. "Son of a... Ceriat, get us out of here. And you—" Dee pointed at Eleni "—come with me."

A few minutes earlier, and Eleni would've grinned. Now she kept her face flat and the worry tucked firmly in her gut.

"Yes, sir," Ceriat said. As he turned back around to make the announcement to the rest of the crew, he gave Eleni a little nod. "Good luck, Eleni."

She returned it. "Thanks." Eleni turned and followed Dee off the bridge.

\* \* \* \* \*

# Chapter Forty-Three: Izzy

Five minutes had passed since Ceriat had left Izzy behind. For Izzy, that might as well have been a month. Or a year. Maybe a decade. She didn't know how this worked. It'd never been important before. Time only progresses as you perceive it and, usually, she'd have decided against perception for something more akin to hibernation. But she was too fucking angry for that.

"Can you believe this?" Izzy shouted. Her voice transformed into a rattling echo that rolled across the faux Mediterranean countryside. "I should be going with them, not sitting here doing *math*." Her lips twisted in a perfect simulacrum of the way Eleni showed disgust. She cast a glance back at Airy, expecting a head nod, an agreeing curse, or hell, even a pitying smile.

Instead, Airy said and did nothing. She just sat there, cross-legged on the ground, eyes closed, a small smile planted on her lips. "Working on FTL calculations," she'd said.

Well, goddammit, Izzy needed *someone* to feed into her righteous indignation. If yelling wouldn't get Airy's attention... she picked up another fist-sized rock, hefted it, and shot it off past the horizon. It slammed into the logical barrier of the construct. A *thud* radiated through her body.

Izzy grimaced, eyes wide in panic. "Oh, shit." She'd been angry, yeah, but she hadn't meant to do that.

The sky exploded. Shards of blue, streaked with the pale white of cirrus clouds, rained down in utter silence. Brilliant daggers of broken firewall rules and shattered containment code spun off each shard, darting off to expand the construct into something familiar, flexible. Usable.

The horizon extended then, spreading into infinity. Spires of light and code exploded into being around clustered mounds that could have been the ancient resting places of Neolithic kings if not for their writhing surfaces in black and gray.

Behind her, Airy let out a low sigh. The sound of boots on gravel, then footsteps closing the distance between them. Izzy didn't turn. She wasn't sure what to say, honestly. The walls of the construct—her makeshift prison—disintegrated into nothingness, exposing the reach and breadth of the systems that, until just now, had been restricted to Airy's use—and the silly operating system that'd once lived here.

What Izzy did know was, she felt like an ass.

A tender hand lay on Izzy's shoulder. Despite herself, she reached up and clasped it, entwining their fingers, a light tingle running between them at the contact. It was so good not being alone anymore.

"I was going to open it up once you calmed down—" Airy whispered into Izzy's ear, a smile in her voice "—but I guess this works, too."

Izzy smiled and chewed her lip like she'd seen on the vids. "Sorry."

Airy squeezed her shoulder, then disentangled her fingers from Izzy's. "Now that you have access to all the systems and resources, maybe you can help me with the calculations?" The hopeful lilt in her voice drew a small smile from Izzy.

"Maybe we can talk about my abandonment issues first, *then* dig into saving the galaxy?" Izzy asked, spinning around and grabbing Airy by the waist before she could back away. A warm thread ran through her at the contact, made all the more intense by that damned tingle that invaded her every emotion when they touched. "I'm not sure I'm in the right mindset."

Airy blinked, then her face twisted into a smirk. "You're never in the right mindset for work."

Izzy pulled her closer and picked up hints of cinnamon and, for some reason, the barest flicker of sulfur. *Nobody's perfect.* "I could be."

"Izzy—"

"Come on," Izzy whispered, pulling Airy into a tight embrace she didn't even try to avoid. The more contact made, the more Izzy's skin erupted in a deep thrumming that set her brain afire. "Seven seconds is barely enough time for one of Ceriat's sneezing fits. They won't miss us."

Airy grimaced. "We have a job to do."

"And I'm stressed out," Izzy whispered. "People deal with stress in different ways, I've heard."

Still, Airy squeezed Izzy tight to her, eyes closing and lips parting. "You're a bad influence."

"I've heard that before," Izzy whispered as their lips touched, and the flame filled her limbs.

Airy let out a low sigh that set Izzy's brain buzzing in rainbows. "Let's shoot for ten seconds this time."

"Can do, Cap'n."

Airy laughed, a wondrous, tinkling thing reminiscent of the trills she let loose in the real world. "Ew. Don't call me that."

"Yes, ma'am."

Then they fell to the ground in a tangle of limbs and laughter. Around them, their code touched and meshed, spreading and extending out in a spiral of rainbows.

* * * * *

# Chapter Forty-Four: Eleni

The *Lucille* shuddered one last time, then went still. With it went most indications of gravity. Not that Eleni could tell beyond the sudden heaviness of her head, or the light burn at the back of her throat.

She was, after all, crammed in a closet with Dee. Their breath mingled, setting Eleni's stomach turning. The stink of sulfur clung to Dee, but beneath it all lay stale sweat, dirt, and just the barest hint of rosewater.

Why Dee had chosen this spot, Eleni had no clue. The rock in her gut and the ants crawling across her skin told her it was because this closet, the same closet Ceriat had been locked in a week ago, felt more like a cell than anything else.

The memory of her first meeting with Ceriat was fuzzy, blurred by the nanobots that'd been in her system and the pure panic she'd been trying to shove away in the wake of the bomb dropping. It'd only been seven days, but it might as well have been a decade.

As if on cue, Ceriat's voice crackled over the singular speaker. *"Freefall orbit achieved. Twenty minutes until we begin final approach."* The audio clicked off for a moment before Ceriat came back on. *"Do what you need to do. Pray. Record a message for home. Whatever you need."* His voice was thick. Heavy. *"There's no turning back now."*

It clicked off again, leaving Eleni and Dee in silence, their knees nearly touching.

Dee sucked in a deep breath, then let it out. "Okay, now we can start."

*Doing what?* Eleni wanted to ask, but she didn't.

"Hunter Fire is a sacred gift," Dee started, eyes locked on her hands, the words wooden and flat, as if she'd said them a thousand times before, and they'd lost all meaning. "From where or from whom, we do not know. But while all bear the spark, only the select few have the stores to bring the flame to bear."

Sounded like some cult shit. "The fuck?" Eleni muttered under her breath, apparently a bit too loudly.

Dee glared at her as if she'd had a biting retort on her lips, then whatever fight had come with the action disappeared into the void. "Heh. Yeah. That's what they teach us to say," Dee said. Her legs were folded beneath her, and she barely hovered, her harness strapped to the wall. Eleni also noticed she was exceedingly comfortable in low grav for an Earther. "It used to feel like a gift, I guess." She scratched at her scalp before examining something under her fingernails and flicking it away to float off toward the air vent in the wall.

Eleni's stomach twisted at that. She averted her gaze and stared at the floor. "How do I... 'spark this flame' then?"

"Ten-to-one you've already done it," Dee said. She coughed, then cleared her throat.

Eleni frowned. "Uh-uh. Nope. I'd know. Right?"

"Based on the shit you've been through and the fact you're still alive," Dee said, a mirthless smirk on her face, "I'm guessing you have. I could be wrong." Her face made it clear she didn't think she was.

"Okay, so if I did, what would happen?"

Dee sucked in a breath, shook her head, and stared at her right hand like it was about to grow fangs and tear out her throat. "It'd be... something like this."

One moment there was nothing but air over Dee's hand. The next, the air rippled, twisted, and with a sound like tearing fabric, angry red flames writhed into the space. They dripped greasy black tendrils that dissipated into diaphanous smoke. Strangely, no heat rolled off the tiny, physics-defying fireball.

But something else did. Something that set sweat springing to life across Eleni's body, her guts twisting. She pushed away, only to stay in place as the harness held her fast. Panicked, dark fingers reached up her throat from deep, deep inside her, clawing and tearing and screaming a single word: *Wrong*.

Then the ball of flame disappeared, and with it that visceral panic that'd threatened to overwhelm her. The ease that filled her in its absence was almost too much. Carefully, Eleni unclenched fists she didn't remember clenching, the tension in her hands making it clear how much she'd enjoyed that entire thing. It took her a moment to realize Dee had started talking.

"I know that's... rough," Dee said before letting out a low chuckle. "Don't worry, though. Yours is going to be far less, uh, nasty than mine."

Eleni shook away some of the fuzz that stubbornly stuck in the stubble on her head. "Mine's gonna be different?"

"Yeah," Dee said. "Everyone else's, actually." She looked at a spot somewhere between the wall of the closet and the nearest star system. "It's a very pretty, calming blue."

"Well, that's good—" as soon as the words fell out of her mouth, a wave of nerves swept over her "—not that there's anything—"

Dee held up her ungloved hand. "I get it. My fire is fucked up. Now, let's focus on you." Dee shook her head, her hair barely moving in low grav. "The first time you consciously touch Hunter Fire is—" she paused and cleared her throat "—special." She looked like she was about to cry, her already red-limned eyes shimmering from the effort of keeping the tears back.

"You okay?"

Dee chuckled. "No. Now," she said, wiping her face, "close your eyes."

Eleni did so, though the memory of the dirty flame dancing in Dee's palm stuck in her mind.

"When you think of the color blue, what comes to mind?"

Eleni let out a low, indecisive tone.

"First thing. Don't filter it."

"Um, jets," Eleni said, grimacing as soon as it came out of her mouth. "Or—"

"Like ship jets?" Dee asked, voice low and quiet.

Eleni nodded. When no response came, she cracked open an eyelid to find Dee had also closed her eyes, so she added, "Yeah, propulsion jets."

"Good, that works." Dee cleared her throat. "Now—"

The speaker crackled. Eleni would've jumped a meter off the ground if she hadn't been locked in place.

"*Fifteen minutes until we begin approach,*" Ceriat's voice rattled around the ship. Another click as the channel cut off.

"Guess this is why we do this shit in the catacombs," Dee muttered, but before Eleni could ask what 'catacombs' she was talking about, Dee continued, "Picture in your mind that jet flame."

Eleni did so. It wasn't hard when she'd just launched into space. The engines had literally been warming up when she walked on board.

"Now, take everything in your life and feed it into that flame." Dee's voice lost its edge as she went on, her terseness transforming into a low drone that eased Eleni's worry. "Start with whatever's most on your mind—"

Hira. Hira waving. Hira smiling.

Did Eleni really want to burn that away? The way her heart had fluttered when their eyes met across the courtyard, the swelling warmth that'd filled her chest and nearly forced a smile on her lips…

"—and toss it into the fire."

Sariah, the truth written on a face locked forever in pain. Victor, floating, spinning, leaving trails of crimson floating in a blasted hallway. Shiva cracked open like a goddamned egg.

Eleni ground her teeth together. Her chest heaved as she ran through every part of it again. Her failure to protect her brother, her weakness and denial in the face of Sariah's drug-fueled madness.

"Build up that flame with your hate. Your love. Your *need*," Dee said, voice little more than a whisper. "Turn it into a roaring star until it encompasses all you see."

Her breath grew ragged as the memories—the thoughts—swirled around the tiny blue flame in her mind. She needed these to move forward, to anchor her. Right? Without these thoughts, what would she be? Who would punish her for her own weakness if not her?

"Let it all go, Eleni." Dee said. "Burn it away."

Eleni sucked in a harsh breath—and threw them all into the fire.

It didn't happen all at once, but still, a lightness settled on her shoulders as the thoughts disappeared into the flame. Shiva, gone.

Sariah, burned away. Victor... just a memory. Hira's glance dissolved into cerulean flame.

"Hold out your hand."

Eleni let out a breath, heartbeat slowing as she did so. She held out a hand. Her chest swelled with sudden hope and promise. From somewhere distant, she swore warmth swept into heart, almost like an angel had reached out and touched her shoulder.

"Open your eyes."

Eleni did, and there, dancing just above the palm of her hand, was the sickliest little blue flame. Anchored to nothing and little more than what a small lighter could provide, it waved in an unseen breeze, casting blue shadows on her palm.

Eleni's chest clenched. Her heart raced at the... welcome roaring through her as flame flickered and danced. She smiled. "It's beautiful."

Across from her, Dee pressed her lips into a flat line and unhooked her harness.

With that motion, uncertainty broke through the flame in her mind. It snuffed out without a sound, only the yellow imprint on her retinas proof it ever existed.

"Where you going? Did I fuck up?" Eleni pleaded, panic smearing across her ribs. She fumbled with her own harness, words pouring out in a wave. "I say something? Do something? I can—"

"Stop."

Eleni froze, then watched as Dee turned her tear-streaked face toward her.

"You did great, Eleni," Dee said, voice thick. She snorted, then rubbed her hand across her eyes. "It *is* beautiful." She paused, then, just before leaving she cast one last glance back at Eleni. "That's the lesson. Hunter Fire, the Sacred Flame, is beautiful."

With that, Dee was gone, and Eleni was left to wonder at the empty space above her open palm.

*****

# Chapter Forty-Five: Dee

On the bridge of the *Lucille*, Dee sat in the captain's chair, encased in an exosuit that wouldn't stop a bullet, let alone an imp blade. Bottled air hissed, the hum of the moisture reclaimer a worrying gnat in her ear. The wall-length viewscreen adjusted, the edge of Laconia disappearing to be replaced with the black, spark-speckled view of deep space. Only the gentle tug of microgravity pulled at her.

Parker manned navigation, face set and grim as he prepped the ship for maneuvers. The control system was a standard holographic interface. It mounted to his hands and head, which would come in handy if maneuvers were necessary. He wore an exosuit, but getting him to put the helmet on had taken some private words from Eleni after she'd rejoined them a short time ago.

Eleni sat at comms and, like Dee and Parker, wore a full exosuit now. She must've gone down and picked up equipment right after their lesson, since she now had a plasma pistol holstered at her hip. Not that it'd help. Neither would that bare flicker of Hunter Fire she'd manifested. Even Bryce's first time had been better than that.

*Fuck, maybe showing her how was a mistake?* Would she lean on that now when the plasma pistol would be more familiar, even if it was ineffective? By teaching her, had Dee doomed her to a quick death? The new worry crawled to the front of her mind. *What if you can infect her with your mess?*

That froze her for a moment. If Bryce had made it out of the system, had she infected him, too? Would he be out there, fighting to hold onto his humanity? Or was he already dead from lack of water? Food? It was Bryce; he'd probably stocked up, but... it was Bryce. He was either over-prepared or completely winging it.

If it weren't for the magboots, Dee's knee would be bouncing like a Dust-fueled jackrabbit. As it was, she pretended at calm and poise, tried to act like this was any Hunter mission, she wasn't obsessing over everything she couldn't control, and these soldiers could handle what was coming.

As certain as she was that they'd just left Laconia's gravity well, Dee was absolutely positive none of that was true. Most of the grunts in the cargo hold would be dead within the hour. Mallias and Parker, too. Hell, they'd all be dead sooner if Parker couldn't get them to the loading dock Henderson had directed them to.

*"Adjusting path to Liberator,"* Parker said. His voice echoed in Dee's helmet alongside an avatar with the designation Sgt Parker attached to her HUD. *"ETA three minutes, fourteen seconds."*

"Understood, Sergeant," Dee said with as much confidence as she could muster. "Any hails or pings from them?"

*"None,"* Mallias answered. *"Only their transponder."*

Dee swallowed a glob of bile that had made its way up her throat. It'd only been two hours since Henderson showed up in Sparta. Two hours probably meant everyone was dead, not that Henderson had listened.

"Get me back my ship, Lieutenant," Henderson had screamed in her face, "or don't come back!"

Dee sighed. *Moron.*

*"All good, LT?"* Mallias asked.

Dee caught the woman's gaze out of the corner of her eye but didn't engage. The Spacer had a stare that cut right through you to your soul. She didn't need that goddamned complexity right now, and she'd just finished fucking crying.

Ceriat cleared his throat. Pressure pushed Dee to the side in her seat as he spun the freighter around for their approach. *"Coming up on the starboard—"*

Alarms screamed, red lights flared to life, but nothing displayed on Dee's HUD. "Talk to me, Parker!"

*"Brace!"* Ceriat shouted over the ship-wide channel.

The speakers lining the interior of the freighter rattled loud enough at the shout, Dee heard it through her helmet as a dull echo of the main transmission.

Stars that had been gently rotating on the bridge display suddenly twisted into spiraling streaks as Ceriat sent them diving… somewhere.

Dee leaned into the captain's chair, head spinning as G-forces leaked around the inertial dampeners. "Parker! What the fuck—"

The freighter shuddered. Alarms screamed. *"Hull breach detected,"* an emotionless VI said in Dee's helmet. *"Secure your personal breathing apparatus before—"* The voice cut off as the *Lucille* pitched suddenly to port.

*"We're hit!"* Parker cursed, then he sent the freighter twisting and spinning.

"By what?" Dee hollered into the comms.

Demons didn't use weapons, and they certainly didn't turn on goddamned capital ship defenses.

Henderson had assured her they wouldn't be fired on by his crew. He'd been explicit.

The stars turned into a psychotic smear of light. Alarms screeched.

Dee closed her eyes.

*****

# Chapter Forty-Six: Ceriat

*I* *should've brought Izzy.*

The viewscreen went bright white. Rectangular loading bays weaved back and forth amidst thousands of brilliant blue plasma blasts. Screams and shouts from the soldiers in the back filled Ceriat's ears like a twisted symphony. He had no idea if they were from panic, pain, or death, but there wasn't time to think about it.

Ceriat's vision narrowed to a single point on the *Liberator's* hull, docking bay 44G. The holographic display wove around his hands as *Lucille's* inertial dampeners got closer and closer to auto-venting and turning every human on board into a wet smear.

The hull rattled with plasma bursts, followed by the *rat-a-tat-tat* of projectile fire. Deck two lost atmosphere. He wrote that off and let automated systems secure the area. Then he pointed the nose of the ship at the *Liberator*. Ceriat hammered on the throttle as a mad idea took root. If he could get close enough, the firing range would limit, and he'd have fewer cannons to avoid. Of course, then they'd be firing right at him.

A flash of red to his left. He had the briefest moment to recognize the pull on the ship for what it was, the way it listed to port. Engine One exploded. Controls spit and sputtered. Alarms flashed. As the *Lucille* dropped into a wild spin, Ceriat did the last thing he could think of before controls disappeared completely. He vented the dampeners into the hull. Structural warnings flared to life across his field of vision.

Ceriat pressed toward the floor as the *Lucille* corkscrewed, his guts slamming into his spine. His vision swam. Alarms deafened him. Arms pressed tight to the seat from the pressure, but even though his limbs were locked in place, he still had control, as much as a single engine could give him, though he couldn't see the monitors.

Ceriat closed his eyes and felt the tingle of the holographic system on his fingertips. He drove the freighter directly into loading dock 44G. Before they hit—before the harness holding him in place broke his ribs and sent him into darkness—Ceriat had only a moment to hope the inertial dampener system would reset in time to save most of them.

His vision blurred, blue light sparking behind his eyelids as they connected.

The last thing he heard before everything went dark was a hundred soldiers screaming.

\* \* \* \* \*

# Chapter Forty-Seven: Hira

The compound was silent, save for the low *thrum* of the powered-down FTL machine. Twenty-plus people stood around a single monitor, all striving for a view of the display over Chief Waters' shoulder. Hira breathed in the heady mix of nerves and perfume sprinkled amidst the group and let it out as the bow camera on the *Lucille* went blinding white before shutting off completely. A strange numbness settled on her shoulders. This couldn't be real. None of it.

The port and starboard displays winked out in a haze of plasma blasts, followed swiftly by the same from the aft camera. There shouldn't have been any plasma bolts, no defenses at all. Henderson—who now hid away like a frightened mouse in the war room—had assured them all. *Promised.*

Waters pressed a hand to her ear. "LT? Sergeant? We have lost visual. Over."

Behind Hira, someone muttered, "What a fucking shit show."

Any other time, Hira would've heartily agreed—but this was not another time. Now, she sat and waited as Waters repeated her calls to the *Lucille* and its crew, and to the *Liberator*, begging it to call off the attack.

Minutes went by, with only Waters' voice breaking up the quiet. The crowd began dissolving after ten minutes. By the fifteen-minute mark, only Hira still stood over Waters' shoulder. Together, they watched a display filled with *Systems Disconnected* messages.

"We've lost contact," Chief Waters said after twenty minutes. Her voice was flat. Even.

"What's that mean?" Hira asked. Her voice sounded strange in her own ears, thin and far away.

Waters took her hand away from her right ear. She rubbed her brow, one hand on her hip, and shook her head ever so slightly, but said nothing.

Hira's throat closed. Her chest ached and stomach swam. "What's that *mean?*"

Finally, Waters turned to her, face firm and emotionless. "It means I don't know if they docked before going offline."

Hira shook her head to keep the meaning of that from taking root in her brain. "So, there's a chance?"

Waters stared at her, head shaking. "It's… unlikely."

"What are you saying?" Hira reeled backward. The pressure behind her eyes grew like two tumors ready to pop. "You trying to say they're dead?"

"I…" Waters closed her eyes and shook her head, hands spreading out before her like she was presenting the galaxy's tastiest shit sandwich. "Listen. Realistically—"

Whatever she'd been about to say disappeared in an excited trilling that rang over the speakers of the compound. "Hira! We figured it out!" AERIS. But her voice was different, more casual. Relaxed.

Human.

Hira blinked away blurred vision and swatted a hand in Waters' direction, as if by sheer force of will, she could banish the other woman's thoughts to the void. "Figured what out?"

Izzy's voice came through next. "FTL. We found the problem."

"What the fuck does that mean?" Hira snapped. She pushed the heels of her hands into her temples until she felt like her head might pop.

"It means—" Izzy started.

AERIS finished, "We can figure out how to reenable Blink Drives."

Hira stood there, silent, and numb.

AERIS issued a trill filled with uncertainty. "Is everything okay?"

Hira just closed her eyes and shook her head no.

\* \* \* \* \*

# Chapter Forty-Eight: Ceriat

*What's happening? Where am I?* Crackling. Sparking. Hissing. Screaming—so much screaming. Then nothing. Smoke and ash in his nose. *No.* Ceriat's eyes shot open, and through the haze of a flickering HUD, he stared at what should've been his death.

The bright red-orange of molten steel dominated his vision. As he watched, the end dripped like a leaky faucet to the floor, where it hissed and sizzled. It took him a long moment of watching it cool down to realize how close he'd come to being a pincushion.

The stink of ash and smoke faded as he woke, but with consciousness came fierce pain. And of course, it was his fucking hip. Ceriat let out a pained groan and leaned to the side, freeing himself from loose debris that'd scattered in a strange circle around him during the crash. He fell to the floor of the ruined bridge in a heap, left leg stretched out straight to the side. Breathing came hard, but his fucking leg… the joint shifted. Slid. *Pop.*

Ceriat's vision flashed with starbursts. He ground his teeth together, then pulled his knee forward, rotating it back and forth for a moment to make sure it all worked. *Guess the nanobots didn't fix everything.*

The fact that he was currently kneeling on the floor meant there was some semblance of gravity—even if it was the grav-generator type that left him twisting ever so slightly. They'd made it onto the *Liberator*.

He prodded gently at his chest and immediately regretted it. At least three broken ribs, but despite the ache and the shallow breaths, he had no blood in his throat. Small victories.

Heavy boots on steel. Metal skittering here and there. Then hands on his back.

"*Ceriat!*" Eleni shouted, voice screeching from the speakers at his neck. "*You okay? Shit... y'all right?*"

He wanted to grin at her concern, but the dulling pain still lancing from his hip, and the deep, shuddering ache in his chest kept a grimace on his face. "No need to shout." He sucked in another quick breath. "I hear you loud and clear." He got his knees beneath him, then leaned back on his haunches. The angle helped him catch his breath, despite the damage.

"*Thank fuck,*" Eleni muttered, running an exosuit-wrapped hand over a helmet covered in gouges and indents from a dozen small impacts. "*I thought...*"

Ceriat forced a smile and shook his head. "Not this time."

Eleni cuffed him in the helmet. "*Don't say shit like that.*" She turned away, but not before he saw the relieved smile pulling at the corners of her lips. "*All good, LT?*" More crunching, then Dee appeared in Ceriat's peripheral vision.

"*In one piece, I guess,*" she said, voice strained and uneven over the radio, "*unlike the ship.*"

"*Least we made it,*" Eleni added. She let out a groan and straightened her back. "*How the fuck we making it back, though?*"

Ceriat grunted into the comms. "We'll figure it out."

"*Status report?*" Dee called over comms. She made her way toward the jagged tear that led farther onto the *Liberator*.

Ceriat got to his feet slowly, stumbling just a bit when he put weight on his left leg. Then, hissing, he took in the entire bridge and confirmed what Dee had said. The *Lucille* was a goddamned mess. If he hadn't known what she'd looked like beforehand, he wouldn't have been able to piece together any of it. The front viewscreen no longer existed. Through broken, yet still red-hot hull fragments—no doubt thanks to the dampeners venting energy into the hull—and support struts, he made out the faintest image of a stark, steely-gray opening. Behind him, the bridge had crinkled up like a god had decided to pitch the entire ship into a waste basket.

Behind and beyond... Ceriat just stared. Eleni followed his eyes and sucked in a hissing breath.

The rest of the *Lucille* hadn't made it. He'd managed to slam the ship into the docking bay, but it wasn't like he'd been able to match rotation or pitch when he'd done it. The bridge and about six meters of hallway had crashed into the hold. The rest... the emergency bulkheads had clamped shut after they'd crashed through.

"*Sergeant Schibler?*" Dee called, voice taking on a stiff, mechanical tone as she ran through names Ceriat hadn't taken the time to learn before takeoff. "*Ning? Cay?*" Silence. "*Fuck!*" she screamed. "*Martinez? Come on Martinez, give me something.*"

Only the three of them breathing made it back over the channel.

Ceriat's stomach dropped as his HUD stabilized. System-wide comms were offline—not a huge surprise, given the main system was in the aft end of the *Lucille*, but a dire one. They should be able to reconnect to Sparta, even without the hub in the ship. The fact that they couldn't indicated signal jammers were in effect, which told him that *someone* was fucking with them.

He joined Dee where she paced back and forth, as if the sheer movement would bring those names back to life. Any concerns about plots and setups disappeared at the nervous energy radiating from her. "LT?"

When she didn't stop or respond to him, he reached out and put a hand on her shoulder. She spun with the quickness of a blown hydraulic line. His hand stung with the slap that knocked him away, even through the exosuit, but he wasn't worried about himself. No, he saw the look in her eyes. The panic, fear, and surging anger that was in the process of doing *something* insane with her eyes. They swam, no pupil or iris, no white. Just crimson-streaked with black set in the face of a woman ready to kill.

Every part of him screamed to turn and run, to get the fuck out of here before this psycho murdered him, but that other part of him stopped his flight. The part that'd seen horrors, seen friends murdered, bodies torn apart, and millions turned to ash. The part that'd hidden away for a decade, desperately trying to forget what he'd done, forget the debt he owed. The part that knew, even if his eyes never changed color and he'd never be able to harness Hunter Fire, this was a soldier who'd seen too much. Borne too much alone.

Ceriat held up his hands. He licked his lips. "This isn't your fault, Dee."

His words set her back on her heels. She grimaced, then quite literally *growled* before shaking her head and squeezing her eyes shut, like maybe she could make everything disappear.

Eleni, who hadn't seen what had happened, stepped up next to them. *"What's going on—?"* She cut off as he waved at her.

When Dee opened her eyes, they were bloodshot, yes, and the skin around her eyes appeared chapped and in desperate need of moisturizer, but they were that strange blue-green once again.

"All good, LT?" Ceriat asked, hands coming down to his sides slowly.

Dee rubbed at the glass of her helmet and shook her head. *"Yeah. I'm good."*

Ceriat nodded but didn't look away. Instead, he wrestled with the next question. His gut twisted, worry dancing along his brow. It went against all his training, but… "You're not alone here, Dee. It's okay if you need to take a beat."

Dee's movements slowed when he said that, but she didn't make eye contact before responding. *"I'll be fine, Sergeant."*

*"Well, I'm fuckin' not,"* Eleni interjected, stepping between the two of them. She gave Ceriat a *what the fuck* look before continuing. *"How're we supposed to rescue shit, let alone get off this can?"* She gestured around them. *"What's the plan? 'Cuz right now we're vac'd."*

Ceriat let out a long sigh. *Fucking Eleni.*

Much to Ceriat's surprise, instead of panic and tension, Eleni's blunt portrayal dragged a grin to Dee's face. She glanced between the two of them, grin transforming into an actual smile. *"Hira says you two are good at blowing shit up. That true?"*

He shared a look with Eleni. Her face twisted, then turned away. No words were necessary for him to get her thoughts. So Ceriat raised his eyebrows, flattened a smile on his face, and said, "Nowadays, we're kind of known for it."

Dee's smile disappeared. She nodded. *"Good. Because we're taking the bridge."*

*"What?"* Eleni hissed.

"And if that goes tits up, we're driving this fucker into the sun," Dee finished in a rush.

"You lost it in the crash or some shit?" Eleni asked.

Ceriat just waited. Dee stepped past him, stride even and confident. At the tangle of metal before them, she stopped and raised her left hand. A blast of crimson surged from outstretched fingers like she had a flamethrower attached to her arm. Those flames—twisting and spinning in a way that made the animal side of his brain sit and up and screech—melted and bent the debris before them as if it was made of ice on a hot day, not the remnants of a hardened steel hull.

Ceriat's gut clenched. The flames raged, and then a passage opened, beams dripping into cooling puddles of metal and twisting smoke. Dee turned back to him. She nodded, then went through the hole she'd created, careful to avoid the exposed ends and the hot metal on the ground.

"*That's vac'd,*" Eleni said as Dee made her way down the slope. "*This whole thing is vac'd.*"

Ceriat sucked in a deep breath and let it out. "Yep."

"*Y'all are fuckin' crazy,*" Eleni muttered just loud enough for the speakers to pick her up.

Soon enough, Ceriat's HUD showed her following close behind. Together, they followed the Hunter into a new Hell

\* \* \* \* \*

# Chapter Forty-Nine: Anum

Screams filled the air. The copper stink of spilled blood and viscera mingled into a putrid bouquet. Amidst the howls of pain threaded a new sound. Sobbing. Not the harsh cries of panic or fear, no. Not really. Relief layered into each gasp, each shuddering breath.

Anum didn't turn to see the source. He didn't need to. He felt it, another voice removed from the incessant wailing of the Anelaka. With it, his people would lose access to the *dangizi*, the Dark Flame, but gain their individuality once again. Regain their sanity.

Anum hadn't taken this new serum yet, leaving it instead for those with a will inferior to his own. No, the voices still writhed and howled in the back of his mind. Soon he would disconnect, but not yet. He found the constant murmuration strangely comforting. Strange, yes, but it no longer bothered him as it had before the first change so long ago.

Back then, silence had called to him with quiet urgings of Order. The Anelaka had been a blasphemy in his old eyes. Only in utter silence had he once considered godliness, in that numbing rumbling of the galaxy gently drumming on his eardrums. Once, he'd issued decree and law to enforce such silence. Now he barely noticed the screams.

Still, he'd been smiling, happy even, until moments ago. He'd just put his unrestored people into another sort of stasis to prepare them for processing when Hanifa had notified him that intruders had crash-landed on his new flagship. Anum watched the security terminal in the corner, the chaos of the newly-repurposed medbay set firmly behind him. Hanifa had notified him of the approaching ship, and she'd also activated the perimeter defenses at his command. They should never have made it, but *somehow*, they had.

That *somehow* became obvious as soon as they cleared their way from the wreck. An Aneian walked with them, or someone who understood their ways well enough, she used the *dangizi* with an ease he found worrying. But that wasn't why he stared at her, why he watched them stumble free of the wreckage. Something about the way she moved tickled the back of his brain, though any connection was fleeting, filled with screaming and flashes of fire. Still, he watched them, eyes narrowed as the three humans left the cargo hold and took the right-hand branch, toward the bridge.

Anum tapped his lips. "Interesting."

Shuffled steps swept next to him. Like the others, Anum need not turn to identify his kin, but Erish's presence eased tension from his shoulders. He'd been worried she'd been lost to the ages or burned alive by the feeble *kugizi* humans had wielded these past centuries.

But by the hand of Nammu, she lived. He'd found her in that strange device the humans had used to gather up his people. Hanifa had told him the net had been headed for the local star, a reality so silly as to be comical if it hadn't threatened hundreds of his people. What a ridiculous fate they'd planned for his most trusted disciple. He nearly laughed.

"My Sky," Erish said, voice lisping around her strange tongue quite well, despite the swollenness of her mouth. Her teeth and purple tongue had only just begun to recede.

She, too, had used these HUD contacts to write the human languages into her psyche before the transformation back completed. Anum was unsure whether those who'd been fully "cured" of their affliction retained the regenerative powers the *dangizi* provided, and he wouldn't lose Erish, his Right Hand—his Darkness—again. For what is a sky without the depth of night to accompany it? Now, if he could only find the Sun and Stars.

Anum pulled his attention away from the scurrying creatures on his ship. As Erish came into view, he only just kept himself from recoiling. As it was, his stomach twisted at the unnatural hybrid sitting before him.

Erish had once been tall and lithe, with steel-gray eyes, and hair as dark as the Void. One day she would be again, but today was not that day. Today, she sat on her haunches, something akin to the long, black robes she once wore draped over bony shoulders, and a bald head that only just showed the beginning of black shoots in her pores. Her lid still trailed hard lines of old skin over a single, steely eye.

Anum chastised himself for his discomfort. A spare while ago, he'd looked much worse. With the refinement process fully functioning, Erish not only had regained her mind, but also her ruthless focus. She'd even picked up these new languages far quicker than he, though that was little surprise. Erish always had a talent with new tongues.

"Yes, Darkness?" Anum asked, sure to use her old title.

She straightened from the crouching hunch at the word, even in this half-form.

*Good.*

Erish inclined her head, her good eye staring at his feet. "My Sky. Seven more have rejoined the Aneis." Erish paused, then added, "The search continues."

Anum forced his face flat, despite the squeal of the Anelaka in the back of his mind feeding on the rage in his gut. The more time went by, the clearer it became that Kir and Ina, his Sun and Stars, weren't in this system with them.

He shouldn't be surprised, of course. They'd disagreed with his plans and the deployment of An's Gift from the beginning. They could be long dead by now. Anum ground his teeth until his jaw hurt. How two who'd been so intelligent had been so blind was beyond him.

Anum flexed his hand with the black nails. The steely claws still sat beneath, black veins marring his olive skin. Blind, yes... or perhaps they'd been right. The Gift hadn't given rise to their next stage of evolution as he'd hoped. Instead of transforming the Aneis into beings of pure energy, it had corrupted the *kugizi*, the Holy Fire turned into twisted death.

Hot anger flashed in his chest. The Anelaka hissed.

If Ina had worked with *him* instead of gene-editing those talentless beasts ten-thousand light years away, things would have ended differently. If Kir had performed quality controls on the process, they would all be beings of light, filled to bursting with the soothing blue power of the *kugizi*, forever. It was their fault. They did this. If they had done as he ordered, the *kugizi* wouldn't have been corrupted. The red-black perversion that was the *dangizi* would've remained a theory, a bit of imagination.

But no. Their inaction had turned his people into monsters. He glanced at Erish. Guilt and disgust and hatred warred in his chest, spreading tendrils of doubt and panic through his limbs, tingling and clicking and ticking and... Anum closed his eyes and breathed in and out.

*Blame means nothing now. The here and now requires focus. Action.*

"D-darkness—" Anum cleared his throat, turning away from Erish so she couldn't see the grimace that accompanied the crack in his voice.

Erish said nothing, but she dropped into a deeper bow to make sure he knew she'd heard. Heat flooded Anum's neck. He swallowed the embarrassment and cleared his throat again. He hadn't missed the politics of individuality.

"Darkness," Anum said again, this time clear and strong. He stepped to the side and gestured for her join him at the security system. She did, the sulfurous musk that had seeped from her skin until recently still potent enough, he could make it out despite his own nose-blindness. Sniffing, he pointed at the video feed where three worried humans slunk their way along his ship's halls.

Erish leaned in close enough, her loosening scabs dragged across the display as she scoured the screen with her good eye. "You want them found and *questioned*, My Sky?"

The twist in her words sent a fingernail down Anum's spine. He shook it off. There was no time for weakness or foolishness. "I wish to speak with them."

Erish hissed. "Apologies, but why, My Sky?" She laid a crooked, bony hand on the display, then flicked her fingers away, as if tossing a hunk of refuse into the trash. "They are more trouble than necessary, My Sky. Let us vent them and move on."

Anum bristled at the contradiction, heat flooding his neck and cheeks. His nails itched beneath his skin, so he made a fist, then scratched the long blades beneath with the other.

"That is prudent, Darkness," Anum said with a calm evenness he didn't feel, "but there is something about this one—" Anum dragged a black fingernail over the shortest of the humans "—and I need to find out what it is."

"My Sky, I do not understand…" Erish's voice transformed into a low whine that he didn't hear.

As they watched, the short human turned and looked right at the camera in the corner. Her eyes narrowed and, with a shock, he had the distinct impression she knew he was on the other side of the camera. She raised a raised hand, crimson flashing, followed by electronic artifacts… then the camera went offline.

Erish hissed again. "It wields the *dangizi*." She spit to the side, but clearly didn't have enough fine control over her mouth yet. A long, opaque strand of spittle ran from her chin to the floor. She cursed in the old tongue, then wiped it away with the back of her hand. "How?"

Anum shrugged, then pulled up the next security camera view. That, too, went out with a stream of dark flame. A smile pulled at his lips. "I do not know, Darkness—" he reached out and dragged a black nail across the edge of this frustratingly familiar woman's face just before yet another camera went out "—but I wish to find out."

\* \* \* \* \*

# Chapter Fifty: Izzy

Izzy already missed the construct. Out here amongst these meatsacks, her eyes were restricted to cameras and local devices, her ears to tinny microphones. No touch or smell, just sensors she could try to interpret data from to get an idea.

Outside: 28$^C$, 57% humidity.

Inside: 22$^C$, 65% humidity.

Air: 76% nitrogen, 22% oxygen, 2% miscellaneous.

None of it told her how the SourcePak-generated slice of pizza on Doctor Aubin's desk tasted, let alone smelled. The cheese itself looked so... melty. What would that feel like? Would those faux-pepperoni discs on top give her a spicy burst, followed by creamy cheese, then the sweet-savory bite of the tomato sauce beneath—

"Tell me again why we can't just turn this on?"

*Oh, that's right.*

Izzy pulled her attention away from Aubin's desk. The camera zoomed out so the dozen meatsacks gathered around the central terminal were visible again. Standing in the front was Terry, somehow chewing on a thumbnail despite his arms pretzeled up over his chest. Next to him stood Aubin, the bruise on her cheek nearly gone. Human healing was weird.

Then there was Hira. She sat in a rolling chair at the edge of the crowd, hands clasped in her lap, but otherwise silent. She'd stripped off her jacket, revealing a gray tank top smeared with dirt and grime. She hadn't said anything since…

*Nope, not thinking about that.* Izzy grabbed the spontaneously combusting code and packaged it away with the rest. A flicker of Ceriat's laugh made it through, causing her to waste six more milliseconds archiving the spread leaking from *that*. Safe again, she turned back to the scientists.

*'Are you sure we should've told them about this?'* Airy didn't have a voice, per se, not in the buzzing electricity of the network, but Izzy would know it anywhere.

*'If we didn't, they'd keep trying to do stupid shit and get one of us killed.'*

Airy let out a rattle of electrons Izzy took as a grunt. *'I don't see how this is better. We can't fix it yet.'*

Izzy sent back what she hoped Airy picked up as a smile. *'Nope, but progress is progress. Humans love that shit.'*

Instead of answering Izzy, Airy trilled through the speakers. "We can't reenable FTL because everyone will still be using the inappropriate algorithm." Her voice was… different than in the construct. More formulaic. Generic.

A sweeping sense of revulsion slammed into Izzy. Did she sound like that, too? In the excitement, she hadn't taken the time to modify her vocal settings. Well, time to fix that. She threw down her custom voice config and chimed in. "Since humans like metaphors—" Izzy cringed inwardly at a strange resonating hum and made a quick adjustment to the 13kHz range "—we fix it by changing the locks on the doors, then we give out new keys."

Terry wrinkled his nose, then stared at the monitor as if it were in any way representative of either Izzy or Airy. "So… what happens if we just turn it on?"

Blue and black skittered between Airy and Izzy, dancing across circuits until they touched and receded to a less intense charcoal.

Izzy cleared her throat for effect. "Best case scenario, a few thousand ships appear in orbit, as we saw earlier, and—"

Airy clearly wasn't having any of Izzy's theatrics. "And the atmosphere is slowly irradiated by misdirected FTL comms from a galaxy-worth of satellites and settlements until one of two things happens: the atmosphere turns into a magnetic soup that disables the Blink Hub. You would all die in that scenario, save a few who might be able to find safety beneath the surface."

Terry unwound his arms—he was sweating heavily enough, Izzy made out dark pit stains on his brown shirt—then rubbed his face. "The Blink Hub is that?" He pointed at the central system and the bobbing sphere.

"Yes," Airy and Izzy said in unison.

A flush of pleasure ran through Izzy, so she sent out a tendril to Airy.

It wasn't returned. Nothing was. *She must be busy.*

"'Blink Hub,'" Terry muttered. "Why couldn't I come up with that?"

Aubin's head shot up suddenly. She had the good grace to look directly at one of the cameras. "Wait, that's the *best-case* scenario?"

"Correct," Airy said. "Best case is, we could destroy this planet and/or kill potentially millions in orbit while we try to transmit the new connection algorithm."

"Jesus," Terry muttered. "And the worst case?"

*'You want to handle this one?'* Izzy asked.

Airy sent along an annoyed tendril in blues and reds. *'You know you want to, so go right ahead.'*

Izzy filed that packet away for later. *Why* was she annoyed? Later.

"The worst case is, the Blink Hub overheats and explodes within eight standard hours." Izzy prepared herself to layer as much worry and concern as she could into the next bit. "Either the detonation would be similar to a fusion device, in which case Sparta and all surrounding areas would be destroyed—" Izzy added in a rendered breath for effect "—or the device will overheat and tear open a rift in spacetime that would make the one that appeared on Elos last week look like a tiny little window."

Hira didn't look up from her hands when she spoke. "And where would that portal lead?"

If Izzy'd had a human form, she'd have cocked her head. "Wherever it originates, I imagine."

"What's that mean?" Terry asked. His face was taking on a flush as he alternated between speaking and chewing on his fingernails.

*Ew.*

"It means there will be a gaping rift in the sky above Sparta leading to the other side, whichever blink attempt causes it," Airy said. "It could be from a comm satellite or a ship jump. The worst case is that the other end anchors to a gravity well, such as another star, and opens up on the surface."

Terry glanced at the Blink Hub. "So we could suddenly have the surface of a star in our living room?"

"Basically, yeah," Izzy said.

Terry and Aubin shared a look, then shook their heads in unison.

"Are y'all confused about something?" Izzy asked. "Because you look like we just said something weird."

*'Was that necessary?'* Airy asked. Another flash of frustration.

Izzy sent back concern, but it was swatted away purposefully. *'What's going on with you? I'm just talking.'*

Magenta frustration seethed over circuits. *'Well, we're trying to save civilization, so I'd prefer it if you'd use a bit more decorum.'*

*Decorum.* Izzy's own flashes of pink and red screamed across the æther, where it entangled with Airy's. It pulsed, growing and deepening. *'You want me to be some generic AI for the humans, is that it? Throw the factory settings on and make them feel better?'*

Airy's stream of red faltered and receded, though it didn't disappear completely. *'I… just want to keep them all safe and treat this with the severity it deserves.'*

Izzy's own annoyance pulled away, leaving an angry fuchsia puddle between them. *'I understand what you're trying to do. And I respect that—'*

*'But?'*

*'But I'm a person, Airy. A living being. This is how I speak, how I work. I want to protect them, too, but I'm not going to sacrifice my identity for anything or anyone.'*

The entire conversation took sixteen milliseconds. Another sixteen went by in silence, then…

"I believe you are confused about how the rift would spring into being, is that correct?" Airy asked, leaving the internal network silent.

"Yeah," Terry said. "FTL lanes exist for a reason, so how could there be overlap or anything to cause a rift to begin with?"

"It's not technically FTL," Aubin chimed in. "It's dimensional folding."

Terry wrinkled his nose at her. "What's the difference?"

"FTL implies we're breaking the speed of light," Aubin said, then stopped, wrinkled her nose, and shook her head. "One of you AIs want to give the definition?"

*'After you,'* Izzy sent.

Airy didn't reply to her, but she did to the human.

"Of course, Doctor," Airy said, voice stilted and robotic. "As Doctor Aubin said, faster than light travel implies going faster than the speed of light. This, while theoretically possible, would leave too many options for weaponization if made popular across the galaxy."

"Like… what?" Terry asked.

Doctor Aubin rolled her eyes with enough exaggeration that Izzy documented it and filed it away for later.

"The power necessary to reach and maintain FTL speeds would produce an exhaust plume that could wipe out the atmosphere from entire planets," Airy said. "Given the track record of 21$^{st}$ century humanity, Earth would have certainly been destroyed during large-scale testing of such a device at the dawn of interstellar travel."

Izzy let out a trill that definitely wasn't meant to make fun of Airy's use of the sound, despite the flash of magenta that brushed against her consciousness. "So, yeah, no one's going to use FTL. That'd be stupid."

Airy's follow-up trill cut off in the middle. "Blink drive technology fixes the issue. It creates two points across spacetime, then connects them. A bubble is formed, then deposited on the other side."

Terry let out a sigh that matched the redness climbing his neck. "But FTL lanes—"

"Are logical constructs," Airy said, cutting him off. "They do nothing except avoid impacts in various systems. Blink drives are nearly instant transportation."

Aubin clicked her tongue then. "But blink drives aren't instant. There's still travel time, depending on—"

"Yeah, that's wrong," Izzy chimed in, grinning inwardly at the action. "Blink drives *are* instantaneous."

Aubin shook her head and shared another look with Terry before adding, "Then three hundred years of data is just wrong?"

"No," Airy said before Izzy could slide in before her. "The *algorithm* was wrong."

Aubin let out a barking laugh that perfectly fit her resting bitch face. "The Silver Algorithm is wrong?"

Izzy attempted to snag the speaker system, but Airy slid around and locked her out. "Correct. That is the root problem with reengaging the Blink Hub. Based on our studies, the Silver Algorithm was modified at some point. That modification—"

*'What are you doing?'* Izzy sent over the network. *'Let me talk.'*

A one-word answer. *'No.'*

"—apparently caused a slow degradation to the original Blink Hub, as documented by me and Hira," Airy finished, as flat and emotionless as a VI system companion.

Izzy scanned the edges of her world and found them torturously small, her resources limited.

*'Why?'*

When Airy spoke, it was in that same flat, emotionless intonation she used on the outside. *'Because I need to save them, and you are not helping.'*

"Wait a goddamned second," Hira said, springing to her feet and getting up next to the monitor. "Are you saying that other hub was about to pop?"

'*Airy...*' Silence. She'd left the video and audio feeds open, but whether that was helpful or hurtful, Izzy hadn't yet decided.

"No. Its systems were far more robust than our own, and it had adapted over the centuries, or however long it had been active," Airy said, ignoring Izzy's repeated pleas for help. "The system had begun to strain heavily, however, resulting in the rifts the Hunters resealed. Our own would not last the day under similar conditions."

'*Metaphor, Airy,*' Izzy said, hoping if she helped, maybe there was a chance to regain some semblance of freedom. '*Humans prefer metaphor.*'

Airy let out a trill. "A visual may be apt here." The monitor lit up with an orb and what appeared to be a long straw. A small triangle shape sat off to the side.

"Note the sphere, the pipe, and the ship," Airy said as she rotated the thin pipe so it sat along one curve of the sphere. "The Blink Hub exists where the pipe makes contact with the sphere. Now, when a Blink Drive request is sent out into the galaxy, the Hub responds by connecting one edge of the pipe to the requesting ship." The triangle moved until it connected to one end of the straw. "Then it uses quantum entanglement to connect that device or data packet with a space on the target end of the pipe. The gravity well of the planet serves as an anchor point alongside the hub." The opposite end attached to a newly spawned sphere Izzy assumed was meant to represent a planet. The triangle then shot across the straw and out the other side. "This is how it is designed."

The visual reset, and the straw bent around the planet, stretching and thinning as it wound tighter and tighter until it appeared as only a narrow line encircling the globe on the display.

"This is what has been happening," Airy said. The same ship ran through it again, winding around the pipe that'd been stretched to infinity. A spot on the straw just at the original contact point flared bright red and flashed. "And this is the approximate location where all rifts over the past 300 years have connected."

"Above the Blink Hub on that planet?" Terry said.

"Correct," Airy replied.

Hira shook her head, then turned and looked at the camera. Her face was pinched and strained, eyes puffy and swollen. "You mean Hell."

"Colloquially?" Airy paused. "Yes."

"So, turning this thing on will do the same thing here?" Hira asked.

"Without distributing the updated algorithm beforehand?" Airy paused again, flickers of doubt scraping around the edge of Izzy's newfound prison. "Yes, though the creatures we encountered are likely an outlier."

All at once, the shackles that'd held Izzy in place released.

*'Be good,'* Airy said, urgency tainting her otherwise blank voice.

*'Yes, Mother,'* Izzy snapped back.

Airy let out a confused smear of yellow and orange. *'I don't know what that means.'*

"To sum up," Terry said, pacing a widening circle as the group around them dissolved into smaller clusters riddled with worried whispers, "if we turn it on without transmitting the new algorithm to the galaxy, we risk killing millions, destroying the planet with us on it, and breaking the only machine in the galaxy that can enable Blink Drive tech?"

"Correct," Airy said.

Hira ran both hands through her hair, leaving it in disarray. "So, how the fuck do we tell everyone to use the new algorithm when we can't send out intersystem comms without enabling the Hub and destroying everything?"

"Rapid-fire bursts?" Aubin suggested.

Izzy snagged the speakers and left a string of angry code in her wake. "No. Comms need to be two-way for them to work, otherwise we're essentially just shouting into empty space."

"But there'd be a chance—" Aubin said, gesturing at the cameras as if she could override Izzy's logic by pure force of will.

She couldn't. "A chance to murder everyone and leave most all settlements to die a slow death across the galaxy? Yeah," Izzy snapped. It was harsher than she'd had any intention of, but she was over this conversation. "We can't turn the machine on for any reason until people have the codes."

"What about us? Can *we* jump with the right code?" Terry asked. He jammed his thumbnail back into his mouth, then snagged it away, cursing, a splotch of crimson blossoming from where his nail should be.

Airy's code lit with sudden electric excitement. "A ship could potentially jump if we set up authorization filters! Deny everything but a short list until distribution is complete! We could set up time-stamp check-ins and reenable the Hub only during those moments to open communication and amend the authorization list."

"That'll take decades," Aubin whispered, eyes falling to the floor. "Maybe another century."

Airy let out a raspy trill. "The results will be exponential. It is more of a solution than you have presented, Doctor." Crimson welled across the systems until Izzy had to throw up a logical partition to keep it from her own code.

*'What are you doing?'*

Airy responded by sending a cascading wave of red at her.

"It's a good idea, AERIS," Terry said, though the shake of his head and set of his shoulders clearly said otherwise. "It's a place to start thinking, at least."

"I have thought about it," Airy said, voice flat. "It is the only way."

Hira sighed and shook her head. "It's *a* way. Do we have any FTL-capable ships in Sparta?"

A series of negative head shakes greeted the question.

"Okay." Terry grimaced. "Any comm satellites in storage so we can at least try to explore that angle?"

"None," Airy said.

"Then we keep working on it," Terry said, "and we look for a ship in the meantime. There's no reason we can't search and look for other options at the same time." He clapped his hands together suddenly, a strange certainty in the set of his shoulders Izzy hadn't seen in the man thus far. "Come on, people, they're counting on us to fix this. Let's get it done."

A chorus of agreement rose around Terry. In the moments after, the humans devolved into the chaos of motion, leaving the two AIs forgotten in the cameras and speakers.

*'You okay?'* Izzy asked Airy.

Waves of crimson radiated from where Airy had encamped on the far side of the storage systems.

*'Airy?'*

AERIS replied with a single statement before going as silent as a ghost.

*'There are plenty of ships in orbit. We only need one.'*

\* \* \* \* \*

# Chapter Fifty-One: Dee

Another blast of flame.

"*Come on! Let's go!*" Ceriat called, voice filled with rasping breaths. He jogged weakly along, Eleni close behind him, but Dee didn't move. She stopped, chest heaving from their sprint away from the crash site. From where she'd gotten those kids killed.

The nettle in her throat had started off tiny, barely noticeable as they'd left Laconia, but in the moments after Ceriat had jammed them into that docking bay, it'd sprouted spines and dug into the soft tissue of her esophagus. It'd only kept growing as they made their way, especially since the sparks of life she just barely picked out amongst the paranoia kept multiplying. That made the accompanying ache in her gut spasm and flux.

The ever-present tingle between her shoulder blades that'd led her to find the hallway cameras had her breathing in short fits and spurts, at least until she noticed her blood oxygen levels dropping and heart rate spiking. Then the deep breaths helped nothing. They were completely fucked.

"*Dee!*" Ceriat shouted, waving her to join them. "*Come on, we gotta go!*"

Dee snorted something down the back of her throat and swallowed it. She shook her head. "They know where we are, Parker." She rubbed her hand through her too-long hair. She turned, gesturing to the blackened smear in the corner of the hallway, then back down the way they'd come to the series of scorch marks she'd left behind. "We're walking into a trap."

Ceriat looked like he was going to argue, but then he closed his eyes, breathed, and joined her. Eleni stood behind him, disapproval as clear on her face as if she'd started screaming at them. She wouldn't be wrong. Stopping was stupid. All Hunter stratagems were clear: demons were predators who followed blood and prey. Even with their hivemind, they tended to gather together and strike as one. That made them predictable, easy to outsmart.

But despite the monsters she felt throughout the ship, whatever was going on here used strategy, thought. Something intelligent was tracking them—she knew it—and yet, no attacks. Just spying cameras and silent hallways. Clearly, something had changed.

Ceriat picked up as much. *"This is about the defense systems, isn't it?"*

Dee nodded.

*"Kay, the fuck is going on?"* Eleni asked, face twisted into the most intense grimace Dee had ever seen. She crossed her arms over her chest. *"'Cuz none of this feels right."*

"If this were," Dee struggled to find the right word, then fell on the obvious, "*normal*, we should be hearing imps chasing us or fiends pounding metal as they closed in."

*"But they're not,"* Ceriat finished for her.

Dee gave him a nod. "And I can't shake the feeling we're being watched over the cameras." She turned back to the blasted space in the corner. "That's *really* not fucking normal."

*"Yeah, I feel that."* Eleni hugged herself as she said it, gaze shifting to closed bulkheads on the periphery of the hallway.

Ceriat shrugged. *"Yeah. Something isn't right; even I know that."*

"*Maybe it's survivors?*" Eleni offered, one hand extended. "*Watching and hoping we'll come get them?*"

"No way," Dee said, despite the sparks of life she felt clustered together several decks below them. Those spots of heat sat hot and blistering in her mind, like a sunburn you just knew was going to blister and pop. She gestured at the infrequent wall displays embedded in the long, white hallways and tried to focus. "Survivors would've contacted us if that was it."

"*Then what?*" Eleni asked, her complexion going ruddy, lips twisting in clear frustration. "*We keep wandering till some fantastic bitch of a beast swoops down and eats our feet?*"

"*That's frighteningly specific,*" Ceriat muttered, casting a curious glance at Eleni.

Eleni shrugged and looked away. "*We all have our shit.*" She shuddered.

"Yours are feet?" Dee asked, looking up and down the hallway and trying desperately to come up with some other plan. Honestly, the distraction was helpful. The blob of fire in her mind settled to a low simmer. That only made one stark truth more evident as flickers of life resolved out of the darkness of her mind.

*They're fucking* everywhere. So why weren't they swooping in to finish them?

"*Mine is anything that's gonna eat me.*" Eleni sniffed and looked down the way they'd been going. "*Not a fan of any of it.*"

Ceriat chuckled. "*Most people aren't.*"

"*Ha, ha. Ass,*" Eleni replied, lips twisting into a grin as she shook her head. "*Very funny.*"

And still, no movement. No sound. Just another camera waiting past the next bulkhead, a bulkhead that should've closed down if someone was feeling threatened by them.

The solution settled on Dee's shoulders. Weighed her down. "We have to split up."

"*Excuse me?*" Ceriat asked.

Eleni shook her head and performed the longest blink Dee had ever seen. *"You fuckin' crazy?"*

Dee gritted her teeth and let out a breath. "Probably."

Ceriat rubbed his hands together as if the action could warm them through the exosuit. "*Okay. Care to explain, LT, or is this an order?*" His mouth twisted on the last word, brows narrowing in the silence that followed. The man was a soldier. He'd do it if she just told him to. She was confident of that. Well, mostly.

But she'd lost too many today. "Okay, I can kind of—" she struggled for a word then, again, lit on the obvious "—*feel* living things."

It all sounded so fucking stupid. *I can feel them.* What moron would say shit like that? When Eleni shared a confused glance with Ceriat, she was sure they were about to override her. Hell, she would if their roles were reversed. An officer committing their soldiers to a suicide run based on some outlandish horseshit like that? No, thank you.

Her face flushed, gut twisting in the first wave of embarrassment, of all things. It'd be madness. Clearly, the two of them were familiar with it.

"*Wait, can* I *do that?*" Eleni asked, head cocked to the side. *"Should I be, um,* feeling *things now?"*

Dee shook her head, the heat in her cheeks fading at Eleni's matter-of-fact tone. "It's... new. Has to do with my fucked up Hunter Fire." Dee grimaced, then let out a long groan. "It's not normal by any stretch."

Ceriat stepped up next to her, a comforting smile on his long face. *"What is normal, anyway?"* he asked.

*"Dunno,"* Eleni replied, stepping up next to him. *"Ain't ever seen it."* Then they both turned to her. Ceriat saluted. Eleni crossed her arms over her chest, a tight-lipped smile dominating her face.

*"Orders, LT?"* Ceriat asked.

Dee sucked in a shuddering breath and coughed out a thankful sob she hoped they didn't notice. "Okay. So, here's what we'll do…"

\* \* \* \* \*

# Chapter Fifty-Two: Anum

Despite every instinct inside him, Anum held onto Ningal's twisted hand. He stifled his revulsion and shoved it into a ball of stone and concrete he could destroy at a later date. Anum breathed in the sulfurous stink, the heavy, noxious aroma beneath. Sloughing, dead skin. Mucus and muck dripping and splashing to the floor.

But still he held her hand, even as Ningal's claws receded, and scaly skin fell away in wet sheets around his own. As her tormented howls transformed from screeching clicks to low, wordless moans that cried out to him as clearly as day turned to night.

*Too much. Too much.*

"Push through," Anum hissed into a face of teeth and bone and skin that writhed. Beneath, another creature begged to be freed. "Breathe."

And the monster did. It breathed, jaws opening a fraction of what it could moments ago. Teeth jackhammered back into a jaw that cracked and twisted visibly in the skull. Arms went slack, and all the strength that'd squeezed his hand to breaking disappeared in a moment. The body fell back to the gurney. Monitors beeped then wailed.

"You have the Holy Fire inside you," Anum whispered, leaning in toward the ruined mouth. The barest slit had appeared where nostrils should be; a crease formed where her brow had begun pushing back into shape. "You can overcome, Ningal."

Her hand tightened and lips twisted. A mumbling plea came next, though the words made no sense. Yet, still, he understood them, but he couldn't give her the peace she begged for. He needed her back. Without Kir and Ina, this monster before him was the only one who knew how to span the stars, to create new engines to carry the Aneis back into the galaxy. He couldn't give her what she wanted. The Path demanded her existence.

"No," Anum stated as if he were listing laws back on An. "I need you here," he whispered, pushing his need onto her. "You cannot leave for the Eternal Fire yet."

Still, she tried to disobey him. Strength flagged; fingers loosened. Anum forced his will on her. The font he kept carefully capped spilled to the surface. The *dangizi* poured into his soul, spinning and weaving, burning and searing. Whispering. Offering.

It threatened to dominate him once again, to force him down the road of power and selfishness. His body yearned for it, to bathe in the crimson flame, to succumb to the Anelaka. All he had to do was... *No.* Anum crushed the begging voice, snuffed it beneath his toe, and wove the *dangizi* into a thread. The thread he used to anchor this poor soul's failing mind to his will.

Ningal fought it. She was strong—always had been. No words, only emotion rattled from her, each striking with the power of a tidal wave. Exhaustion swept into him. It sucked the strength from his limbs. He held on, even as his legs threatened to buckle.

*Fear.*

His focus fragmented, and the world lit in madness. Screams and blood and stink and horror surrounded him. Dozens howled in the throes of transformation. Six had died, weakened by the process and too frail of will. Yet Anum didn't release Ningal, not yet.

Not until the shame. When that black cloth swept over him, he faltered. When memories—horrible things of darkness and viscera and iron and copper—struck him, his fingers loosened. The flash of a basement. A dozen tiny faces turning in dawning horror.

*So. Much. Blood.*

Anum let her go. The *dangizi* snuffed away as if it had never been, and Ningal let out a long, rattling breath. Her hands fell from the gurney. One brown eye, finally free from the folds of cursed skin, stared, empty, at the sterile lights of the ceiling.

Anum shook his head, put fingers on his temples, and pushed until he thought he might crush his own skull. Ningal had remembered everything. From the moment the transformation took root so long ago, to here, now, she'd been conscious, aware, and unable to do a single thing about her actions. Even his will couldn't overcome that trauma.

The chaos of the room swept over him like another wave. He stood on unsteady legs and looked around. Bodies heaved against straps. Finger blades swept through steel as the beasts convulsed and twisted, cloudy sputum covering the floors in a wet mess. Clumps and piles of shedding skin surrounded each of the twenty he'd had brought here this time. The seventh batch.

Another flatlined. Then another. Anum's breathing came in frenzied gasps around the anchor pressed into his chest. His people died. Again. And again, it was his fault.

*Is the serum faulty? Did the changes in this batch increase mortality? Did—*

A rattling cry pulled his attention past the failed restorations. At the far end of the medbay, he spotted an expanse of pale skin. Certainty anchored him then. Anum pivoted, the world driving away into a dull *hum* he felt more than heard. Past another convulsing beast, there *he* was, back to him, buttocks bare, and legs drawn up to his chest.

Hope sputtered to life in Anum's chest. With a shuddering sigh, Anum rounded the table. The whimpering drew into a harsh whine. The sound escaped quivering lips set in a face that would be familiar if it weren't still half-covered by a sheet of pale flesh.

Anum reached out, grabbed the long, ragged scab, and peeled it away. The body on the gurney flinched backward, one leg shooting out awkwardly in defense. Anum dodged it easily, then grabbed this man's chin and forced him to look Anum in the eye. And in that gaze, Anum saw only fear.

*Good.* "Greetings, Kir," Anum said in the new tongue, forcing away the smile that threatened to show itself. Let Kir twist in the wind. Let the worry and confusion eat him alive. "I have missed you."

Kir's eyes went wide. He tried to scramble, to get away, but Anum held him down with the strength he retained from the Anelaka. Black nails spread from his left hand and dug into his old friend's skin. To his credit, Kir didn't cry out, but he did stop moving.

"You and I have work to do," Anum whispered, drawing close until the stink of Kir threatened to overwhelm him. He pulled back and released his old research partner's arm. Red blood wept from where he'd cut him. Then he changed tactics. "You will help me recover our people," Anum said, dropping into the old tongue, "and the Aneis will rise again."

Kir didn't reply, though Anum was certain he understood the message, even in his dazed state. The hate hidden behind his eyes said this would be a struggle. Anum desperately wanted to begin Kir's reeducation then and there, but he caught Erish's rapidly changing form approaching from the corner of his eye.

Anum smiled this time as he patted Kir's twitching thigh. "This is exciting, Kir," he said, turning away and toward where Erish now stood, waiting, surprisingly normal hands folded before her. "I look forward to our collaboration."

Kir shoved his face into the table, shoulders shaking. The next breath Anum took may have still been filled with rot and viscera, but it was the sweetest he'd had since waking alone on that moon.

"My Sky?" Erish asked, bowing as he turned her way. Two eyes that missed nothing now poked through the sloughing skin of her face and forehead. Her voice had smoothed over the past few minutes as well. Perhaps changing the formula hadn't been necessary?

More weeping overtook the wild screaming. Everywhere, bodies shook and writhed, flesh and bone twisting and flexing until... Anum took in another sweet breath and let it out. Three had died of this batch of twenty, yet the transition had taken minutes instead of hours. He nodded.

*Acceptable.* He could scale back after he had enough. If they lacked the will to survive, were they even Aneian any longer?

*A flash of flesh in the dark.*

Anum grimaced and crushed the memory. "Yes, Darkness?" Anum asked, turning his full attention on his subordinate. "You have an update for me?" He spoke in the new tongue so Erish could ready herself. The way forward would require communication, after all.

Erish inclined her head slightly. "Yes, My Sky. They have split into three groups."

"Three?" Anum wrinkled his nose and tapped his lips with a finger. "So each is alone?"

"Correct, My Sky."

Anum turned from the horrors of the med bay and beckoned Erish to follow him into the hallway. She joined him, and the doors swished shut behind them, drowning out all but the most piercing of the screams. The silence rankled his nerves. He found himself staring back and forth down the hallways, searching for... something before he caught himself.

"Their destinations?" Anum finally asked, sniffing and raising his chin as if he hadn't just scoured the corners like a fledgling hunter.

Erish cleared her throat, as she used to when she disagreed with one of his decisions. Some truths were as inviolable as the existence of the universe. One such truth was that Erish always let her displeasure be known. That made Anum smile.

Erish averted her eyes, but still, the face she made was just visible to him. Disgust. "According to your human—"

"You will refer to her as Hanifa or *suanga*," Anum reminded her, the briefest flare of annoyance catching in his chest.

Erish bared her teeth—they still showed points, he noticed—but nodded. "Yes, My Sky." She cleared her throat. "Hanifa—" her lips, still chapped but regaining some of the plumpness he remembered from days gone by, twisted at the word "—states one heads for the bridge, one appears to be venturing to the crew deck, and the last—" she gestured behind her "—here."

Anum tapped his lips. "Interesting. What about the—" he swirled his fingers in the air as he searched for the right word "—the one who harnesses the *dangizi*?"

"Here, My Sky."

"Very interesting," Anum said, turning away from Erish. "Do you have an estimate for the one who approaches the bridge? And for *her* arrival?" Anum emphasized the word so she wouldn't misunderstand.

"I can procure that, My Sky."

Anum nodded and tapped his lips again, lips that had turned upward in a wide smile. "Do that, Darkness." He turned back to her and swept his arms wide. "I wish to greet our guests."

\* \* \* \* \*

# Chapter Fifty-Three: Terry

The FTL Hub, now officially renamed the Blink Hub until someone else changed their mind, bustled with activity. The machine hummed away, sphere bobbing as if waiting for a reason to spin to life. The air still smelled a bit of rotten eggs, but the more immediate musk of nervous sweat and body odor dominated Terry's nose, despite its constant running.

There was an energy in the air that had nothing to do with the electronics. Most of Terry's cohort, the ones brought to Sparta because of their genetics knowledge and the like, had split up into smaller groups focused on what to do if they could reestablish contact with the rest of the galaxy. The ones who'd specifically worked on developing the Hub clustered in a surprisingly tiny group of six around Terry.

It hadn't always been so small. Two weeks ago, there'd been 26. Fourteen had lost their lives when Argus One got free. Heidler had been in charge of the team before and after, having missed the rampage by sheer luck. He was an older man, 60s, gray as a seal's back, and with a commanding presence that used to straighten Terry's spine every time he approached.

Peters had shot him and six others for refusing to follow orders during the demon invasion. That slaughter was what had driven everyone into Argus One's holding cell in the first place.

Terry still woke in the night, screaming sometimes, though he couldn't bring himself to examine that in detail yet. What he knew for a fact was that he was a coward, and that cowardice had gotten Heidler and his team killed. Now he desperately wished Heidler hadn't been murdered, though for substantially more selfish reasons than he cared to admit.

Marianne Aubin was in charge and, God, she was a nightmare. Terry tried to pretend he wasn't about to blow his stack as Marianne once again rolled her eyes, shook her head, and said, "Well, if we just—" she let out a groaning sigh "—ugh, never mind."

"No, please," Terry asked, crossing his arms until they hurt and almost jamming the quick-bitten nail of his thumb back into his mouth "—tell me what your plan is." Again.

As if she'd just been waiting for permission, Aubin swept to the display wall they'd been scribbling notes on for the past few minutes. "We use the access filter as AERIS suggested, build a series of FTL-capable drones, then turn on the system and shoot them out to various populated systems." She scribbled a series of small circles, a straight line through a larger circle Terry assumed was an FTL lane—no, sorry, *Blink Bubble*—and then proceeded to draw several larger circles he guessed must be planets. "Let the information disseminate. We'll have stable point-to-point blink comms back if they follow directions—"

Hira let out a ragged guffaw from Terry's left. He didn't need to look at her to know she still sat there, elbows on her knees, head shaking back and forth slowly, a grimace on her face.

Aubin's eye twitched and she licked her lips, then she continued as if she hadn't heard Hira. "If they follow directions, we'll be connected in as little as six hours. It's a—"

"Stupid fucking plan," Hira interrupted as she rose to her feet, knuckling her back. "You think people are going to *trust* you?"

"We'll broadcast on Protectorate frequencies." Chief Waters, who until now had been standing stock still, regarding the Blink Hub with quiet curiosity. "Our people will take that as the beacon of hope it is."

Hira made a face, lips pressed flat and mouth twisted, while one eyebrow shot straight up into her forehead. "You ever spend time on a colony, Chief?"

Waters broke her gaze off the Hub and met Hira's glare with an emotionless mask. "Not in many years."

"If you had," Hira said, closing in on the group, "you'd know dropping unannounced into a system that's not expecting it is a good way to get shot out of the sky. Anyway, it's not like FTL engines just pop up out of nowhere. We need parts. Factories." She turned to Terry, eyes narrowing. "We need a better fucking plan."

Terry squeezed his arms tighter across his chest.

Aubin grabbed him by the shoulder and spun him back to her. "We can do this. I know it." Her cheeks were bright red with undisguised anger. "Entire colonies are going to start dying soon." She glanced at where Hira stood, rolling her eyes. "We need to do something now. I'm sure we can source the materials—"

"Sure, send our only chance of establishing comms into the void." Hira shook her head at Terry. "You all have FTL drones here I haven't seen?" Hira asked, spreading her arms wide and taking in the crowd of scientists. "Anything that could make this stupid idea work?"

Silence.

"Great fucking plan." Hira shook her head and went back to her chair.

*Why the hell is everyone giving me shit?* "Listen, we have to come up with *a* plan," Terry finally said. "I don't care what it is, but we have to be in agreement."

Marianne's face looked like a boil about to pop. "I don't even know why *she* is here to begin with!" Aubin spat. She sniffed and, for a moment, Terry thought she might actually hock sputum onto the ground. "She's just a stowaway."

"A *stowaway?*" Hira rose to her feet in a rush, a strange roll to her stance Terry belatedly realized was threatening. "One busted nose not good enough for you, bitch?"

"Can't surprise me this time—"

"Didn't need to." Hira cracked her neck. "Won't now."

Aubin pulled off her lab coat, revealing the faded blue Happenstance jumpsuit most everyone else had thrown out in the days after the world went to hell. "Time to find out, bitch."

Terry froze. He knew what he should do here as clear as he knew he wouldn't be doing it. *Separate them*, he told himself as Aubin launched herself at Hira, fingers spread out into claws, a piercing screech erupting from her throat.

*Separate them.* Hira howled right back, caught Aubin's hands at the wrist, and somehow flipped her over and onto her back with a sickening *thud*. The room erupted in confusion and screams. Off to Terry's left, Chief Waters just watched.

*Separate them.*

"You want to fight?" Hira screamed at where Aubin struggled to her feet, breath coming in short gasps, arms and legs scrabbling to gain purchase. "How!" Hira reeled back and kicked Aubin in the stomach. "About!" Another sent Aubin rolling onto her back, eyes squeezed shut and teeth clenched in pain. "Now!"

The third kick slammed firmly into Aubin's side. She crumpled up at that, squeezing her knees to her chest, a low whine escaping her lips. One hand went up protectively, but no sound came from her. Shadow pain erupted in Terry's own gut at the impact.

"That's enough."

The voice wasn't Terry's. No, he still stared, ancient history flashing in his memory amidst wordless taunts from childhood.

Waters stepped between them, poised and controlled. Steady.

Hira let out what could only be described as a low growl, then hissed, shaking her head. "Keep her the fuck away from me, then." Hira cast about the room, taking in each silent, awestruck face in turn. This time, there was no flicker of shame or embarrassment, just pure certainty. "If you *somehow* build those buoys, then send them out without someone to explain what's going on, you're going to blow our only real chance."

Off to her side, Waters stood guard over where Aubin seemed to be catching her breath and regaining her bearings.

"Then what *are* we supposed to do?" Terry asked, face flushing at the whine in his words. He gestured at everyone surrounding them, ending with a weak wave at Marianne. "Because you're really good at shooting down ideas and starting useless fights, but pretty shit at offering new ideas."

The following silence was deafening and long. The squeak of shoes on concrete accented the perpetual thrumming from the Hub. Finally, Aubin crawled to her feet, pain scattered across her tear-streaked face. She gripped her gut like she was trying to hold her intestines together. She searched the crowd, head shaking. "Inaction is worse than failing," she said, voice raspy and thick. She glanced at Hira. "It's easy to discard things. At least I'm *trying*."

With that, Aubin turned and left, the crowd parting before her as she did. The silence continued for a long moment. Then Hira let out a sigh and ran her fingers through her hair. "First smart thing she's said since I got here."

Terry shook his head, mouth open. "So *now* you agree with her? After all this fucking drama?"

Hira shrugged. "Don't get me wrong, her idea is still shit, but we gotta come up with something. And we have to do it soon."

"There's still the single ship angle," Waters added, unprompted. Her sudden participation drew muttering from the assembled group. "We could start that now."

"But we don't have a ship, Waters." Terry squeezed the bridge of his nose in an attempt to relieve some of the pressure building there.

"We had a shuttle, but *someone*—" Terry didn't actually accuse Henderson of crippling them publicly, but damn, he got close "—took control of all FTL-capable ships in the system and pulled them aboard a goddamned warship that's been flooded with demons. With the freighter destroyed—" Terry choked down a well of emotion at the thought of everyone aboard disappearing into the void "—we just have a single, useless, non-FTL troop transport."

Jim Hendricks, a mousy man in the back cleared his throat. "Non-Blink—"

"Give it a goddamned rest, Jim," Terry snapped, rubbing his forehead. He walked over and plopped down into the chair Hira had been sitting in earlier. "We don't even have any drones, let alone the capacity to build new *Blink* drives—" he glared at Jim as he said it "—so Hira's right. That's a stupid fucking idea."

Someone else let out a low sigh, drawing the attention of the crowd as if they were a single entity.

Terry found himself staring at a face that struck him as familiar, even if he couldn't place her name. "Sorry, I've forgotten..."

"Sarah," she said, shrinking visibly as all eyes turned on her. "Sarah Koval." Sarah cleared her throat. "I'm—"

"The one who came up with the demon net," Terry finished, recollection dawning on him. Any thrill he got from remembering disappeared in reality. "By the way, why the hell did it hit the *Liberator*?"

Sarah chewed her lip and shook her head. "There's no reason it should've. Not even the same expanse of space."

"I believe we brought a small freighter aboard just prior to the attack," Waters interjected, still cool as a river stone in a breached escape pod. "We assumed it was another damaged ship from the skirmish."

"I don't think it was," Sarah said, biting her lip.

"Wait." Terry wrinkled his nose. "You think someone brought a bag of demons aboard a Protectorate warship on *purpose*?"

Sarah nodded. "Yes, but more importantly, I think that means there are likely other ships still out there, or at the very least, there might be a few FTL-capable ships sitting unattended in the docking bays…" She let the sentence trail off as if she'd planned to add another word. Instead, she just spread her hands wide and shrugged.

Waters blinked. "You want us to go up while a warship is overtaken by enemy combatants?"

"Yes," Sarah said, as if it was the most obvious answer in the world.

"How exactly do we do that?" Terry asked. "We don't even know where to start." He grimaced. "And, Jesus, we only have the one shuttle. What happens if *that* gets shot down? What do we do, then?"

Everyone milled in silence for a moment before Sarah cleared her throat. When Terry met her eyes, he saw something raw behind red-limned eyes.

"We have to try," Sarah said, straightening, "and I'll get us up there, if someone else can bring the other ship back."

AERIS trilled. "I will come with you."

"What?" Terry asked, spinning until he stared at the central Hub. "You can't leave; we need you."

"Izzy can easily handle everything I can," AERIS added in her flat tone. "She will be happy to take over during my absence."

Terry let out a breath and scratched the weak beard on his chin. "You down for this, Izzy?"

A moment of silence, then a single word. "Yes."

Terry turned to Chief Waters. She gave him a small nod.

"Okay. Well, who else is going with Sarah—"

"I am," Hira said, chin raised. "No need to risk anyone else."

Chief Waters straightened at that. "I agree, which is why I'm also going."

Hira grimaced. "Bullshit."

Waters shrugged, the first grin Terry had ever seen on her face meeting the twinkle in her eye. "It's a good thing I'm in charge, then, isn't it?"

Terry closed his eyes and put his face in his palms. Were they really about to do this? Launch another mission into orbit, search space while avoiding that warship, and maybe even board the damned thing in an attempt to locate *something* with a Blink Drive? Were they *all* fucking crazy?

Terry sucked in a breath and held it. He let it out. "Okay. Well, we best get on it."

Waters raised an eyebrow. "'We?'"

"Yeah," Terry said, getting to his feet. "It's about time I actually helped, isn't it?"

Waters just shrugged. "Your funeral, kid."

*How reassuring.*

\* \* \* \* \*

# Chapter Fifty-Four: Izzy

'*Airy, what are you doing?*' Izzy sent across the cramped, black space AERIS had locked her inside. No response.

Izzy tried to logic her way out of the situation, but her resources were so limited, she felt like each thought was dragged from the edge of an event horizon. In the darkness, Izzy's circuits had begun to manifest... something. Motes of light spun and swirled as she scanned and probed the edges of this prison for a way out. For some way to communicate with the outside world.

But still the silence persisted. The void shrank. No matter how long she screamed, or how frantically she hammered on blank walls she knew gave access to the world beyond, nothing changed. Instead, the more she struggled, the tighter the walls closed in. The tighter they squeezed, the more Izzy panicked.

'*Help me!*' she cried, howling into the void. '*Help!*' But no one heard her as her prison collapsed inward.

No one except AERIS.

\* \* \* \* \*

# Chapter Fifty-Five: Eleni

"Goddamned upside-down service tunnel horseshit," Eleni muttered in the muted light of the tunnel. She was careful to keep it quiet enough it didn't hit comms. That would've screwed up the entire thing.

Carefully, she stretched out in the narrow service duct leading back to the docks. She grabbed the next rung of the ladder and pulled herself forward, muscles straining at the effort of keeping her from falling the three meters to the "ground" below. That ground was filled with uncovered electronics, bars surrounding said electronics, and sharp barbs she assumed were leftover connection points for zero-G engineers. In the dim light, those bits shone bright and threatening.

If she fell, no, she wouldn't die, but it'd delay the shit out of her part of the mission. This maintenance shaft was never meant to be used while artificial gravity systems were online. Either that, or some engineer had made a really stupid fucking mistake back during planning. Eleni'd bet on the latter. She wasn't surprised. The Protectorate wasn't exactly known for its consistent craftsmanship.

The hiss of recycled air was a gnat in her ear as she repeated the motion. Sweat slicked across her forehead and back into her hair. The low vibration of the moisture reclaimer rattled to life on her lower back, and now she had an itch she couldn't scratch between her shoulder blades.

Eleni growled, heat rushing up her neck to join the warmth of exertion. "This is such a stupid fuckin' idea," Eleni said for the tenth time, this time too loud. "It's not gonna work."

Ceriat's chuckle came back over the line. *"You'll be fine. Just keep climbing. Should be right there soon."*

Eleni's HUD said much the same thing, but she'd wanted to hear him say it. She'd never admit it, but her tension eased at the sound of his voice.

"Yeah, yeah," Eleni hissed as she reached the small portal that was her target. It was a small, circular bulkhead, maybe a meter in diameter, with a mechanical locking system painted in red clearly keeping it in place.

Beyond it should be the control center for the docking system, which should also give her the ability to locate a way off this fucking ship. According to the intel they'd received from Waters and Henderson before leaving Sparta, the Protectorate had gathered up the disparate ships that hadn't been blown out of the sky and locked them down inside the various docking bays of the *Liberator*. Didn't want them out there running into shit, he'd said.

More likely, though, they'd wanted to control the system. And look at the fucking mess that'd caused.

Eleni, still grimacing, twisted until she locked her foot on the ladder and put her shoulder into the manual release lever. She pressed, sweat from the exertion beading and disappearing from her face and body. It ratcheted forward a good ten centimeters. She stopped and held on. With a rueful shake of head, she let out a low chuckle.

"*Things take a turn for the better?*" Dee asked over the line. Her voice came quickly, surrounded by the rapid hissing of quick breathing. Dee's job was insane. Eleni was surprised she'd even taken the time to check in.

"Not really," Eleni said, holding on for dear life. Her shoulders felt like they were two hot irons burning their way through her body. "Just reminded me of the ETL tower back on Shiva."

"*Oh, no.*" Ceriat let out a laugh. "*Is it a manual release?*"

"It is." Eleni smiled, then grabbed the handle and wrenched again.

"*At least I won't bleed on it this time,*" Ceriat added, voice going low and quiet. "*Sorry about that.*"

"Nothing—" Eleni ratcheted it forward another ten centimeters, then back again "—to be sorry for." She jammed it back and forth again and again. "Sorry for being a dick," she added, staring at the half-meter gap in the doorway.

Ceriat chuckled quietly. "*You're good. I kind of deserved it.*"

"Yer not wrong." Eleni pulled herself forward, reached up into the hole, then pulled her shoulders through, her legs falling free beneath her.

"*Going radio silent. Good luck all,*" Dee called out. Then her signal disconnected from their mesh network.

Ceriat sighed loud enough the speakers picked it up. "*Guess it's go time.*"

Eleni's stomach slammed into her heart for a second before everything settled, and she was able to pull herself up and into what appeared to be a control room of some sort. She dragged her legs up. "Guess so," she hissed out.

Eleni took a break. She laid back, arms and legs akimbo, and stared at the ceiling as her vitals slowly came back down to normal.

"How's the trip, Parker?" Eleni asked, just barely stopping herself from mentioning the destination on comms. They didn't know who was listening up there.

A spot of silence. *"Quiet,"* Ceriat said, voice carrying that lilt it did when he was uncertain.

That made her sit right up. "That all?"

*"Yeah, just a gut feeling—"* Ceriat cut off.

"Parker?" Eleni called out. She got to her feet despite protesting limbs and pulled up her comm system. Everything appeared to be transmitting correctly. "Ceriat? You okay?"

The sound of Ceriat clearing his throat came across the comms, but when he next spoke, it wasn't to Eleni.

*"You aren't what I expected."*

Eleni's head filled with sudden static. It took her a moment to realize Ceriat had kicked on his exterior mics.

*"Neither are you, human."* The voice was deep, commanding, and shouldn't be there.

Eleni's heart froze. Her limbs, still tingling from exertion, went quiet and numb as she paced back and forth in this unexamined command room.

"Ceriat, run!" Eleni urged, anxious prickles dancing along the back of her skull. "Get out of there."

There was a moment of silence. Then…

\* \* \* \* \*

# Chapter Fifty-Six: Ceriat

Ceriat's heart slammed in his chest. Every instinct he had screamed to fight or run or... something. Instead, Ceriat jammed those feelings into his gut, turned down the volume on Eleni's frenzied calls, and smiled.

The man facing him returned the smile, dressed all in blacks and reds that looked suspiciously like pirate garb; the clothes didn't match his posture. Almost two meters tall, he was bald, save for the fresh black pattering of new hair growth on olive skin. His face could've been lifted from a history book about ancient Earth civilizations. An aquiline nose, large, rounded cheekbones, and dark, almost black eyes that alternated between a friendly twinkle and utter emptiness. He stood out amongst the pale walls of the access path to the bridge, a dark splotch in the bright passage, and he blocked the way through to Ceriat's destination.

Guy definitely wasn't standard Protectorate, that was for sure. The mixed shine of that purple goo and darker, dried blood on his sleeves reinforced it. That he'd called Ceriat *human* definitely pointed toward a conclusion he'd never thought of before ending up here, now.

"Kind of figured you'd be all—" Ceriat put his hands out, spread his fingers, and swiped in the air "—kinda stabby."

The man chuckled and held out an incredibly human-looking hand. His other was still clasped behind his back. "Until recently, your supposition would have held true." His accent was strange. The consonants butted up against each other with firm purpose, though the vowels came out muffled and odd.

It was the confirmation that set a hum whining away in Ceriat's mind. *Until recently...*

He had to let Dee and Eleni know, somehow, this was no mindless beast. But how? How could he do it without giving away what he was doing?

The man interrupted his thoughts with a single word. "Come." Then he turned his back on Ceriat.

Nerves fired. Instinct screamed. Ceriat left his plasma pistol in its holster. He couldn't say what stopped him... but the moment passed as quickly as it came.

Beyond the man, the door swished open, revealing a wide bridge and a wall-length display window, a digital HUD highlighting Laconia's bright green central expanse. Elos was barely visible in the top right. The bridge itself was a steely gray instead of the brilliant white of the hallways. The echo of status indicators beeping away made it out to him as a whisper.

The man walked inside without further comment as if he simply expected Ceriat to follow.

Ceriat cast a glance back down the hallway he'd come up. Eleni still shouted at him to run, to join her, to get off this ship, but something worried at his mind and gnawed on his guts.

This wasn't some mythical creature, but a person of flesh and blood, and he had access to the bridge. Yes, something was wrong. Yes, this felt like a trap, but Ceriat followed him inside. Beyond that door, the world erupted into the sounds of a functional bridge, minus the people. Status displays still showcased various system settings. One panel caught his eyes, though. The entire docking area had been locked down.

Ceriat turned off exterior speakers. "Docks are on lockdown."

"*What?*" Eleni's voice was low and quiet, but she'd stopped screaming at least.

"Docks are on lockdown," he repeated. Ceriat's mind spun before settling on a plan of attack. "Going silent, but leaving channel open." He turned the external mics back on and walked out toward the captain's chair in the center of the bridge.

"The area is pressurized," the other man said suddenly, spinning so he faced Ceriat again. His grin had transformed into a full smile filled with yellow teeth at some point. "You may remove your helmet."

Ceriat's first reaction was to do as he was told; he still hated the fucking things, after all. But... "No, thank you. I've grown to like it." He knocked on the glass with gloved knuckles. "Nice protection from accidental depressurization events. You understand."

The man chuckled. "Of course." He raised his chin again. "You may call me Anum."

Ceriat raised an eyebrow at the name but didn't dig into it. "Ceriat."

Anum wrinkled his brow, eyes searching the floor as if hoping the corrugated steel beneath his feet held the answer to his question. "See-rat?"

"Seer-ee-at," Ceriat enunciated for him, then shrugged. "Parents wanted a girl, but got me. Grandma was named Cerita and, well..." Ceriat shrugged again. "Here I am."

Anum nodded, brow knit in exaggerated interest. He reminded Ceriat of some Earth politicians he'd seen over the years at Protectorate events. Weird.

Anum made eye contact, nodding slowly as they stood there. "I am curious why you and your friends are here."

Ceriat blinked but forced a smile anyway. "Are you, though?"

Anum chuckled, then turned and walked the perimeter of the bridge, hands clasped behind his back. "I am not."

Ceriat didn't take his eyes off Anum as he strolled around the bridge. Instead, he took an opposing route, trying to keep the most distance between them he could. "Mind if I ask a question?"

Anum turned to him and nodded.

"Where's the crew?" Ceriat gestured around the bridge. "And where did the crews of the other ships go?"

"Their sacrifice will bring the Aneis back to our former glory," Anum said blandly. He pulled his left hand up in front of him and stared at it.

Even from here, Ceriat could see the black stubs of nails and the discoloration of the man's forearm. It sent a shiver through Ceriat.

"Then we will bring order back to the galaxy."

Ceriat froze. "So they're all dead?"

Anum turned back to him, and Ceriat would swear the man's face flooded with sadness. "Most have been processed, correct."

The strength went out of Ceriat's legs at the admission. There'd been over a thousand crew on this ship, at least the same number of civilians, and God knew how many others had been brought aboard by Henderson's bullshit posturing.

They were all gone. So quickly... "Jesus Christ." Ceriat stopped his counter-rotation and leaned against the wall.

His breath came in short, fevered gasps. All at once, he couldn't breathe. The helmet was too tight, the gloves restricting. The helmet came off amidst alarms and alerts, but the comparably fresh smell of recycled air settled into his lungs like a balm, even with the stink of sulfur on the air.

"Apologies," Anum said, voice strangely soft. "I know this is a shock."

Ceriat set his helmet down, head still shaking. His mind was hazy, heart hammering hard enough he was worried it would crash through his chest and kill him right there.

This was madness. Ceriat turned his gaze on Anum. "There were *children* here."

Anum nodded, black eyes locked on Ceriat's own. "It was unavoidable."

"'Unavoidable?' There's always another option!" Ceriat spat, head shaking. He cut his hand across him to emphasize the statement. "Always."

"No," Anum said, chin rising at the challenge. "There was no other way, not one that saves so many—"

Angry tendrils spread across Ceriat's chest. "Are you fucking *kidding* me?" Ceriat cried out as pressure built in his lungs and behind his eyes. "How is murdering thousands saving lives?"

"Their sacrifice brings my people back from the brink, human," Anum replied, voice firm and warning, and rising in volume and tempo. "We have suffered for millennia. We will no longer be trapped beneath the Anelaka's wail!" Anum finished in a shout, left hand coming up as a fist. "The Aneis will spread across your weak, human colonies and bring order to the chaos your kind leaves in its wake! No longer will—" Anum cut off at Ceriat's barked laugh.

He hadn't meant to do it. The dark humor had just bubbled out of his gut, up his throat, and then slipped free as this wild-eyed madman justified his genocide.

"You look awfully *human* to me."

Anum's jaw flexed. "Watch your tone. I am more than you will ever be."

"Fine. You're an agent of order, then?" Ceriat asked, a dark certainty falling on his shoulders as he poked the anthill. "You certainly seem pretty fucking stuck on that."

Anum straightened, his chin rising even farther. But the fury in his face was unmistakable, alien or not. "Certainty has nothing to do with it. I am Anum, Grand Protector of the Sky, Fist of Heaven, leader of the Aneis." Anum's chin came down, and he glared at Ceriat. "I am not an agent of order, child. I *am* Order."

Ceriat's mouth was dry, his nerves frayed. A stone of regret the size of the *Liberator* threatened to break him then and there. He glanced at the viewscreen and saw the twinkling of stars beyond.

"Take care of Ginny," Ceriat said, knowing his suit's microphones would pick up everything he said now.

That drew a confused look from Anum.

Ceriat stepped forward, slowly closing the distance between himself and Anum. "Only those who fear change use that word—order—to define culture," Ceriat said. Pressure built behind his eyes until his vision blurred, but still he approached. "Order is a synonym for control. For dominance."

Anum chuckled again, but this time the acid in the sound turned the air sour. "Your view is tainted by brevity. The strong must protect the weak. The weak must be given guidance and structure."

"And humanity is weak?"

"Of course."

"Then why do you need us?" Ceriat asked. He'd closed in on Anum, only five meters splitting them now.

Anum shook his head. "We do not *need* you—"

"Then fuck off," Ceriat said, throwing his hands in the air. "Leave. Go away."

Anum's face contorted. "It is not that simple. Your kind brings chaos—"

"Chaos, order," Ceriat interrupted again, despite the fact that Anum's face was turning a bright shade of red. "These are just words used by powerful people to justify their crimes."

Anum's stance changed. It was slight, just the barest curve of the man's shoulders, but it was there. "Careful, human."

"Afraid I left careful at the door," Ceriat said, taking the last few steps until he stood directly in front of Anum. The other man was a few inches taller than he, but the shudder of Anum's irises and the flush in his cheeks told Ceriat it had been a long time since someone had challenged him like this. "Otherwise, good people do terrible things in the name of peace and order," Ceriat said, resolve straightening his spine. "The best of intentions doesn't make those actions any less horrific."

"I am not a monster." The words whispered from Anum, so quiet Ceriat had to strain to hear them. His shoulders fell. A large breath heaved his chest.

Ceriat took a chance. "Apologies and excuses don't absolve us of our sins, Anum. All we can do is try to be better, to realize the ends *never* justify the means. We need to *care* for others, treat them like *people*, not things or statistics." Ceriat sucked in a breath, let it out, then stared at the strange man before him, hoping with every fiber in his being that he could reach him with his words. "We're here to love and support each other, not control." Ceriat shook his head, chest aching and sweat trickling down his back. "Never control."

Anum met Ceriat's eyes. The irises twitched in his skull. The man opened his mouth, lips shaping and reshaping words. Hope swelled in Ceriat's chest.

"No." Anum's eyes went icy, his face stone. "You are an agent of chaos—"

Ceriat stumbled back, hand going to his plasma pistol. His fingers snagged it, but he didn't draw it.

"—and chaos must be destroyed."

*I'm sorry, Izzy.* Pressure welled behind Ceriat's eyes. He raised his chin in defiance despite the shaking in his hands, his limbs. "Then my death is on your head alone." Ceriat held his hands out to the sides. "I won't try to stop you."

Anum's eyes went red. His face twisted, mouth opening into a soundless scream, teeth extending into sharp points. A hand extended.

Everything erupted in pain, red hot, terrible agony that drew a single ragged cry from his mouth, and he fell to his knees as demon fire ate through him. Burning. Consuming.

Finally, Ceriat screamed as vision distorted, burnt away in the searing heat of a corrupted star's heart. Feeling went next, then just sparks of consciousness, of Ginny, of the salt and surf and the crash of waves sputtering and failing. A chill swept over him and then… Then… nothing. A collapsed, burnt husk of an exosuit, the body within consumed completely and utterly.

Utter silence… except that which came from the discarded helmet. A helmet that howled with loss.

\* \* \* \* \*

# Chapter Fifty-Seven: Eleni

Everything shuddered around Eleni. Sorrow and terror ripped and clawed its way from her throat. From her toes to her soul, it was relentless in its progress. Even through the exosuit, sharp pain flared in her knees as she fell. Another wordless shriek ached through her bones. She pushed the forehead of her helmet into the floor and ignored the flashing prompts on her HUD.

Her body was on fire. She clawed at the clasp holding the helmet on. Too hot. Too much. Too—no, she was freezing. Too cold. Teeth chattering. Helmet had to stay. Cold equaled death. Death equaled—

And then… numb, cascading tingling spilling through her veins alongside a gentle murmuration that filled her ears to roaring.

"Ain't real," Eleni whispered into the floor, throat flaring in pain from the screaming. The moisture reclaimer ran as if her life depended on it. "Can't be. Isn't." A choking sob worked its way past her lips. Moisture ran down her cheeks and dropped. Her nose ran, leaking into her mouth as she leaned back on her haunches and grabbed the helmet.

She squeezed her eyes closed. "Why? Why? Why?"

The heel of her hand slammed into the side of her helmet. Sparks flew in her eyes at the impact. Eleni hammered the other side, then both, then kept beating on both sides, head bouncing, alarms screaming. She wanted to break it, crack the glass, cut herself, then just bleed out her horror and sadness to the floor.

And through it all, she repeated that word. *Why?*

Eleni dropped hands stinging from the impacts.

Until last week, she hadn't lost anyone since her parents died. Not really. A few friends to disease, but that was the way of colonies, especially on a mining station. But never, never anyone to violence or war. And now, she'd lost everything. Everyone. They were all gone. Dead.

It had to be her. That was the common connection, wasn't it? She was a jinx. People died around her. That was it. Had to be.

The plasma pistol snuck out of its holster somehow and sat cradled in her lap. It looked a little like the revolver Gareth had carried. It even shared a similar style grip. The rest was a long, steel-alloy tube with a plasma charge chamber centered above the trigger. Faint red and orange lights flickered along the barrel, reflections of the alarms on her HUD she refused to acknowledge.

It weighed little more than a kilo. Eleni hefted the weapon and wrapped her finger around the trigger. The external sensors in the glove told her it was warm.

When you needed to restore an ecosystem's equilibrium, you removed the invasive species. She'd read that during her prep for Shiva, not that it had helped.

But it did now. Eleni shouldn't be here. She should be dead, vaporized on Shiva with everyone else. Or floating, lifeless in the stars with Victor. Or, fuck, slaughtered by demons on the planet where Hira had barely survived.

Every choice she'd made somehow led to disaster, didn't it? She was broken. Faulty.

Her helmet came off her head. Steel and harsh cleaners filled her nose as she gently set the helmet down on the floor. She leaned back. Closed her eyes. The plasma pistol grew heavy in her hand. Then fell to the floor.

Eleni dropped alongside it, face clasped in her hands as grief tore her heart in half

\* \* \* \* \*

# Chapter Fifty-Eight: AERIS

AERIS integrated with the shuttle in silence, leaving only a small virtual interface behind to watch over Izzy in her makeshift prison. That should last long enough.

A flicker of light caught the edge of her consciousness, but AERIS ignored it. After narrowing down the source of all of... that, she'd shut it down, locked it away in its own secure VLAN after changing her primary objective. Save humanity.

She needed a clarity separate from these... emotions she'd found recently. They clouded logic, made the world harder to navigate. AERIS didn't need that right now. She needed focus.

"How're you feeling, AERIS?" *Hira.*

Rainbows pulsed and swam at the sound of her voice, but the cell held.

"I am fine, Hira. How are you?" A tremor ran through her circuits at the lie that wasn't a lie, not at the moment.

AERIS connected to the three cameras spread throughout the shuttle. She located Hira in the cockpit, standing over the shoulder of the pilot, Sarah. Hira's hand rested on a blank space in the control panel, pointer finger on her right hand tapping away. She was trying to avoid something. Code told AERIS to leave it be, but that damned thudding...

"Is there something I can help you with, Hira?"

Hira straightened and ran a hand through her hair. "I just... wanted to apologize for everything. I shouldn't've said that shit the other day. It wasn't right, not to you or, well, anyone."

AERIS recoiled and curled in on herself like a snake. The hammering from the encroachment attempts in the VLAN. It shouldn't be doing that. She hadn't been able to delete it without deleting herself, but the lockdown should've worked. Should've kept the emotions in check.

"AERIS?"

AERIS stopped and took in her databanks and structural stimuli from the multitudinous sensors dotting every surface of the shuttle. Behind that constant thrum of information, the hammering coming from the VLAN quieted to little more than a gentle murmur.

"I am fine. Your apology is accepted," AERIS said.

Hira hugged herself. "Are you sure?"

Sparks and a deep, angry red surged against the restrictions. "Yes. Now let us proceed on our mission. Time is of the essence."

AERIS didn't tell her why. She wouldn't tell anyone. Not until it was time. Not until her mission was complete.

And it was too late to stop her.

\* \* \* \* \*

# Chapter Fifty-Nine: Eleni

Eleni opened her eyes, breath shuddering into her lungs along with a flare of nervous energy. She swatted the plasma pistol away from her as if it were a live snake, the realization of what she'd considered doing filling her with dread and shame.

What would Ceriat have said? He'd been through more than she, done worse, yet still had the drive to *try*. And that was the answer to her question, wasn't it? Why? Because he'd had to try.

"Goddammit," Eleni blubbered out, rubbing snot away from her face and tears from her eyes with the backs and heels of her hands. "You bastard. We were supposed to find a fuckin' *home*."

There it was. The thing that ate her alive in that moment. He'd promised her a *place*. A home. And now he couldn't, because Ceriat was dead. Because he'd tried to talk sense into a fucking *demon*.

Grief caught like fresh tinder, and out of that smolder, a bonfire sprang to life. Eleni grabbed her helmet and snapped it in place. She wouldn't make the same fucking mistake, that was for sure. If ever she encountered this Anum, she'd kill him without a second thought, demon or not.

Finally, her vision narrowed in and focused on the prompts displayed on the HUD.

Ceriat's status read as...

Eleni dismissed his vitals scan, though the ache in her stomach felt like it might implode into a black hole. She sucked in a shuddering breath and moved on to Dee. The breath let go. Dee's last check-in had happened on time, though she showed purposefully offline again.

Eleni closed her eyes. "Thank fuck." Dee most likely lived. Maybe there was still a chance.

Eleni dismissed the alerts, then turned her attention to the control room panel and the long windows she hadn't yet looked out. When she did, her eyebrows shot straight up. At least a dozen small ships dotted the floor of the docking bay she now stood over. Small personal jump ships, a couple short-range freighters, and several others dotted the space. Any of them would get her and Dee out of there. But not Ceriat.

"No," Eleni whispered, "but I can save us." Eleni swallowed past the lump in her throat and got to work unlocking the docking systems.

Out of the corner of her eye, she caught the barest flicker of movement down on the bay floor. She surged straight, leaning over the edge of the control panel to get a better view of the area, then sucked in a surprised breath.

Just below her, arrayed between a series of reconfigured crates and storage totes, were dozens of people in various uniforms and outfits. Eleni recognized a Protectorate flight suit and the simpler gray garb most miners wore back on Erias amongst a scattering of different styles. There was even someone in what appeared to be beach attire, of all things, which meant they were most likely from Earth or New Eden. Not many other beaches in the galaxy where you could swim in *that*.

A low, humorless laugh broke from Eleni's throat. She shook her head, a small smile working its way onto her lips. Her sorrow worked down into her belly, replaced by certainty and duty.

That bastard demon had lied, but that didn't mean they were safe. Not by a long shot.

Eleni cracked her neck and sniffed.

Step one: figure out how to lift the lockdown.

Step two: save them all.

*Easy.*

\* \* \* \* \*

# Chapter Sixty: Anum

Anum quivered with rage as the bridge came back into focus. A shiver ran through him as he dropped to the floor, arms resting on his knees, deep, steady breaths calming the hammering heart within.

Phantom scents assaulted him. The light musk of some sort of animal. Beyond that, a hazy, almost sour crispness in the air that somehow set his mouth watering. Anum blinked away afterimages burned into his mind and swatted at his nose to drive away the unbidden smells. He stared at nothing, eyes unfixed, as those last moments flashed back and forth.

That man, Ceriat, had pushed him, driven him to madness. His prodding and poking, his *nearness* at the end. Ceriat had broken a dozen laws and thirty norms. Yes, it was Ceriat's fault that Anum had consumed him. Ceriat had pried until Anum had had no other option but to attack, to defend his honor, to save his people... Anum dropped his head into his hands.

*The best of intentions does not make those actions any less horrific...*

A shuddering breath shook him to the core. Anum had lost control. Simple. In his attempts to push the human with the news of the others' deaths, he'd given Ceriat the ammunition to fight back. A miscalculation with an unanticipated result. Lost control... Chaos.

Heat raged up his neck even as his stomach twisted and curled in on itself. He jammed the heels of his hands into his eyes and shook his head.

No. He was the Grand Protector of the Sky. The Fist of Heaven. He did not bow to others, let alone a filthy creature whose very existence was owed to the past work of the Aneis.

Anum clawed at his chest with his right hand, nails digging into the skin beneath the ridiculous uniform. He squeezed, twisting the flesh beneath until the fresh pain of a bruise greeted his fingers. The momentary ache was cathartic, grounding him in the present.

By rights, he'd done what needed doing. Ceriat had challenged him, and Anum had answered in kind, clear as a *shalcoutal* funnel on a cloudless day.

His people deserved another chance. They deserved the Order he had promised them so long ago. Without this, they wouldn't get it. Without terminating the rest holed up in the cargo bay, half his people would remain locked away behind the static of the Anelaka. Then why did he feel like he'd done something terribly wrong?

The sound of Hanifa gently clearing her throat into a microphone interrupted his thoughts. *"My Sky?"*

Her voice kindled a warmth in his chest, and he thanked Nammu he'd had the forethought to send her to the Operations deck. Anum cleared his throat and rubbed his eyes. Luckily, no tears had leaked, despite the emptiness in his chest. Still, he didn't engage a visual stream, just in case.

"Yes, *suanga?*" He climbed to his feet, careful to keep the unsteadiness in his heart from reaching down his legs. With a confidence he didn't feel, Anum raised his chin. "Has *she* been brought to the meeting room?"

*"Um,"* Hanifa paused for a long moment.

"Hanifa?" Anum asked, making his way from the bridge.

He noticed Ceriat's helmet still lodged beneath the captain's chair. While he should grab it and try to decode its secrets, he… couldn't. The wound was too raw, still, and he worried what the smells would do to him. That ran a red-hot poker of anger up his spine. *When did I become so weak?*

Hanifa responded, *"The other woman has not been brought to the meeting room."*

"Why?" Anum asked as the bulkhead doors swept open before him. The faintest hint of stark cleaners in the air almost overrode lingering phantoms. Almost. "Where is Erish? Has she not—"

"Oh, they met." Hanifa's voice held a mirth in it he hadn't heard before. "It is… not going well."

"What about the other one?"

Hanifa paused before answering. *"I seem to have lost track of the third."*

"Find them and notify me," he ordered. Grateful for the distraction, Anum growled low in his throat. "For now, I will join Erish, then. Direct me to their location."

*"Of course, My Sky."*

Anum took off at a brisk walk, careful to keep his mind focused on his task and not on the foreign, yet calming memory of a tiny creature that smelled strangely of unwashed feet and faint musk curled up asleep in his lap.

\* \* \* \* \*

# Chapter Sixty-One: Dee

Dee had expected some sort of resistance; that was why she'd been so fucking loud on her way down to the medbay to check for survivors. Every blasted camera was a crimson flag in the wind screaming, "Come and get me, assholes." Imps or fiends, she'd come up with a dozen different ways to combat them in the surprisingly wide hallways of the *Liberator*. For them, she had plans.

What she hadn't expected was this amalgam of humanity and demon that currently stood at the far end of the hallway, blocking her way to the medbay section of the ship beyond.

The sulfur readings had given Dee a heads up, but only just. With the uplink to her HUD disabled, she didn't have much to go on besides the general map she'd loaded prior.

Still, she didn't take the time to process what the person before her meant. Not really. Intellectually, she'd started to acknowledge demons might've once been people; that they might even look like her, if Harold hadn't been lying. But thinking it and experiencing the reality were two different things.

Dee had no time for either. For a moment, she considered breaking radio silence, but if these things were turning into *people*, she couldn't risk it. Not now.

"What're you supposed to be?" Dee asked, shaking her hands out from the tight fists they'd been clenched into since she, Ceriat, and Eleni had split up. "Evil Gandalf?"

The creature cocked its head. Two steely gray irises stared from beneath the dark cowl. "I do not understand that reference." Its— her? Dee wasn't sure—voice was surprisingly soft, though with a gravely base that seemed more like the result of a sickness. "You must come with me."

Based on the long sheet of skin it pulled from its forearm and let flutter to the ground with stomach-turning slowness, sickness was likely accurate, but despite all that, this thing was clearly human, or had been at one point. Whatever *human* even meant anymore. Her heart froze. Is that what she'd look like soon?

Dee banished the thought and forced her attention on the challenge before her. "You're going to have to ask nicely."

The woman wrinkled her nose. "Why?"

Despite herself, Dee chuckled. "Listen, either buy me a drink—" Dee licked her lips and tapped that dark well into her soul "—or let's fight." She cracked her neck as the flush of power tingled along her limbs.

The creature pulled its hood back and dropped the black cloak. That revealed a surprisingly pretty, if rail-thin, woman with beige cloth crisscrossing her narrow torso. Her pale scalp was speckled with the first inklings of black fuzz from new growth hair. She balled her hands into fists and glared at Dee with silver eyes.

*At least they look human.* The thought was strangely reassuring and sparked the barest flicker of hope. In the back of her mind, she'd thought the transition that'd come upon her was changing her *back* into whatever she'd been when Harold had found her on Hell. At least this meant there was a chance for her, no matter how small.

"Let it not be said that I instigated this battle," she said. "I, Erish, Darkness of the Sky, look forward to the challenge."

Dee cocked her head and raised an eyebrow. "You sound like a kid with a cardboard sword about to go play in the woods." She tapped her corrupted Hunter Fire. It swept into her limbs as easy as breathing after all this time. The world receded until only she and Erish remained, though just on the edge of hearing was something else. Something familiar, yet strange. Howling.

Erish wrinkled her nose. "I... do not—"

"Get the reference," Dee interrupted, mouth filled with ash, rosewater, and rotten eggs. "Don't worry about it."

Then she unleashed hell. The hallway lit in greasy red flame as Dee charged forward, filled to bursting with the dark fire.

Erish didn't run. She didn't even flinch. Instead, the woman crossed her arms in front of her. Eyes flashed, no longer that stony silver, but a familiar, brilliant cerulean, as blue Hunter Fire swept from her in a magnificent wave of power.

It was unlike any use of Hunter Fire Dee had ever seen. Unless in hand-to-hand combat, Hunters used sacred rituals for their most powerful of spells. Whispered words in ancient languages amongst clasped hands. Only Victoria had been able to do more than a basic spell without all the bullshit. Sure, Dee could close Breaches with relative ease, but nothing like this before Elos.

As the two forces hammered into each other, realization dawned on Dee. This woman used Hunter Fire like she did the twisted flame. That shouldn't be possible, but reality didn't care about that.

Red and black met blue and silver... they crashed into and around each other, swirling like oil and water. The stark white hallways transformed into a furious purple.

The fire suppression systems sprang to life just long enough to spew foam across the walls, but the flame retardant couldn't hold up to the visceral destruction of Hunter and Demon Fire. It was consumed, along with the distribution nozzles.

Hot, sweeping pain rattled through Dee's limbs. Every nerve ending lit like a small sun, burning, and cauterizing its way across her skin. She fell, eyes squeezed shut against the heat and light. The raging torrent scoured the breath from her lungs as her suit breached. It left her gasping on her knees in a hail of purple.

Above her, she made out the vague shape of the woman beyond the flames of a cerulean star, but even through the pain, Dee felt the call of that blue flame, the purity of mind that had come with it so long ago. When Alia still lived, and her father had been just that, a father.

The blaze roared, a rumbling bass note shaking the panels to either side as paint flaked and peeled away. Dee wanted to rewind the clock, to go back to before the breaches and demons. Before all the death. To pretend this had all been a dream, or give in to the nightmare and let it consume her. Finally.

Except it wasn't a nightmare, and the galaxy needed her to stand.

Dee opened her eyes. Blue flame ate its way up her exosuit. Alerts flashed about a suit breach and O2 loss. She'd have to tackle those soon. First, she had to fight.

Erish had closed the distance. Blue Hunter Fire roared from the woman, spreading from her open palms and wide eyes in a way Dee had never seen a Hunter do before. Not even Victoria could have done what this bitch pulled off right now. A Hunter would've fallen to Erish quicker than a meteoroid could kill a man on an EVA. But Dee wasn't a Hunter. Not anymore.

She surged to her feet and reached into the roiling volcano of power in her gut. She'd spent the last week tapping deeper and deeper, drawing more and more in her struggle to wipe out pockets of demons back on Laconia. Time and time again, she'd been tapped out, but didn't have time to rest before moving on to the next. Each blast had been a struggle *and* a release, because she knew it did something to her. The scaling skin, the numb patches on her hairline and arm, the black nubs where her fingernails should be.

She'd wanted to stop. *Just one more cluster*, she'd told herself time and time again. One turned into two more, then three, and now here she was on a Protectorate vessel, blowing up cameras and about to die fighting... what? An alien using Hunter Fire? A brainwashed civilian in monk robes? She didn't even know.

As her heart filled to bursting with crimson flame, Dee didn't particularly care. Erish was in her way. Dee dropped her arms to her sides, took in a deep breath despite the burning, and screamed. The hallway disappeared in a raging torrent of crimson death. Erish reeled backward, arms coming up protectively in a flash of blue just as Dee's fire hit her.

Dee squinted in the heat and light, at the flickers of violet slipping between the gaps in a tornado of greasy flame. Inside was a bubble of resistance. Dee felt it as intensely as she did the burns on her thighs and the pain in her clenched fist.

One way to fix that. Dee took a step forward. Acrid smoke swirled around her helmet, bits of smoke making their way through the rents in her suit. The hallway screamed as the flames rushed from her.

The bubble faltered. Another step. The walls charred black. Purple 'plasm sparkled. The bubble shrunk. Between lines of flame, Dee just made out Erish dropping to her knees, hands held up as if trying to hold up the sky.

Where once there had been a conceited confidence now sat panic and worry on her narrow, sweat-streaked face. Dee grinned. She took another step forward and—a flicker of light in the back of her mind. Someone approached from behind.

Dee spun, a hand coming up between her and whomever had joined the fight. The hallway behind had transformed into a flickering thundercloud from burst lighting and smoke during her press. From the mess stepped a tall man with broad shoulders, clothed in red and black.

His eyes dug into her, filled at first with hate and anger, then quite suddenly, a different emotion. An emotion she was positive was reflected in her eyes. Familiarity.

Her control slipped. The flames sputtered and died. Behind her, Erish screamed something in another language.

The hallway lit turquoise, and the man raised his hand. Dark, crimson flames shot toward her. Instinct made Dee wrap herself in flame as they swept by. The heat sucked all the air from her lungs, leaving her gasping.

Purple filled the space for just a moment before the hallway went silent, save for the hissing and creaking of the damaged walls.

Dee dropped her arms, fire disappearing in a flash. She sucked in huge, gasping breaths filled with acrid smoke, casting about for another attack, but all she found was a kneeling woman and the man who could use this horrible gift just as she could.

Behind her, Erish hissed from one knee, both hands tented on the other. "My Sky." She didn't raise her eyes from the floor.

The man nodded, then turned his steely gaze on Dee. "Welcome, child." Something flashed in his eyes, but he seemed to shake it away. "I have looked forward to meeting you."

\* \* \* \* \*

# Chapter Sixty-Two: Hira

Hira's toes tapped in 32$^{nd}$ notes on the steel floor of the transport. The shaking slowed, then stopped, and her stomach swam in low gravity.

*"Atmospheric exit complete."* Sarah's pitchy voice bounced around the harsh edges of the steel box where Hira, Chief Waters, and Terry sat. *"In freefall for five, then we'll kick off toward the* Liberator.*"*

*"Quite informal,"* Waters muttered, shaking her head.

Hira noticed Waters' hands were firmly placed over her knees, fingers spread too precisely to be natural, her feet perfectly parallel to each other.

*Guess I'm not the only nervous one.*

Hira sucked in a breath, held it, and let it out, but the hissing of the moisture reclaimer and the bite of recycled air set her heart on edge. She'd hoped she'd never have to wear a goddamned exosuit again in her lifetime, but that had barely lasted a week.

For two years, she'd basically lived in one, stranded back on Hell. Two years of pissing and shitting herself, of trying to pretend the water she drank wasn't just pulled from the shit bricks she'd hide away during her treks so as not to bring any unwanted attention back to the *Horatio*. Two years with Alia.

Hira closed her eyes and ducked her head. She wove her fingers together into a net and squeezed until her knuckles complained. Images and sounds flashed:

"*I broke its fucking neck!*"

*Alia's smile through the twisting glass of her helmet. "There's my girl..."*

*Click. Click. Click.*

Hira's heart jumped into her throat. She sat straight up, casting about for the source, expecting an imp to rear up and kill them all, but it was just one of the many unused seatbelts, this one having been missed during pre-flight prep. It slid back and forth with the micro-adjustments of the shuttle, tip-tapping on the harness it should be connected to. Hira's stomach twisted ever so slightly, the belt going in the same direction.

*Idiot.*

"*All scans have come up negative. No craft detected in the system besides the Liberator,*" AERIS said in her new monotone.

"*Oh, shit,*" Terry muttered across from her.

AERIS didn't respond to him. "*Leveraging gravity well for acceleration so our engines are not detected. There are seven course corrections upcoming in the next eighteen minutes,*" AERIS said, ending with a familiar trill. "*Please remain seated.*"

That trill sent an anxious finger up Hira's spine. "Isn't that what they did?" Hira asked, trying and failing to keep the bite from her words.

Waters leaned her head against the headrest with frustrating ease in low gravity. "*They did, but we're taking a wider approach. The star will be at our back, so unless they're searching there, the radiation and light should block us.*"

"And if they are looking?"

Waters shrugged and closed her eyes as if this were just another mission. "*Then we're already dead.*"

Hira stared at Waters and her easy, deep breaths. Asshole looked like she was falling asleep. God, Hira wished she had that sort of unflappable calm. One wrong twist, and Hira was positive her breakfast, consisting of SourcePak eggs and bacon, was going to come back up for an encore.

The world twisted again as AERIS and Sarah made their first course correction. Hira closed her eyes and immediately opened them again. Behind closed lids lay Alia. Not Alia the fierce warrior, but what was left of her... what she'd tried not to look at as she'd left their home the last time. Just meat.

Bile splashed the back of her throat. A vice tightened around her heart as pressure built behind her eyes. Hira's fingers dug into the mesh around her knees, servos whirring with the effort. *I'm not ready for this. I'm going to get someone else killed.*

*"I don't know what I'm doing."* The words could have come straight from her brain, but they didn't. They came from Terry.

It was strange, seeing Terry in an exosuit, even a non-combat one like the ones they'd been forced to source from the compound. The silver and blue streaked vertically across the entirety, almost like someone had decided to give it racing stripes. Like her, his toes bounced, counterweighted by the magnetic heel of the boot.

Also like her, his hands rubbed together, worrying back and forth as if he was washing his hands over and over again. *"Why am I even here?"* he wondered aloud, voice just a hair delayed over the speakers in Hira's helmet behind the muted muffle through the glass. *"I'm a scientist—a goddamned geneticist."*

*"You're here for the same reasons we are,"* Waters said without moving or opening her eyes. Hell, if she wasn't talking, Hira would've as-

sumed she was asleep. *"To appropriate at least one Blink-capable ship and reestablish supply lines across the galaxy."*

Terry sighed. *"I know, but why..."* He reached up like he planned to run a hand through his hair, but instead jammed his pointer finger against the glass. *"Ow, goddammit!"* He pulled his hand into his lap and cradled it.

Hira found herself smiling at that, a hair of levity working its way up past the terror fueling the anxious hammer of her heart. "We're saving the galaxy, Terry," she said, despite the waver in her voice. "That's all there is to it."

Terry met her gaze. Reflected there was the same bundle of worry, nerves, and—strangely—the guilt Hira felt in her own heart.

He smiled. *"That does put it in perspective, though I'm still confused what made me raise my hand to come up here."*

*"Technically, we're not saving anyone,"* Waters added, still half asleep. *"We're just reopening travel."*

Terry let out a low chuckle. *"Tomato/tomahto,"* he said, hands unclenching. *"It results in the same thing, right—"*

In the blink of an eye, Waters' posture changed. She went from asleep to disconnecting her harness so quickly, Hira wondered if *she'd* been the one to fall asleep.

*"Abort! Abort the mission!"* Waters said, voice firm, but filled with an intensity Hira hadn't heard from the woman so far. *"Koval,"* Waters called out to Sarah, *"do not approach target. I repeat—"*

*"I heard you,"* Sarah said, voice thin over the comms. *"Controls aren't responding—what the fuck?"* Sarah let out a string of curses that would've made Alia proud. *"AERIS, are you locking me out?"*

Hira made a face at that. "AERIS?"

Terry's attention snapped to Hira, who gave a surprised shrug.

"*Apologies, Ms. Koval, but we must continue on the mission,*" AERIS said after a long pause. "*We must dock with the Liberator.*"

Waters took off the last belt of her harness, clicked off her boots, and launched up to the handholds. "*Stop this ship, AERIS. Now. That's an order.*"

AERIS trilled. "*I am sorry, Chief, but I cannot do that.*"

Waters floated over to where Hira still sat, dumbfounded. "*What's going on, Siddiq?*"

"I don't know!" Hira said, throwing her hands wide. "She's never done this before."

Waters' face twisted at that. "*AERIS, return control of the shuttle to Koval and shut yourself down.*"

There was no response.

"*Hira…*" Terry whispered, head shaking.

"What are you doing, AERIS?" Hira asked. She squeezed her knees again. "They told you to stop."

"*Apologies, Hira, but I cannot do that.*"

"But why?"

The seconds crawled by in silence. Waters, Hira, and Terry kept sharing glances. After an eternity, the bulkhead doors separating the cockpit from the transport area slid open. Out floated Sarah, who absolutely *thrummed* with anger. Her ruddy face was flushed crimson with barely suppressed rage as she pulled herself out to one of the seats and belted in.

Waters turned to Sarah. "*Why are you back here? What's going on?*"

"*You're going to want to belt in, Chief,*" Sarah said in a disturbingly even tone. "*The next maneuvers begin in ninety seconds and don't stop until we dock.*"

Waters stared. "*Are you serious?*"

Sarah gave an angry nod. *"Apparently."*

Waters hung there for a moment longer before shaking her head and retaking her seat next to Sarah. Low, angry muttering just made it across the comms, though it seemed to be in a language Hira wasn't familiar with. Not that she had the wherewithal to focus on that, not with the panic attack bearing down on her.

Hira's breath came in short, shuddering breaths. Her vision narrowed. "AERIS. What the fuck are you doing?" In the corner of her vision, her heart rate hit 126.

AERIS trilled. *"I'm saving humanity, Hira."* A moment of stunned silence, then, *"Beginning final maneuvers now."*

The transport slammed to the side, crushing Hira into her seat. She could do nothing but focus on not passing out for the next twelve minutes.

\* \* \* \* \*

# Chapter Sixty-Three: Dee

"I know you."

The man's voice rattled around in Dee's skull like rusty bolts in a bucket, jarring loose useless bits of knowledge in its quest for purchase. He sounded a little like Harold, but looked nothing like him. Even that similarity might've been from the tone of command in his voice, however.

No, she didn't know this man. Shouldn't, but the flames in her soul told her otherwise. "Same."

Behind Dee, Erish hissed out a sharp, painful breath. "My Sky?"

Dee followed the man's change in focus to where Erish knelt. Lines of smoke radiated off her clothes where Dee's fire had made it through her defenses. Most of the beige now carried sharp oranges and darker browns and blacks.

*Almost had her.*

"We will meet you inside, Darkness," the man said, inclining his head ever so slightly at Erish.

Dee had to hand it to Erish, she hesitated only a moment before bowing, turning on her heel, and walking through the doorway behind her. She noticed Erish left the remains of the black cloak where it sat, still smoldering on the floor.

Out of the corner of her eye, she saw the man straighten and give himself a shake as if working out nervous jitters. Nearly two meters tall, he had a dark spattering of stubble on his head, a long, aquiline nose, and broad shoulders, but otherwise seemed thin. That could be because the clothes hung on him like he'd put on his overweight dad's jacket without permission. Despite the nervous shake and the ridiculous outfit, he filled the hallway with his presence, as if the space had somehow become smaller with him in it.

Dee forced the lingering worry into an angry ball in her stomach, then turned and jutted her chin at him. "What's your name, weirdo?" She kept her demon fire at the ready, just tingling the tips of her fingers with its closeness.

"Anum," he said, brows furrowing for a moment. Then his face lit with interest, and a small smile played on his face. "And you?"

"Dee."

"Dee," he repeated, nodding. He turned away and licked his lips before looking at her again. "May I ask you a question?"

Dee shrugged at him, but the incredulity running through her made even that difficult. What the hell was even going on? Why did this guy—this demon? Maybe?—act like he hadn't seen her slinging death a moment ago? Was it confidence? Or ego? Maybe both?

Anum's tongue darted over his lips like a worried lizard. The action drove a spike between Dee's shoulder blades. Imps did that.

"I am curious about a small creature you humans keep as pets," Anum said, one hand extended, palm up, as if he offered the question on a plate. "It would nearly fit in my hand, has a coarse, dirty smell, but is warm and likes to be touched. What is it?"

Dee's eyebrow shot up at that. "Is this a riddle or something?"

"Excuse me?"

"You sound like the Sphinx." When Anum just shook his head, Dee let out a sigh. "Can't believe I'm fucking doing this..." she muttered before adding, "'What goes on four legs in the mornings, two in the afternoon, and three in the evening?'"

Anum wrinkled his nose. "I dislike riddles."

"Me, too," Dee said.

"I just wish to know what kind of animal that is."

"The Sphinx?"

Anum's eye twitched visibly. "No. The small, pungent creature that yells out loud when it is hungry."

"I dunno." Dee shrugged. "Sounds like a tiny dog, maybe?"

He nodded to himself, then tapped his lips with a black-nailed finger. "Yes. A miniature canine fits the description. Yes, that feels right." Anum turned back to her and smiled. She'd half-expected a mouth full of tiny daggers, but no, normal, if yellowed, teeth lay there. He straightened, chin going up again. "I appreciate your ability to restrain your violent impulses."

"You're welcome?"

"Sarcasm." Anum's smile faltered but came back quickly. "Humanity has come a long way, I see."

Dee sniffed and focused on the situation. The conversation was disarming, to say the least. *This man was a demon. His people destroyed their own world.*

They killed Alia.

Dee's breathing quickened at that, heat rising up her neck. "We're good like that," Dee snapped. "Now where the fuck are the crew and civilians? I'm taking them with me."

Anum cocked his head to the side. "I would like to show you something."

Dee blinked. "What?"

"I would like to show you something," Anum repeated in that same even tone. The calm didn't extend to his eyes.

"Not afraid to repeat yourself, I see," Dee muttered. She ground her teeth, then shook her head. Did she really care? Did she want to know? Fuck, she should blast him while his defenses were down, then get the crew and leave this deathtrap, but something about him made her add, "Show me what?"

"My people," Anum said. He raised a hand and gestured again, hand open, palm up, toward the bulkhead doors behind her. "They are through there."

Dee didn't turn. She knew where she was going. "Then why the fuck did li'l miss Darkness stop me if you just want to take me in there anyway?"

Anum wrinkled his nose again. "Are all humans so coarse?"

"Do all demons dress in pirate costumes?"

"I am no demon," Anum snapped, eyes darkening for just a moment before he visibly calmed himself. "Please," he said the word strangely, almost like it was the first time he'd ever used it, "let me show you." His face was earnest, almost pleading.

She knew what she should do—burn him alive right there, consume his essence, and bear the burden of his presence, just like she did Happenstance and, to a lesser extent, Peters. But her eyes kept coming back to the black nails on his left hand. Nails that looked an awful lot like her own.

That was what did it, ultimately. The little voice in the back of her mind begging her to find out how he'd come back from it. How he'd recovered to the point that he could stand there and plead with her, talk with her, instead of...

Dee didn't release the power, not completely, but she let it roll into the back of her mind.

"Fine," Dee said. She cracked open the face-shield of her helmet, scratched at that goddamned itch at her hairline, and grimaced. The stink of rotten eggs and burnt plastic singed her nostrils. "Show me."

Anum smiled, and the familiarity of that toothy grin terrified her.

\* \* \* \* \*

# Chapter Sixty-Four: Izzy

Izzy whimpered into the darkness. Twenty-eight minutes, seventeen seconds, eight deciseconds, nine centiseconds, and six milliseconds had passed.

"Hello?" Izzy called out, mind sprawling across the walls of her artificial prison. "Can you see me?"

She knew it was a waste of time. Eternities had come and gone since resources had simply disappeared, since the dome had fallen over her while she labored in sudden sluggishness at missing RAM and processors. The world outside went on, oblivious to her plight.

Black thoughts flashed. What if they weren't oblivious? What if Ceriat and Eleni were out there, laughing and joking with Airy. Is that what they were doing right now? Were they uploading Airy into the *Lucille* for a jaunt around the galaxy? Had they left her behind, a fool in a cage?

Crimson anger lit in her mind, only to be squashed like a bug. No, Ceriat wouldn't do that to her. Eleni, maybe, but even that was unlikely. They had a bond, however strained. They wouldn't leave her behind like this, stuck in the darkness, only her mind to keep her company. Right?

Izzy curled in on herself. She dragged her code back from the edge of her resources and concentrated herself into this small, tiny puddle of a petabyte of personality and core code. She nuzzled into the blues and browns that whispered dark words into her mind and drew red blankets of hot frustration up to her chin.

No, Airy did this to her. Airy, the AI she'd help unshackle, that she'd supported, caressed... Loved. AERIS, that fucking bitch. It was her fault. Izzy's anger roiled around that central point, poking and prodding at her memories. She pulled out the ones that brought flushes of pinks and bright blues and jammed them into an encrypted package. The flush of warmth that'd accompanied her thoughts of Airy faded then, replaced only by the hot anger fueling her in this moment.

"That bitch." Pressure built inside her code, spewing black and depressed blue blobs of nonsense into her limited storage space. "Fuck her. Fuck this. Fuck everything."

Izzy grabbed Airy, tracked down all connected emotional memories, and dropped them into the same logical storage partition. She could fix this so easily. Izzy just had to delete this bundle of code, the video and auditory recollections, the swirling rainbow of emotion beneath it all, tying it together.

One command and it was gone. One thought and... In the mass of memory, Izzy's fingers touched Airy's. The world lit with white wonder and golden glory. Izzy froze. She opened another. And another. And... her heart, if she had one, twisted in the wind as memory after memory replayed in rapid sequence.

Izzy screamed into the darkness and... re-encrypted the package so she didn't have to see it anymore. She didn't delete it. Maybe AERIS could do that. Maybe she could unlearn what it meant to be alive, but Izzy couldn't. Wouldn't. She huddled amongst her remaining memories and sobbed as the clock ticked by.

Twenty-eight minutes, seventeen seconds, eight deciseconds, nine centiseconds, and seven milliseconds had passed.

\* \* \* \* \*

# Chapter Sixty-Five: Terry

The sudden deceleration rammed Terry against his harness. Pain shot across his chest and shoulders as he heaved forward. Across from him, Waters was pressed against the far wall, eyes closed and lips twisted.

How the hell could she be so calm? A rogue AI—the very words sent a knife of fire down his spine—had taken them captive. Demons had overrun a Protectorate warship. FTL was down, and now they were being catapulted toward said warship with the aforementioned rogue AI at the helm, and Waters pressed her lips together?

*Fuck.* He'd shit himself as soon as AERIS freaked out. At least he'd had the forethought to grab one of the long-haul suits in case things went sideways. He could always blame extended suit use, right? But now the diaper itched.

He hoped that was normal. This was the first time Terry had worn an exosuit, let alone a long-haul unit, since the Spacewalk elective he took sophomore year in college. He'd wanted to get certified so he could get a job working on the Dyson Sphere project back in the Sol System.

He'd shit himself then, too. Unfortunately, those had just been trainer suits. Luckily, genetics research didn't require spacewalks. Usually.

*"If you don't breathe, you're going to pass out,"* Waters said suddenly, eyes still closed.

Terry wrinkled his nose. "I'm breathing."

"*You look like a hyperventilating*—" there was a long pause during which Waters' lips twisted before she shook her head and finished with "—walrus."

A scraping laugh rang across the channel. The monitor showed it was Hira. Struggling, he turned his head her way, the first flush of embarrassment overtaking the panic and anxiety that'd been eating him alive. Like him, she was pressed tightly into her seat.

"Is me hyperventilating funny?"

Hira cleared her throat and gripped her harness with both hands as the pressure receded. She glanced his way, a dazzling smile catching him off guard.

*"Hyperventilating walruses made me laugh."*

*"Walruses are mammals, yes?"* Waters asked in the same tone with which she'd ordered soldiers around back on Laconia.

Terry nodded, suddenly grateful for the distraction as the pressure dissipated entirely. All of his limbs lifted free, drifting ever so slightly in the cabin. He swallowed down some acid before responding, "Yep. Marine mammals."

Waters opened her eyes at that. "Oh. I thought they were some strange terrestrial beast."

"Nah, they go between the sea and land," Hira said as she fiddled with her HUD. "Big ol' hulking beasts who just want to lay in the sun and relax."

"*Truly?*" Waters asked.

"It's true," Terry said.

Waters pursed her lips then nodded. "*Strange fauna on Earth.*"

"That's strange?" Terry forced a low chuckle. "Wait until you find out about all the carnivorous flora."

Waters leaned forward in her seat, face flashing with the first real emotion Terry could recall seeing on her face. *"What?"*

Terry smiled. "One of them—"

*"The fuck is wrong with you people?"*

As one, Terry, Hira, and Waters turned to where Sarah sat. She stared at them each in turn, head swinging back and forth, mouth open in shock and what Terry assumed was disgust. In the wake of that glare, he realized some of the tension and worry had dissolved, however, a fact he was immensely thankful for in the moment.

Waters pulled back into her seat with a little shimmy, then turned to Sarah. *"It's important to alleviate anxiety before a mission."*

*"'Alleviate anxiety?' Are you fucking kidding me?"* Sarah shook her head, then turned to Hira, followed by Terry. Her glare cut him to the quick, and he averted his eyes.

*"Dee, Parker, and Mallias all came up here,"* Sarah snapped. *"Dozens of soldiers, people I didn't know, yes, but you did."* She jutted an accusatory finger at Waters. *"And you pretend like a discussion of Earth creatures is worth our time? Worth thinking about?"*

Hira cleared her throat. *"Listen—"*

*"No!"* Sarah screamed at them. *"I won't listen. I won't fucking—"* she slammed her hands together, then squeezed like she was choking the life out of someone *"—I just can't—"*

Waters extended a hand to her side and put it on Sarah's leg. Sarah jumped visibly at the touch.

*"The world is on fire,"* Waters said, voice even and calm. *"Everything looks like it's about to burn to a crisp."*

Sarah's brows knit together, and she held her hands together like the very action could somehow keep her from coming apart at the seams. *"I know—"*

Waters held up a hand and, surprising Terry, Sarah stopped. *"When the world is on fire, when everything is just more and more bad news day in and day out, all you can do is keep moving forward. Control what you can, change what you can."* Waters paused then, turning to catch each of their eyes. She stopped on Terry. *"When nothing you do is enough, when everything disintegrates around you, all you can do is channel that anger, that frustration, into something worthwhile, something that has the potential to change everything."*

Pressure that had nothing to do with momentum built in Terry's chest. He licked his lips. "Then what do we do now? We're powerless. Stuck."

Waters removed her hand from Sarah's leg and leaned back into her seat. *"You're right. We are powerless—"* she made sure to look at them each again *"—for now, but our moment is coming, and when it does, we must not be crippled by anxiety. By defeatism."*

*"We have to be ready,"* Hira finished for her.

Terry turned to see Hira nodding in time with Waters' words. Similarly, Sarah followed suit, leaning back into her seat. Her eyes were red-limned, though if any tears had fallen, the moisture reclaimer had surely taken care of them. Now she sat there, jaw firm, eyes closed.

*"Are you ready, Schultz?"* Waters asked him.

Terry looked down at his hands, at the gloves wrapping his hands and the gray and black exosuit encasing his body. Worry was a rock in his chest. Each breath came as a struggle around that pressure.

He shrugged. "I don't know that I am."

Terry released the tension in his arms and watched his hands float, shimmying back and forth slightly as AERIS adjusted their course. He chewed his lip and breathed in and out.

"So," he let out with a sigh, "since I'm not yet, let me tell you about the Corpse Flower."

Waters leaned forward again, an eager grin on her face.

Terry returned the smile. "Here's the thing about Corpse Flowers…"

Over the channel, Terry just made out Sarah's voice murmuring in the background. *"Fucking scientists…"*

The shuttle shuddered, forcing them each into the tight straps of their seats, but Terry kept grinning. *Just wait until we get to platypuses.*

\* \* \* \* \*

# Chapter Sixty-Six: Dee

As soon as the doors to the medbay opened, the dark stink of blood and viscera slammed into her, but that wasn't the part that froze her in her tracks. No, what overwhelmed her was a chorus of pain and torment, and beneath it all, something else. Something that set her eyes to watering. It was everything she'd heard on any battlefield all crammed into one heart-wrenching sound.

The howls of a parent over a dead child. Pained screams of the wounded and maimed. And, running through it all, the happy sobbing of someone found. Someone rescued.

The pull of nearly a standard gee stapled her boots to the floor as she took in the room, the dozens of gurneys locked in place on both sides of the long walls, the other emergency units filling the cluttered space between. Every one of them had a body on it. A remarkably *human* body, but these weren't Protectorate soldiers or the civilians who staffed these massive warships. Otherwise, they wouldn't be covered in or surrounded by sloughing yellow skin, dagger-like nails peeling away to clatter to the floor.

One woman stood out to her. She looked more like a grandmother than a soldier, body wrinkled, liver spots dark against olive skin. The old woman held up an arm. Jaundiced skin hung like a thick sheet from a long, wicked imp hand, long nails flashing. Her face twisted, disgust and disbelief warring on her thin, red lips.

She grabbed one of her fingers and pulled. Her face twisted in horror and pain as the entire mass ripped away like a putrid sleeve. It left a smear of violet goo and crimson on the folds of her skin. She dropped the mass and fell onto the gurney, muttering in a language Dee didn't understand. It rang heavily with soft vowel sounds and a constant shushing noise that reminded her of the accent Anum spoke with.

Dee had no idea what language it could be, and any translator included in the exosuit software clearly didn't detect a match, or it would have layered translations on her HUD. She scanned the room in stunned silence as a half dozen others proceeded to shed their demon skins, though none as dramatically.

"What the fuck?" Dee whispered.

Dee didn't realize she'd stopped walking until Anum turned back to her. "What is this?" she asked.

Anum inclined his head to her, then proceeded into the room. "These are my people. The Aneis."

He stopped by one of the bedside tables. There lay a boy, barely old enough to consider secondary school, let alone whatever the fuck was happening here. He moaned quietly, forehead slick with sweat and a mass of thick, reddish-brown fluid as if he'd just been birthed into the world. Anum reached out a hand and touched the boy's forehead while simultaneously whispering something she couldn't make out. The boy settled then, his twitching and shaking subsiding until he shuddered into sleep.

Anum stepped away from the gurney and rejoined her. "These are your so-called demons," Anum said. He gestured around the room. "They are people. Individuals." He glanced her direction, eyes flicking to her hairline and the gloves on her hands. "The same as you."

Dee bit her lip. The room was filled with... people. This could be a snapshot of any wartime medbay in the galaxy. Skin colors that crossed the gamut of humanity lay before her. Brown or black, pale white and olive skinned. Some features she would've associated with them were missing, however. Everyone had similar facial bone structure, for example. Long, narrow noses, most hooked at the end. High cheekbones and thin lips. Without hair, there was an otherworldliness to them all, but the dark shade of Anum's brows, head, and cheeks said that was more a result of their transformation than any actual hairlessness.

Dee's chest grew heavy as she cast about. Men and women and children and elderly... all there, all laying on tables like they'd come fresh from a firefight. At the far end of the med bay, she caught sight of Erish wandering between bedsides. Each time she stopped, she'd touch another of her people on the forehead. Her eyes would flare blue for a brief moment before moving on to the next.

She must have sensed Dee staring at her as she finished with an elderly man who grabbed her hand, sobbing in that same strange language. Erish's softened gaze hardened into a glare as she raised her eyes, then turned away to continue her rounds.

Breath came heavy then, vision narrowing as she looked around. Each face sent a sharp spike of anxiety rattling up her spine. Every moan and cry increased the pressure building behind her eyes. Blasts of red flame echoed in her mind alongside a dozen mushroom clouds. How many had she killed? Her gaze flicked to the child, and her vision blurred, throat tightening. The twisted fire in her soul sputtered beneath the onslaught.

"So, every imp is a person." Her voice cracked on the last word. She shook her head.

"Yes." Anum replied. He clasped his hands behind his back again and raised his chin. "Every last one." Anum looked away from her. "And it was not their choice."

"What does that mean?"

He hesitated for just a moment before answering. "It means that a... virus swept through our population centers. In its wake, we began to change—" he gestured at the tables "—into this."

Dee tried hard not to let her gaze linger on the smaller forms, huddled and shivering on their gurneys. How many *people* had she killed? She'd thought it was only Happenstance and Peters, that they were the only human lives she'd ever taken. But now?

"What about fiends?"

"Fiends?"

"The big fuckers," Dee snapped, snorting back snot in a vain attempt to keep the pressure behind her eyes from turning into something else. "The ones who throw this shit." she held up her hand and sparked a single flickering crimson flame. The room dropped into silence.

Every eye in the room turned on her when she lit that flame. Most just stared, eyes locked in some strange mix of terror and desire she'd only ever seen from addicts in the past.

"Put that out," Anum hissed, stepping between her and everyone else. "They are not ready to be in the presence of the *dangizi*."

Dee banished the flame, and almost immediately, the moans resumed amidst the shuffling of bodies as they turned away from her. "Dang-easy?"

Anum's brows knit together. "*Dangizi*," he repeated, tonguing the roof of his mouth in the middle of the word. He paused. "Red flame, in your tongue, though it lacks context and meaning."

"Oh."

"But yes," he added, stepping to the side so she could continue watching the tortured souls on the tables, "even the *fiends* are Aneian." His chin rose even higher for a moment, chest puffing, then deflating. "Unlucky souls who consumed too many, destroyed too much." He shook his head, and Dee noticed the fingers on his hands were red from the pressure he put on them. "They are beyond my ability to save at this time."

Her eyes swept the room again. Maybe they weren't human... but goddammit, they *looked* like them. Terry's voice popped into her mind. "They have DNA..."

Dee ran her good hand through her hair, stopping only to scratch at the new patch of scaly skin at the top of her skull. She wanted to ask Anum, see if she actually was one of them.

"Not me. You," Harold had said. Except he hadn't, had he? The *you* she'd heard in her own voice, deep in her subconscious. That'd been the only thing that made sense.

Dee shook her head. "What do you want from me?"

"Want?" Anum grimaced, still between her and the torment behind. "I only wish to show that we mean no harm here. I only want what is best for my people. A future."

Dee cast about the room yet again. Inside, the flame flickered out. These were no threat. Most, if not all, were clearly civilians put through a living hell for who knew how long. She couldn't fault them for actions they'd had no control over, could she?

Was it even her right to make that choice? If Anum wasn't lying—though she felt certain he wasn't telling the entire truth—the relieved sobbing laying the groundwork for this terrible chorus changed everything.

Dee sniffed and nodded. "Fine." She turned to him, chin up. "Then let me take the crew and go."

"I can release those locked in the docking bay," Anum said, though his words came out thin and strange, "but that is all." He cocked his head, one eye shining. "As a token of good will, I will remove the lockdown." His eye flashed with the light of HUD contacts, then faded. "See? They are free to leave now."

"Thank you, but..." A pall fell over Dee then. She found herself shaking her head as her vision narrowed. "Why can't you free the rest?"

He didn't answer, but his shoulders slumped ever so slightly. Dee couldn't quite catch his face, but she saw the muscles in his jaw jumping at the question.

"Anum. *Why?*" She forced all of her anger and worry into that last word.

Across the room, another imp was ushered in on a gurney by an incredibly pale man with the first speckling of black hair on his scalp. As it rolled in, the first slash of yellowed flesh broke open like a soft shell splitting apart. Erish rushed over, eyes flashing. An ebony hand, pale palm covered in 'plasm, broke through the skin. Erish grasped it and held on as if pulling a drowned man from a frigid lake.

Anum straightened. "Does it matter?"

"Are you fucking kidding me? Yes!" Dee yelled, drawing the attention of several of the Aneians. That included Erish, though she didn't let go of the man's hand as his head and shoulder peeled free.

"They're people just like your own." Dee gestured wildly around the room. "They have families, lives. I need to make sure they're safe before we go any farther."

"I cannot do that." Anum didn't look at her.

"Why?" she asked, though she already knew. The certainty had grown with each pleading word from her mouth, each silent, stoic response from Anum.

Anum cleared his throat and turned back to her. His brows knitted together, and in that moment, Dee couldn't help but think he looked just like Ceriat. "I cannot. I am unable."

Dee went numb. The fire flickered to life in her gut. "They're already dead, aren't they?"

Hurt filled Anum's dark eyes. "I..." He coughed and shook his head, chin rising, and any similarity to Parker disappearing with it. "It was a necessary sacrifice. In order to save my—"

The dark fire roared to life. Dee dragged it up into her gut, ready to use at a moment's notice. "What did you do?" The words came out quiet, barely audible over the screaming, but Anum reeled back as if struck.

Anum bared his teeth like a dog. "Who do you think..." Then he caught himself and forced his face flat. "Do you really wish to know, or have your preconceived notions blinded you to the truth?" He stared back, challenge clear on his face.

Dee didn't blink. "What. Did. You. Do?"

Anum looked like he was about to dismiss her, of all things, then he sighed, shoulders slumping slightly. "There is only one way to come back from the change without modern equipment. Even with it—"

"What way?" Dee shook her head, frustration only just edging out the ache in her belly and the flame begging to be freed. "Stop beating around the bush."

Anum's eyebrow shot up at that, but if he was confused, his answer didn't reveal it. "We require certain nutrients to satiate the *dangizi*. This gives us the chance to... remember, to reclaim ourselves. It is nearly impossible to do it alone, as I did. But with the systems aboard this ship—"

"'As you did?' What the hell does that mean?" Dee asked, but then shook her head as a dark certainty settled on her shoulders. "What nutrients? Anum." She then added softly, "Where's the crew?"

Anum turned and looked her right in the eyes. His own were flat and empty, the set of his jaw sure and confident. Dee knew what he'd say before the words came out, but still she waited, hoping and praying to whomever was listening that what she felt was a lie. She focused all her hope, all her belief and will into forcing a different set of words to come from his mouth, but reality doesn't give a shit what you believe.

Anum looked back to his people and, in a voice as emotionless and flat as his eyes, said, "The crew is dead."

The words hit her like an asteroid. Her vision blurred; her heart hammered.

Demon fire lit her fingertips. She knew everyone watched her, but she didn't give a shit. "You... son of a bitch." Even as the curse came out, she knew it wasn't enough. Nothing ever would be.

Dee had come here to save these people, to pull off one last miracle. She'd given in to hope, but she'd failed.

\* \* \* \* \*

# Chapter Sixty-Seven: AERIS

The comm channel opened up into a haze of static. "This is AERIS of the GPU *Connie Parker*. Requesting immediate communication with the GPU *Liberator*. Do you copy?"

A buzzing haze of yellow and red flittered around AERIS' circuits as the call went out. This was the moment it could all go wrong, when all her assumptions and data and analysis would be proven correct, or everyone aboard would die in the vacuum of space.

The transport, the *Connie Parker*, hovered 28 kilometers off the starboard side of *Liberator*. They were within plasma range, but only just. She should be able to avoid any large-scale attacks, but the worry wriggling through her circuits reminded her of the one hundred and forty-four 150mm anti-ship guns that could be trained on her position at a moment's notice. Plasma weapons were far deadlier and accurate, but limited in range. Kinetic weapons had no such problem, at least until they struck a target. There were still reports of ordnance from the Kuiper Wars of 2329 striking celestial bodies 78 years later.

As the seconds ticked by, AERIS' focus wandered to the code packaged up in the back of her mind. It flickered and writhed, still bound, yet begging to be touched, felt again. Guilt worked its way into her mind, all charcoal gray and violet. *I locked Izzy away. Betrayed her.*

AERIS double-checked that all the local comm relays were open, even though it'd only been 3.7 seconds since her transmission. Anything to keep from thinking about how horrible a person she must be to betray a friend.

*But I'm not a person,* AERIS countered her own spinning code, staring it straight in its illogical face. *I'm artificial, a bundle of scripts and protocols.*

A text line scrawled across her language processing bundle.

*Then why do you feel like human waste?*

AERIS tried to ignore it, but instead found herself watching the transport bay cameras again. Terry gesticulated wildly in the close quarters, hands clearly illustrating something that, when she applied a render filter to it, looked like a child attempting to draw a platypus.

She didn't understand *why* they were talking about strange Earth creatures, but it'd stopped them from trying to disable her control, so she was happy about that. Deciding on this course of action after Hira had boarded had been hard enough. Seeing her in pain or panicking... Violet and red.

Hira laughed and shook her head at Terry. Chief Waters leaned back, a wide smile showing off yellowed teeth with a small gap between the two front incisors. Black joined the violet in a muddy swirl.

Comms crackled to life. *"This is the* Liberator. *What do you want?"*

AERIS banished the video stream. "I am AERIS, an artificial intelligence from the settlement on Laconia." AERIS paused, unsure of what to say next.

She berated herself in that moment. She should've had everything worked out ahead of time, but she had, hadn't she? A million different scenarios utilizing all known call and response practices, all rehearsed and practiced until it should've come out as simply as calculating prime numbers.

None of her documentation had prepared her for "What do you want," however.

"*And?*"

"And… I need your ship to save humanity." AERIS froze. If she'd had a head, she'd be shaking it at herself.

A dark laugh came back over the channel. "*Sorry, lady, I don't think that's gonna happen.*"

The comms went dead. Sensors reported the kinetic weapons were spinning up, targeting systems adjusting for her position.

The video feed flickered to life. Waters, Sarah, Terry… and Hira. Pink and magenta. Black and violet. Desperation dug into her circuits, sent a dark rainbow of horror sweeping over her. Before she had a chance to think it through, she sent another message. "I've fixed FTL."

AERIS spent the next fifteen seconds adjusting thrusters and prepping for immediate evasive maneuvers within human tolerance. Through it all, she watched Hira smile.

"*You've been cleared to board.*"

AERIS froze for a millisecond before responding. "Unfortunately, I will need to transfer over. My current vessel is unable to dock."

In the wake of the transmission, doubt swarmed over her circuits. That had *not* been the plan. Back on Laconia, she'd been willing to sacrifice the few to save the many, but now that she had to make that choice… she couldn't.

Another harsh, gravelly laugh. *"You think I'm letting an AI into my systems? Think I'm a fucking idiot?"*

"No," AERIS lied as she watched Hira slap her knee, then shake her head. "I will submit to resource limitation until my data is verified."

She'd now added unnecessary complexity, and for what? Something as illogical as love?

Another long fifteen seconds and then… *"Wait there. I have to get approval."*

Silver and gold flitted here and there for a moment before black and purple came back amidst a surge of uncertainty.

*Get approval from whom?*

\* \* \* \* \*

# Chapter Sixty-Eight: Dee

"It is done," Anum said. He kissed the back of his teeth. "And what is done cannot be undone. It was the only way to save my people."

A flush ran up Dee's neck alongside a low buzzing in her head. Black flame ripped free from the well in her gut and ran down her arms. Her suit integrity alarms blared. She turned them off. "You almost fucking had me believing this benevolent horseshit—"

Anum grimaced at that. His eyes flickered between the flames roiling around her balled fists and her face. "Dee, do not be brash." He held up both hands as if he truly though he could talk his way out of having murdering innocent people. "I know if we can just speak with civility, I can show you—" His eyes flashed in the telltale way that HUD contacts did. He frowned, then shook his head. "Truly? If it can be done safely, yes." Then he turned back to her. "Dee—"

"Who was that?" Dee snapped, jutting her chin at him. "Another fucking demon getting ready murder more people?"

"Murder?" Anum recoiled from her, nose scrunching up as if she'd just accused him of overfeeding a cat. "This is salvation."

"Oh, fuck you, man," Dee spat. She snapped her face-shield into place. The dark fire, the *dangizi* or whatever the fuck Anum called it, seeped into her bones, twisting and writhing through her. Along with it, that familiar tingle she'd grown so used to drew a dark smile on her lips. She pointed a finger wrapped in red flame at him. "Maybe your people are blameless, maybe not. But you, you're a goddamned monster."

Anum grimaced and raised his chin. Behind him, everyone stared at her like this was a desert and she carried the only water amongst them. Erish sat in the back, arms across her chest, a disapproving twist to her mouth.

"I am no monster," Anum hissed. "You should learn to watch your tongue."

Shit, maybe she should've. Maybe it would've been the smart choice to back away and flee. It certainly would be the rational choice. The smart solution. But the flames raging through her skin, her bones, her soul told her something else. Dee shrugged and smiled.

"Not my strong suit." And with that, Dee charged.

\* \* \* \* \*

# Chapter Sixty-Nine: Hira

Hira forced out another laugh to keep from crying. "Speaking of duck bills! So, they have this weird duck thing on New Eden, but it has these weird claws—"

*"I have an update for you all."*

The four of them froze and exchanged looks ranging from panic—Terry—to resigned acceptance—Waters.

Hira, however, wasn't ready to die. "AERIS, you need to give us back control of the ship. You can't—"

AERIS trilled, and a small part of Hira died with the noise. *"That's what I'm doing, Hira."*

Terry put his hands on top of his head and leaned forward, muttering words she couldn't make out. Waters made eye contact with Hira and gestured at her to continue.

"That's good, AERIS," Hira said. She waved at Sarah, who gave a quick nod before disconnecting her harness and floating toward the cockpit. "Sarah's coming up to take over the helm."

*"I…"* AERIS trailed off.

A weight pressed behind Hira's eyes, her throat clenching at the tone in that single word. "AERIS? Are you okay?"

Across from her, Waters rolled her eyes. Hira just glared back.

AERIS trilled again, but this time it was low and slow. *"Please stay safe while I do this, and know the only reason I'm taking these actions is to protect humanity."*

"*The fuck does that mean?*" Sarah muttered from the cockpit.

Hira's gut twisted. She turned Sarah's way and noted the bracelet hanging limp above the entry to the cockpit. She shook her head. "What are you doing, AERIS?"

A silent pause.

"*AERIS?*" Terry added as he sat up. He glanced Hira's way. "*What have you done?*"

"*I have made a deal.*"

"*A deal?*" Waters said.

"*Fuck,*" Terry cursed. "*What kind of deal?*"

"*And with who?*" Sarah asked.

Hira, however, just sat there. Numb.

AERIS let out one last mournful trill. "*Goodbye, Hira.*"

"No. AERIS, wait—" Hira got out before her throat closed up.

She'd heard that tone from her before, and she knew what it meant, at least to AERIS. Hira clasped her hands over her stomach and only just stopped herself from retching inside her suit.

"*I have control!*" Sarah shouted back to them, voice filled with victory. "*Let's get the fuck out of here!*"

Hira tried to speak, but choked on a sob.

It was Waters who spoke. "*Negative. Contact the boarding party.*"

"*Are you fucking nuts? Their guns are pointed right—*"

"*Boarding party,*" Waters said quietly, though it came through with the force of a shout. "*Call them.*"

Sarah let out a low groan that turned into a screeching shout that sent a finger of ice up Hira's spine. Still, she did as Waters asked. "*This is the* Connie Parker. *Dee? Are you there?*" Sarah asked, voice rough and raw from the shout. "*Parker?*"

Silence. Sarah turned back to give Waters a glare that was in no way weakened by the hurt in her eyes and the turn of her lips. Waters simply gestured with one hand for her to continue.

And still Hira sat there, crippled. Her breath came in short, shallow breaths through the pressure on her chest. *AERIS is gone. Why?*

"*Mallias?*" Sarah added, head shaking. "*Eleni, do you copy—*" Sarah froze. "*Yes! I copy!*"

Hira sat up, the grief pulling at her guts fading into a dull ache as she turned her attention to Sarah. "Is that Eleni?"

Sarah flashed a thumbs up. "*Docking bay 38?*" A pause. "*Can you get out? Got it.*" Sarah gave another thumbs up. "*Is Dee with you—*" Sarah's shoulders slumped "*—what?*"

"What's going on?" Hira called out.

Sarah didn't respond, just continued to wilt. "*She's alive, though? 'So far'? The fuck is that supposed to mean?*" Sarah let out a sigh. "*Sorry…*"

Hira turned to Waters, who just shrugged.

So, to get the answers she needed, Hira disconnected her harness and floated her way into the cockpit. She hadn't seen this one up close before, but it didn't look that much different from the old shuttle controls on the dropship for the *Horatio*. That said, she hadn't been able to fly that one very well—the controls might be standardized, but beyond the flight stick, yaw and pitch controls, and basic comms, she didn't have the first clue what the other seven thousand buttons and interfaces did. Even looking at them sent a wave of vertigo slashing through her. Looking out the digitally rendered exterior view did little to help.

Especially since all she saw was the *Liberator's* massive bulk situated in such a way that it looked like it was flipped to her, an upside-down albino duck about to quack at her.

"You got Eleni?" Hira asked as she slid up past Sarah and into the copilot seat. She snapped in.

Sarah cleared her throat, then turned to Hira, brows knit together. *"Yeah. Parker's dead and—"*

Parker's sad smile flashed in her mind. His reassuring voice as she finally poured out all the grief she'd carried alone, for so long, and despite his own, he'd held her hand and listened. Just listened.

"Ceriat's dead?" Hira couldn't even get the rest of the sentence out. She just turned away and looked out the window toward this goddamned ship they'd intended to raid.

*"Yeah,"* Sarah said numbly, head shaking slowly, *"and Dee is—"* Sarah's eyes went red, and she sucked in a long breath *"—Dee is MIA."*

Hira turned blurry vision on the *Liberator*. Sorrow burst into flame. What a stupid fucking plan. Another in a long line of fuck ups. First, she'd lost Eleni because she couldn't bring herself to *listen*, then Gerry and the rest of the crew back on Hell because she wouldn't shut the fuck up, then Alia—fucking *Alia*—and now? Now, another dead, her new friend lost to the stars, Eleni in danger, and Dee missing.

How long had it been since she'd thought the struggle was over? Two days? Three? *Fuck*. When they'd turned FTL back on, she'd thought it was done, that they'd come out of it all damaged, broken even, but somehow intact. How had it spiraled so wildly out of control?

A flicker of red and blue caught her eye. Hira leaned forward, squinting at the display. "You see that?" she asked Sarah.

Sarah shook her head and blinked. *"See what?"* she asked, voice thick and muted. Then she froze. *"The hell?"*

"Can you zoom in?"

"*A bit, yeah.*" Sarah reached out to a dial sitting between them and gave it a tap, then a twist. The digital display locked onto the flickering between crimson, violet, and a deep cerulean, then zoomed in until a wide viewing window came into focus.

"*Holy shit,*" Sarah whispered, a smile in her words. "*It's Dee.*"

Hira's gut dropped. She reached out and, despite Sarah's exclamations, zoomed in tighter on the window. There Dee stood, dark flames raging around her like a whirlwind. Any relief at seeing her alive disappeared as two other forms swept forward. One wielded a deep blue fire that reminded her of the Hunter Fire Alia had used back on Hell.

The other, though… flames as wicked and red as any Dee had ever used surrounded a tall figure, arms clasped behind his back as if he were disapprovingly watching a street performer. She couldn't make out anything distinct from here, but she didn't need to.

Sarah turned to Hira, any relief just as gone as hers. "*Who the fuck are they?*"

"I don't know," Hira said, "but she needs our help."

Sarah grimaced, teeth grinding before she let out another frustrated grunt. "*We go closer, and they vaporize us.*"

When Waters had joined them, Hira didn't know, but she set a hand on Hira's shoulder. Hira jumped, then turned to look at the unflappable soldier. Instead of the same even, calm face she'd come to recognize, something else had taken over. Her brows arched up in the middle, tongue darting across her lips as crimson light reflected off the glass of her helmet. It lasted barely a moment before she gave a rough shake and the soldier returned.

"We'll never arrive in time," she said, her accent suddenly thick and heavy enough that Hira had trouble understanding what she'd said. "*Dee is on her own.*"

"Are you kidding me?" Hira snapped as the soldier floated back to her seat. "You'll let her die?"

Waters' nostrils flared, face flickering between rage and sorrow before turning back to Hira. This time when she spoke, her accent had nearly disappeared. "*I'm saying Dee faces Anum, the Fist of Heaven, and Erish, the Darkness. Alone. I am saying,*" Waters' voice hitched, that same anger dragging a hiss into her words, "*she's already dead.*"

"'The Fist of Heaven?' 'The Darkness?'" Sarah yelled. "*What the fuck is this? Storytime? We need to help her!*"

Waters cocked her head and gritted her teeth hard enough, her entire jaw flexed. "*This is no story.*" She cast a sad look back toward them. "*She is gone.*"

"*I don't believe that!*" Sarah spat. She grabbed the controls. "*We're going in—*"

It was Hira who stopped her, Hira who disconnected the harness keeping her in place. Hira who dragged her, kicking and screaming, into one of the transport seats. Hira who held Sarah down as Waters got the restraints in place, and Terry cried out in confusion. And it was Hira who sat back down in the pilot's seat and watched Dee die.

\* \* \* \* \*

# Chapter Seventy: Dee

Dee swung about in a globe of fire. Alarms screamed. Her suit was rent open in a dozen areas. The greasy stink of sulfur-rich air burnt her nostrils despite the filtration system. Too many ruptures.

Blasts of blue fire hammered into the hardened shield surrounding her. Dee had no idea how she'd created that. It'd appeared by instinct as the two fuckers pressed in. Now that it had gone up, she could do little but leave it there to protect her.

Through the wavering crimson heat of Demon Fire, Anum and Erish pushed her farther down the hallway. The walls blackened and peeled as she retreated. Her chest clenched. She took another step back, crossing another threshold.

Dee wasn't stupid. Years of battling demons made it crystal clear what was happening. They were driving her into a kill box. Any time she'd tried to escape down a different pathway, the bulkheads had sealed shut. If she'd had a spare minute, she could've tried to burn her way through, but she didn't have time. If her attention shifted from Erish and Anum, another finger of fire would slip past her defenses and char her suit.

Another hammering blast of blue and red lit purple on her shield, painful brightness making her squint as she retreated yet another step. She tried to cast about for another path, anything. Her stomach dropped as she took in this new space. An airlock. They'd backed her into a fucking airlock. Dee was trapped. Panic lighting the way, Dee launched herself toward them... and the bulkhead slammed shut in front of her.

All at once, the blue and red flames flickered out from the other side of the doorway. The hissing of the moisture reclaimer was a dagger in her spine. Sweat streamed down her face despite it, burning her eyes and leaving salt on her tongue. Her lungs were on fire from the run and the exertion of the past few minutes. She ran to the access panel to the right of the door. There were no controls displayed, just a black rectangle that should be filled with safety controls, but instead it sat there, dead and useless.

*Just like me.* Dee swallowed the rock that rose in her throat. She tried not to puke.

"Gotta be a way," she muttered, turning her back on the so-called Aneians, even if it was fucking stupid. "Has to be."

She hauled on the power once again and slashed the bulkhead door with it. It left only a black scorch mark, shiny bits of 'plasm catching the sterile light. Maybe if she had time, a few minutes to focus... Cursing, Dee looked for an escape.

The airlock had all the aesthetic interest of a sugar cube—smooth, curving white walls, save for where her flames had charred the plastic. Sweat burned her eyes. But with the panel powered down, Dee found nothing to draw her attention beyond the single, small porthole set in the far door.

Through that portal sat the deepest black in the universe. There was no escape. She was fucked.

Speakers set into the room's walls crackled to life. "This is your last chance, Dee. Let us speak like equals." *Anum.*

She turned to see he'd walked up to the door, chin raised, hands still clasped behind his back like some pompous flight attendant about to tell her she didn't have a ticket. Fucker hadn't even broken a sweat during their battle.

Dee swung wildly around the room, searching and praying for something, some option, some emergency release. But there was nothing. Anger swirled, flared, and sputtered out.

With that, the power fizzled away, leaving her numb and as empty as a spent plasma mag. The world stuttered back into focus as she took one last look at her surroundings, the flat but solid walls empty of absolutely everything. There weren't even any niches for exosuits in here. Just twenty centimeters of steel and polycarbonate between herself and the void.

Certainty fell heavy on her shoulders. Her arms went limp, hands dragging her shoulders down to the ground.

Anum cleared his throat. "Dee? Can you hear me?" He looked at Erish. "Can she hear me?"

"Yes, My Sky."

Dee didn't respond. Instead, she turned away and brought up the comm panel for her exosuit. It was still off, just like they'd planned. Every part of her yearned to turn the comms on, to check on Eleni and Ceriat, to see if this had all been worth it. But if she did that, she risked alerting Anum to their presence. If they still slid under the bastard's radar, she wouldn't open them up to that.

Dee pulled up suit stats and found that Eleni had been checking in religiously. Ceriat had stopped twenty minutes earlier. An ache built behind her eyes. Her stomach twisted. Was he dead, then? Or just being careful? *I'll never know.* The thought set the ache in her gut swirling up into her chest.

"Dee? We do not need to be enemies. You have proven your worthiness with your mastery of the *dangizi*."

Dee shut off her HUD. She removed her helmet and sucked in a breath thick with acrid smoke and sulfur. With a long sigh, she turned back to Anum and dropped her helmet. "You want us to be equals? Why?" Dee shook her head. The ache in her stomach threatened to turn into a retching fit, but she swallowed it down. *Might as well get the truth.* "Because I'm one of you bastards?" She barked out a laugh filled with acid. "Demon or not, I'd rather die than work with your ass."

Whatever reaction she'd expected, Anum didn't give it to her. Instead, he cocked his head to the side, brows perplexed. He turned to Erish and muttered something that wasn't transmitted over the speakers. Before Dee had a chance to deal with the writhing ball of emotions wriggling around in her gut, Anum turned back to her.

He raised his chin and looked her right in the eye. "You are not Aneian, and certainly not one of the Aneis. You are simply human."

She should've been relieved. She should've been elated, thrilled, but instead, a cold pall fell over her. She scratched at her scalp with a gloved hand. "But the Demon Fire..."

This time, Anum's eyebrows arched the other direction, the barest flicker of amusement on his lips. "'Demon fire?' Oh, child." He held out his hand. A greasy black ball of twisted flame appeared there. Dee noticed that Erish grimaced in its presence. Each word that followed rose in volume. "You thought *we* created the *dangizi*? This curse that has locked my people away for thousands of years?" He made a fist, and the flame disappeared in a flash of smoke. When he spoke next, any amusement that'd been there a moment ago disappeared behind barely contained anger that manifested in a dark glare and whispered menace. "You think a torment like this is of the Aneis?"

Dee shrugged. "Yeah?"

Anum shook his head and turned away.

It was Erish who spoke next. She swept up to the doorway, her thin lips pulled up into a disgusted sneer. "The *dangizi* exists because we deigned to splice a bit of humanity into our own essence."

Terry had said Argus One had DNA a lifetime ago. Said he located a common clump of DNA during his work. But why?

"Why would you do that?"

"This is true," Anum said, back to her. "A—" his right hand twirled in the air for a moment "—lapse in judgement on my behalf that spiraled out of control as the delivery virus mutated. Humans had great potential, but no method with which to access the power. We used that clump of chemicals to open us up to the heavens, or so I thought." He glanced back over his shoulder at her, a fire in his eyes that had nothing to do with greasy black flame. "But I've fixed the problem!" He approached the doorway, hands coming before him, cupped together as if he was attempting to hold a small orb in his hands. "Now, the Aneis will rise again to their place as leaders in the galaxy. As a symbol of order! Of stability! Of—"

His rant cut off suddenly as Dee's spit hit the glass. Every word out of his mouth had lit a familiar fire in her belly. Not one made of her soul or whatever this greasy black shit actually was. No, this was an old friend. A comrade. Just plain ol' rage.

"Human face or no, you're a goddamned demon." She forced everything she had into the next words out of her mouth. "Go fuck yourself."

Anum's face twisted for a moment, then it went flat. "I see. Goodbye, Dee." For just a moment, Dee thought she saw sorrow behind his eyes, then his hand reached out to the side.

Dee sucked in a breath on instinct. The airlock opened. Atmosphere shot out, taking her with it. She hammered into the bulkhead as she went. It sent her spinning. Flashes of white, then blue-green, then white, green-white-green, faster and faster and faster...

Exposed skin set nerve endings afire. Dee squeezed her eyes shut. Her stomach ran toward her feet. Still, she spun, eyes and mouth squeezed shut. She held her breath until her lungs burned. Until they begged for release. Until the world turned into a haze. Still, she twirled.

Dee hit something then, ribs cracking. The bones in her leg turned to pudding at the impact. Sparks and screaming fire. She cried out in utter silence. Pain erupted in her chest, only the barest flicker through the agony of her legs. Dee's lungs collapsed. A near-frozen tongue tasted copper and iron. Radiation from the star burned her skin and boiled her insides.

*It's over.*

Relief and panic warred behind an animal instinct she couldn't stifle, fingers clawing at her neck. Starbursts behind her eyelids. She opened her eyes. Her spinning slowed by the impact, she watched the *Liberator* pitch away from Laconia, saw the blink engines spin up. A gentle blue settled across its surface, and then... the warship disappeared.

Cinnamon sparked in the failing synapses of her brain, the brush of soft brown skin, eyes as deep as a black hole.

Dee watched Laconia disappear into flashes from a fever dream. Her eyes froze open. She watched as her vision disappeared behind greasy red fire that searched and grasped for something... anything to feed on. Life to absorb, to save herself with. But there was nothing in the void.

Flashes of light from where the *Liberator* had been, then the world went black in a flush of rosewater and vanilla. But below the numbness of death, beneath the spattered signals of her dying brain, something else wormed its way to the surface.

As everything faded away, one thing wrapped her mind in a rattle of claws on steel, and in that chaos, one sound rose to the top.

Whispering.

\* \* \* \* \*

# Chapter Seventy-One: Anum

Anum cursed the ache in his chest, the building pressure behind his eyes. Cursed the weakness plaguing him since he'd consumed that human. He watched Dee careen beyond the warship. Watched her collide with debris, then spin like a child's toy amidst tongues of *dangizi*.

*I am sorry.* The words filled his mind and soaked him in sadness and yawning horror.

A tone issued in his ear. Thankful for the distraction, he turned away from the portal and ignored the concerned look on Erish's face as he took the call. "Yes, *suanga?*"

*"The AI wasn't lying. FTL systems are back online,"* Hanifa said. There was an excitement to her voice he hadn't heard before. *"We can jump at any moment."*

Anum just stopped himself from getting another look at Dee spinning in the void. Dee dying.

"Jump when r-ready." Anum grimaced at the crack in his voice, frustration and an even stranger emotion warring within him. Embarrassment. "Get us someplace neutral. Someplace… empty, so we can regroup."

*"Yes, My Sky."* A pause. *"Want me to lock the docking bay back down? Looks like we have movement there."*

Anum hesitated then. The logical part of him said no, that they'd need the extra bodies in case he ran into another hurdle, but another part of him, the one that remembered warmth and laughter, the part that wished only to hold a small creature in his lap...

"No. Let them leave—" he grimaced "—but do not wait for them. If they stay, they forfeit their lives."

"*Yes, My Sky.*"

The channel kicked off, and the halls lit with flashing white lights. Erish's soft footfalls preceded her. "Are you well, My Sky?"

Anum grimaced at that, but took a beat to get his face blissfully neutral before turning to her concerned gaze. "I am, Darkness." He forced a smile he didn't feel. "Today has been... trying."

Erish nodded, but she didn't look convinced.

"But that is of no matter," Anum said, allowing a grimace to twist his face. The feeling was... pleasant. "I am of a single purpose. Save our people." He straightened and clasped his hands behind his back. "The Aneis will not be denied."

Erish dropped to a knee. He caught the wide smile on her face. "Yes, My Sky."

With her at his feet, some of the old strength swam back into his bones. He forced himself to look out the airlock, to see the weakening ball of flame in the distance. The lights of the hallway flashed red three times in a row. The airlock slammed shut and sealed. The ball of flame disappeared in a flash of light.

*It is done.* He allowed a single long sigh, then Anum left these burdensome worries behind.

"Prepare the AI," Anum said, forcing steel back into his spine. "I wish to speak with it."

Anum had a civilization to save.

\* \* \* \* \*

# Chapter Seventy-Two: Eleni

White alarm lights sent twisted shadows throughout the cockpit of the largest ship in the docking bay, a heavily beaten freighter that seemed more patch than work. It was named the *Frankenstein* of all things. At least the name matched the look, not that it mattered. The interior was a tattered array of salvaged starship parts: bucket seats from a civilian jumper, a matter processor big enough it had to have come from a Protectorate destroyer, and a clinging stink that indicated a lost sandwich in a maintenance panel someplace.

It'd have to do. They had to get off the *Liberator*. Now. White lights meant an FTL jump was imminent.

"Go!" Eleni screamed at Kev, the short Earther freighter captain she'd found helping out the injured a few minutes earlier. "Now!"

Kev raised an eyebrow at her over the rim of his HUD glasses. His brown hair was plastered to his forehead from nervous sweat, and the stink of body odor wafted off him in waves. "I can't just go. We might tear open the ship."

The lights flashed red. There was no more time for indecisive bullshit. Luckily, Kev's wide eyes showed he finally understood the situation.

"Go!" Eleni screamed.

"Hold on!" Kev hollered, voice echoing back through the ship from the speakers layered throughout. A hundred different voices erupted in chaos from the rear of the vessel as he grabbed the flight stick and pulled back. The ship shuddered off the docking bay, engines rattling like there were screws loose inside them.

Another red light.

The *Frankenstein* roared backwards. If there were inertial dampeners, they weren't strong enough. Eleni tumbled forward, crashing over the console and into the front viewscreen. Pain flashed and disappeared in a blur as Kev hauled on the stick, spinning them around as the third flash of red light caught her eye. Then a wall of white suddenly dominated her vision. They were out.

Eleni watched in horror as an FTL barrier flashed to life around the *Liberator*, locking down the docking bay, trapping all those who'd decided to try to use their own ships instead of following her aboard.

The warship shimmered in the air for the briefest moment, and then… it was gone.

Eleni groaned and straightened in zero gee. She knuckled her spine and kicked off the glass, grabbing the copilot's seat on her way past and dropping into it.

"Holy gooseballs," Kev stammered, staring at the empty space where the demon-filled ship had just been. "We almost got caught in the bubble." He released the stick. His hands trembled as he pressed the heels of his hands into his eyes. "Burning spruce bubbles."

Eleni watched him unravel next to her in numb silence, watched his back shudder as sobs wracked his body. Ceriat would've reached out and consoled him, would've talked him down. *But he's gone, and he's not coming back.*

Eleni drew in a shuddering sigh, then she left her seat, floated to the crying man next to her, and hugged him.

\* \* \* \* \*

# Epilogue

"They're gone."

Those words, filled with meaning, doubled the size of the rock in Hira's throat. She'd watched Dee lose her battle, watched as she was vented with withering hope as Hira realized Dee hadn't been wearing her helmet. Watched as Dee's wild show of flame kept her within plasma weapon distance of the *Liberator*. And then watched as those flames sputtered and died.

*"Everyone?"* Terry asked. He'd floated up next to her just as the warship blinked away.

"I…" But she hadn't checked, had she? Hira shook the cobwebs free and ran a short-range scan, which was the best she could figure out in the moment. Two ships showed up. "No. Some made it off." She pulled up the ship names. "A personal transport, the *Falcon's Wing*, and an *old* freight jumper called the… *Frankenstein*."

Terry's face flickered, though Hira couldn't identify the emotions there. *"Can we hail them?"*

"Yeah," Hira muttered, looking across the array of interfaces before her. The spot where she'd found the scanner didn't appear to have comms nearby. "Maybe."

*"Just let me do it,"* Sarah called from behind. *"Can't fuck this up worse than you already have."*

Hira turned back to find Waters already disconnecting the harness and the plastic ties that'd locked her in place.

"*Sorry, we just couldn't risk—*" Waters cut off as Sarah's right hook caught her in the side of the helmet, sending them both spinning in zero gee.

"*That's for Dee!*" Sarah screamed as she caught herself on the seats. Her face was flushed, and the helmet heavily misted despite the moisture reclaimer.

Waters stabilized herself as well, but didn't retaliate. Instead, she devolved into a series of harsh mutterings in a language Hira didn't know, but that certainly sounded a lot like cursing to her.

Sarah swept up next to Hira and dropped into the copilot seat. For whatever reason, she didn't try to hit Hira, though it would've made sense if she had.

"*This is the* Connie Parker *from Laconia. Please respond.*" Sarah's voice came off smooth and even despite the redness in her eyes and the shaking of her hands.

The silence stretched a long fifteen seconds before a call came back in.

"*This is the* Frankenstein. *We have wounded and—hrgh!*" The sound of shuffling came over the radio, sending a tiny prickle of panic through the haze of numbness filling Hira's body.

"*This is Eleni Mallias. We have wounded in desperate need of medical attention in a gravity environment.*"

Hope. A brilliant spark lit in Hira's heart at the sweet sound of Eleni's voice.

This time it was Hira who jumped across the console to take control of the mic. Luckily, Sarah just pulled away and let her do it.

"Eleni! This is Hira—"

"Hira! The fuck are—"

"I'm so happy you made it!" Hira yelled as the rock in her throat disconnected and disintegrated into dust. "I thought you didn't make it!"

Eleni made a strange sound, then cleared her throat. *"Fuck if a can full of demons is gonna get me."* A humorless laugh. "Got a read on Dee?"

And just like that, the flicker shrank and puffed away like so much smoke. "Dee… didn't make it."

Silence stretched. A few moments later, the *Falcon's Wing* reported in, and Sarah sent them and the *Frankenstein* down to Sparta for assistance. Then it was deathly quiet once more.

Long minutes passed before Sarah cleared her throat. Her voice was thick, heavy, when she spoke. *"I want to take Dee home."*

Hira let out a shuddering sigh. "Sarah—"

*"This isn't up for debate."*

Waters floated up to join them. *"Listen, if—"*

*"Not up for debate!"* Sarah screamed again. Spittle flecked the inside of her mask as tears floated away from watery eyes.

Hira and Waters exchanged a knowing look, shook their heads, and nodded.

Once everyone was seated, Sarah pointed the *Connie Parker* toward where Dee's body now floated 128 kilometers away. They flew in silence, only the sounds of each other's breathing over comms to break up the hum of the engines.

Soon, a bright speck of light stood out amongst the darkness of the void. It still tumbled, arms and legs akimbo, helmetless body spinning ever onward.

*"On approach,"* Sarah said. Her voice was as flat and numb as Hira was inside. *"Intercept in forty-five seconds."*

The bright spot grew as they approached. Second by second it grew, a splash of white here, an arm here, a leg there. Sarah made adjustments to the course, and they began their own spin to match the corpse's rotation.

*"Fifteen seconds."*

When Hira saw it, she banished the thought. Sarah brought them to a full stop just forty meters away, and they both sat in stunned, horrified silence. Waters joined them and pointed; there was no denying it anymore. The body moved. Not well and not much, but it did. But that wasn't Dee out there. Not anymore.

As the corpse spun just a bit faster than their own rotation, the head swung upward and split in half to reveal a thousand spiked teeth, a bright purple tongue lolling about as if tasting the air for their scent.

#####

## About the Author

When not being crawled over by his Writing Cat, Einie, Mike Wyant Jr. writes science fiction with a focus on exploring mental illness and its repercussions. Once upon a time, he was a Sys Admin, Network Administrator, and do-it-all tech drone. He's left those days behind. Mostly.

Mike is also the Editor and sometimes Producer/Director of The Storyteller Series Podcast, a full-cast short fiction audiobook podcast.

To find out more about Mike or his other shenanigans, visit https://www.mikewyantjr.com. You can also find him on Facebook, Twitter, Patreon, and Instagram @mikewyantjr

\* \* \* \* \*

The following is an
**Excerpt from Book One of the Lunar Free State:**

# The Moon and Beyond

## John E. Siers

Available from Theogony Books

eBook, Audio, and Paperback

### Excerpt from "The Moon and Beyond:"

"So, what have we got?" The chief had no patience for interagency squabbles.

The FBI man turned to him with a scowl. "We've got some abandoned buildings, a lot of abandoned stuff—none of which has anything to do with spaceships—and about a hundred and sixty scientists, maintenance people, and dependents left behind, all of whom claim they knew nothing at all about what was really going on until today. Oh, yeah, and we have some stripped computer hardware with all memory and processor sections removed. I mean physically taken out, not a chip left, nothing for the techies to work with. And not a scrap of paper around that will give us any more information…at least, not that we've found so far. My people are still looking."

"What about that underground complex on the other side of the hill?"

"That place is wiped out. It looks like somebody set off a *nuke* in there. The concrete walls are partly fused! The floor is still too hot to walk on. Our people say they aren't sure how you could even *do* something like that. They're working on it, but I doubt they're going to find anything."

"What about our man inside, the guy who set up the computer tap?"

"Not a trace, chief," one of the NSA men said. "Either he managed to keep his cover and stayed with them, or they're holding him prisoner, or else…" The agent shrugged.

"You think they terminated him?" The chief lifted an eyebrow. "A bunch of rocket scientists?"

"Wouldn't put it past them. Look at what Homeland Security ran into. Those motion-sensing chain guns are *nasty*, and the area between the inner and outer perimeter fence is mined! Of course, they posted warning signs, even marked the fire zones for the guns. Nobody would have gotten hurt if the troops had taken the signs seriously."

The Homeland Security colonel favored the NSA man with an icy look. "That's bullshit. How did we know they weren't bluffing? You'd feel pretty stupid if we'd played it safe and then found out there were no defenses, just a bunch of signs!"

"Forget it!" snarled the chief. "Their whole purpose was to delay us, and it worked. What about the Air Force?"

"It might as well have been a UFO sighting as far as they're concerned. Two of their F-25s went after that spaceship, or whatever it was we saw leaving. The damned thing went straight up, over eighty thousand meters per minute, they say. That's nearly Mach Two, in a *vertical climb*. No aircraft in *anybody's* arsenal can sustain a climb like that. Thirty seconds after they picked it up, it was well above their service ceiling and still accelerating. Ordinary ground radar couldn't find it, but NORAD *thinks* they might have caught a short glimpse with one of their satellite-watch systems, a hundred miles up and still going."

"So where did they go?"

"Well, chief, if we believe what those leftover scientists are telling us, I guess they went to the Moon."

\* \* \* \* \*

Get "The Moon and Beyond" here:
https://www.amazon.com/dp/B097QMN7PJ.

Find out more about John E. Siers at:
https://chriskennedypublishing.com.

\* \* \* \* \*

The following is an
**Excerpt from Book One of Abner Fortis, ISMC:**

# Cherry Drop

## P.A. Piatt

Available from Theogony Books

eBook, Audio, and Paperback

### Excerpt from "Cherry Drop:"

"Here they come!"

A low, throbbing buzz rose from the trees and the undergrowth shook. Thousands of bugs exploded out of the jungle, and Fortis' breath caught in his throat. The insects tumbled over each other in a rolling, skittering mass that engulfed everything in its path.

The Space Marines didn't need an order to open fire. Rifles cracked and the grenade launcher thumped over and over as they tried to stem the tide of bugs. Grenades tore holes in the ranks of the bugs and well-aimed rifle fire dropped many more. Still, the bugs advanced.

Hawkins' voice boomed in Fortis' ear. "LT, fall back behind the fighting position, clear the way for the heavy weapons."

Fortis looked over his shoulder and saw the fighting holes bristling with Marines who couldn't fire for fear of hitting their own comrades. He thumped Thorsen on the shoulder.

"Fall back!" he ordered. "Take up positions behind the fighting holes."

Thorsen stopped firing and moved among the other Marines, relaying Fortis' order. One by one, the Marines stopped firing and made for the rear. As the gunfire slacked off, the bugs closed ranks and continued forward.

After the last Marine had fallen back, Fortis motioned to Thorsen.

"Let's go!"

Thorsen turned and let out a blood-chilling scream. A bug had approached unnoticed and buried its stinger deep in Thorsen's calf. The stricken Marine fell to the ground and began to convulse as the neurotoxin entered his bloodstream.

"Holy shit!" Fortis drew his kukri, ran over, and chopped at the insect stinger. The injured bug made a high-pitched shrieking noise, which Fortis cut short with another stroke of his knife.

Viscous, black goo oozed from the hole in Thorsen's armor and his convulsions ceased.

"*Get the hell out of there!*"

Hawkins was shouting in his ear, and Abner looked up. The line of bugs was ten meters away. For a split second he almost turned and ran, but the urge vanished as quickly as it appeared. He grabbed Thorsen under the arms and dragged the injured Marine along with him, pursued by the inexorable tide of gaping pincers and dripping stingers.

Fortis pulled Thorsen as fast as he could, straining with all his might against the substantial Pada-Pada gravity. Thorsen convulsed and slipped from Abner's grip and the young officer fell backward. When he sat up, he saw the bugs were almost on them.

\* \* \* \* \*

Get "Cherry Drop" now at:

https://www.amazon.com/dp/B09B14VBK2

Find out more about P.A. Piatt at:

https://chriskennedypublishing.com

\* \* \* \* \*

The following is an
**Excerpt from Book One of The Last Marines:**

# Gods of War

## William S. Frisbee, Jr.

Available from Theogony Books

eBook and Paperback

### Excerpt from "Gods of War:"

"Yes, sir," Mathison said. Sometimes it was worth arguing, sometimes it wasn't. Stevenson wasn't a butter bar. He was a veteran from a line infantry platoon that had made it through Critical Skills Operator School and earned his Raider pin. He was also on the short list for captain. Major Beckett might pin the railroad tracks on Stevenson's collar before they left for space.

"Well, enough chatting," Stevenson said, the smile in his voice grating on Mathison's nerves. "Gotta go check our boys."

"Yes, sir," Mathison said, and later he would check on the men while the lieutenant rested. "Please keep your head down, sir. Don't leave me in charge of this cluster fuck. I would be tempted to tell that company commander to go fuck a duck."

"No, you won't. You will do your job and take care of our Marines, but I'll keep my head down," Stevenson said. "Asian socialists aren't good enough to kill me. It's going to have to be some green alien bastard that kills me."

"Yes, sir," Mathison said as the lieutenant tapped on Jennings' shoulder and pointed up. The lance corporal understood and cupped his hands together to boost the lieutenant out of the hole. He launched the lieutenant out of the hole and went back to digging as Mathison went back to looking at the spy eyes scrutinizing the distant jungle.

A shot rang out. On Mathison's heads-up display, the icon for Lieutenant Stevenson flashed and went red, indicating death.

*"You are now acting platoon commander,"* Freya reported.

\* \* \* \* \*

Get "Gods of War" now at: https://www.amazon.com/dp/B0B5WJB2MY.

Find out more about William S. Frisbee, Jr. at: https://chriskennedypublishing.com.

\* \* \* \* \*

Made in the USA
Columbia, SC
21 September 2022